THE WILL OF AN ECCENTRIC

Jules Verne

2015 by McAllister Editions (MCALLISTEREDITIONS@GMAIL.COM). This book is a classic, and
a product of its time. It does not reflect the same views on race, gender, sexuality, ethnicity, and
interpersonal relations as it would if it was written today.

CONTENTS

Anonymous translation, 1900

First published in 1899, this adventure novel is based on the board game *Game of the Goose*. The narrative features William J. Hypperbone, an eccentric millionaire, who resides in Chicago, has left the sum of his fortune, $60,000,000, to the first person to reach the end of "The Noble Game of the United States of America."

CHAPTER I. A WHOLE TOWN IN FESTIVITY

A STRANGER arriving in the chief city of Illinois on the morning of the 3rd of April, 1897, would have had good reason for considering himself the most fortunate of travellers. His note-book that day would have had entries enough to yield copy for many sensational articles. And assuredly if he had prolonged his stay in Chicago by a few weeks before and a few months after, he would have taken a share in the emotions, palpitations, and alternations of hope and despair, of the feverishness and bewilderment even, of this great city which for the time was beside itself.

Since eight o'clock an ever-increasing crowd had been streaming towards the twenty-second quarter. This is one of the wealthiest, and is comprised between North Avenue and Division Street on the north and south, and on the east and west, between North Halstead Street and Lake Shore Drive which skirts the waters of Michigan. As you know, the modern towns of the United States lay out their streets conformably to latitudes and longitudes, and make them as regular as the lines on a chess-board.

"Well!" said a member of the municipal police, on duty at the angle of Beethoven Street and North Wells Street, "are all the people going to invade this quarter?"

A man of tall stature was this policeman, and of Irish origin like most of his colleagues of the corporation — gallant fellows in fact, who spend most of their salary of a thousand dollars in combating the inextinguishable thirst so natural to the natives of green Erin.

"It will be a fine day for the pickpockets," replied one of his comrades, no less tall, no less thirsty, no less Irish.

"And so," said the first, "let everyone see to his pocket, if he does not want to find it empty when he goes into a house, and that as we know — "

"There will be plenty to do to-day," concluded the second, "nothing but offering your arm to the ladies at the street crossings — "

"I will bet on a hundred being run over," added his comrade.

Fortunately one has the excellent habit in America of looking after oneself without calling on the administration for an assistance it is incapable of giving.

But what a crowd there would be in this twenty-second quarter if only half of the people of Chicago went there! The city did not then contain less than seventeen hundred thousand inhabitants of whom about a fifth were born in the United States. Germany could claim nearly four hundred thousand, Ireland almost as many. As for the rest, the English and Scotch numbered about fifty thousand, the Canadians about forty thousand, the Scandinavians a hundred thousand, the Bohemians and Poles about the same number, the Jews fifteen thousand, the French ten thousand, the smallest number in this agglomeration.

Besides, the town, as Elisée Reclus observes, does not yet occupy all the municipal territory that the legislators assigned for it on the shore of Lake Michigan, an area of 471 square kilometres, almost equal to that of the Department of the Seine. It is not impossible and it is even probable that its population will increase to occupy these forty-seven thousand hectares.

It was evident that on this occasion the sightseers were streaming from the three sections which the river Chicago forms with its two branches from the north-west and south-east, from the north side as from the south side, considered by certain travellers as being the first the Faubourg Saint-Germain, the second the Faubourg Saint-Honoré of the great city of Illinois. It is true that the influx was also taking place from the angle comprised on the west between the two branches of the river. Though they dwelt in a less fashionable section, the people were none the less disposed to furnish a contingent to the crowd, even from the miserable houses in the environs of Madison Street and Clark Street, in which swarm the Bohemians, the Poles, the Italians, and a number of Chinese escaped from the folding screens of the Celestial empire.

All this exodus was thronging towards the twenty second quarter, tumultuously, noisily, and the eighty streets which it contains, would not suffice for the accommodation of such a crowd.

And very different classes of the population mingled in this human swarm, — functionaries of the Federal Building and of the Post Office; magistrates of the Court House; higher officials of the County Hall; municipal councillors of the City Hall; the staff of that immense caravansary, the Auditorium; in which the rooms are in thousands; clerks from the great stores and bazaars, those of Marshall Field, Lehmann and W. W. Kimball; workmen from the factories of lard and margarine which produce a butter of excellent quality at ten cents the pound; men in the great car factory of the celebrated Pullman come from their distant suburb in the south; assistants from the important retail establishment of Montgomery Ward & Co., three thousand of the workmen of Mr. MacCormick, the inventor of the famous reaping and harvesting machine; some from the furnaces and rolling mills of the Bessemer steel factories; some from the shops of Mr. J. MacGregor Adams who work in nickel, tin, zinc, copper, and refine gold and silver; some from the shoe factories, where a boot and a half is made every minute; and in addition to all these the eighteen hundred workmen of the Elgin factory which puts on the market two thousand watches a day.

To this long list we might add the staff engaged in the elevators of Chicago which is the leading market of the world in the grain trade. With them should be mentioned the railway men from the network of lines which by twenty-seven different ways and more than 1300 trains carry 175,000 passengers daily through the town, and to these we may join the men employed on the steam and electric tram cars, rope cars and others which carry 2,000,000 people, and finally the boatmen and sailors of an extensive port dealing inwards and outwards with sixty vessels a day.

You would have had to be blind not to have seen in this crowd, the managers, editors, compositors, reporters of the 540 journals, daily and weekly, of the Chicago press. You would have had to be deaf not to have heard the shouts of the brokers, the bulls or operators for a rise, the bears or operators for a fall, as if they had been in full swing at the Board of Trade or the Wheat Pit, that is, the Grain Exchange. And with all this noisy crowd were the clerks of all the banks, national or state, the Corn Exchange, Calumet, Merchants' Loan Trust, Fort Dearborn, Oakland, Prairie State, American Trust and Savings, Chicago City, Guarantee of North America, Dime Savings, Northern Trust Company, etc., etc.

And how could we forget in this public demonstration the students of the colleges and universities, the Northwestern University, Union College of Law, Chicago Manual Training School and so many others, or forget the performers at the twenty-three theatres and casinos of the town, such as the Grand Opera House, Jacob's Clark Street theatre, the Auditorium and the Lyceum, or forget the people from the twenty-nine principal hotels, or the waiters and servants of the restaurants large enough to accommodate 25,000 customers an hour, or the packers or butchers of the Great Union Stock Yard, which, on account of the houses of Armour, Swift, Nelson, Morris and a number of others, kill millions of cattle and pigs at two dollars a head. And can you be surprised that the Queen of the West holds the second place after New York among the industrial and commercial towns of the United States, its volume of business reaching a total of thirty milliards.

Chicago, like the other great American cities, rejoices in a liberty as absolute as democratic. Decentralization is complete, and yet, if we may say so, what was it that caused it to centralize on this day around La Salle Street?

Was it towards the City Hall that its population was pouring, in tumultuous masses? Was there an irresistible current, what is here called a boom, in some lands speculation? Was it one of those electoral contests which drive crowds to fury, a meeting of conservative republicans or liberal democrats in the precincts of the Federal Building? Was it to inaugurate a new World's Columbian Exhibition, to recommence under the shady trees of Lincoln Park and along the Midway Plaissance the solemn pomps of 1893?

No, it was for a ceremony of quite a different kind, the character of which ought to have been profoundly sorrowful if its organizers had not, in accordance with the wishes of the person concerned; carried it out amid universal festivity.

At this hour La Salle Street was quite clear, thanks to the police posted in great numbers at each end. The procession which was to pass down the street, would thus have no obstacle to meet with.

If La Salle Street is not sought after by rich Americans as the equal of Prairie, Calumet or Michigan Avenues with their opulent mansions, it is none the less one of the most frequented thoroughfares in the city. It bears the name of a Frenchman, Robert Cavelier de La Salle, one of the first travellers who came in 1619 to explore this region of the lakes — a name very justly celebrated in the United States. Towards the middle of La Salle Street the spectator who had been able to get through the double barrier of policemen, would have seen at the corner of Goethe Street, a car drawn by six horses, standing before a house of magnificent appearance. In front and behind this car was a procession arranged in perfect order waiting only for the signal to move.

The first half of this procession comprised several companies of militia, all in review order, under the orders of their officers, a band of not less than a hundred performers, and a choir of singers amounting to as many, who would occasionally mingle their voices with the music of the instruments.

The car was decked with draperies of brilliant red, relieved by borders of silver and gold, on which were, sparkling with diamonds, the three letters W. J. H. Heaped on the car was a profusion of bouquets, or rather armfuls of flowers, which would have been rare anywhere else than in a town generally known as Garden City. From the top of this vehicle, worthy of appearing at some national festivity, garlands were hanging held in the hands of six people, three on the right, three on the left.

A few steps behind was a group of some twenty people, among whom were James T. Davidson, Gordon S. Allen, Harry B. Andrews, John I. Dickinson, Thomas R. Carlisle, etc., of the Eccentric Club in Mohawk Street, of which George B. Higginbotham was the President, members of the Calumet Club in Michigan Avenue, the Hyde Park Club in Washington Avenue, the Columbus Club in Munroe Street, the Union League in Custom House Place, the Irish American Club in Dearborn Street, and the fourteen other clubs in the town.

You are not unaware that at Chicago are the headquarters of the Missouri division and the residence of the commandant. It goes without saying, therefore, that the commandant, General James Morris, with his staff and the officers installed in Pullman Building, were in a crowd behind the group mentioned. Then the governor of the State, John Hamilton, the mayor and his assistants, the members of the municipal council, the administrators of the county arrived for the occasion from Springfield, the official capital of Illinois where the public offices are established, and also the magistrates of the Federal Court, who differ from the other functionaries, in not being appointed by universal suffrage, but by the President of the Union.

Elbowing each other at the end of the procession were merchants, manufacturers, engineers, professors, barristers, solicitors, doctors, dentists, coroners, sheriffs, to whom would be added an immense concourse of the public when the procession debouched from La Salle Street.

With a view to protect this tail end from being lost in the crowd, General James Morris had massed strong detachments of cavalry with drawn swords, whose standards floated in the breeze.

This long description of all the bodies, civil and military, of all the societies and corporations which took part in this extraordinary ceremony, should be completed by this very significant detail: those present, without an exception, wore in their button-holes a gardenia given to them by the major-domo in a black suit, who stood on the steps of the mansion.

The house itself had every appearance of festivity. Its girandoles and electric lamps streaming with light contended with the brilliant rays of an April sun. The windows wide open displayed their multi-coloured draperies. The servants in their best liveries were on duty on the marble steps of the principal staircase. The drawing-rooms were prepared for a solemn reception. The dining-rooms were set out with tables on which glittered the massive silver plate and marvellous ware of the millionaires of Chicago, with the crystal cups full of wines of the best vintages and champagnes of the best brands.

At last nine o'clock sounded from the clock of the City Hall. There was a fanfare of trumpets at the end of La Salle Street. Three cheers, given unanimously, filled the air. At a signal from the superintendent of police the procession began to move with banners flying.

At first, from the formidable instruments of the band amid the enlivening strains of the Columbus March by Professor J. K. Paine, of Cambridge, with slow and measured step the procession moved up La Salle Street. Almost immediately the car started, drawn by its six luxuriously caparisoned horses, plumed with tufts and aigrettes. The garlands of flowers were held in the hands of the six privileged persons, whose choice seemed to be due to the fantastic caprices of chance.

Then the clubs, the authorities, military, civil, and municipal, the masses which followed the detachments of cavalry, advanced in perfect order. Needless to say, the doors, windows, balconies, the roofs even, of La Salle Street were thronged with spectators of every age, of whom the greater number had taken up their positions the evening before.

When the first ranks of the procession had reached the end of the street they inclined a little to the left so as to take the avenue that skirts Lincoln Park. What an incredible swarm of people were gathered on the two hundred and fifty acres of this admirable enclosure, bounded on the east by the rippling waters of Lake Michigan, with its shady alleys, its thickets, its lawns, its wooded dunes, its Winston lagoon, its lofty monuments to the memory of Grant and Lincoln, and its parade ground, and its zoological department, in which the wild beasts howled and the monkeys capered to be in unison with all this popular agitation. As the park is almost deserted during the week, a stranger might have asked if the day were not Sunday. No, it was a Friday — the miserable unlucky Friday — that fell this year on the third of April.

But the people hardly gave this a thought as they exchanged observations with each other while the procession went by, regretting doubtless, that they did not take part in it.

"Certainly," said one, "it is as fine as the dedication ceremony of our exhibition."

"True," said the other, "and that was as good as the closing on the 24th of October in Midway Plaisance."

"And the six who walk near the car — " said a boatman from the Chicago River.

"And who will return with their pockets full," remarked a workman from McCormick's factory.

"There are the winners of the big prizes," grunted an enormous brewer, who sweated beer from all his pores.

"I would give my weight in gold to be in their place."

"And you would not lose by it!" announced a strong slaughterman from the Stock Yards.

"Bundles of bonds for them to-day!" said those around them, "Yes: their fortunes are made!"

"And what fortunes!"

"Ten million dollars to each — "

"You should say twenty million dollars!"

"Nearer fifty than twenty!"

Started in this way, the good people ended by reaching a milliard — a word in current conversation in the United States. But it should be noted that all this was based on mere hypothesis!

Was this procession going to make the tour of the town? Well, if the programme included such a perambulation the day would not have sufficed for it.

Anyhow, always with some demonstrations of joy, always amid the loud outbursts from the orchestra and the singing of the choir who had just given "To the Son of Art" amid the cheering of the crowd, the long unbroken column arrived before the entrance to Lincoln Avenue on which abuts Fullerton Avenue. It then took the road to the left and went westward for about two miles to the northern branch of the Chicago River. Between the sidewalks, black with people, there was enough width for it to move along freely.

Crossing the bridge the procession, by way of Brand Street, reached that magnificent artery which bears the name of Humboldt Boulevard for a length of eleven miles and descends again towards the south after running towards the west. It was at the angle of Logan Square that it took this direction as soon as the police, not without difficulty, had cleared the road between the quintuple hedge of spectators.

From this point the car proceeded to Palmer Square and appeared before the Park which also bears the name of the illustrious Prussian scientist.

It was noon. A halt of half an hour was made in Humboldt Park — a halt quite justifiable, for there was still a long way to go. The crowd could disperse at its ease over its green expanse which has an area exceeding two hundred acres and is watered by running streams.

The car stopped. The band and choir attacked "The Star Spangled Banner," which was received with applause as if it had been at a music hall.

The point furthest west which the programme assigned for the procession, was reached about two o'clock at Garfield Park. We can see that there is no want of parks in the great city of Illinois. At least fifteen principal ones can be enumerated — Jackson Park does not contain less than five hundred and eighty-six acres — and altogether they cover two thousand acres of underwood, thickets, shrubberies and lawns.

When the angle made by Douglas Boulevard as it turns towards the east had been passed, the procession followed the same direction so as to reach Douglas Park, and thence by the south-west cross the southern branch of the Chicago River and the Michigan Canal which runs alongside it further up. It then descended to the south along Western Avenue for about three miles to reach Gage Park.

Three o'clock then struck and a new direction had to be taken so as to return towards the eastern quarters of the town.

This time the band grew furious, playing with extraordinary vigour the liveliest two-fours, the maddest allegros, chosen from Lecocq, Varney, Andran and Offenbach. It was almost incredible that the people did not break out into a dance under the influence of these ball-room airs. In France no one could have resisted them.

The weather was magnificent although rather cold. In the early days of April the wintry period is far from having come to an end in the climate of Illinois, and the navigation of Lake Michigan and the Chicago River is generally interrupted from the beginning of December to the end of March.

But although the temperature was rather low the air was so pure, the sun pursuing his course in a cloudless sky gave forth such dazzling rays that he also seemed to be making holiday, as the reporters said, and everything went magnificently to the close of the day.

The masses of people showed no tendency to diminish. If the spectators no longer came from the northern quarters, they came from the southern, and these were as good as the others in their demonstrative animation and the enthusiasm of their cheering as the procession passed along.

In its various groups the procession remained as at its start from the mansion in La Salle Street, and such it would remain until its long journey had finished.

Coming out of Gage Park the car returned towards the east by Garfield Boulevard.

At the end of this boulevard there stretches in all its magnificence Washington Park, which occupies an area of three hundred and seventy-one acres.

The crowd covered it as they had done a few years before when the Great Exposition was held in its vicinity. From four o'clock to half-past four o'clock there was a halt here, during which, amid the applause of the innumerable audience, the choir performed Beethoven's "In Praise of God."

Then the procession went on again under the shade of the trees to the park which, with Midway Plaisance, comprised the surroundings of the World's Columbian Fair within the spacious limits of Jackson Park on the very shore of Lake Michigan.

Was the car going to this already famous place? Was there to be a ceremony to recall to remembrance this memorable event in the annals of Chicago? Was there to be an annual festival to prevent its ever being forgotten?

No. After passing round the Washington Park Club by Cottage Grove, the leading ranks of militia halted before a park which the railways enclose with their network of steel in this populous quarter.

The procession stopped, and before advancing beneath the shades of the magnificent oaks, the instrumentalists played one of Strauss's most exhilarating waltzes.

Was this park then that of a. casino, and was there some immense hall prepared for an evening festival in which all these people were to take part?

The gates had just opened wide, and the police could only with great effort keep back the crowd that were here more noisy and overflowing than ever.

This time they had not invaded the park which was guarded by detachments of militia, so as to permit the car to enter it at the end of its fifteen miles of route through the immense city.

The park was not a park. It was Oakwood Cemetery, the largest of the eleven cemeteries of Chicago. And the car was a funeral car which bore to his last home the mortal remains of William J. Hypperbone, one of the members of the Eccentric Club.

CHAPTER II. WILLIAM J HYPPERBONE

BECAUSE James T. Davidson, Gordon S. Allen, Harry B Andrews, John I. Dickinson, George B. Higginbotharn, and Thomas R. Carlisle have been mentioned among the distinguished crowd walking behind the car, it need not be inferred that they were the most prominent members of the Eccentric Club.

In fact, to tell the truth, there was nothing eccentric in their manner of living in this world, except in their belonging to the said club in Mohawk Street. These eminent sons of Jonathan, grown wealthy in their multiple and profitable businesses in land, salt provisions, petroleum, railways, mines, stock raising, stock slaughtering, may have intended to astonish their compatriots in the fifty-one States of the Union and the new and old worlds by their ultra-American extravagances; but their existence, public and private, offered, it must be admitted, nothing of a kind to attract the attention of the universe? They were there, some fifty or so," worth a good deal for taxes, "paying a high subscription, going little into Chicago society, regular attendants in the reading and play rooms, reading a number of journals and reviews, playing more or less heavily as in all clubs, and saying to themselves occasionally with regard to what they had done in the past and what they were doing in the present, —

"Decidedly we are not at all eccentric!"

One of the members, however, seemed to show more tendencies towards originality than his colleagues. Although he had not yet distinguished himself by a series of notorious extravagances, there was evidently a chance that in the future he would justify the name prematurely adopted by the celebrated club.

But, unfortunately, William J. Hypperbone had just died. It is true that what he had never done when living he had just done in a certain fashion after his death, for it had been his express wish that his funeral should take place amid general hilarity.

The late William J. Hypperbone, when his life had suddenly ended, had not passed his fiftieth year. At this age he was a well-built man, tall of stature, broad of shoulder, strong of chest, rather stiff in his bearing, not without a certain elegance, a certain nobleness. He had chestnut hair, which he wore short, a fan-shaped beard in which the silky threads of gold were mingled with a few threads of silver, eyes of a dark blue with glowing pupils beneath the thick eyebrows, the mouth with its dental furniture complete, lips rather tightly closed with their corners slightly raised — the sign of a disposition inclined to raillery and even to disdain.

This superb specimen of the North American rejoiced in vigorous health. Never had a doctor felt his pulse, examined his tongue, looked at his throat, sounded his chest, listened to his heart, nor taken his temperature with a thermometer. And yet there is no scarcity of doctors in Chicago, nor of dentists, all of them of great professional ability, which they had never had an opportunity of displaying in his case.

It might have been said that no machine — ever of a hundred doctor power — would have been able to drag him from the world and transport him to another, and yet he was dead, dead without the help of the Faculty, and having passed from life to death here was his funeral car standing before the gate of Oakwood Cemetery.

To complete the portrait of this physical personage by the portrait of the mental personage it may be added that William J. Hypperbone was of a nature very cool, very positive, and that he never lost control of himself. That he found life pleasant was because he was a philosopher; and philosophy is easy when a large fortune and freedom from every care for wealth or family allows of benevolence being joined to generosity.

It will be asked if it were logical to expect anything eccentric from a nature so practical and well balanced. Had there been anything in this American's past to lead one to suppose so?

Yes, there had been such a circumstance.

At the age of forty, William J. Hypperbone had made up his mind to marry the most authentic centenarian of the New World, whose birth dated from 1781, the very day when, during the Great War, the Capitulation of Lord Cornwallis had obliged England to recognize the Independence of the United States. Just as he was going to ask her to be his wife the worthy Miss Anthonia Burgoyne was carried off by an attack of infantine whooping-cough, so that he was not in time to be accepted. Faithful to the memory of the venerable lady, he remained a bachelor, and that perhaps may pass as an example of eccentricity.

Henceforth nothing troubled his life, for he was not of the school of the great poet, who has said in magnificent verse: —

"Oh death, dark goddess, unto whom Returneth all and their own selves efface, Receive thy children in thy starry breast, Free them from time, from number and from space, And give them that which life hath troubled — rest."

In truth, why should William J. Hypperbone have thought of invoking "the dark goddess"? Time, number, space, had they ever wearied him in this world? Had not, on the contrary, everything succeeded with him? Had he not been the great favourite of fortune who had always and everywhere heaped its favours on him?

At twenty-five he had rejoiced in a fair share of wealth, he had doubled it, increased it ten times, a hundred times, by lucky speculations without a single disaster. A native of Chicago he had but to follow the prodigious development of this town of which the forty-seven thousand hectares — declares a traveller — were worth two thousand five hundred dollars in 1823 and are now worth eight milliards. It was under these easy conditions, by buying at low prices and selling at high ones the plots of ground that purchasers acquired at the rate of two or three thousand dollars the square yard for the construction of houses of twenty-eight stories, and by also taking shares in railroads, oil wells and mines, William J. Hypperbone was able to enrich himself sufficiently to leave after him an enormous fortune. Really Miss Anthonia Burgoyne was unwise to lose the chance of so grand a marriage.

After all there was nothing astonishing in inexorable death carrying off a centenarian of that age, but it was remarkable that William J. Hypperbone, who was not even half a centenarian, in the prime of life, in the fulness of his strength, should go to join her in a world which he had no reason for thinking a better one.

And now that he was dead, to whom would come the millions of the honourable member of the Eccentric Club?

At the outset it had been asked if this club would not be the sole legatee of the first of its members who had quitted this life since its foundation — to encourage, perhaps, his colleagues later on to follow his example.

It should be said that William J. Hypperbone lived more at the club in Mohawk Street than at his home in La Salle Street. There he took his meals, his ease, his amusements, of which the greatest please note this — was the game not of chess, nor backgammon, nor tricktrack, nor cards, neither baccarat, trente-et-quarante, lansquenet, poker, not even piquet, écarté, or whist, but that which he had introduced himself into the club and which he preferred to all the rest.

This was the Royal Game of Goose, the noble game that has come down to us in a more or less altered form from the Ancient Greeks. It would be impossible to say how passionately he was fond of it — so fond that he had succeeded in imparting some of his enthusiasm for it to his colleagues. Great was his excitement in leaping from one division to another at the caprice of the dice, hurling himself from goose to goose to reach the last of these denizens of the poultry-yard, walking on "the bridge," resting in "the inn," falling down "the well," losing himself in "the maze," casting himself into "the prison," stumbling against "the death's head," visiting the compartments of "the sailor,"

"the fisherman,"

"the harbour,"

"the stag,"

"the mill,"

"the snake,"

"the sun,"

"the helmet,"

"the lion,"

"the rabbit,"

"the flower-pot," etc.

It goes without saying that among the opulent personages of the Eccentric Club, the fines to pay according to the rules of the game were not small, that they amounted to thousands of dollars, and that the winner, however rich he might be, experienced considerable pleasure in transferring the respectable total to his pocket.

For about twenty years William J. Hypperbone had been spending his days at the club, satisfying himself with a walk or so along Lake Michigan. Without any of the inclination of the Americans for running round the world, his travels were limited by the United States. Then why did not his colleagues with whom he was on such excellent terms, succeed to what he had left? Were they not the only people to whom he was bound by ties of sympathy and friendship? Had they not every day joined in his immoderate passion for the Royal Game of Goose, and contended with him on this field where chance brought so many surprises? At least he might have conceived the idea of founding an annual prize in favour of his fellow member who had won the greatest number of games between the first of January and the thirty-first of December.

It should be said here that the deceased possessed neither family nor direct or collateral heir, nor any relation near enough of kin to be his heir, and if he had died without disposing of his fortune it would have gone to the federal republic, which, like any monarchical State, would have accepted it without any pressing.

Anyhow, if you wished to know what were the last wishes of the deceased you had only to go to No. 17, Sheldon Street, to Mr. Tornbrock, the notary, and ask if William J. Hypperbone had left a will, and if so, what were its clauses and conditions, "Gentlemen," said Mr. Tornbrock to George B. Higginbotham, the president, and Thomas R. Carlisle, who had been delegated to call at the office of the worthy notary, "I expected your visit. I am honoured by it."

"And we are equally honoured," said the two members of the club with a bow.

"But," continued the notary, "before troubling ourselves about the will, we must see about the funeral of the deceased."

"With regard to that," said George B, Higginbotham, "should it not be conducted with a magnificence worthy of our late colleague?"

"I can only conform to the instructions of my client which are contained in this cover," replied Mr. Tornbrock, showing an envelope of which he had broken the seal.

"And what sort of a funeral is it to be?" asked Thomas R. Carlisle.

"Pompous and lively, gentlemen, accompanied by a band and a choir so that the people will join in cheers of delight in honour of William J. Hypperbone."

"I should have hoped no less of a member of our club," replied the president, with an approving nod of the head.

"He could not be interred like a simple mortal," said Thomas R. Carlisle.

"Likewise," continued Tornbrock, "William J. Hypperbone has signified his wish that the entire population of Chicago should be represented at his funeral by a delegation of six members drawn by lot under special circumstances. With this project in view he had for some months been collecting in an urn the names of all his fellow-citizens of Chicago of both sexes between the ages of twenty and sixty. Yesterday, as his instructions required me, I proceeded to draw the lots in the presence of the Mayor and his assistants. The first six individuals whose names were drawn I have informed by registered letter of the intention of the deceased, and I have invited them to take their places at the head of the procession, and entreated them not to decline the duty of rendering him the last honours."

"Which they will take good care not to decline," exclaimed Thomas R. Carlisle," for there is reason for believing that the testator has left them something to their advantage, if he has not left them the whole of his property — "

"That is possible," said Mr. Tornbrock," and I should not be surprised if it were so."

"And what conditions have to be fulfilled by the people who have been chosen by lot? asked George B. Higginbotham.

"Only that they should have been born and reside in Chicago."

"What! nothing else?"

"Nothing at all."

"That is, understood," said Thomas R. Carlisle," and now, when are you going to open the will?"

"A fortnight after the death."

"In a fortnight only?"

"That is all — as is directed in this note which accompanies it. Consequently on the 15th of April — "

"Why the delay?"

"Because my client desired before making the public acquainted with his last wishes that no doubt should exist of his having passed from life to death."

"A practical man, our friend Hypperbone," said George B. Higginbotham.

"One cannot be too careful in such circumstances," said Thomas R. Carlisle," and unless you are cremated — "

"Or," added the notary, "burnt alive — "

"Of course," added the president, "but then you are at least certain of the death."

But nothing had been said about cremating the body of William J. Hypperbone, and beneath the draperies of the funeral car the body lay ready for burial.

As may be imagined, the news of the death of William J. Hypperbone had produced a prodigious sensation. The earliest accounts were as follows: —

On the 30th of March, in the afternoon, the member of the Eccentric Club was seated with two of his colleagues before the Game of Goose table. He had just made the first throw, nine, made up of a six and a three, the most fortunate beginning, which sent him on to the fifty-ninth square.

Suddenly his face became congested, his limbs grew stiff. He tried to rise, he tottered as he did so, stretched out his hands and would have fallen on the floor if John T. Dickinson and Harry B. Andrews had not caught him in their hands and laid him on a sofa.

A doctor was at once called in. Two came. They said that William J. Hypperbone had succumbed to congestion of the brain, that all was over, and Dr. H. Burnham, of Cleveland Avenue, and Dr. S. Buchanan, of Franklin Street, were not likely to make a mistake in pronouncing a man to be dead.

An hour afterwards the deceased had been removed to a room in his own house whither Mr. Tornbrock, to whom the news had at once been conveyed, had hastened without losing a moment.

The notary's first care was to open the packet containing the deceased's dispositions with regard to his obsequies. In the first place he was requested to draw by lot the six people who were to take part in the procession, and whose names were contained with hundreds of thousands of others in an enormous urn that stood in the centre of the hall.

When this extraordinary arrangement became known it may easily be imagined what hosts of journalists assailed Mr. Tornbrock. To him came the reporters of the *Chicago Tribune,* the *Chicago Inter-Ocean,* the *Chicago Evening Journal,* which are republican or conservative, those of the *Chicago Globe,* the *Chicago Herald,* the *Chicago Times,* the *Chicago Mail,* the *Chicago Evening Post,* which are democratic or liberal, those of the *Chicago Daily News* the *Daily News Record,* the *Freie Presse,* the *Staats Zeitung,* which are of independent politics. The house in La Salle Street was crowded with visitors for half the day. And what these news-hunters, these fact-providers, these editors of sensational chronicles, these reporters, wished to get at was not the details of Hypperbone's death, which had occurred so unexpectedly at the famous throw of nine by six and three — No! it was the names of the six privileged ones that had just been drawn from the urn. Mr. Tornbrock, overwhelmed by the numbers, got out of the difficulty like a practical man — practical as so many of his countrymen are to an unusual degree. He offered to put the names up for auction, to hand them over to the journal which would pay the highest price, with the understanding that the sum paid should be divided between two of the twenty-one hospitals of the town.

The *Tribune* was the purchaser at ten thousand dollars. The bidding ran to ten thousand dollars after a prolonged competition with the *Chicago Inter-Ocean.*

They rubbed their hands that day, did the managers of the Illinois Charitable Eye and Ear Infirmary, 237, W. Adams Street, as did those of the Chicago Hospital for Women and Children, Paulina Corner, W. Adams Street.

But next day what a success was made by the powerful journal, and what a profit it realized by its extra edition of two million five hundred thousand copies, for it had to supply them by hundreds of thousands to the fifty-one States of which the Union was then composed.

"The names!" shouted the newsboys — the names of the mortals fortunate above all, who had been chosen by lot from among the population of Chicago.

They were the six "chancers" as they were called, coining a word for the occasion, which would have to find its way into the dictionary — or, more briefly," the six."

The *Tribune* was accustomed to these audacious outbursts, and what could dare to do so with a better grace than the well-informed journal of Dearborn and Madison Streets, which is run with a capital of a million dollars, the shares of which were issued at a thousand dollars, and are now worth twenty-five thousand.

In addition to this issue of the 1st of April, the *Tribune* published the six names on a special list which its agents distributed in profusion to the most distant towns of the Republic of the United States.

Herewith, in the order in which chance had designated them, are the names which were to be heard in the world for many months in connection with such extraordinary vicissitudes as were never imagined by the most imaginative of French romancers.

Max Real.

Tom Crabbe.

Hermann Titbury.

Harris T. Kymbale.

Lizzie Wag.

Hodge Urrican.

It will be seen that of these six persons, five were of the stronger sex and one of the gentler sex — supposing that this qualification is correct when speaking of American women.

Public curiosity was not, however, entirely satisfied at the outset. Who were the bearers of these names? where did they live? to what class of society did they belong? This information the *Tribune* was not at first in a position to give its innumerable readers.

Were they even still alive at this time, the elect of this posthumous lottery? That was an important question.

In fact, the names had been in the urn for some time, some months already, and some of those on whom chance had chosen might have died or left America.

But if they were able to do so, although they had never been consulted on the subject, they would come and take their places round the car — there was no doubt about that. Was it likely that they would reply by a refusal to the strange but serious invitation of William J. Hypperbone — an eccentric, at least, after his death — that they would renounce the advantages reserved for them, as was almost certain, in the will deposited with Mr. Tornbrock! No! they would all be there, for they had every reason to consider themselves the heirs to the large fortune of the deceased, and a heritage would assuredly not be allowed to fall to the greedy authorities of the State; and that was clear enough when, three days later, the "six," without knowing one another, appeared on the steps of the mansion in La Salle Street before the notary, who after proving their identity, placed in their hands the garlands of the car.

Of what curiosity they were the object, and, equally, of what envy! By the orders of William J. Hypperbone all signs of mourning had been proscribed at this extraordinary funeral, and they had conformed to this injunction, as published in the newspapers, and appeared in their best holiday clothes — clothes, which by their quality and cut, denoted that their wearers belonged to very different grades of society.

They took up their positions in the following order: —

In the first rank: Lizzie Wag to the right, Max Real to the left.

In the second rank: Hermann Titbury to the right, Hodge Urrican to the left.

In the third rank: Harris T. Kymbale to the right, Tom Crabbe to the left.

A thousand cheers greeted them when these positions had been taken up — cheers which some acknowledged by an amiable bow and to which others made no reply.

Thus it was they had begun their walk as soon as the signal had been given by the superintendent of police, and thus it was that for about eight hours they had passed along the roads, avenues and boulevards of the great city of Chicago.

Assuredly these six guests at the funeral of William J. Hypperbone were quite unacquainted with each other, but that would soon be altered. And who knows, for human avidity is insatiable, if these candidates to the succession were not already looking upon each other as rivals and feared that after all the fortune was to fall to one of them instead of being divided among the six.

We have seen how the funeral had proceeded through a prodigious concourse of people from La Salle Street to Oakwood amid music and singing, in which there was nothing funereal, and exclamations of delight at every turn in honour of the deceased.

And now it had only to enter the cemetery and place in the depths of the tomb, to sleep an eternal sleep, him who was William J. Hypperbone of the Eccentric Club.

CHAPTER III. OAKWOOD

The name of Oakwood indicates that the site occupied by the cemetery was formerly covered with a forest of oaks, the principal tree of these vast solitudes of Illinois, formerly called the Prairie State on account of the exuberance of its vegetation.

Of all the monuments it contained — many of them erected at great cost — none could be compared with that which William J. Hypperbone had built some years before for his own use.

As we know, these American cemeteries, like English Cemeteries, are regular parks. Nothing is wanting which can please the eye, neither lawns, nor shady walks, nor running streams. It seems as though there could be no sadness in them. The birds warble more joyously there than elsewhere, perhaps, because their safety is complete in these fields consecrated to supreme repose.

The mausoleum built on the plans and by the care of William J. Hypperbone stood close to a small lake of calm clear water. In Anglo-Saxon architectural taste it combined all the fancifulness of that Gothic style which extended into the Renaissance. In its front surmounted by a clock tower rising a hundred feet from the ground it resembled a chapel, in its roof and its stained glass windows in the shape of miradors it had the look of a large villa.

The clock tower ornamented with crosses and finials and supported by the buttresses along the front, contained a bell of powerful sonorousness, which struck the hours for the illuminated clock at its base. The metallic voice of this bell when it escaped through the pierced and gilded louvres, could be heard beyond the boundary of Oakwood as far as the bank of Lake Michigan. The monument measured a hundred and twenty feet in length and sixty in breadth at its transept. Its plan was that of a Latin cross terminated by an apse. The railing that surrounded it, a beautiful example of aluminium metal work, was supported at intervals by lamp columns. Beyond were grouped magnificent evergreen trees which served as a frame to the superb mausoleum. The gate of this railing, then open, gave access to a path bordered with clumps and clusters leading to a staircase of fine steps of white marble. At the back of the wide landing was the doorway with its two bronze doors decorated with a pattern of interlacing fruits and flowers.

This entrance led into an antechamber furnished with gold-studded couches and ornamented with a flower vase of Chinese porcelain, the flowers in which were frequently changed. From the centre hung an electrolier of crystal with seven branches. Through copper orifices arranged at the angles there was introduced the pleasant equable temperature of a hot-air stove, looked after during the cold season by one of the attendants at Oakwood. In this way warm air was provided in the interior of the monument.

Opening the glass panels of a door facing the entrance from the steps you stood in the principal apartment of the building. It was a spacious hall, circular in form, in which was displayed all that extravagant luxury possible to an arch-millionaire who desires to continue after his death the opulent surroundings of his life. Abundant light was given from the ceiling of ground glass which closed in the upper portion of the vault. The surface of the walls was ornamented with arabesques, scrolls, annulets, embossments, floral designs, vermiculations as finely designed and carved as those of the Alhambra. The lower part was hidden by couches of startling fabrics. Here and there were bronze and marble statues of fauns and nymphs. Between the pillars of dazzling stucco on which rested the ribs of the vault were a few pictures by modern masters, mostly landscapes, in gold frames picked out with luminous points. Thick strips of soft carpet covered the pavement which was decorated with glittering mosaics.

Beyond the hall, at the back of the mausoleum, was an apse, lighted by a large window in which the splendid stained glass glowed like a flame when the sun as he set struck it with his oblique rays. This apse was fitted with modern furniture. Easy chairs, chairs, rocking-chairs, sofas, encumbered it in the wished for disorder. On a table were thrown in confusion books and pamphlets, journals and magazines, home and foreign. Behind its glass doors a sideboard equipped with china and so forth provided cold refreshments, always ready and renewed every day, delicate sweetmeats, unctuous sandwiches, dry cakes, flagons of fine wines, bottles of liqueurs of illustrious brands. An admirably arranged place it must be admitted for a read, a siesta or a luncheon.

In the centre of the hall, bathed in the light which the dome allowed to enter through the glass, rose a tomb of white marble encircled with fine sculptures, with heraldic animals at the corners. This tomb, surrounded by a circle of incandescent lights, was open, the stone which closed it having been drawn back. Here was to be placed the coffin in which the body of William J. Hypperbone lay on its padded cushion of white satin.

Assuredly such a mausoleum was not suggestive of ideas of mourning. Gladness rather than sadness was what it evoked. Through the pure air that filled it there was no feeling of that rustling of the wings of death as over the tombs in a cemetery. And was not the monument worthy of the eccentric American to whom was due the anything but sorrowful programme of his funeral which was nearing its end, in which songs of gaiety had mingled with the joyful cheers of the crowd?

It should be noted that William J. Hypperbone never failed to come twice a week, on Tuesdays and Fridays, and spend a few hours inside his mausoleum.

From time to time many of his colleagues had accompanied him. It was one of the quietest and most comfortable places for conversation. Stretched on the couches of the apse, seated before the table, these people read or chatted about the politics of the day, the market prices of stocks and goods, the progress of jingoism, otherwise chauvinism, in the different classes of society, the advantages or disadvantages of the McKinley Bill, with which thinking people occupied themselves unceasingly.

While they talked in this way they were served with luncheon, and when the afternoon had been spent in this agreeable way the carriages came up Grove Avenue and took away to their houses the members of the Eccentric Club.

It need scarcely be said that no one but the owner could enter his "cottage at Oakwood," as he called it. The keeper of the cemetery, to whom the care of the said cottage was entrusted, alone possessed a second key.

Certainly if William J. Hypperbone was scarcely distinguished from his fellows by the actions of his public life, his private life divided between the club in Mohawk Street and the mausoleum at Oakwood, afforded a few singularities that admitted of his being classed among the eccentrics of his time.

It would have crowned all and pushed eccentricity to its furthest limits if Hypperbone were not really dead. But his heirs, whoever they might be, could rest assured in this respect. Here was no case of apparent death but of unmistakable death.

The ultra X-rays of Professor Friedrich of Elbing (Prussia) had at this period been brought into use, which rays possess a force of penetration so intense that they traverse the human body and rejoice in the singular property of producing different photographic images according as the body is living or dead.

These rays were tried on William J. Hypperbone, and the images obtained left no doubt in the minds of the doctors. The "defunctuosity" — such was the word they used in their report — was indubitable, and there could be no danger of error in a too hasty burial.

It was a quarter to six o'clock when the car entered the gates of Oakwood. It was in the middle of the cemetery, at the end of the lagoon, that the monument was placed. The procession in the same order as before, increased by a more jostling crowd that the police had great difficulty in restraining, made its way under the foliage of the large trees towards the lagoon.

The car stopped before the gate where the electric arc lights mingled their dazzling rays with the first shades of evening.

The interior of the mausoleum would hold a hundred people at the most, if therefore the programme of the obsequies included any more items they would have to be gone through outside, and, in fact, this was what occurred.

The car stopped, the ranks closed up, there being no crowding on the six holders of the garlands who were to accompany the coffin to the tomb. A confused noise arose from the crowd, eager to see, eager to hear. But gradually the tumult subsided, the groups became motionless, and silence reigned around the railings.

Then, the Rev. Mr. Bingham, who had followed the deceased to his last home, declaimed the words of the Liturgy. The crowd listened to them reverently, and at this moment, and this moment alone, the obsequies partook of a religious character.

To these words, given in a penetrating voice that could be heard afar, succeeded the performance of a celebrated march by Chopin, which has such an impressive effect in ceremonies of this kind. But perhaps the orchestra gave it a rather more lively movement than was warranted by the indications of the Master Symphonist — a movement more in accord with the character of the audience and of the defunct, whose feelings were considerably different from those with which Paris was inspired at the funeral of one of the founders of the Republic, when the Marseillaise, which has so striking a tonality, was played in a minor key.

After this work of Chopin's, the principal feature of the programme, one of the colleagues of William J, Hypperbone, who had been bound to him by the ties of closest friendship, the president, George B. Higginbotham, stepped out from the group, placed himself in front of the car, and in a brilliant oration retraced in apologetic terms the life story of his friend.

"At twenty-five years of age, already possessed of a moderate fortune, William J. Hypperbone had discovered how to increase it — And his fortunate acquisitions of land, every square yard of which was now worth as much gold as would cover it — And his elevation to the rank of one of the millionaires of the city — that is to say, one of the great citizens of the United States of America — And the sagacious shareholder in the mighty railroad companies of the Federation — And the prudent speculator in industrial enterprises bearing a high rate of interest — And the generous giver, always ready to subscribe to the loans of his country whenever his country wanted to borrow, which was a want he himself had never experienced — And the distinguished colleague that the Eccentric Club had lost in him, the member on whom they had reckoned to make it famous, the man who, if his life had been prolonged, would have astonished the universe, — And he was one of those geniuses who do not reveal themselves until they are no more, — To say nothing of his funeral, conducted in the way they had seen amid the concourse of the whole population, there was reason for supposing that his last wishes would impose exceptional conditions on his heirs, — No doubt his will would contain clauses of a nature to provoke the admiration of the two Americas, — which alone was worth more than the other four quarters of the globe!"

Thus spoke George B, Higginbotham, not without producing general emotion. It seemed as though William J. Hypperbone had just appeared to the eyes of the crowd, flourishing in one hand the testamentary document which was to immortalize his name, and with the other pouring on the heads of the "six "the millions of his fortune.

To the discourse of the most intimate of his friends the public responded by flattering murmurs, which gradually spread to the outermost ranks assembled within the cemetery. Those who had heard communicated their impressions to those who could not hear, and who were not the least attentive of the audience.

Then the choir and the band in vocal and instrumental union of the loudest performed the formidable *"Hallelujah"* from Handel's "Messiah."

The ceremony was nearing its end, the programme had been completed, and yet it seemed as though the public were awaiting something extraordinary, something ripe, matured. Such was the excitement that no one would have been surprised at a sudden modification of the laws of nature, at some allegorical figure appearing in the sky, as when the cross and *in hoc signo vinces* appeared to Constantine, or for the sun to stand still to shine on this great manifestation for an extra hour, or for something miraculous which the fiercest free-thinker could not deny —

But this time the laws of nature remained unchanged, and the universe was not troubled by phenomena of a superior order.

The moment had come to remove the bier from the car to take it into the interior of the hall, to deposit it in the tomb. It was to be carried by eight domestics of the deceased in their best liveries. They approached it, they removed the coverings, they placed it on their shoulders and approached the gate.

The "six "marched in the order and position they had maintained since their departure from La Salle Street. Those on the right held in their left hands, those on the left held in their right hands the silver handles of the coffin as they were asked to do by the Master of the Ceremonies.

The members of the Eccentric Club, the civil and military authorities walked behind. Then the gate was closed, and it was with difficulty that the antechamber, the hall and the apse of the mausoleum could hold them all.

Outside were grouped the others who had received invitation to join the procession; the crowd straggled off in different ways, and human grapes hung themselves on the branches of the trees which surrounded the monument.

At this moment the trumpets of the militia blared forth loudly enough to burst the lungs of those who filled them with their breath, and there was let loose an immense flight of birds decorated with many coloured streamers, who flew off in different directions over the lake and above the trees uttering joyful cries of deliverance, and it seemed as though the soul of the deceased, carried off in their flight, was borne away through the depths of the sky.

As soon as the steps had been mounted the coffin passed through the first door, then through the second and stopped close to the tomb in which the bearers placed it.

The voice of the Rev. Mr. Bingham was again heard praying that the celestial doors might be opened to the late William J. Hypperbone.

"Honour to the honourable Hypperbone!" said the clear loud voice of the Master of the Ceremonies.

"Honour — honour — honour — !" repeated the gathering.

And outside thousands of mouths hurled this last farewell into space.

Then the "six" passed in procession round the tomb and received the salute of George B. Higginbotham in the name of the Eccentric Club, and prepared to leave the hall.

All that had to be done was to replace the heavy marble lid on which were inscribed the name and titles of the deceased.

Mr. Tornbrock stepped a few paces in front, and taking from his pocket the note that referred to the funeral, read the last lines as follows: —

"My wish is that my tomb shall remain open for twelve days, and that when this delay has elapsed, in the morning of the twelfth day the six persons designated by lot who have followed my funeral come and lay their visiting cards on my coffin. Then the stone can be put in place, and Mr. Tornbrock will the said day at noon precisely in the hall of the Auditorium read my will which is in his hands.

"WILLIAM J. HYPPERBONE."

Evidently the defunct was an original, and who knew if this posthumous originality were the last?

The assembly retired, and the keeper of the cemetery closed the doors of the monument and the gate of the railing.

It was nearly eight o'clock. The day had been fine throughout. The serenity of the sky appeared to be still more complete amid the early shades of night. Innumerable stars sparkled in the firmament, adding their gentle light to that of the lamps which glared round the mausoleum.

The crowd slowly dispersed through the cemetery gates, longing for rest at the close of so tiring a day. For a little a tumultuous sound of footsteps troubled the neighbouring streets, and at last tranquillity reigned in this distant quarter of Oakwood.

CHAPTER IV. THE SIX

Next day Chicago returned to its numerous occupations. The different districts had resumed their daily physiognomy. If the population no longer passed, as they had done the day before, along the avenues and the boulevards as the funeral passed by, they took no less interest in the surprises that were doubtless in store in Hypperbone's will.

What clauses did it contain, what obligations, fantastic or otherwise, did it impose on the "six," and how were they to be put in possession of their heritage, providing that it was not all to end in some mystification beyond the tomb worthy of a member of the Eccentric Club?

But this was an eventuality that no one could admit. People refused to believe that Miss Lizzie Wag and Messrs. Urrican, Kymbale, Titbury, Crabbe and Real were to get nothing out of the affair but deception, and much ridicule.

There was a very simple way of satisfying public curiosity on the one hand, and on the other, of saving those interested from the uncertainty which threatened to deprive them of appetite and sleep. All that had to be done was to open the will and ascertain its contents. But it was distinctly forbidden to do this before the 15th of the month, and Tornbrock would never consent to infringe the conditions imposed by the testator. On the 15th of April, in the theatre of the Auditorium, in presence of the numerous assemblage it would contain, he would read Hypperbone's will — the 15th of April at noon not a day sooner or a minute later.

They must resign themselves to circumstances, and this could only increase the mental excitement of Chicago, as the fateful day approached. Added to this, the two thousand two hundred journals, the fifteen thousand other publications, weekly, monthly, fortnightly, of the United States were engaged in keeping up this excitement. And if they could not, even by supposition, forecast the secrets of the deceased, they could at least submit each of the six to the tortures of the interview, and discover their social position.

Considering that photography would not allow itself to be outstripped by journalism, portraits, large and small, full length, head only, head and shoulders, having been put into circulation by hundreds of thousands, it will be admitted that the six were destined to rank among the best known people in America.

The reporters of the *Chicago Mail*, who called on Hodge Urrican at 73, Randolph Street, got a very bad reception.

"What do you want with me?" he replied, with a violence that was in no way put on. "I know nothing! I have nothing to tell you! I was invited to follow the procession, and I followed it! And there were five others there, as I was, near the car — five of whom I knew no more than Adam or Eve. And if it ends badly for some of us, I shall not be astonished. I was there like a barge in tow of a tug, with no chance of steaming at my ease as I blew off my temper. Ah! this William Hypperbone, if he has deceived me, if he forces me to strike my flag before these five intruders, let him take care of himself, and dead as he is, and buried as he is, if I have to wait for the last judgment, I'll — "

"But," objected one of the reporters, bowing to this storm, "there is nothing, Mr. Urrican, to lead you to believe that you will be exposed to a mystification, that you will have to regret being one of those chosen by lot. And if your share is only a sixth of the heritage — "

"A sixth — a sixth!" replied the hot-headed Urrican in a voice of thunder; "and this sixth, am I sure of getting it in full?"

"Calm yourself, please"

"I will not calm myself. It is not in my nature to calm myself. I am accustomed to storms, and I am always more stormy than — "

"There are no storms about," said the reporter, "the horizon is serene,"

"That is what we shall see, sir," shouted the irascible American; "and if you are going to tell the public about my looks and my actions and my gestures, take care what you say, or you will have to reckon with Commodore Urrican."

He was in fact a Commodore, Hodge Urrican, an officer of the United States Navy, retired six months before, to which he could not reconcile himself, a good and brave sailor who had always done his duty before the fire of the enemy as before the fire of the heavens. Notwithstanding his fifty-two years, he had lost nothing of his natural irritability. Imagine a man vigorously built, of tall stature, powerful shoulders, strong head with large eyes rolling beneath bushy eyebrows, forehead rather low, hair close cut, chin square, with a billy-goat beard that he stroked unceasingly with a feverish hand, arms not idly hung, legs regularly bowed, and giving the body that rolling motion peculiar to seafarers. Of a fiery temper, always flying into a passion, incapable of restraining himself, as disagreeable as a human creature could be in private as in public, and — without a friend. It would have been surprising for such a man to have been married. And he was not; and "What a chance for a woman!" would be jokers exclaimed. He belonged to that class of the violent whom anger renders pale by causing a spasm of the heart, whose body is carried forward as if in attack, whose glowing pupils are in a perpetual state of contraction, and whose voice has a hardness in it when they are calm and a roar when they are not.

When the reporters of the *Chicago Globe* knocked at the studio at 3997, South Halsted Street — the street is a good length, it will be noticed — they found no one at home except a young negro of seventeen, who was in the service of Max Real and opened the door to them.

"Where is your master?" they asked.

"I don't know."

"When did he go out?"

"Don't know."

"When is he coming back?"

"Don't know."

And it was a fact that Tommy did not know, for Max Real had gone out early in the morning without saying anything to Tommy, who was as fond of sleep as a child, and whom his master did not care to wake up at so early an hour.

But because Tommy could not answer the questions of the reporters, it need not to be inferred that the *Chicago Globe* was without information regarding Max Real. No! this particular "sixer" had already been the subject of interviews widely published in the United States.

He was a young painter of talent, a landscape painter, whose pictures had begun to sell at good prices in America, and for whom the future had in reserve a high position in the domain of art. Born at Chicago, if his name was of French origin it was because he was descended from a Canadian family of Quebec. In that city still lived Madame Real, a widow for many years, who was preparing to take up her abode near him in the metropolis of Illinois.

Max Real adored his mother, who held him in similar adoration — an excellent mother and an excellent son. And so he had not lost a day in telling her what had passed and how he had been selected to take a special place at the obsequies of William J. Hypperbone. He assured her at the same time that he troubled himself very little about the testamentary dispositions of the deceased, which seemed "droll "to him, that was all.

Max Real had just reached his twenty-fifth year. From his birth he had the grace, distinction and elegance of the. French type. He was rather above the medium height, dark brown in hair and beard, eyes of dark blue, head high without haughtiness or stiffness, mouth smiling, walk deliberate, indicative of that internal contentment whence sprang his cheery unshaken confidence. That he had a fund of open-heartedness was apparent in his courage and generosity.

Having made himself known as a painter of real merit, he had decided to leave Canada for the United States. His father had left him but a small patrimony, and he had made up his mind to acquire a fortune more for his mother than himself.

In short, when it was stated that Max Real was not to be found at No. 3997, South Halsted Street, there was no need to question Tommy about him. The *Chicago Globe* knew enough to satisfy the curiosity of its readers with regard to the young artist. Max Real might not be in Chicago to-day, but he was yesterday, and certainly he would be back on the 15th of April to be present at the reading of the famous will and complete the group of six at the Auditorium.

It was another sort of thing when the reporters of the *Daily News Record* presented themselves at the home of Harris T. Kymbale. There was no necessity for them to hunt him up at 213, Milwaukee Avenue, for he would have come of his own accord to deliver himself over to his colleagues.

Harris T. Kymbale was a journalist, the reporter-in-chief of the popular *Tribune*. Thirty-seven years old, medium height, robust, sympathetic face, nose like a ferret, piercing little eyes, fine ears made to hear everything, impatient mouth made to repeat everything. Vivacious, active, clear-headed, restless, talkative, patient, indefatigable, energetic, and quite an artist at brag in the

American style. Thoroughly aware of his powers, always in an attitude of action, gifted with a persistent will always ready to manifest itself, he had remained a bachelor, as was best for a man who daily scaled the walls of private life. A good companion in short, very sure, very much esteemed by his comrades, who in no way envied the good fortune which had called him to figure among the six, supposing that he was to share in the worldly goods of William J. Hypperbone.

No! There was no need to interrogate Harris T. Kymbale, for he at once saved them the trouble by beginning: —

"Yes, my friends, it is really your humble servant who figured in the Council of Six. You saw me yesterday walking in my place near the car. Did you notice how I bore myself worthily and properly, and the pains I took to dissemble my delight, for never in my life did I take part in such a lively funeral? And when I think that he was then near me, laid in his coffin, this eccentric defunct! Do you know what I said to myself? If he were not dead, this worthy man! If he is going to start from the depths of his bier! If he is going to appear all alive oh! Well, believe me, I did hope that that would happen, that Hypperbone would, arise in his full height and, like a new Lazarus, break open the tomb; and I should have thought none the worse of him for his untimely resurrection! You have always the right, haven't you, to come to life, provided you are not dead?"

So said Harris T. Kymbale, but you should have heard him!"

"And what do you think," they asked, "will happen on the 15th of April?"

"What will happen" he replied, "will be that Mr. Tornbrock will open the will at noon precisely"

"And you do not doubt that the six will be declared the sole heirs of the deceased?"

"Naturally! Why, pray, did Hypperbone ask us to his funeral, unless he was going to leave us his fortune?"

"Who knows?"

"It would be too much of a good thing for him to have taken up our time without paying damages! Think of it — eleven hours of procession — "

"But is it not supposable that the will may contain some more or less curious provisions?"

"That is likely, considering that he was an original. Well, if he asks what is possible it shall be done, and if it is impossible it must do itself; anyhow, my friends, you can reckon on Harris T. Kymbale, he will not draw back an inch."

No! For the honour of journalism he would not draw back; that was clear enough to those who knew him, and those who did not know him, if they were among the people of Chicago. No matter what were the conditions imposed by the defunct, the chief reporter of the *Tribune* would accept them and fulfil them to the end! If he had to start for the moon, he would start, and unless respiration failed him for want of air, he would not stop on the road!

What a contrast between this resolute American and his co-heir of a sixth, known by the name of Hermann Titbury, who lived in the commercial quarter traversed from south to north by the long thoroughfare of Robey Street.

When the envoys of the *Staats Zeitung* rang the bell at No. 77 they were not allowed to cross the threshold. "Mr. Hermann Titbury" they said through the half-open door," is he at home?"

"Yes," replied a sort of giantess of slovenly appearance with her hair in disorder, a kind of female dragon.

"Can we see him?"

"I will tell you when I have asked Mrs. Titbury."

For there existed a Mrs. Kate Titbury, aged fifty, that is, two years older than her husband. And the reply made by this matron and transmitted faithfully by the servant was:

"Mr. Titbury has no wish to see you, and is astonished that you should have allowed yourselves to disturb him.

There was no question of having access to his office or his dining-room to ask him for particulars about himself, or of taking a seat at his table. The house remained closed and the reporters of the *Staats Zeitung* had to return reportless.

Hermann Titbury and Kate Titbury were the most avaricious couple ever united to traverse together this vale of tears, in which they had never let fall the least drop in pity for the fate of the unfortunate. Two strong, callous hearts, they were made to beat in unison. Happily heaven had disdained to bless their union and their line would become extinct with them. They were wealthy, but their fortune was derived neither from commerce nor industry. Together — for the lady worked as hard as the gentleman — they had carried on a clandestine business as pawnbrokers, lending on pledges, buying securities for as near to nothing as they could get them, being usurers of the lowest kind, sharks who live on plunder and yet manage to keep within the limits of the law — that law which a great French romancer has said would be a fine thing for scoundrels if God did not exist!

In tracing back their line of ancestors, you would at the outset have met with the progenitors of German origin, justifying the Christian name of Hermann borne by the last representative of this Teutonic tribe.

He was a short, stout man, red-bearded as his wife was red-haired. Enjoying a health that never failed them, they had never had to spend half a dollar on drugs or doctor's visits. Provided with stomachs capable of digesting anything — such as honest people ought only to have — they lived on nothing, and their servant accommodated herself to what she could get. Since Mr. Titbury had retired from business he had had nothing to do with outside affairs and allowed himself to be completely managed by Mrs. Titbury, a masterful woman as detestable as she could be, and who "slept with his keys," as the popular phrase goes.

The couple occupied a house with windows as narrow as their ideas, iron-barred like their hearts, and which resembled a private strong-box. Their door never opened for a stranger, nor for a member of the family, as they had no family, nor for a friend, as they had no friends. And on this occasion, before the disgusted seekers after information it remained obstinately closed.

It is true that, without interviewing Titbury directly, nothing could be easier than to appreciate his state of mind on the day he took his place among the group of six. What were his feelings when Hermann Titbury read his name in the famous issue of the *Tribune* on the 1st of April! But were there not other people of the name in Chicago? None, at least at 77, Robey Street. As to supposing that he was the victim of some practical joker, he would have none of it. He saw himself already in possession of a sixth of the enormous fortune, and his great regret, his vexation even, was that he was not the only one designated by lot. And it was more than envy that he felt for his five co-heirs, it was hate — as with Commodore Urrican — and what he and Mrs. Titbury thought of these intruders had best be left to the reader's imagination.

Assuredly luck had committed one of those gross errors it is accustomed to in calling on this in no way interesting, in no way sympathetic personage to receive a share of the fortune of William J. Hypperbone, if such had been the intention of that eccentric individual.

The morning after the funeral, at five o'clock in the morning, Mr. and Mrs. Titbury had left their house and gone to Oakwood Cemetery. There they had called up the keeper and in a voice that betrayed the most intense anxiety had asked:

"Anything fresh — last night?"

"Nothing fresh," replied the keeper.

"And so he is realty dead?"

"As dead as he can be, never fear!" declared the good man, who vainly expected a gratuity for his good news.

The deceased had not awoke from his eternal sleep and nothing had troubled the repose of the gloomy guests of Oakwood.

Mr. and Mrs. Titbury returned home, but once again in the afternoon and again in the evening they made the long journey to assure themselves that William J. Hypperbone had not returned to the sublunary world.

And that is enough regarding this couple destined to figure in this singular story, whom not even one of their neighbours complimented on their good fortune.

When the two reporters of the *Freie Presse* arrived in Calumet Street, not far from the lake of this name, situated in the southern part of the town amid a populous and industrial district, they inquired of the police where they would find the house of Tom Crabbe.

Tom Crabbe's house, or rather that of his trainer, was No. 11. In fact it was John Milner who assisted him in those memorable encounters from which gentlemen most frequently emerge with eyes bunged up, jaw bones dislocated, chest knocked in here and there, and mouth relieved of a few teeth for the honour of the National Boxing Championship.

Tom Crabbe was a professional prize-fighter, the then Champion of the New World, owing to his having vanquished the famous Fitzsimmons, who that year had vanquished the no less famous Corbett.

The reporters without difficulty obtained admission to John Milner's house, and were received on the ground floor by the said trainer — a man of ordinary stature, of extreme leanness, mere skin and bone, but all muscles, all nerves, penetrating eyes, pointed teeth, smooth face, active as a chamois, artful as a monkey.

"Tom Crabbe?" they asked.

"He is finishing his first breakfast," replied he in a harsh voice.

"Can we see him?"

"Regarding what?"

"Regarding the will of William J. Hypperbone, and to say something about him in our newspaper."

"When you want to talk to Tom Crabbe," replied Milner, "Tom Crabbe is always visible."

The reporters entered the dining-room and found themselves in that personage's presence He was devouring his sixth slice of ham, his sixth hunch of bread, his sixth pint of half-and-half while awaiting the tea which was being made in a huge kettle, and the six small glasses of whisky which generally ended his first meal, that which he took at half-past seven, which was followed by five others in the course of the day. You will notice the important part played by the figure 6 in the life of the famous boxer, and perhaps it was to its mysterious influence that he came to be counted in the group of heirs of William J. Hypperbone.

Tom Crabbe was a colossus measuring six feet ten in height and three feet from shoulder to shoulder, his head was voluminous, his hair hard and black, cut close as if shaven, big bull's eyes under thick eyebrows, forehead low and retreating, ears prominent, heavy jaw bones, heavy moustache cut off at the corners of his lips, all his teeth, for the formidable blows he had received had not removed one, a body like a hogshead of beer, arms like connecting rods, legs like pillars made to support this enormous human structure.

Is human the proper word? No, it should be animal, for there was nothing but animality in this gigantic product. His organs worked like those of a steam engine when the fire is lighted — an engine which had for its engineer John Milner. He was celebrated in the two Americas and knew nothing of his celebrity. To eat, drink, box, sleep — that included all the acts of his existence, without any intellectual expenditure.

Did he understand what chance had done for him in introducing him among the "six"? Did he know why the day before he had marched with heavy step close to the funeral car amid the applause of the multitude? Vaguely; but his trainer understood it for him, and all that came from the stroke of fortune would John Milner turn to his own profit.

Hence it follows that it was Milner who gave the replies in the interview the reporters had with Tom Crabbe.

He furnished them with all the details likely to interest the readers of the *Freie Presse:* his personal weight, 533 lbs. before a meal and 540 after it; his height, exactly 6 feet 10 inches, as we have said; his strength, measured by the dynamometer, 75 kilogrammeters, that of one horsepower; the maximum force of contraction of his jaws, 234 lbs.; his age, 30 years, 6 months, 17 days; his parents, a father who was a packer or slaughterer at Armour's, a mother who had been a strong-woman in a Swansea circus.

And what more could they ask to write an article of a hundred lines on Tom Crabbe?

"He hardly speaks" said one of the journalists.

"As little as possible," said John Milner. "What is the good of using your tongue?"

"Perhaps — but does he not think?"

"What is the use of thinking?"

"None, Mr. Milner."

"Tom Crabbe is merely a fist" said the trainer — " a closed fist, as prompt in attack as in defence!"

And when the reporters of the *Freie Presse* had left them:

"A brute!" said one.

"And what a brute!" replied the other.

And certainly it was not of John Milner they were speaking.

Going to the north-west of the town, after passing the Humboldt boulevard you enter the twenty-seventh quarter. Here there is less bustle in the streets, the people are not so busy. The visitor might believe himself in the provinces, although the phrase has no meaning in the United States. Beyond Wabansia Avenue is the lower part of Sheridan Street. Reaching No. 19, you find yourself before a house of modest appearance, of seventeen floors, inhabited by a hundred tenants. It was here, on the ninth floor, that Lizzie Wag occupied a little flat of two rooms, to which she returned after her day spent as under-cashier in the linendraper's shop of Marshall Field.

Lizzie Wag belonged to a respectable family of slender means, of whom she alone remained. Well brought up, educated as are most young American girls, after reverses of fortune and the death of her father and mother, prematurely carried off, she had had to go out to work to gain the means of livelihood. Mr. Wag had lost all he possessed in a disastrous matter of marine assurance, and the liquidation persisted in the interest of his daughter had produced no result.

Lizzie Wag, endowed with an energetic character, sound judgment, shrewd intelligence, quiet and self-controlled, had moral strength enough not to lose courage. By the intervention of a few friends of the family, she was recommended to the head of the house of Marshall Field and for fifteen months had held a good situation there.

She was a charming girl who had just reached her twenty-first year, of medium height, fair hair, dark blue eyes, a good colour indicating good health, carrying herself gracefully, features rather serious, animated occasionally by a smile, across which gleamed her beautiful teeth. Amiable, affable, obliging, kindly, she had none but friends among her companions.

Of tastes very simple and humble, without ambition, without giving way to the dreams which have led so many others astray, Lizzie Wag was by far the least excited of the six when she heard that chance had called her to figure at the funeral. At first she would have refused. This kind of exhibition was not at all to her liking. To have her name and herself the object of public curiosity inspired her with deep repugnance. And it was much against her feelings that, with a heavy heart and blushing forehead, she took her place by the side of the car.

It should be said that the most intimate of her friends had done everything to overcome her resistance. This was the lively, cheery, laughing Jovita Foley, twenty-five years old, neither ugly nor pretty — and she knew it — but with a face sparkling with archness and humour, very refined, very acute, of excellent nature in fact, and whom the closest affection united to Lizzie Wag.

These two girls occupied the same flat, and after the day spent in the shops of Marshall Field, where Jovita Foley was chief saleswoman, they returned together. One was seldom seen without the other.

But if Lizzie Wag under such circumstances ended by yielding to the irresistible solicitations of her companion, she by no means consented to receive the reporters of the *Chicago Herald* who presented themselves that very evening at 19, Sheridan Street. In vain Jovita Foley entreated her friend to be less disagreeable; she would have nothing to do with an interview. After the reporters would come the photographers, who would aim at her with their unceremonious lenses — after the photographers would come inquisitive people of all sorts. No! better shut the door on the first of these importunates. Whatever Jovita might say, it was the wisest, and the *Chicago Herald* was unable to provide its readers with a sensational article.

"So be it" said Jovita, when the disappointed journalists had retired, "You have shut your door, but you will not escape the attention of the public! Ah! if it had been I! I warn you, Lizzie, I will make you comply with all the conditions of the will! Think, my dear, this share of such an extraordinary heritage — "

"I scarcely believe in it, Jovita," replied Lizzie Wag, "and if it is only the freak of some practical joker, I shall not regret it much."

"But, my Lizzie," said Jovita Foley, drawing her towards her, "not regret it very much! When it means a fortune — "

"Are we not happy?"

"Agreed: but if it had been I!" repeated the ambitious young person.

Well — if it had been you!"

"To begin with, you should have your share in it, dear Lizzie."

"As I shall do, you need not fear!" replied Lizzie, laughing at the contingent promises of her enthusiastic friend.

"Would it were the 15th of April," continued Jovita. "How long the time seems! I am beginning to count the hours, the minutes — "

"Spare me the seconds," said Lizzie. "There are too many of them."

"Can you jest about so serious a matter — millions of dollars to bring home with you?"

"Or rather, millions of annoyances, of worries, as I have had all this day — "

"You are difficult to please, Lizzie!"

"Cannot you see, Jovita, that I am anxious as to how it is going to finish?"

"It will finish at the end," exclaimed Jovita, "as does everything else in the world."

Such, then, was the sixth of the co-heirs — there was hardly a doubt that they would be called upon to share the enormous estate — whom William J. Hypperbone had invited to his funeral. These mortals, privileged above all, had only to remain patient for a fortnight.

At last the two long weeks rolled by and the 15th of April arrived. That morning, in accordance with the conditions imposed, in the presence of Mr. George B. Higginbotham, assisted by Mr. Tornbrock, Lizzie Wag, Max Real, Tom Crabbe, Hermann Titbury, Harris T. Kymbale and Hodge Urrican came to place their visiting cards on the tomb of William J. Hypperbone. Then the sepulchral stone was put in its place. The eccentric deceased was to receive no further visitors at Oakwood Cemetery.

CHAPTER V. THE WILL

From dawn on that eventful day, the nineteenth quarter was invaded by the crowd. The public excitement seemed to have in no way decreased since the long procession had taken William J. Hypperbone to his last home.

The thirteen hundred trains a day of Chicago had been pouring thousands of visitors into the town since the evening before. The weather promised to be superb. A fresh morning breeze had cleared the sky of the mists of the night. The sun hung on the distant horizon of the lake, which, streaked with a few ripples on its blue surface, caressed the shore with a gentle surf.

By Michigan Avenue and Congress Street, the tumultuous mob made their way to an enormous edifice surmounted at one of its corners by a massive square tower 310 feet in height.

The list of the city's hotels is long. The traveller's difficulty is not to find one, but to choose among so many. It matters not whither the cabs at twenty-five cents a mile take him, he never fails to find accommodation. He can get a room in the European style at two or three dollars a day, in the American style at four or five.

Among the principal hotels are the Palmer House in State and Monroe Streets, the Continental in Wabash Avenue and Monroe Street, the Commercial and Fremont House in Dearborn and Lake Streets, the Alhambra in Archer Avenue, the Atlantic, the Wellington, the Saratoga, and a hundred others. But in importance, in management, in the amount of its business, in its well-ordered service, in its power of accommodating its visitors in either the European or American manner, the most noted is the Auditorium, a vast caravansary whose ten floors rise one above the other at the corner of Congress Street and Michigan Avenue, opposite Lake Park. And not only can this vast edifice give shelter to a thousand travellers, but it contains a theatre large enough to hold eight thousand spectators.

During the matinee — the expression comes from the other side of the Atlantic — it would hold more than the maximum, and this expression is as justly applicable with regard to the takings. Yes, the takings; for after the happy thought of putting the names of the six up to auction, Tornbrock had decided to make everybody pay for places who wished to hear the reading of the will in the Auditorium. By this means the poor would benefit to the amount of some twelve thousand dollars, to be shared between the hospitals of the Alexian Brothers and the Maurice Porter Memorial for Children.

The charge for seats made little difference to the inquisitive crowd. On the stage were the mayor and the municipal authorities; a little behind them were the members of the Eccentric Club, around their president, George B. Higginbotham; a little in front were the six in a line near the footlights, each in the attitude most fitting to his or her social position.

Lizzie Wag, really ashamed at being exhibited in this way before thousands of greedy eyes, sat in her arm-chair with her head bowed, endeavouring to make herself as inconspicuous as possible.

Harris T. Kymbale expanded between the arms of his chair, waving salutes innumerable to his journalistic friends of every degree.

Commodore Urrican, rolling his ferocious eyes, seemed to be seeking a quarrel with everyone who took the liberty of looking him in the face.

Max Real carelessly looked around at all these people swarming up to the very roof, devoured by curiosity which he in no way shared, and if the truth must be told, looking principally at the charming girl seated not far from him, whose evident embarrassment inspired him with keen interest.

Hermann Titbury was calculating how much the takings would amount to — a mere drop of water amid the millions of the heritage.

Tom Crabbe, hardly knowing why he was there, was seated, not in an arm-chair — which could not have contained his enormous mass — but on a large sofa, the legs of which bent beneath him.

We need scarcely say that in the first row of spectators figured his trainer, John Milner, Mrs. Titbury, who every now and then made incomprehensible signs to her husband, and the nervous Jovita Foley, without whose intervention Lizzie Wag would never have consented to sit in the presence of this terrible public in the body of the theatre.

In the circles and amphitheatres, in the remotest tiers of seats, in every place where a human body could find room and in every hole through which a head could peep, were piled up men, women, and children belonging to the different classes of the population who could pay for admission.

And outside, along Michigan Avenue and Congress Street, in the windows of the houses, in the balconies of the hotels, on the pavements, in the roadways, where the traffic had been stopped, were massed a crowd overflowing like the Mississippi at the time of its floods, with its outermost undulation reaching beyond the furthest limits of the district.

It was estimated that on that day Chicago had received a crowd of fifty thousand visitors from different parts of Illinois and the neighbouring states, and also from New York, Pennsylvania, Ohio, and Maine. A continued uproar, increasing and tumultuous, floated above this part of the town, filled the enclosure of Lake Park and died away on the sunny surface of Lake Michigan.

Noon sounded. A tremendous whisper of "Ah!" escaped from the Auditorium. The same instant Tornbrock arose, and the whisper, as a breeze through foliage, reached the crowd outside.

Then there was profound silence — a silence as of that between a lightning flash and the growl of the thunder.

Tornbrock, standing before the table which occupied the centre of the stage, with his arms crossed and a serious look on his face, waited until the last stroke of twelve had struck.

On the table was laid an envelope sealed with three red seals bearing the initials of the deceased. This envelope contained the will of William J. Hypperbone, and probably, from its dimensions, other testamentary papers. A few lines of writing indicated that the envelope was not to be opened until a fortnight after the death, and stipulated that the opening was to take place in the theatre of the Auditorium at noon.

Tornbrock with a feverish hand broke the seals and drew from it a parchment on which appeared the well-known large handwriting of the testator; then he drew forth a card folded in four, and then a small box about an inch square and half an inch high.

And then in a loud voice, that could be heard in the furthest corners, Tornbrock, after running his eyes, armed with aluminium spectacles, over the first lines of the parchment, read as follows: —

"This is my last will, written entirely by my own hand, done at Chicago the third day of July, one thousand eight hundred and ninety-five.

"Sound in body and mind, in all the plenitude of my intelligence, I have drawn up this deed, in which are set forth my last wishes. These wishes Mr. Notary Tornbrock, together with my colleague and friend George B. Higginbotham, president of the Eccentric Club, will carry out in all their details, as well as all that is to be done with regard to my funeral."

At last the public and those interested knew what was coming. Now were to be solved all the questions asked during the fortnight, all the suppositions and hypotheses that had arisen during these two weeks of feverish expectation.

Tornbrock continued: —

"Up to now undoubtedly no member of the Eccentric Club has made himself remarkable by notable eccentricities. The writer of these lines has, like his colleagues, never ventured beyond the commonplaces of existence. But what he has failed to do when living he can by his last will do after his death."

A murmur of satisfaction ran round the ranks of his audience. He waited until this had died away before he resumed the reading thus interrupted for half a minute. And this was what he read: —

"My dear colleagues have not forgotten that if I ever experienced a passion it was only for the noble Game of Goose, so well-known in Europe, and particularly in France, where it is said to have been revived from the Greeks, although Hellas never saw it played by Plato, Themistocles, Aristides, Leonidas, Socrates, or any other historical personage. I introduced this game into our club. It has caused me the most lively emotion by the variety of its details, the unexpectedness of its throws, the caprice of its combinations, in which pure chance guides those who struggle for victory on the field of battle."

For what object did this Game of Goose intervene in this unexpected fashion in Hypperbone's will? A very natural question. The notary continued: —

"This game — everyone in Chicago knows it now — consists of a series of divisions placed side by side and numbered from one to sixty-three. Fourteen of these divisions are occupied by the figure of a goose, the animal so unjustly accused of stupidity, and which should have been restored to favour from the day it saved the capitol from the attack of Brennus and his Gauls."

A few of the more sceptical of the audience began to ask themselves if the late Mr. Hypperbone were not slyly poking fun at the public with this unseasonable eulogium on this typical example of the anserines.

The will continued in this way: —

"On account of the above arrangement, by cutting off fourteen divisions there remain forty-nine, of which six only require the player to pay a fine, the first fine being at the sixth, where there is a bridge leading to the twelfth; two fines at the nineteenth, where he has to stay at the inn until the other players have had two throws; three fines at the thirty-first, where there is a well, at the bottom of which he must remain until another comes to take his place; two fines at the forty-second, where is the labyrinth he must immediately leave to return to the thirtieth, where is displayed a nosegay of flowers; three fines at the fifty-second, where he must remain in prison until he is replaced by another player; and three fines at the fifty-eighth division, in which there is a death's head, from which the player is sent back to begin the game over again."

When Tornbrock stopped after this long sentence to take breath many murmurs arose, but they were promptly repressed by the majority of the audience, who were evidently partial to the deceased. But everybody had not come to be crushed at the Auditorium for the purpose of listening to a lesson on the noble Game of Goose.

The notary continued: —

"There will be found in this envelope a board and box. The board is that of the noble Game of Goose, arranged with a new set of divisions according to a little idea of my own with which the public should be made acquainted. The box contains two dice similar to those I have been in the habit of using at my club. The board on the one hand, the dice on the other, are intended for a game to be played on the following conditions."

What! a game? Was there to be a Game of Goose? Decidedly the man was a practical joker! He was nothing but a humbug, as they say in America!

Loud cries of silence were addressed to the malcontents and Tornbrock resumed his reading.

"This is what I've done in honour of my country, which I love with a patriot's ardour, and of which I visited the various states as they increased in number and added to the stars in the flag of the American Republic!"

Here a triple salvo of cheers awoke the echoes of the Auditorium, followed by a deep calm, for curiosity was at its zenith.

"Without counting Alaska, situated outside its territory, the Union consists of fifty states, extending over an area of nearly eight million kilometres.

"By arranging these fifty states in the divisions one after the other and repeating one of them fourteen times, I have obtained a board of sixty-three divisions, identical with that of the noble Game of Goose, which thus becomes the noble Game of the United States of America."

Those of the audience who were familiar with the game in question understood Hypperbone's idea without difficulty. Indeed, it was a happy thought to distribute the States of the Union among the sixty-three squares; and the audience abandoned themselves to enthusiastic applause, and soon the streets resounded with acclamations at the testator's ingenious invention.

Tornbrock continued his reading.

"It remained to be determined which of the fifty states should figure fourteen times on the board. Could I do better than choose that of which the waters of Michigan bathe the superb shores, that which prides itself on a city such as ours, that which has robbed Cincinnati for more than half a century of the title of Queen of the West, that Illinois, the privileged region which Michigan borders on the north, the Ohio on the south, the Mississippi on the west, the Wabash on the east — a state at the same time continental and insular, and now in the first rank of the great federal republic!"

Renewed thunder of cheers, which made the theatre walls tremble and were taken up outside by the crowd, now at the very height of their excitement. This time the notary suspended his reading for several minutes. When calm was at length restored, he read: —

"The next thing is to select the persons who are to play the game over the immense territory of the United States, according to the board enclosed in this envelope, and which should be printed in millions of copies in order that every citizen of the republic should follow the game's vicissitudes These players, to the number of six, have been chosen by lot from among the population of our city and should be assembled at this moment on the stage of the Auditorium. These are the people who will personally betake themselves to each state indicated by the number of points obtained, and to the very spot indicated by my executors according to the note annexed."

And so this was the part assigned to the six. The caprice of the dice was to send them moving about the surface of the Union. They were the chessmen of this extraordinary game.

If Tom Crabbe did not understand Hypperbone's idea, it was otherwise with Commodore Urrican, Harris T. Kymbale, Hermann Titbury, Max Read and Lizzie Wag. They looked at each other and were already looked upon as extraordinary creatures placed beyond the bounds of humanity. But there remained to be ascertained the final arrangements proposed by the deceased.

"A fortnight after the reading of my will," he said, "and continuing every other day in this place in the Auditorium, at eight o'clock in the morning, Tornbrock, in the presence of the members of the Eccentric Club, will shake the box, throw the dice, announce the number, and send it by telegraph to the place where each player should be found under pain of being excluded from the game. Considering the facility and rapidity of communication within the boundaries of the republic, which none of the players are allowed to cross under penalty of being disqualified, I have estimated that a fortnight will suffice for each move, however long a journey it may mean."

It was evident that if the six decided to take part in this noble game they would have to strictly conform to the rules. Under what conditions then were they to undertake these mad careerings across the United States?

"At their own expense," said Tornbrock, amid a profound silence, "the six will travel, and out of their own finds will they pay the fines required when reaching such and such a division, otherwise such and such a State; the fines being fixed at a thousand dollars each. Any player failing to pay any one of these fines will thereby retire from the game."

A thousand dollars. And if this had to be paid several times — as ill luck might have it — it might amount to a considerable sum. We need not be surprised that Hermann Titbury made a grimace, which was reproduced at the same instant on the bloated face of his wife. Evidently the obligation to pay this fine of a thousand dollars when payment was necessary was not of a nature to inconvenience all, or at least some of the players. Assuredly lenders would come to the aid of the one who seemed to have the best chances. Did this not afford a new field to the speculative ardour of the citizens of speculative America?

The will contained further interesting matter. To begin with this declaration relative to the financial position of William J. Hypperbone.

"My fortune in properties built or not built upon, in shares, in industrial companies, in bank shares and railway bonds, the securities for which are deposited in the hands of Mr. Tornbrock, can be estimated as being of the value of sixty millions of dollars."

This declaration was received with a murmur of satisfaction. People were gratified that the deceased had left a heritage of this importance, and the amount appeared respectable even in the country of Gould, Bennett, Vanderbilt, Astor, Bradley-Martin, Hetty Green, Hutchinson, Carroll, Prior, Morgan, Slade, Lennox, Rockefeller, Schemeorn, Richard King, May Goelet, Ogden Mills, Sloane, Belmont, and other millionaires, kings of sugar, grain, flour, petroleum, railways, copper, silver, and gold! Anyhow, him, her, or those to whom the fortune would fall in whole or part would be quite contented with it! But under what conditions would it be awarded? To that question the will replied in the following lines: —

"In this Game of Goose, as you know, the winner is the one who first reaches the sixty-third square. This square is not definitely reached if the number of points yielded by the last throw of the dice takes him beyond it. If he exceeds it the player must go back just as many points as he obtained in excess. Having conformed to all these rules, the inheritor of my entire fortune shall be the player who first takes possession of the sixty-third square, otherwise the sixty-third State, which is that of Illinois."

And so there was to be one winner — the first to arrive! Nothing to his companions, after so many fatigues, so many excitements, so many expenses —

Wrong! The second was to be compensated and reimbursed to a certain extent.

"The second," said the will, "that is to say the one who at the end of the game is nearest to the sixty-third square, shall receive the sum produced by the fines of a thousand dollars that the chances of the game may bring up to a considerable sum, which he will know how to turn to good and profitable use."

This clause met with neither a good nor a bad reception from the assembly. Such as it was, there was no disputing it.

Then William J. Hypperbone added: — "If for one reason or another, one or several of the players retire before the end of the game, it will continue to be played by those who remain. And in the event of their all abandoning it, my heritage shall devolve on the city of Chicago as my sole legatee, to be employed in the best way for its interests."

At last, the will ended with these lines: —

"Such are my formal wishes, the execution of which will be superintended by George B. Higginbotham, president of the Eccentric Club, and Notary Tornbrock. They must be observed in their strictness, as shall also be the rules of the noble game of the United States of America. And now may Heaven control the game, determine the chances, and favour the worthiest."

A cheer received this final appeal to the intervention of Providence in favour of the players, and the audience were about to retire when Tornbrock, claiming silence by an imperious gesture, added these words: —

"There is a codicil."

A codicil! Was it going to destroy all the arrangements of this testamentary work and finally reveal the mystification which some still expected of this eccentric deceased?

The notary read as follows: —

"To the six players designated by lot there shall be added a seventh of my own selection, who will figure in the game under the letters XYZ, enjoy the same rights as the others, and submit to the same rules. His real name will only be revealed in the event of his winning the game, and the information regarding the throws which concern him shall be sent to him only under these letters. Such is my final wish."

This was strange. Whom did this codicil conceal? But there was no disputing it more than the others, and the crowd, much impressed, as the reporters said,' left the Auditorium.

CHAPTER VI . THE BOARD IS PUBLISHED

That day the evening newspapers, and next day the morning newspapers, were snatched at double and treble prices from the vendors and the stalls. If eight thousand spectators had been able to hear the reading of the will, Americans by the hundred thousand at Chicago and by millions in the United States, devoured by curiosity, had not had that fortunate opportunity.

But although the articles, interviews, and reports were of a nature to satisfy the masses in a great measure, general opinion imperiously required the publication of the card which accompanied the will.

This card was the board on which was to be played the noble game of the United States as arranged by William J. Hypperbone, which was exactly similar to that of the Royal Game of Goose. How had the honourable member of the Eccentric Club arranged the fifty states of the Union? Which were they which caused the stoppages, short or long; which of them sent the players back to begin over again; which of them sent them back so many points, and required the payment of single, double, or triple lines? There need be no surprise that, even more than the public, the six and their personal friends were particularly desirous of ascertaining this.

By the diligence of George B. Higginbotham and Notary Tornbrock, the card or board, faithfully reproduced after that of the deceased, was drawn, engraved, coloured, and printed in less than twenty-four hours, and many millions of its copies scattered throughout America at a cost of two cents each. It was thus within reach of everybody who could pin out each throw and follow the progress of this memorable game.

Here is the order in which he had numbered and arranged the fifty states of which the republic was composed at this epoch: —

1. Rhode Island. 33. North Dakota.

2. Maine. 34. New Jersey.

3. Tennessee. 35. Ohio.

4. Utah. 36. Illinois.

5. Illinois. 37. West Virginia.

6. New York. 38. Kentucky.

7. Massachusetts. 39. South Dakota.

8. Kansas. 40. Maryland.

9. Illinois. 41. Illinois.

10. Colorado. 42. Nebraska.

11. Texas. 43. Idaho.

12. New Mexico. 44. Virginia.

13. Montana. 45. Illinois.

14. Illinois. 46. District of Columbia.

15. Mississippi. 47. Pennsylvania.

16. Connecticut. 48. Vermont.

17. Iowa. 49. Alabama.

18. Illinois. 50. Illinois.

19. Louisiana. 51. Minnesota.

20. Delaware. 52. Missouri.

21. New Hampshire. 53. Florida.

22. South Carolina. 54. Illinois.

23. Illinois. 55. North Carolina.

24. Michigan. 56. Indiana.

25. Georgia. 57. Arkansas.

26. Wisconsin. 58. California.

27. Illinois. 59. Illinois.

28. Wyoming. 60. Arizona.

29. Oklahoma. 61. Oregon.

30. Washington. 62. Indian Territory.

31. Nevada. 63. Illinois.

32. Illinois.

Such was the order assigned to each state in the sixty-three numbers, Illinois being mentioned-fourteen times.

To begin with, it is convenient to note which of the squares necessitated the payment of a fine and which of them obliged the unfortunate players to remain stationary or to effect a no less regrettable retreat.

They were six in number: —

The sixth, New York, corresponded to that of the bridge in the Game of Goose, and the player who reached it had to leave it at once and betake himself to the twelfth, New Mexico, and pay a single fine.

The nineteenth, Louisiana, corresponded to that in which figures an inn, and here the player had to remain for two turns without playing, and pay a double fine.

The thirty-first, Nevada, corresponding to that of the well, at the bottom of which the player remained until another player took his place, the fine being a triple one.

The forty-second, Nebraska, corresponding to that in which are drawn the multiple sinuosities of a labyrinth whence, after the payment of a double fine, the player goes back to the thirtieth, that of Utah.

The fifty-second, Missouri, corresponding to that of the prison in which the player has to remain on payment of a triple fine until another player takes his place and pays a similar fine.

The fifty-eighth, California, corresponds to that which displays a death's head, and which by the pitiless rule compels the player to abandon it, after paying a triple fine, so as to begin again at No. 1, that is, Rhode Island.

Regarding the State of Illinois, appearing fourteen times on the map, the numbers 5, 9, 14, 18, 23, 27, 32, 36, 41, 45, 50, 54, 59, and 63 borne by it corresponded to those of the geese. But the players could never stop there, and according to the rule they doubled the points obtained until they lighted on a number not reserved for the sympathetic animal whom Hypperbone wished to rehabilitate.

It is true that if the first throw of the dice yielded the number 9, the player could proceed from goose to goose direct to the sixty-third square, that is, to the end. In consequence of this, as the number 9 could only be obtained in two ways, either with a 3 and 6 or a 5 and 4, the player in the first case had to go to 26, that is, Wisconsin, and in the second to 53, that is, Florida. This, it will be seen, was a great advantage for this favoured player. But the advantage was more apparent than real, for the last number had to be reached by the exact, number of points, and the player was obliged to go back if he went beyond.

Again, when one player was followed by another on to the same number, he had to give up his place to him and return to that which the other occupied, and pay a single fine to the pool — unless he had already left the number the day the other should have arrived there. This exception had been introduced by the testator in consideration of the delays necessitated by having to make more than one move.

There remained a secondary question — and a most interesting one assuredly — which a study of the map was unable to solve. In each state, what was the place to which the players had to go? Was it the capital, the official chief town, or the metropolis, generally the more important, or any other locality remarkable from a historical or geographical point of view? Was it not presumable that the deceased, profiting by the experience of his own travels, would prefer the places most talked about? A note annexed to the will indicated these places, but the information was only to be given to those interested when they received the telegram announcing the result of the throw. This telegram Tornbrock was to send to the place where the player should be at the time.

Of course the American newspapers published their observations with the reminder that, according to the will, the rules of the Game of Goose were to be strictly followed.

The lapse of time allowed for the players to reach the places denoted was more than sufficient, although a throw was to take place every other day. As there were seven players, each was allowed twice seven, that is fourteen days, and in that time he could easily get from one end of the Union to the other, for instance, from Maine to Texas or from Oregon to the furthest part of Florida. In these days the network of railroads covered the entire surface of the country, and with the aid of the time-tables and maps the journeys could be made very quickly.

Such were the rules, which admitted of no discussion. As the saying goes, they could either be taken or left.

And they took them.

That all the six took them with the same eagerness and enthusiasm was certainly not the case. Commodore Urrican's interest in the matter was about on a par with that of Tom Crabbe, or rather John Milner, and that of Hermann Titbury. As to Max Real and Harris T. Kymbale, they regarded the whole affair more from a tourist point of view, one as affording subjects for pictures, the other as matter for articles. As to Lizzie Wag, this was what she was told by Jovita Foley:

"My dear, I have asked Mr. Marshall Field to give a holiday to you and to me also, for I will go with you to the sixty-third square."

"But that is foolish!" said Lizzie.

"On the contrary, it is wise," replied Jovita. "And as it is you who will win the sixty millions of dollars of the Honourable Mr. Hypperbone — "

"Me?"

"You, Lizzie — you ought to give me half of it for my trouble."

"All — if you wish."

"Agreed!" answered Jovita Foley, as seriously as could be.

Mrs. Titbury of course would follow Hermann in his peregrinations, although it doubled the expense. As they were not forbidden to start together, they would start. It would be better for both of them. Mrs. Titbury insisted on it, as she had also insisted on Mr. Titbury consenting to be a player, for such running about and its cost quite frightened the good man, who was as timid as he was avaricious. But the imperious Kate had given him to understand that she had made up her mind, and Hermann had to obey.

It was the same with regard to Tom Crabbe, whose trainer would never leave him, and would take good care to train him, entrain him and detrain him to the best of his ability, as may be imagined.

As to Commodore Urrican, Max Real, and Harris T. Kymbale, would they travel alone or take a servant with them? They had said nothing about this as yet. No clause in the will prevented them from doing so. On the contrary, anyone could accompany them who liked, and bet on them if they chose, as men bet on racehorses.

It would be superfluous to add that the posthumous eccentricity of William J. Hypperbone produced an enormous sensation in both continents. There was no doubt that the Americans in their eagerness for speculation would venture enormous sums on the chances of this exciting game.

With their private resources, Hermann Titbury and Hodge Urrican, who were wealthy, and also John Milner, who would make a good deal of money by exhibiting Tom Crabbe, would never be defaulters in the payment of fines. As regards Harris T. Kymbale, the *Tribune* — what an advertisement for this newspaper! — was prepared to open the necessary credits for him.

Max Real did not worry himself about these financial obligations which might or might not occur. He would think of that when the time came.

With regard to Lizzie Wag, Jovita Foley was content to say to her:

"Fear nothing, my dear; we will use our savings to pay our travelling expenses."

"Then we shall not go far, Jovita."

"Very far, Lizzie"

"But if our luck makes us pay any fines — "

"Luck will make us win!" declared Jovita, in so resolute a tone that Lizzie Wag refrained from arguing with her.

Nevertheless it was probable that neither Lizzie Wag nor perhaps Max Real would become favourites among the American speculators, as the non-payment of a fine would exclude them from the game, to the advantage of the other players.

In some people's opinion there was one thing in Max Real's favour, and that was that fortune chose him to be the first, to start. At this Commodore Urrican was furious to the verge of absurdity. He could not reconcile himself to having the sixth place, after Max Real, Tom Crabbe, Hermann Titbury, Harris T. Kyrnbale, and Lizzie Wag. And yet a little reflection would have shown that this was of no importance.

Could not, for example, the last player distance the rest by a throw of 5 and 4, and thus go on to 53, which meant Florida? For such are the possibilities of these wonderful combinations, due, if we admit the legend, to the subtle and poetic mind of the ingenious Greek.

It was evident that the public, interested as they were from the very outset, would see nothing of the difficulties, still less of the fatigues of the journeys the game entailed. Doubtless it might be over in a few weeks, and yet it might last months or even years. None knew this better than the members of the Eccentric Club, who had seen the lengthy games played daily in the club-rooms by William J. Hypperbone. By prolonging the moves and making them so hurried and rapid it was to be feared that some of the players would fall ill and have to stay in one place, so as to be obliged to give up the chance of reaching the end, to the benefit of the more energetic or those more favoured by fortune.

No good was to be obtained by thinking of these eventualities. Everyone was eager for the game to begin, and then when the six were on the road they could share in their emotions, accompany them in their imagination and even in reality as amateur cyclists in a professional race, and follow them in their numerous journeys across America. And that is what would satisfy the greed of the hotel-keepers of the states that were crossed by the lines of travel.

But if the public would not reflect on the hindrances of all sorts that would arise, a very natural reflection occurred to some of the players. Why should they not come to an arrangement between themselves — an arrangement by which the winner would undertake to share his winnings among those whom fortune had not so favoured? Or rather, if he kept half the enormous fortune, why should he not give the other half to the less fortunate? Thirty millions of dollars for himself, and the rest shared among the losers! That was tempting. To be sure in any case of gaining several millions seemed to many practical and unventuresome minds an offer worth serious consideration.

On the whole there was nothing in it contrary to the wishes of the testator, as the game would be carried on all the same under the prescribed conditions, and the winner could certainly deal with his prize as he thought fit.

And so those interested, at the invitation of one of their number — evidently the wisest of the six — were called together to discuss the proposal. Hermann Titbury advised its acceptance — think of several million dollars guaranteed to each of them! As an old gambler, Mrs. Titbury hesitated, but finally yielded. After reflection, for he was of an adventurous character, Harris T. Kymbale was of the same opinion; so was Lizzie Wag, at the advice of her patron, Mr. Marshall Field, and in spite of the opposition of the ambitious Jovita Foley, who wanted all or none. As to John Milner, he asked nothing better than to support it on behalf of Tom Crabbe; and if Max Real required a little pressing, it was because these artists have generally a grain of foolishness in their brain. Besides, he did not wish to run contrary to Lizzie Wag, whose position interested him greatly, and he announced that he was ready to sign the engagement with the other players.

But for this engagement to be definite all the six must sign. But if five had consented, there was a sixth whose obstinacy no argument could triumph over. As may be guessed, this was the terrible Hodge Urrican, who refused to listen to reason. He had been designated by lot to play the game and he would play it to the end. The agreement could proceed no further, the commodore taking refuge in impregnable obstinacy, in spite of the threat of a mighty blow Tom Crabbe was preparing to give him, at John Milner's orders, and which would have bulged him out in several places. And in addition it will not have been forgotten that, according to the codicil, the players were no longer six, but seven. There was this unknown, this XKZ chosen by William J. Hypperbone. Who was he? Did he live in Chicago? Did even Tornbrock know who he was? The codicil declared that the name of this mysterious personage would not be revealed unless he was the winner. There indeed was something for people to think about which threw a new element of curiosity into the affair. And as this XKZ could not be found to acquiesce in the proposed arrangement, it was impossible to carry through the proposal even if Commodore Urrican had consented.

Nothing then could be done but to wait for the first throw of the dice, the result of which would be announced at the Auditorium on the 30th of April.

We are now at the 25th, six days only from the fateful day. For preparations there was plenty of time for Commodore Urrican, who was to start sixth, as well as for the four others, Hermann Titbury, Harris T. Kymbale, Tom Crabbe, and Lizzie Wag, who would take their departures before he did.

Would it be believed that it was the first who was to get away who was the least concerned about the journey? The fantastic Max Real seemed to take no thought about it at all. When Madame Real, who had quitted Quebec and now lived at the house in South Halsted Street, spoke to him about it, —

"I have plenty of time" he said.

"Not too much, my child."

"And after all, what is the good of my going on this absurd adventure?"

"What, Max! surely you would not lose the chance —

"Of becoming a great millionaire?"

"Undoubtedly," continued the excellent lady, who dreamed all that mothers dream for their children. "You must get ready for your journey."

"To-morrow — dear mother, the day after to-morrow — the evening before I start — "

"But tell me at least what you think of taking with you."

"My brushes, my colour box, my canvases, and my knapsack like a soldier."

"Do you forget that you may be sent to the far end of America?"

"Of the United States, rather," replied the young man, "and with no more than a handbag I would make the tour of the world."

It was impossible to extract any other reply from him, and he returned to his studio. But Madame Real intended he should not lose so good an opportunity of making his fortune.

Lizzie Wag had plenty of time, as she was not to start until ten days after Max Real — hence much complaining on the part of the impatient Jovita Foley.

"How unfortunate, my poor Lizzie," she repeated, "that you are number five!"

"Do not worry yourself, my dear friend," replied the girl, "it is quite as good as the others — or quite as bad."

"Do not say that Lizzie! Do not have such ideas! It will bring us ill-luck."

"See here, Jovita — look at me — do you seriously believe — "

"Believe that you will win?"

"Yes."

"I am sure of it, my dear, as sure of it as that I still have my thirty-two teeth!"

And then Lizzie Wag gave such a shout of laughter as made Jovita tempted to strike her.

We need not dwell on Commodore Urrican's state of mind. He lived no longer. He had decided to leave Chicago ten minutes after the number thrown for him had been announced. He would not wait a day nor an hour even if he were sent to the depths of the Everglades in the Florida peninsula.

As to the Titburys, they only thought of the fines they might have to pay, if luck would have it so, and still more of a sojourn in the prison of Missouri or the well of Nevada. But perhaps they would have the happiness of avoiding these fatal places.

In conclusion, a word about Tom Crabbe. The boxer continued to take his six meals a day without troubling himself about the future, and hoping that nothing would interfere with so good a custom during his travels. Large eater as he was, he might always find hotels that were sufficiently provisioned even in the smallest towns. John Milner could be there and could see that he wanted nothing. It would cost a good deal, undoubtedly, but what an advertisement for the Champion of the New World, and why should he not get up a few pugilistic entertainments on the road which would yield honour and profit to the celebrated jawbreaker?

If the impatience of the public had been great between the 1st and 15th of April — the day of the reading of the will — it was none the less so between the 15th and 30th of April, the day of the first throw of the dice on William J. Hypperbone's board. The people who intended to bet on the event were only waiting for that to take the six, or now the seven, at so much to one, or evens. On what grounds, the odds? There were none as in the case of racehorses, neither a series of victories already won, nor an illustrious hippie pedigree, nor reports from trainers. All there was to base an opinion on was the personal characters of the players — a moral and not a physical basis.

Under any circumstances, Max Real, it must be confessed, conducted himself in a way to obliterate any sympathy the sporting gentry might have for him. Will it be believed that on the 28th of April, the evening before the dice were to indicate his route, he had left Chicago? For two days, with his painter's kit on his shoulder, he had been absent in the country! His mother, in the greatest anxiety, could not say when he was coming back. Ah! If he were to be detained, no matter where, if he were not present next day to answer to his name, what satisfaction to the sixth player, who would become the fifth! And this fifth would be Hodge Urrican, who would be already exulting at the thought that his turn would advance a step and that he would only have five rivals to beat.

In short, no one could say if Max Real on the 30th of April had returned from his excursion, or even if he were in the Auditorium.

As twelve o'clock struck, before the tumultuous crowd of spectators, Notary Tornbrock, assisted by George B. Higginbotham, surrounded by members of the Eccentric Club, shook the box with a firm hand and rolled out the dice on to the board.

"Four and four," he shouted.

"Eight!" replied the audience with one voice.

The number was that of the square assigned by the testator to the State of Kansas.

CHAPTER VII . THE FIRST TO START

The next day the great railway station at Chicago was a scene of intense excitement. What was the reason of this excitement? Evidently the presence of a traveller in a tourist suit, with an artist's kit on his back, followed by a young negro carrying a light portmanteau and with a bag slung across his shoulder, who had come to catch the 8.10 train.

There is no scarcity of railroads in the federal republic. They run through the country in all directions. The capital of the railroads of the United States exceeds fifty-five milliards of francs and seven hundred thousand men are engaged in working them. At Chicago alone, there are three hundred thousand passengers a day, besides the ten thousand tons of newspapers and letters that are carried every year.

Consequently it mattered not whither the caprice of the dice would send them across the States, none of the seven players would find it difficult to get there or would meet with much delay on the road. And in addition to their railroads there were the steamers and boats on the lakes, canals and rivers. Chicago is easy to get at and not less easy to leave.

Max Real had returned the night before from his excursion and was standing among the crowd which encumbered the Auditorium, when the numbers four and four were proclaimed by Tornbrock. No one knew he was there, for no one was aware of his return. When his name was called there was an ominous silence, broken by the powerful voice of Commodore Urrican, who shouted from his place:

"Absent!"

"Present!" was the reply.

And Max Real, greeted with applause, mounted the stage.

"Ready to start?" asked the president of the Eccentric Club, approaching the artist.

"Ready to start, and to win!" replied the young painter with a smile.

Commodore Urrican, like a Polynesian cannibal, would have eaten him alive.

That excellent fellow Harris T. Kymbale stepped up to him and said without bitterness, —

"A pleasant journey to you, comrade!"

"A pleasant journey to you also, when the day comes for you to pack your things!" replied Max Real. And they shook hands cordially.

Neither Hodge Urrican nor Tom Crabbe, the one furious, the other as stupid as usual, thought it necessary to join in the journalist's compliments.

As to the Titburys, they had but one wish, that all the worst luck of the game should fall to this first starter, that he might fall into the well of Nevada or thrust himself into the prison of Missouri and stay there for the rest of his life.

As he passed Lizzie Wag, Max Real bowed respectfully and said:

"Allow me, miss, to wish you good luck — "

"But that is to speak against your own interest, sir," said the girl, somewhat surprised.

"Never mind that, miss; rest assured that I really mean it."

"I thank you, sir," replied Lizzie Wag.

And Jovita Foley whispered into her friend's ear the very judicious remark, "He is rather good-looking, this Max Real, and if, as he wishes, he lets you arrive first, he will be better looking still, The proceedings being over, the Auditorium was gradually evacuated, and the result of the throw of the dice immediately spread through the town.

The "Hypperbone match," as it was called by the public, had begun.

In the evening Max Real completed his preparations — simple as they were — and the next morning he embraced his mother after a formal promise to write to her as often as possible. Then he left 3997, Halsted Street, preceded by the faithful Tommy, and arrived on foot at the railway station ten minutes before the departure of the train.

That the railroads radiated from Chicago on all sides he was well aware, and all he had to do was to choose between the two or three lines that went to Kansas. This state does not adjoin Illinois, but is only separated from it by the state of Missouri; thus the journey imposed by fate on the young painter did not exceed five hundred and fifty or six hundred miles, according to the route he selected.

"I do not know Kansas," he said to himself, "and here is an opportunity for me to see the American desert, as they used to call it. Among the farmers there the French Canadians are not badly spoken of. I shall be at home there, for there is nothing against my going as I like, providing I get to the place picked out for me.

There was nothing against his doing so. Such was the opinion given by Tornbrock when he was consulted on the subject. The memorandum drawn up by William J. Hypperbone required Max Real to go to Fort Riley in Kansas, and it was enough for him to be there within a fortnight after his departure, so as to receive by telegram the number of the second throw which concerned him — that is the eighth in the game. In fact, among the fifty states placed on the board in the order we know, there were but three to which the player had to go as quickly as possible, to be there in the event of chance sending another player to replace him by the next throw. These were Louisiana, the nineteenth square, assigned to the inn; Nevada, the thirtieth square, assigned to the well; and Missouri, the fifty-second square, assigned to the prison.

Nothing could be better than for him to be able to go to his destination in the schoolboy way, as the French have it. But we can hardly suppose Commodore Urrican or Hermann Titbury spending their patience and their money by loitering on the way. They would drive on at full speed, little desirous of *transire videndo*.

The route adopted by Max Real was this. Instead of going the shortest way to Kansas City, by crossing Illinois and Missouri obliquely from east to west, he took the Grand Trunk, the railroad 3786 miles long which runs from New York to San Francisco — "Ocean to Ocean", as they say in America. A run of about 500 miles would take him to Omaha, on the Nebraska frontier, and from there on board one of the steamboats which descend the Missouri he could reach the metropolis of Kansas. Then as a tourist, an artist, he could arrive at Fort Riley on the day appointed.

When Max Real entered the station he found there a crowd of spectators. Before they wagered heavy sums on the game about to be played, the people who were going to bet wished to see with their own eyes the first of the players to get off. Although the odds depending on probabilities of more or less importance had not yet been quoted, it was desirable to have a view of the young painter at the moment of his departure. Did his looks inspire confidence? Was he in form? Was there a chance of his becoming a favourite notwithstanding the possibility of the fines to pay stopping him on his journey?

It must be confessed that Max Real did not please his fellow-citizens by carrying his painter's kit. Jonathan is a practical man, and thought that Real need not have troubled himself about seeing the country or making pictures; he should have travelled as a player in the game and not as an artist. In the opinion of the majority, the game invented by William J. Hypperbone was raised to the height of a national question and should be played seriously. If any of the seven did not play the game with all the ardour they could muster it would be a breach of the conventionalities with the immense majority of the citizens of free America. And the result was that among the disappointed spectators not one decided to go by train with Max Real, as far at least as the first station, to give him a good send off, as it is called. The cars were occupied entirely by passengers whom the requirements of commerce or industry called away from Chicago.

Max Real, quite at his ease, installed himself in one of the seats, and Tommy sat near him, for the time had gone by when whites would not remain in the same compartment with people of colour.

At last the whistle was heard, the train began to move, the powerful locomotive puffed from its wide mouth great showers of sparks amid the steam.

And amid the crowd remaining on the platform there was noticed Commodore Urrican glaring threateningly on the first to start.

From the weather point of view the journey began badly. Do not forget that in America at this latitude — and it is on much the same parallel as northern Spain — winter does not end until the month of April. Over these vast territories which no mountain shelters it is prolonged to this season of the year and the atmospheric currents from the polar regions are freely unloosed over it. If the cold began to give way before the rays of the sun of May, storms were still troubling the air. Dense low clouds, from which fell heavy showers, hung in confused masses on the horizon and shut it in. An unfortunate circumstance for a painter in search of sunny landscapes. Far better to have toured through the states in the early days of spring. Later the heat would become insupportable. After all there was reason for hoping that the bad weather would not last beyond the end of the month, and there were already signs of better meteorological conditions.

And now a word with regard to the young negro who had for two years been in the service of Max Real and was to accompany him on a journey that would probably be fertile in surprises. He was, as we know, a boy of seventeen, and consequently born free, for the emancipation of the slaves dated from the war of secession, which ended thirty years before, to the great honour of the Americans and of humanity.

Tommy's father and mother, who lived in the slavery times, were born in this state of Kansas, where the strife was so violent between the abolitionists and the Virginian planters. His parents — and stress should be laid on this point — had not to undergo too rigorous a fate, and their life had been much easier than that of most of their kin. Living under a good master, a man thoughtful and just, they had considered themselves as being of the family, and when abolition was proclaimed they had no more desire to leave him than he had to get rid of them.

Tommy then was born free, and after the death of his parents and their master — was it the influence of atavism or the remembrance of the happy days of his childhood? — he was much embarrassed at finding himself alone in face of the necessities of life. Perhaps his young mind did not grasp the advantages of this great act of emancipation when he had to trust to his own resources to get along with, when he had to think of to-morrow, who had never before thought of the future and to whom the present was everything. And were they not more numerous than was thought, these poor people who regretted as the children they still were that they had become free servants after having been slaves?

Fortunately Tommy had the opportunity of being recommended to Max Real. He was fairly intelligent, open-hearted, well-behaved, and ready to love those who showed the slightest affection for him. He became attached to the young artist, with whom he found a permanent situation.

One regret, one only, he had — and he did not conceal it — that he did not belong to him in a more complete way, in body as well as soul, and he often said so.

"But why?" Max Real would ask.

"Because, if you were my master, if you had bought me, I should belong to you."

"And what would you gain by that, my boy?"

"I would gain that you could not send me away, as you can do with a servant who does not please you."

"But who talks of sending you away? Besides, if you were my slave I could always sell you."

"It does not matter, master, it is very different, and I should be safer — "

"In no respect, Tommy,"

"Perhaps — perhaps — and as for me, I should not be free to go away!"

"Well, be easy; if I am satisfied with your services, I will buy you one day."

"And from whom — for I do not belong to any one?"

"From yourself, when I am rich, and as dearly as you like."

Tommy nodded his head, his eyes glowed in their dark orbits as he disclosed a double row of teeth of startling whiteness, happy in the thought of selling himself some day to his master, and wishing for nothing better.

Needless to say, he was delighted to accompany him during this journey about the United States. He would have had a heavy heart to see him set out alone, though it might have been for only a few days. And who knew how long this game would last if the winner took weeks, and perhaps months, to reach the sixty-third square?

Whether the journey was short or long, it was certainly very disagreeable during this first day between the windows clouded with steam and rain. The country had to be traversed without being seen. Everything was lost in the grey tones abhorred by painters; the sky, the birds, the villages, the houses, the railway stations, the landscape of Illinois appeared confusedly through the mists. All that could be identified were the high chimneys of the Napiersville flour-mills, and the roofs of the Aurora match factory. Nothing could be seen of Oswego, of Yorkville, of Sandwich, of Mendoza, of Princeton, of Rock Island, of its superb bridge across the Mississippi, whose waters surround the island; nothing of that State property transformed into an arsenal where hundreds of guns lie side by side among the green thickets and flowering shrubs.

Max Real was much disappointed. In passing through these storms he would find nothing worth remembering for his art. He might just as well sleep all the day — as Tommy was doing conscientiously.

Towards evening the rain ceased, the clouds rose into the higher zones, the sun set in cloths of gold on the horizon. This was a feast for the artist's eyes. But almost immediately the shades of twilight invaded the sky over the region separating Iowa from Illinois, and so the crossing of this country, although the night was clear enough, gave no satisfaction to Max Real, who soon closed his eyes and did not open them again until dawn next day.

And perhaps he was right in regretting that he had not stopped the night before at Rock Island.

"Yes, I was wrong, evidently wrong," he said to himself when he awoke. There was plenty of time, and I am not in a hurry for twenty-four hours. The day I thought of spending at Omaha I should have spent at Rock Island. From there to Davenport, that riverside city of the Mississippi, there is only the big river to cross and I should have seen this Father of Waters, which I am perhaps called upon to see all the way down now that fate has sent me across these central states."

It was too late to indulge in such reflections. The train was now running at full steam across the plains of Iowa. Max Real could not see Iowa City in the valley of that name, which for sixteen years was the capital of the state, nor Des Moines, the present capital, an old fort built at the junction of the river of that name and the Racoon, now a city of fifty thousand inhabitants, camped amid a network of railroads.

At last the sun rose as the train was about to stop at Council Bluffs, almost on the state's boundary and three miles only from Omaha, an important town of this Nebraska of which the Missouri forms the natural frontier.

There formerly was "The Rock of Council," where the tribes of the Far West assembled. From there started the expeditions of conquest or commerce which were to open up the regions intersected by the multiple ramifications of the Rocky Mountains and New Mexico.

It cannot be said that Max Real ran through this first station of the Union Pacific as he had run though many others since the previous evening.

"Let us get out," he said.

"Have we arrived?" asked Tommy, opening his eyes.

"A man has always arrived — when he is anywhere!"

And after this astonishingly positive reply, the two, one with knapsack on his back, the other with the portmanteau in his hand, stepped out on to the platform of the railway station.

The steamer would not leave Omaha before ten o'clock in the morning; it was now six, and there was plenty of time to visit Council Bluffs, on the left bank of the Missouri. This was what they did after a short halt for the first breakfast. Then the future master and the future slave went off between the two iron roads which lead to the two bridges over the river and form a double communication with the metropolis of Nebraska.

The sky had cleared. The sun was shooting a sheaf of morning rays through the rift in the clouds that a light breeze from the east was gently driving above the plain. What satisfaction, after twenty-four hours' imprisonment in a railroad car, to swing along in this way with free and freshening stride!

True, Max Real could not think of stopping to sketch on the way. Before his eyes lay long and barren beaches with nothing about them to tempt an artist's brush, and so he walked straight on towards the Missouri, that grand tributary of the Mississippi which was formerly called Mise Souri, Peti Kanoui, that is to say in the Indian language," the muddy river, "which up to here is three thousand miles from its source.

Max Real had an idea which doubtless would never have occurred to Commodore Urrican, nor the trainer of Tom Crabbe, nor even Harris T. Kymbale: it was to keep away as much as he could from public curiosity. It was on this account that he had not announced his route when he left Chicago. The city of Omaha was no less interested than the others in this noble Game of the United States, and if it had known that the first to start had arrived that morning within its walls it would have received him with the honours due to a personage of such importance.

A considerable town is this Omaha, and including its southern suburb it contains at least 150,000 inhabitants. It was owing to "the boom" — that which Réclus justly describes as "the period, of puffery, of speculation, of stock-jobbing, and at the same time of furious work — that in 1854 it rose among the solitudes like so many others with all its equipment of industry and civilization." Gamblers by instinct, how could the Omaha people resist the temptation to bet on one or other of the players whom blind destiny was dispersing among the States of the Union? And here was one of them disdaining to reveal his presence among them! Evidently this Max Real was doing nothing to win the favour of his fellow-citizens. At a modest hotel, without giving his name or occupation, he took his repast. It was possible, besides, that hazard might send him several times to Nebraska or the states which the Grand Trunk serves to the westward.

At Omaha begins that long iron road called the Pacific Union between Omaha and Ogden and the Southern Pacific between Ogden and San Francisco. As to the lines which put Omaha in connection with New York, there are so many that travellers find their only difficulty in making their choice.

There, unrecognized, Max Real walked about the principal quarters of this town, which is just as much like a chess-board as its neighbour, Council Bluffs, there being fifty-four blocks, all rectangular and all bounded by rectilineal lines.

It was ten o'clock when Max Real, followed by Tommy, returned towards the Missouri by the north of the town and went down to the quay near the steamboat wharf.

The *Dean Richmond* was ready to start. Her boilers were snoring like a drunken man, her engine beam was only waiting for the order to begin to move above her spar-deck.

The day would suffice for the *Dean Richmond* after a run of 150 miles to reach Kansas City.

Max Real and Tommy installed themselves on the upper gallery near the stern. Ah! if the passengers had only known that one of the players in this famous game was to descend in their company the Missourian waters as far as the town of Kansas, what an enthusiastic welcome he would have had! But Max Real continued to keep the strictest incognito, and Tommy was not allowed to betray it.

At ten minutes past ten, the hawsers were cast off, the powerful paddle wheels were put in motion and the steamboat started down the river, which is dotted with floating pumice stone from its sources in the gorges of the Rocky Mountains.

The banks of Missouri are flat and green and have none of that strange aspect given them higher up by the gigantic rocks of which they there consist. Here the yellow river is no longer interrupted by cataracts, weirs, locks, nor troubled with falls and rapids. Swollen by the material brought down by its tributaries from the furthest regions of Canada, it owes much to its numerous affluents, of which the chief is the Yellowstone River.

The *Dean Richmond* sped rapidly down the river among the flotilla of steam vessels and sailing vessels, which are not found above this owing to the course being hardly navigable, ice encumbering in winter, and drought making it shallow during the summer.

They reached Platte City, on the river which gives one of its names to the state, for it is also called the Nebraska. But really that of the Platte is more suitable, owing to its meandering between grassy banks that are very bare, and its bed is of little depth. Twenty-five miles further on the steamboat stopped at Nebraska City, which town is practically the port of Lincoln, the state capital, although that is twenty leagues to the west of the river.

During the afternoon Max Real was able to get a few sketches about Atkinson and at a remarkable spot near Leavenworth where the Missouri is spanned by one of the most-beautiful bridges along its course. Here in 1827 was built the fort destined to defend the country against the Indian tribes.

It was nearly midnight when the young painter and Tommy landed at Kansas City. They had still a dozen days to get to Fort Riley, the place indicated in this state by William J. Hypperbone's memorandum.

Max Real soon selected a hotel of decent appearance, where he passed a good night after twenty-four hours in a railway train and fourteen on a steamer.

The next day was devoted to visiting the town, or rather the two towns, for there are two Kansases, situated on the same right bank of the Missouri, which here has a sharp bend, but separated by the Kansas River, one belonging to the State of Kansas, the other to that of Missouri, The second is by far the more important, with 130,000 inhabitants, while the other has but 38,000. In reality they would form but one and the same city if they were in the same state.

Max Real had no intention of staying more than a day in Kansas of Kansas or Kansas of Missouri. The two towns are as much alike as two chess-boards, and if you have seen one you have seen the other. And so in the morning of the 4th of May he started for Fort Riley, and this time it was as an artist that he travelled. True, he took the railroad, but he intended to alight at the stations that pleased him in search of landscape studies which he could turn to profitable use, if he were not the first to arrive although the first to start.

This is no longer the American desert of former times. The vast plain gradually rises towards the west to an altitude of 400 feet on the frontier of Colorado, and its successive undulations are cut up by wide wooded bottoms, separated by the steppes as far as the eye can reach which a hundred years ago were roamed over by the Kansas, Nez Percés, Otea and other Indian tribes.

But what has brought about the complete transformation of the country is the disappearance of the cypress groves and fir groves, the planting of millions of fruit trees on the savannahs, and the establishing of nurseries to supply the orchards and vineyards. Immense tracts are devoted to the cultivation of sorghum used in the manufacture of sugar, alternated with fields of barley, rye, buckwheat, oats, wheat, which make Kansas one of the richest states of the Union.

There are many different species of flowering plants, and particularly noticeable on the banks of the Kansas are the innumerable clumps with cottony leaves, some herbaceous, some frutescent, that impregnate the air with an odour of turpentine.

In going from station to station, in strolling off for four or five miles across country, in sketching in several canvases, Max Real spent a week in reaching Topeka, where he arrived during the afternoon of the 13th of May.

Topeka is the capital of Kansas. It derives its name from the wild potatoes which abound on the slopes of the valley. The town occupies the southern bank of the stream and has a suburb on the opposite bank.

A half day's rest was taken as necessary by Max Real and the young negro — rest which was interrupted next day by a visit to the capital. Its 32,000 inhabitants were unaware that they had amongst them the celebrated player whose name had already begun to appear on the newspaper contents bills, but they were waiting to greet him on his way. They never imagined that to get to Fort Riley he had taken any other way than that which skirts the Kansas and runs through Topeka. They were waiting in expectation, and Max Real departed at dawn on the 14th without his presence being suspected for an instant.

Fort Riley, at the confluence of the Smoky Hill and Republican rivers, is some sixty miles away. Max Real could get there that evening if convenient, or next morning if the fancy took him to linger on the way, which was what he did, having left the train at Manhattan. But he had a narrow escape of being stopped at the outset of the game and losing the right to continue. The artist was almost too much for the chess-man that chance was moving across this region. In the afternoon Max Real and Tommy got out at the last station but one, three or four miles from Fort Riley, and made for the left bank of the Kansas. As half a day was enough to allow for this distance, even if they had to walk it, there was nothing to be anxious about.

The charming landscape that suddenly greeted his eyes tempted Max Real to stop on the river bank. In an angle of the stream amid varied light and shade stood one of the survivors of an old cypress grove, its branches overhanging from one bank to the other. At its base were the remains of an adobe hut, and behind extended a vast prairie studded with flowers, principally showy sunflowers. Beyond the Kansas was a depth of verdure, mostly in heavy shadow, pierced here and there by the brilliant rays of the sun. As a composition the picture was perfect.

"What a beautiful view," said Max Real. In two hours I can finish a sketch of it. And as we shall see immediately, it was not the sketch but himself that was nearly finished.

The young painter was seated on the bank, his little canvas fixed in the lid of his colour-box, and he had been working away for forty minutes without intermission when a distant noise — the *quadrupedante sonitu* of Virgil — was heard to the eastward of him. It seemed like a rush of horsemen across the plain that bordered the left bank.

Tommy was lying at the foot of a tree when this increasing noise woke him from the half sleep into which he had so willingly subsided.

His master hearing nothing, and not even turning his head, he rose and walked up the bank a little way so as to get a better view.

The noise then got louder, and on the edge of the horizon rose clouds of dust, which the breeze, then freshening, was driving towards the west.

Tommy returned hastily, and seized with alarm, said:

"Master!"

The painter, absorbed in his work, did not reply.

"Master!" repeated Tommy in an anxious voice, placing his hand on his shoulder.

"Eh! What is up, Tommy?" replied Max Real, busily mixing with the tip of his brush a little sienna and vermillion.

"Master — do you not hear that?" said Tommy.

He would have been deaf not to have heard the rumbling of this tumultuous gallop.

Instantly Max Real arose, put his palette on the grass, and ran to the edge of the bank.

Five hundred yards away was a vast assemblage of horses raising clouds of dust and vapour and neighing furiously, a sort of avalanche precipitated on to the plain. In a few moments the avalanche would be at the river.

The only possible flight was towards the north. Gathering up his kit, Max Real, followed or rather preceded by Tommy, ran off in that direction.

The horde which approached at full speed was composed of many thousands of horses and mules which the state formerly bred in a reserve on the bank of the Missouri, but since autocars and bicycles had come into fashion these hippomotors had been left to themselves and wandered about the country. These had evidently taken fright, and perhaps had been on the gallop for several hours. No obstacle had stopped them; the fields, the cultivated lands had been devastated on their path, and if the river did not oppose an insurmountable barrier, where would they go?

Max Real and Tommy, although they ran with all their might, were nearly caught, and would have been trampled to death under those terrible hoofs if they had not climbed up into the lower branches of a vigorous walnut tree, the only tree within reach.

It was then five o'clock in the evening.

There they remained in safety, and when the last of the herd had disappeared along the river —

"Quick! Quick!" said Max Real.

Tommy was in no hurry to leave the branch on which he sat astride.

"Quick, I tell you, or I shall lose sixteen million dollars, and shall not be able to make you a vile slave!"

Max Real was joking; there was no risk of his being late at Fort Riley. For this reason, instead of returning to the station, which was now some distance away, and where he might not have caught a train, he proceeded quietly on foot, and, when the evening came, walked towards the distant lights that shone on the horizon.

In this way the last part of the journey was accomplished, and eight o'clock had not quite struck when Max Real and Tommy found themselves before the *Jackson Hotel* The first to start was thus at the spot chosen by William J. Hypperbone in the eighth square. And why this choice? Probably because, if Missouri, situated in the geographic centre of the Union, has been called the Central State, Kansas, on the other hand, might be as justly called so from its occupying the geometric centre, and Fort Riley is in the very centre of this state. And as marking this, a monument has been built near Fort Riley, just at the junction of the Smoky Hill and Republican rivers.

At last Max Real was safe and sound at Fort Riley. Next morning he went out from the *Jackson Hotel,* where he had put up, and called at the post office and asked if a telegram were waiting for him.

"Your name, sir?" asked the clerk.

"Max Real."

"Max Real — of Chicago?"

"In person."

"And one of the players in the noble Game of the United States of America?"

"Quite so."

Impossible this time to maintain his incognito, and the news of Max Real's presence spread through the town.

It was then amid much cheering, but to his great annoyance, that the young painter returned to the hotel. There he would receive as soon as it arrived the telegram announcing the result of the second throw, and which would send him — where? Wherever he was required to go at the caprice of impenetrable destiny!

CHAPTER VIII . TOM CRABBE ENTRAINED BY JOHN MILNER

Eleven by the five and six is not a throw to be despised when the player does not bring off nine by the six and three or the five and four and go to the twenty-sixth or fifty-third square.

Perhaps it was to be regretted that the State indicated by the number happened to be a long distance from Illinois, and no doubt Tom Crabbe was rather disgusted at it — or at least his trainer was.

Fate had sent them to Texas, the largest of the States of the Union, which alone has an area larger than that of France. This State, situated in the south-west of the confederation, borders on Mexico, from which it was not separated until 1835, after the battle gained by General Houston over General Santa Anna.

Tom Crabbe could get to Texas in two ways. He could on leaving Chicago go to St. Louis and take the Mississippi steamers to New Orleans, or take the railway to the metropolis of Louisiana by traversing the States of Illinois, Tennessee, and Mississippi. And from there he could ascertain the shortest way to reach Austin, the capital of Texas, the place indicated in William J. Hypperbone's memorandum, either by railroad or on board one of the steamers which run between New Orleans and Galveston.

John Milner decided to take Tom Crabbe to Louisiana by railway. But under any circumstances he had no time to lose like Max Real, nor leisure to loiter on the road, as he had to reach the end of the journey by the 16th.

"Well," asked the reporter of the *Freie Presse* after result of the throw had been announced on the 3rd of May in the Auditorium," when do you start?"

"This evening."

"Is your luggage packed?"

"My luggage is Crabbe," replied John Milner. He is packed, shut, corded, and I have only to take him to the station — "

"And what does he say?"

"Nothing. As soon as his sixth meal is finished we shall go together to the train, and I should put him in the luggage van if I were not afraid of having to pay excess."

"I have a presentiment," continued the reporter, "that Tom Crabbe will be favoured with the same luck — "

"Do not doubt it," declared John Milner.

"A pleasant journey to you."

"Thank you."

The trainer had no intention of imposing an incognito on the champion of the New World. A personage so considerable — from a material point of view as Tom Crabbe could not be passed unseen. His departure was consequently in no way kept secret. There was a crowd that evening on the railway platforms to see him hoist himself into his car amid cheers. John Milner entered after him. Then the train started, and probably the engine felt the increase of load due to the transport of the weighty pugilist During the night the train covered 350 miles, and in the morning it reached Fulton, on the Kentucky frontier.

Tom Crabbe scarcely troubled himself to look at the country he was passing through — a State relegated to the fourteenth rank in the Union. Undoubtedly if Max Real or Harris T. Kymbale had been in his place, they would not have omitted to visit Nashville, the present capital, and the battle-field of Chattanooga, on which Sherman opened the roads to the south to the Federal armies. And then, one as artist, the other as reporter, why should they not have taken a run to the right for a hundred miles, to Grand Junction, so as to honour Memphis with their presence? This is the only important city the State possesses on the left bank of the Mississippi, and it has a fine appearance, situated on the cliff which dominates the course of the superb river strewn with islets of rich verdure.

But the trainer did not think he was called upon to diverge from his direct route to permit the enormous feet of Tom Crabbe to tread this city with an Egyptian appellation. And so he had no opportunity of asking why some sixty years ago, although Memphis is so distant from the sea, the government there established arsenals and workshops which are now abandoned, nor to hear the reply: in America they make these mistakes, as they do elsewhere. The train continued to carry the second player and his indifferent companion across the plains of the State of Mississippi. It went through Holly Springs, Grenada and Jackson. This last town is the capital, of little importance, of a region which the exclusive culture of cotton has left far behind in the industrial and commercial advance.

There, however, for during an hour at the railway station the arrival of Tom Crabbe produced a great effect. Several hundred spectators wished to see the celebrated prize-fighter. To be sure he did not possess the stature of Adam, to whom was attributed, before the rectifications of the illustrious Cuvier, a height of ninety feet, nor that of Abraham, eighteen feet, nor even that of Moses, twelve feet, but he was a gigantic type of the human species all the same.

Among the spectators was a man of learning, the Honourable Kil Kirney, who, after measuring with extreme precision the Champion of the New World, considered he was justified in offering a few depreciatory remarks, and this was what he did not hesitate to declare *ex professo:* "Gentlemen, in connection with the historical researches to which I am devoted, I have got together the principal statistics of measurement given by giganto-graphers and reduced them to the decimal system. In the seventeenth century appeared Walter Parson, who had a height of two metres, twenty-seven. In the eighteenth century appeared the German, Muller of Leipzig, who measured two metres, forty; the Englishman Burnsfield, who was two metres, thirty-five; the Irishman, Magrath, who was two metres, thirty; the Irishman O'Brien, who was two metres, fifty-five; the Englishman Toller, who was two metres, fifty-five; and the Spaniard Elacegin, who was two metres, thirty-five. In the nineteenth century appeared the Greek Auvassab, who was two metres, thirty-three; the English Hales, of Norfolk, who was two metres, forty; the German Marianne, who was two metres, forty-five, and the Chinese Chang, who was two metres, fifty-five. Now, from the sole of the feet to the crown of the head, I would inform the honourable trainer that Tom Crabbe is only two metres, thirty — "

"What do you want me to do?" replied the trainer rather sharply. "I cannot make him any longer."

"No, undoubtedly," replied Mr. Kil Kirney, and I don't ask you to do so. But, anyhow, he's inferior to — "

"Tom!" said John Milner. "Give him one in the breadbasket, so that he can measure the force of your biceps."

The learned man did not wish to assist at an experiment which would have left him without the regulation number of ribs, and he retired with dignity.

Tom Crabbe was none the less greeted by the acclamations of the public when John Milner issued a challenge in his name to the local amateurs. But the challenge was not taken up, and the Champion of the New World hauled himself back into his car, while wishes of good luck rained around him.

After crossing the State of Mississippi from north to south the railway reaches the frontier of Louisiana at Rocky Comfort.

Following the course of the Tangipaoha river, the train descends to Lake Pontchartrain, the western bank of which it passes by the narrow strip of land which separates this lake from that of Maurepas, on which is the Mauchac viaduct. At Carrolton station it reaches the river, here 900 yards across, which curves so as to encircle the Louisianan city.

At New Orleans, Tom Crabbe and John Milner left the railway after a journey of nearly nine hundred miles from Chicago. Arriving in the afternoon of the 5th of May, they had thirteen days to get to Austin, the capital of Texas — time enough, although they must allow for possible delays either by land in availing themselves of the Southern Pacific or by way of the sea.

In any case it would not have done for John Milner to take his Crabbe through the town to look at the sights. If chance sent here another of the "seven" he would acquit himself of the task much better. Austin was still four hundred miles away, and John Milner's only thought was to get his Crabbe there by the shortest and safest route.

The shortest would have been the railway, for there is direct communication between the two towns, providing the trains fit in. After running westward by Lafayette, Rarelant, Terrebone, Tigerville, Ramos, Brashear, towards Lake Grand, it reaches, a hundred and eighty miles beyond, the frontier of Texas. From this point, at Orange, the line runs on to Austin, a distance of two hundred and thirty miles. Nevertheless — perhaps he was wrong — John Milner preferred to go another way, and thought it better to embark at New Orleans for the port of Galveston, which is united by a railroad to the Texan capital.

He found that the steamer *Sherman* would leave New Orleans for Galveston the following morning. Here was something of which he could take advantage. Three hundred miles of sea on a boat travelling at twelve miles an hour meant a day and a half — two days if the wind were not favourable.

John Milner did not think it worthwhile to consult Tom Crabbe on the subject any more than a man consults his luggage when it is ready to start. Having finished his sixth repast, at a hotel near the harbour, the eminent boxer wanted nothing but to sleep till the morning.

It was seven o'clock when Captain Curtis gave the order to cast off the hawsers of the *Sherman*, after he had welcomed the illustrious Champion of the New World with all the respect due to the second player in the Hypperbone match.

"The honourable Tom Crabbe," said he, "I am honoured in having the honour of your presence on my ship."

The boxer did not seem to understand what Captain Curtis said to him, and his eyes wandered instinctively towards the door of the dining-room.

"You may depend upon it," continued the captain, "that I will do my utmost to get you there with the least possible delay. I shall not stint my coal nor economize my steam. I will be the soul of my cylinders, the soul of my beam, the soul of my wheels, which will run at their highest speed to assure you of glory and profit."

Tom Crabbe's mouth opened as if to reply and closed again immediately, to open again and shut again. That indicated that the hour of the first breakfast had struck in the stomachic-time-piece of Tom Crabbe.

"The ship is at your disposal," declared Captain Curtis, "and rest assured we shall land in time in Texas, if I have to shut down the valves and blow up the ship — "

"Do not blow it up," said John Milner with that good sense which distinguished him. "It would be a mistake — on the eve of winning sixty million dollars."

The weather was fine, and besides, there was nothing to fear in the New Orleans channels, although they are subject to capricious changes which are under the surveillance of the harbour authorities. The *Sherman* took the south channel, between the reeds and rushes of the low-lying banks. Perhaps the olfactory nerve of the passengers was disagreeably affected by the hydrogenous exhalations of innumerable particles engendered by the fermentation of organic matters at the bottom, but there was no danger of running aground in this channel, which has become the main entrance of the great river.

They passed many factories and warehouses grouped on both banks in front of Algiers, in front of Point à la Hache, in front of Jump. At this period of the year the river does not run low. In April, May and June the Mississippi is swollen by regular floods and its waters do not reach their minimum until November. The *Sherman* consequently kept on at full speed, and without a check reached

Port Eads, from the name of the engineer who so much improved this southern channel.

Here the Mississippi becomes absorbed in the Gulf of Mexico after a course estimated at 4500 miles.

The *Sherman,* as soon as she had doubled the last point, laid her course to the westward.

How had Tom Crabbe borne this part of the voyage? Very well. After feeding at his usual times he had gone to bed. In the morning he appeared hale and hearty, when he resumed his place on the after-part of the spar-deck.

The *Sherman* was then fifty miles out at sea and the coast to the north was only just visible very low down.

It was the first time that Tom Crabbe had ventured on a sea voyage. And consequently he looked astonished at the rolling and pitching.

This astonishment produced on his large face, which was generally so red, an increasing paleness, which John Milner, who was thoroughly seasoned, very soon noticed.

"Is he going to be ill?" he asked himself as he approached the seat on which his companion sat.

And shaking him by the shoulder, he said, "How are you getting on?

Tom Crabbe opened his mouth, and this time it was not hunger which put his masseters into motion, although the hour of his first breakfast had struck. And as he could not shut it in time, a mouthful of salt water was dashed down his throat as the *Sherman* gave a deep roll on the surge.

Tom Crabbe was thrown off the seat and fell on the deck.

It was evidently judicious to take him to the center of the steamer, where the oscillations are not so marked.

"Come, Tom," said John Milner.

Tom Crabbe would have risen, but he tried in vain, and fell back with all his weight.

Captain Curtis, noticing the concussion, came aft.

"I see that it is," he declared, " — nothing, in fact, and the honourable Tom Crabbe will be all right. It is not possible for such a man to be sea-sick. It is good silly women at most; but it would be terrible for a man so strongly built."

Terrible it was, and never did passengers behold a more lamentable spectacle. Nausea is the natural lot of the weakly and the miserable. The phenomenon developed in the usual way. But in a case of this corpulence and vigour! With him it was as with those monuments that are more damaged by an earthquake than the frail Indian hut. One resists, the other is shaken to pieces.

And Tom Crabbe was shaking to pieces and looked as though he would become a heap of ruins.

John Milner, greatly annoyed, intervened.

"We shall have to haul him up," said he.

Captain Curtis called the boatswain and twelve sailors to undertake the job. The united efforts of the party were not equal to lifting the Champion of the New World. It was necessary to roll him along the spar-deck as if he were a cask, then to lower him below by means of a block and tackle, then to drag him to the skylight of the engine room, where he remained completely prostrate.

"There," said John Milner to Captain Curtis, "it was that abominable salt water which Tom got in his mouth! If it had been alcohol — "

"If it had been alcohol," replied the captain judiciously, "the sea would have been drunk to the last drop long ago, and no navigation would be possible."

It was, indeed, unlucky. The wind was coming from the westward, and had gone right round, and blew hard, the rolling and pitching being thereby increased. Steaming against a head sea made a considerable diminution in speed. The length of the voyage would be doubled — seventy or eighty hours instead of forty. In short, John Milner passed through every phase of anxiety while his companion passed through every phase of his most unpleasant affliction. In a word, to quote an expression used by Captain Curtis, "Tom Crabbe was only fit to be scraped up with a shovel."

At last, on the 9th of May, after a furious squall which happily was of short duration, the coast of Texas, bordered by white sand-hills, defended by a string of islands over which flew flocks of enormous pelicans, appeared about three o'clock in the afternoon. There had been a great saving in provisions, owing to Tom Crabbe, although he had often and too often opened his mouth, having eaten nothing since he took his last meal when opposite Port Eads.

John Milner cherished the hope that his companion would recover himself, that he would overcome the abominable sickness, that he would resume his human form, that he would at least be presentable, when the *Sherman,* in shelter from the open sea in Galveston Bay, would be clear of the oscillations of the surge. But no! The unfortunate man did not recover in the least, even in smooth water.

The town is situated at the end of a sandy point. A viaduct connects it with the continent, and brings to it the goods it exports, which are principally cotton and are of considerable importance.

The *Sherman,* as soon as she had come up the channel, was brought alongside to her landing-stage.

John Milner was simply furious, as well he might be. Several hundred spectators were on the quay. Hearing by telegraph that Tom Crabbe had embarked at New Orleans for Galveston, they had been awaiting his arrival.

And what was his trainer going to present to them in place of the Champion of the New World, the second starter in the Hypperbone match? A shapeless mass that resembled more an empty sack than a human creature.

John Milner made another attempt to pull Tom Crabbe together.

"Well — it's all over now?"

The sack remained a sack, and truth to tell, the sack had to be carried on a stretcher to the Beach Hotel, where apartments had been secured.

A few jests, a few gibes were heard on the way, instead of the cheers to which he was accustomed and which had greeted his departure from Chicago.

But all was not lost. Next morning, after a good night's rest and a series of meals cleverly combined, Tom Crabbe would probably recover his vital energy, his normal vigour, and would no longer look —

So John Milner thought, but he was again mistaken. The night brought no modification in the state of his companion. The prostration of all his faculties was as profound as on the previous day. And yet what was required of him was no intellectual energy, of that he was incapable, but a mere animal effort. It was useless. His mouth had remained closed ever since he had touched land. And he had made no call for food at his accustomed hours.

In this way the 10th of May went by, then the 11th, and it was on the 16th he must be at Austin. John Milner took the only step he could. Better arrive too soon than too late. If Tom Crabbe was to emerge from this prostration, he would emerge as well at Austin as at Galveston, and, at least, he would be at his post.

So he was wheeled on a truck to the railway and put into a car as if he were a bundle. At 8.30 that evening the train started, while groups of sporting men refused to venture the very smallest sum — not even twenty-five cents — on a player in such awful form.

It was fortunate that the Champion of the New World and his trainer had not to travel over the 75,000,000 of hectares of which the Texan area consists. They had but to cover the 160 miles which separated Galveston from the capital of the state.

Assuredly it would have been desirable to visit the regions watered by the magnificent Rio Grande, and so many other rivers, the Antonio, the Brazos, the Trinity, which flows into Galveston Bay, and the Colorado and its capricious banks strewn with pearly oysters. A magnificent country this Texas, with immense prairies, on which formerly camped the Comanches; in the west it is covered with virgin forest, rich in magnolias, sycamores, acacias, palms, oaks, cypresses, cedars; in profusion are its orange trees, nopals, cactuses, the most beautiful of its flowers; its mountains in the north-west which represent the Rockies are superb; it produces sugar-cane superior to that of the Antilles, Nacogdoches tobacco superior to that of Maryland or Virginia, cotton superior to that of Mississippi or Louisiana; it has farms of 40,000 acres with as many head of cattle, and ranches reckoned in hundreds of miles on which are raised the finest specimens of the equine race.

But what was there in all that to interest Tom Crabbe, who saw nothing, and John Milner, who saw nothing but Tom Crabbe?

In the evening the train stopped two hours at Houston, where a few vessels could be seen on an insignificant stream. Here is the centre for merchandise arriving by the Trinity, the Brazos, and the Colorado.

Next day, the 13th of May, very early in the morning, Tom Crabbe got out at Austin station, having ended his journey. It is an important industrial centre where the waters of the river are held back by a dam, and is built on a terrace to the north of the Colorado in a region abounding with iron, copper, manganese, granite, marble, gypsum and clay. The city, which is more American than many others in Texas, was chosen to be the seat of the State legislature and contains 26,000 inhabitants, nearly all of Saxon origin. It is one town, while the towns of the Rio Grande are double — with houses of wood on one side of the river and huts of adobe on the other — such as El Paso, El Presidio, which are half Mexican.

Thus at Austin Americans only were attracted by curiosity — perhaps with a view to making a bet or so — to gaze at the second player whom a throw of the dice had sent them from the distant regions of Illinois. And these were more favoured than the people of Galveston and Houston. When he set foot on the pavement of the Texan capital, Tom Crabbe had at last got rid of that disquieting torpor over which the attentions, supplications, and objurgations of John Milner had been unable to triumph. At first the Champion of the New World may have appeared a little stale, a little limp, a little slack in his action, but how could you be astonished at that, considering he had absorbed nothing but sea-air since the *Sherman* got out to sea? Yes! The giant had been reduced to requiring food to merely keep him alive, but even reduced to this he would have to take a good deal of nourishment for some days.

What a meal he made that morning — a meal which lasted till the evening, quarters of venison, mutton and beef, odds and ends of pork, vegetables, fruit, cheese and half-and-half, gin, whisky, tea and coffee! John Milner felt rather scared when he thought of the hotel bill he would have to meet at the end of his stay.

And it went on the next day and the day after, and in that way arrived the 16th of May. Tom Crabbe had again become the prodigious human machine before whom Corbett, Fitzsimmons, and other no less celebrated boxers had so many times bitten the dust.

CHAPTER IX. ONE AND ONE MAKE TWO

This very morning a hotel — or rather an inn, that of *The Sandy Bar* and not one of the best — received two travellers, arrived by the first train in Calais, a town in the State of Maine.

These two travellers — a man and a woman evidently suffering from the fatigue of a long and painful journey — gave their names as Mr. and Mrs. Field. The name, like that of Smith and Johnson and a few others in current use, is one of the commonest among families of Anglo-Saxon origin. And you would have to be endowed with extraordinary qualities — to have gained a considerable position in politics, the arts or the sciences, to be a genius in a word — to attract public attention under this common patronymic. Thus Mr. and Mrs. Field told nothing, indicated in no way persons of distinction, and the innkeeper wrote it in his book without asking any questions.

At this time throughout the United States no names were better known, none more repeated by millions of mouths than those of the players and that of the fantastic member of the Eccentric Club. Now, not one of the seven was called Field, and at Calais they thought no more of these Fields than any other travellers. Besides, their faces did not favour them, and the innkeeper wondered if he would be favoured in another way when the time came for him to present his bill.

Whence came these strangers to this little town situated on the extreme edge of a state which is itself situated at the north-east extremity of the Union? Why had they added two units to the six hundred and sixty-one thousand inhabitants of this state, the area of which occupies half the region commonly called New England.

The room on the first floor given to Mr. and Mrs. Field was not particularly comfortable — a bed for two, a table, two chairs, a washstand. The window opened on to the St. Croix river, the left bank of which is Canadian.

The only portmanteau, placed at the entrance from the passage, had been brought by a porter from the railway station. In a corner stood two big umbrellas; and an old travelling bag lay open.

When Mr. and Mrs. Field were alone, after the departure of the innkeeper who had shown them their room, as soon as the door was shut and bolted from the inside, they placed their ears against it to make sure that no one could hear them.

"At last," said one, "we are at the end of our journey."

"Yes," answered the other, "after three days and three nights since our departure."

"I thought it would never end," said Mr. Field, letting his arms fall as if his muscles were unable to move them.

"It is not finished," said Mrs. Field.

"And how much will it cost us?"

"It is not what it will cost us, said the lady sharply," but what it will bring us."

"At least," added the gentleman, "we had a good idea in not travelling under our real names."

"My idea."

"An excellent one! We should have been at the mercy of all the hotelkeepers, innkeepers, cabmen and fleecers who fatten on those who pass through their hands, and that under the pretext that millions of dollars are about to fall into our pockets."

"We have done well," said Mrs. Field," and we will continue to keep down our expenses as much as possible. It was not at the railway bars that we threw away our money during the last three days — and I hope we shall continue — "

"Never mind, but we might have done better to decline altogether — "

"Enough, Hermann!" declared Mrs. Field in an imperious tone. "Haven't we as many chances as the others of getting in first?"

"Undoubtedly, Kate, but the wisest of us would have signed the agreement to divide the heritage."

"That is not my opinion. Besides, Commodore Urrican objected, and this XKZ was not there to give his consent."

"Well — you remember what I say," replied Mr. Field, "I am more afraid of him than all the rest. We do not know who he is, nor whence he comes. No one knows. He calls himself XKZ. Is that a name? Is it likely that anyone is called XKZ?"

Thus Mr. Field expressed himself. But if he had not hidden himself under initials had he not changed Titbury into Field? — for the reader has already discovered this from the few remarks exchanged between him and the fictitious Mrs. Field in which they both revealed their abominable instincts of avarice.

Yes, it was Hermann Titbury, the third player, whom the dice by one and one had sent to the second square, the State of Maine. And how unfortunate, for the throw only took them two steps on the sixty-three and obliged them to go to the extreme north-east point of the United States.

Maine borders on Canada. It entered into the Confederation in 1820, and has for its eastern boundary Passamaquoddy Bay, into which the St. Croix sends its waters, just as the state, which is divided into twelve counties, sends two senators and fifty deputies to Congress, the national bay into which flow the political rivers of the U.S.A.

Mr. and Mrs. Titbury had left their squint-eyed house in Robey Street on the 5th of May and were now at this one-eyed inn at Calais. We know why they had adopted an assumed name. Having told no one of the day and hour of their departure, they had accomplished their journey in the strictest incognito, as also had Max Real, though from very different motives.

This was very embarrassing to the sporting people, for it must be confessed Hermann Titbury had a good record for this match for the millions. There was no doubt that he would become one of the favourites. Was he not one of those privileged people with whom everything had succeeded up to now, being little scrupulous as to the means he used to bring his success about? His wealth permitted him to pay the fines, if luck imposed them on him, and however large they might be, he would not hesitate to settle them cash down. Besides, he would not abandon himself to any distractions or fancies as he moved from place to place, as might Max Real and Harris T. Kymbale. Was it likely to be his fault if any delay occurred in getting from one state to another? No, and it was absolutely certain that he would be at the place indicated on the day required. Undoubtedly there was much in favour of Hermann Titbury, to say nothing of his own luck, which had never failed him during his business career.

The worthy couple had managed to combine the quickest with the least expensive route across this inextricable network of railroads, stretched like an immense spider's web over the eastern states of the Union. Thus without stopping, without exposing themselves to be plundered at the bars of the railway stations or the restaurants of the hotels, depending only on the provisions they had brought with them, passing from one train to another with the precision of a ball from one hand of a juggler to the other, taking no more interest in the attractions of the country than Tom Crabbe, always absorbed in the same reflections always pursued by the same anxieties, writing down their daily expenses, counting and re-counting the money they had brought with them for the purposes of the journey, dozing by day, sleeping by night, Mr. and Mrs. Titbury had crossed Illinois from west to east, then the State of Indiana, then that of Ohio, then that of New York, then that of New Hampshire, and in this way they had reached the Maine frontier in the morning of the 8th of May, at the foot of Mount Washington of the White Mountains, whose snowy summit amid hail-showers and rain-showers bears to an altitude of 5750 feet the name of the hero of the American Republic.

From there Mr. and Mrs. Titbury reached Paris, then Lewiston on the Androscroggin, a manufacturing city, doubled by the town of Auburn, which competes with the important town of Portland, one of the best ports in New England, sheltered in Casco Bay. The railroad then took them to Augusta, the official capital of Maine, the elegant houses of which are scattered along the banks of the Kennebec. From the station at Bangor they went north-east to Backahogan, where the railway tops, and took the stage coach to Princeton, which an outlying portion joins on to Calais.

In this way, with frequent and disagreeable changes of train, they had accomplished the crossing of Maine, to which the tourists flock to visit the mountain glens, the fields of moraines, the lacustrine plateaux, the deep and inexhaustible forests of oaks, hemlocks, maples, ashes, beeches, and other northern species which furnished the wood for the workshops before the adoption of iron in shipbuilding.

Mr. and Mrs. Titbury, — alias Field — arrived at Calais early on the 9th of May, and well in advance, for they had to stay there until the 19th. This made some ten days to be spent in this town of a few thousand inhabitants, a mere coasting port. How would they occupy their time until the telegram from Tornbrock was sent to them?

But what charming excursions are offered by a region so varied as Maine! Towards the north-west there is the magnificent country dominated by Mount Katahdin, 3500 feet high, an enormous block of granite emerging from a dome of forests in the region of the lake plateaux. And this town of Portland of 36,000 people, the birthplace of the great poet Longfellow, with its important trade with South America and the Antilles, its monuments, its parks, its gardens which its very artistic inhabitants keep up with such taste. And this modest Brunswick with its celebrated Bowdoin College, the picture gallery of which attracts so many connoisseurs! And more to the south, along the shore of the Atlantic, the seaside resorts so much in vogue among the opulent families of the neighbouring states, who would lose caste if they did not devote a few weeks amongst others to that marvellous Mount Desert Island and the refuge of Bar Harbour.

But to ask such excursions of two mollusks torn from their natal bank and transported nine hundred miles away would have been almost useless. No! They would not leave Calais for a day or for an hour. They would remain together, calculating their chances, cursing their fellow players, and arranging what they would do with their fortune if chance made them millionaires. But would they not be embarrassed?

Embarrassed — these two — with millions! Do not alarm yourself. They would know how to place it in high-class bonds, shares in banks, mines, and industrial companies, and they would collect their enormous revenues, and would not dissipate them by charitable foundations, and would re-invest them without spending any for their comfort, or pleasure, and they would live just as before, concentrating their existence on the love of money, devoured by the *auri sacra fames,* misers as they were, mere money barrels as they used to say, masses of meanness and stinginess, skinflints and save-alls, perpetual members of the Academy of Curmudgeons!

If chance favoured this dreadful couple there must be reasons for it, but what they were is difficult to imagine. And it would be to the detriment of the players more worthy of the fortune of William J. Hypperbone who would make better use of it — without excepting Tom Crabbe, without excepting Commodore Urrican.

Here they are then at the far end of the States in this little town of Calais, hidden under the name of Field, weary and impatient, watching the fishing boats go out each tide and return with their loads of mackerel, herring, and salmon. Then they would return to their room at the *Sandy Bar,* forever trembling at the idea of their identity being discovered.

Calais was not so far lost in the depths of Maine for the report of the famous match not to have reached its inhabitants. They knew that the second square had been assigned to this New England state, and the telegraph had informed them that the third throw of the dice — one and one — obliged the player, Hermann Titbury, to stay in their town.

Thus passed the 9th, 10th, 11th, and 12th of May, in profound dulness in this anything but recreative place. Max Real himself could not have survived it without difficulty. Walking along the roads bordered with wooden houses, lounging on the quays, the time seemed to be interminable. And this telegram indicating a new journey which would not be sent before the 19th, what patience it required to wait for it during seven long days more!

But the Titburys might easily manage a tour in foreign parts by crossing the river St. Croix, the left bank of which belongs to Canada.

So said Hermann Titbury to himself, and on the morning of the 13th he made the following proposal: —

"Evidently Hypperbone chose the most disagreeable town of Maine to send there the players who had the bad luck to throw a two at the beginning of the game."

"Take care, Hermann," said Mrs. Titbury in a low voice."

"If any one heard you. Chance has brought us to Calais, and whether we like it or not we must stay in Calais".

"Are we not allowed to leave the town?"

Certainly, but on condition that we do not leave the States."

So we have no right to go to the other side of the river?

"On no account, Hermann. The testator expressly prohibited us from going out of the United States."

"And who would know it?" asked Mr. Titbury.

"I do not understand you, Hermann," replied the lady in a louder voice. Is it really you who are speaking? I no longer recognize you! If later on they learnt that we had crossed the frontier? If some accident were to keep us there? If we did not return in time — the 19th? Besides — I won't have it!"

And she had reason in her "won't", had the imperious Mrs. Titbury! Does one ever know what is going to happen? Supposing there had been an earthquake — that New Brunswick had been, detached from the continent — that this part of America was shaken to pieces — that an abyss opened between the two countries. How could they find the telegraph office on the proper day? Would there be no risk of their being put out of the match?

"No — we cannot cross the river," declared Mrs. Titbury peremptorily.

"You are right, that is forbidden us," replied Mr. Titbury. "I do not know how I could have had such an idea. In truth, since our departure from Chicago I have not been myself. This cursed journey has made me stupid. For people who have never budged from their house in Robey Street to take long journeys at our time of life! We had much better have remained at home — and declined the game — "

"Sixty millions of dollars!" said. Mrs. Titbury," that is worth some inconveniences! Hermann, you say the same things over again a little too often!"

And so St. Stephen, the Dominion town which occupies the other bank of the St. Croix, was not honoured by the Titburys.

It seemed as though such minute care, such excessive prudence which gave such advantages over the other players, would have sheltered them from any vexatious accident, that they never would be taken unawares, that nothing could happen to put them in difficulties — but chance loves to sport with the cleverest set snares that all our caution cannot avoid, and chance must be reckoned with.

Now, in the morning of the 14th, Mr. and Mrs. Titbury conceived the idea of going for an outing. Do not be alarmed: it was only two or three miles outside Calais. Let us remark, by the way, that the town received its French name from being at the extremity of the United States, just as its namesake is at the extremity of France; and as to the State of Maine, its name comes from the first colonists, who settled there in the reign of Charles the First.

It was stormy weather, heavy clouds were rising on the horizon, and towards noon the heat became overwhelming. It was a bad day for a walk along the right bank of the St. Croix.

Mr. and Mrs. Titbury left the inn about nine o'clock and walked along the river beyond the town under the shade of the trees, among the branches of which thousands of squirrels were at play.

The Titburys had been previously assured by the innkeeper that no wild beast was to be found in the surrounding country. No, neither wolf, nor bear — a few foxes only. They could thus venture in perfect confidence even through the forests which formerly made Maine an immense fir plantation.

It need not be said that Mr. and Mrs. Titbury did not bother themselves with the landscapes that offered themselves to their view. They spoke only of their fellow players, those who had started before them. Where now were Max Real and Tom Crabbe? And always this XKZ who made them more anxious than any of the rest.

After a walk of two hours and a half, noon approaching, they thought of returning to the *Sandy Bar* for luncheon, but, parched with thirst under the overwhelming heat, they stopped at an inn situated on the bank about half a mile from the town.

Several men were there seated at tables on which were a few pints of beer.

Mr. and Mrs. Titbury sat down away from the rest and considered for a time what they would have. Porter or ale did not seem to be quite to their taste.

"I am afraid it will be a little cold," said Mrs. Titbury. We are streaming, and there might be a risk — "

"You are right, Kate. Pleurisy is quickly caught," replied Mr. Titbury; and turning to the tavern-keeper, he said, —

"A glass of whisky, please."

Immediately the man remarked, —

"Did you say whisky?"

"Yes — or gin."

Where is your permit?

"My permit?" asked Mr. Titbury, astounded at the question.

But he would not have been astounded if he had remembered that Maine belongs to a group of states which have established the principle of the prohibition of alcohol.

In Kansas, North Dakota, South Dakota, Vermont, New Hampshire, and particularly Maine, it is forbidden to make or sell alcoholic drinks, distilled or fermented.

In each locality, however, municipal agents are appointed to sell to those who buy them for medical or industrial use certain drinks which have been first inspected by a State officer. To infringe this law even by an imprudent request is to expose yourself to the severe penalties enacted with a view to the suppression of alcoholism.

And so Mr. Titbury had hardly spoken before a man approached.

"You have no permit?"‘

"No. I have not."

"Then you have committed an offence."

"An offence — in what?"

"In having asked for whisky or gin."

This man was a policeman, a policeman on his round, and he wrote the names of Mr. and Mrs. Field in his notebook and told them they would have to appear next morning before the judge.

The couple returned crestfallen to the inn, and what a day, what a night they passed! If it was Mrs. Titbury who had had the deplorable idea of going into the tavern, it was Mr. Titbury who had had the no less deplorable idea of preferring a glass of whisky to a pint of beer. To what fine had they rendered themselves liable! Hence disputes and recriminations which lasted until daylight.

The judge, a certain R. T. Ordak, was about the most disagreeable, surly, and irascible being that could be imagined. In the morning, when the offenders were introduced into his office, he took no notice of their civilities, and questioned them brusquely and briefly. Your name? Mr. and Mrs. John Field. Where do you live? They replied at hazard, Harrisburg, Pennsylvania. Your profession? Independent means. Then he fined them straight away a hundred dollars for having infringed the prohibition relating to alcoholic drinks in the State of Maine.

This was too much! Self-controlled as he usually was, and in spite of the efforts of his wife, who vainly tried to keep him quiet, Titbury could not contain himself. He lost his temper; he threatened Judge R. T. Ordak, and Judge R. T. Ordak doubled the fine — a hundred dollars extra for contempt of court.

The extra made Mr. Titbury more furious still. Two hundred dollars to add to the expenses already incurred in travelling to the very end of this wretched State of Maine! Wild with rage, the offender forgot all prudence and even sacrificed the advantages his incognito gave him.

With his arms crossed, his face on fire, repulsing Mrs. Titbury with unaccustomed violence, he bent over the judge's table and said to him, —

"Do you know with whom you are dealing?"

"With an unmannerly rascal, whom I gratify with three hundred dollars fine, since he continues in this tone!" replied the no less exasperated R. T. Ordak.

"Three hundred dollars!" exclaimed Mrs. Titbury, falling half fainting on a seat.

"Yes, replied the judge, accentuating each syllable, three hundred dollars for John Field, of Harrisburg, Pennsylvania —

"Well," roared Titbury, banging on the desk with his fist, "know then that I am not John Field, of Harrisburg, Pennsylvania — "

"Who are you. then?"

"Hermann Titbury — of Chicago — Illinois."

"That is to say an individual travelling about under a false name! remarked the judge, as much as to say, "Another crime added to the others."

"Yes. Hermann Titbury, of Chicago, the third to start in the Hypperbone match, the future heir of the immense fortune."

This declaration appeared to produce no effect on R. T. Ordak. The magistrate, as badly informed as he was impartial, made no more fuss about this third player than about no matter what sailor of the port, and, in a sibilant tone as if he sucked each word as he uttered it, deliberately said, —

"Well, then, it will be Hermann Titbury, of Chicago, Illinois, who will pay three hundred dollars fine, and in addition to that, for having presented himself before the law under a name which is not his, I sentence him to go to prison for eight days."

This was the finisher. Mrs. Titbury collapsed on her seat; Mr. Titbury collapsed in his turn.

Eight days in prison! And in five days the expected telegram would arrive! And on the 19th he must start perhaps for the other end of the United States, and if he were not there on the day fixed he would be turned out of the game.

It must be admitted that it was more serious for Mr. Titbury than if he had been sent to the fifty-second square, State of Missouri, prison of St. Louis. There at least he would have had the possibility of being delivered by one of his competitors, while in the prison at Calais, by the sentence of Judge R. T. Ordak, he would remain shut up until the expiration of his time.

CHAPTER X. A REPORTER ON HIS TRAVELS

"Yes, sirs, yes! I consider this Hypperbone match one of the most astonishing national events with which the history of our glorious country will be enriched! After the War of Independence, the War of Secession, the declaration of the Monroe Doctrine, the passing of the MacKinley Bill, it is the most striking fact that the imagination of a member of the Eccentric Club has imposed on the attention of the world!"

Thus spoke Harris T. Kymbale, addressing the passengers in the train that had on this 7th of May just left the city of Chicago.

The *Tribune* reporter, overflowing with delight and confidence, spoke thus in front of the rear car at the central gangway, then at the next car by the platform between them, then in the front of the train, which was running at full speed along the southern shore of Lake Michigan.

Harris T. Kymbale had started alone. He had declined with thanks the offers of his comrades to accompany him. No, not even a servant — alone, quite alone. It will be seen that he did not seek to get away incognito like Max Real and Hermann Titbury. He took the people into his confidence and would willingly have written on his hat, *Fourth player in the Hypperbone match!* A numerous procession had escorted him to the railway station, honoured with cheers, overwhelmed him with wishes for a pleasant journey. And he was so fit, so confident, so wide awake, and at the same time so audacious and determined that already several wagers had been laid on him. These had been taken at two to one and even three to one — which flattered him and was of good augury. If Harris T. Kymbale, however, had refused to take a few friends with him to share the risks of his travels through the Union, he was not going, as we see, to isolate himself in his corner, to indulge in silent thoughts, to deliver himself in mute asides. Far from that, all the passengers with whom he travelled would become his companions. He was to a certain extent one of those people who do not think unless they talk, and it was not of words he would be stingy in the course of his journey, nor of his purse either. The purse of the wealthy *Tribune* was open to him, and he would know how to get his expenses back in interviews, in descriptions, in sketches, in articles of all sorts, for which the vicissitudes of the match would furnish him with ample and interesting matter.

"But," asked a gentleman — Yankee from head to foot — "are you not attaching too much importance to this game invented by William J. Hypperbone?"

"No, sir," replied the reporter; "I think that so original an idea could only have originated in an ultra-American brain."

"You are right," said a portly merchant of Chicago. "The States are all in a ferment over it, and the day of the funeral you could see the popularity the deceased enjoyed the day after his death."

"Sir," asked an old lady in false teeth and spectacles, buried under her wraps in the corner, "were you in the procession?"

"Just as if I had been one of the heirs of our great citizen," replied the man of Chicago, swelling with a puff of pride, "and I could not be more honoured than in meeting with one of his future heirs in going to Detroit — "

"Are you going to Detroit?" asked Harris T. Kymbale, holding out his hand.

"To Detroit, Michigan."

"Well, sir, I shall have the pleasure of accompanying you to this city of so magnificent a future — which I do not know — and which I wish to know."

"You will not have time, Mr. Kymbale, said the Yankee so quickly that it seemed as though he was one of Kymbale's backers. That would make your journey longer, and, I repeat it, you will not have time."

"There is always time to do everything," answered Kymbale in an affirmative tone which did not produce an unfavourable effect.

In fact the car, proud of possessing a passenger of this temper, broke out into cheers, the echoes of which reverberated to the end of the train.

"Sir," said a clergyman of mature age, who with glasses to his eyes was staring at him as if to devour him, "are you satisfied with your first throw of the dice?"

"Yes and no, reverend sir," replied the journalist in a respectful tone. "Yes, for my competitors who started before me have not passed the second, the eighth, and the eleventh square, while I was sent by two and four to the sixth and thence to the twelfth. No, because it is the State of New York which occupies the sixth square, where there is a bridge, as the inscription says, and this bridge is the foot-bridge of Niagara. Now Niagara is too well known. I have been there twenty times already. Used up, you see, done to death like the American fall, the Canadian fall, the Cave of the Winds, Goat Island! And then it is too near Chicago! What I want is to see the country, to be driven about to the four corners of the Union, to do thousands and thousands of miles on my legs-"

"Providing always," said the clergyman, "that you are on the spot at the proper time."

"Quite so. And depend upon it I shall never fail to be at the spot to the minute."

"However," said a merchant in the canned provision trade, whose healthy colour was an excellent advertisement for his goods, "it seems to me, Mr. Kymbale, that you ought to congratulate yourself, for after setting your foot down in New York State you have to be off to New Mexico. They do not quite border on each other."

"Phew!" exclaimed the reporter, "a few hundred miles divide them — "

"And at least," added the Yankee, "to be sent to the land of Florida or the last village of Washington — "

"That is what I should like," declared Harris T. Kymbale," to cross the United States from the northwest to the south-east."

"But," asked the clergyman, "does not the sending you to the sixth square, where there is a bridge, make you liable for the first fine?"

"Bah! a thousand dollars; that will not ruin the *Tribune!* From the station at Niagara Falls I will send off a cheque telegram they will be only too pleased to honour."

"And all the more so," declared the Yankee, "that this Hypperbone match is a business that for them — "

"Will become good business," said Harris T. Kymbale, as though there could be no doubt about it.

"I am so certain of it," said the Chicago merchant, "that if I were to bet I should back you — "

"And you would do well," replied the reporter.

It will be seen from this that his confidence in himself was at least equal to that of Jovita Foley in her friend Lizzie Wag.

"And yet," said the clergyman, "there is one of your competitors who, in my opinion, is more to be feared than the others."

"Which?"

"The seventh, Mr. Kymbale; the one designated by the letters XKZ."

"The competitor of the last hour!" exclaimed the journalist. "He benefits by the mysterious circumstances that surround him. He is the man in the mask in whom the loafers delight, but his incognito will be found out, and if he is the President of the United States in person he is no more to be feared than any other of the seven."

At the same time, it was hardly probable that it was the President of the United States whom the testator had chosen for the seventh player; although in America none would have thought it unseemly for the first personage in the Union to enter into a competition for a fortune of sixty millions of dollars.

About seven hundred miles separate Chicago from New York, and Harris T. Kymbale had to travel only about two-thirds of them to reach Niagara without having to go on to the great American metropolis. He had no desire to visit it, the reason being that he knew it as well as the famous falls before which he had to present himself.

In leaving Chicago, after skirting the lower gulf of Lake Michigan, the train entered Indiana, bordering on Illinois at Ainsworth; and thence it ran up towards Michigan City. Notwithstanding its name, this town does not belong to the State, but is reckoned among the ports of Indiana.

If the confident reporter had chosen this way amid the railway network of the district, if he went through New Buffalo, if he stopped a few hours at Jackson, an important manufacturing centre with twenty thousand people, if he continued to go north-east, it was because he wished to visit Detroit, where he arrived on the night of the 7th of May.

Next morning, after a short sleep in the room of an hotel from which his name spread all over the town, he was called on from soon after dawn by hundreds of inquisitive people — more than inquisitive people, sympathetic partisans — who during the day did not think proper to leave him for an instant.

Perhaps he was sorry he had not sheltered himself under the veil of an incognito, as his object was to go about the town. But how difficult it is to escape celebrity and its inconveniences when you are reporter-in-chief of the *Tribune* and one of the Seven in the Hypperbone match!

It was thus amid a numerous and noisy crowd that he saw the metropolis of Michigan, of which the modest Lansing is the capital. This prosperous city, founded as a little trading port established by the French in 1670, takes its name from the "détroit" or channel, here about half a mile wide, by which Lake Huron pours its waters into Lake Erie. Opposite to it is the Canadian town of Windsor, its suburb, in which the fourth competitor took good care not to set his foot. He had scarcely time to see this town of two hundred thousand inhabitants, who welcomed him with enthusiasm and overwhelmed him with the good wishes that they would doubtless have showered as freely on any of his competitors.

Harris T. Kymbale left that evening. If he had been allowed to travel on the Canadian railways, to go along the south of the province of Ontario, he could, through the long tunnel under the river St. Clair, where it flows into Lake Huron, have taken a more direct route to Buffalo and Niagara Falls. But he was prohibited from entering the Dominion. He had to enter the State of Ohio, descend to Toledo, a growing town built at the southern point of Lake Erie, strike off at an angle towards Sandusky among the richest vineyards in America, and then, skirting the lake shore, go by Cleveland. Ah! the magnificent city, its population of 262,000 people, its streets shaded with maples, its Euclid Avenue, the Champs Elysées of America, its suburbs in terraces on its hills, the wealth that is being incessantly poured forth by the petroliferous basins of the region, and which has naturally made Cincinnati so jealous. Then he touched at Erie City in Pennsylvania, and from this station he proceeded to Northville, to enter the State of New York, then he ran without stopping through Dunkirk, lighted by the hydrogen of its natural wells, and on the evening of the 10th of May he arrived at Buffalo, the second city of the state, where a hundred years before he would have met bison in thousands instead of people in hundreds of thousands.

Certainly, Harris T. Kymbale did well not to linger in this beautiful town, along its boulevards, in its avenues of Niagara Park, around its warehouses and elevators on the borders of the lake which gives passage to the waters of the Niagara. It was necessary that within ten days at the outside he should be in person at Santa Fé in New Mexico — a journey of 1400 miles, in which the railroad does not go all the way.

The next day, therefore, after a short run of about fifty-five miles, he alighted at the village of Niagara Falls.

Notwithstanding all that the reporter could say with regard to this famous cataract, now too well known and too much used for industrial purposes, which it will be more so in the future when its sixteen million horse power is fully utilized, there can be no comparison of the wonders of the Horse Shoe Fall with the Gate of the Adirondacks, that marvellous assemblage of defiles, amphitheatres and forests, with the Palisades of the Hudson, with the Central

Park of the metropolis, with Broadway, or with the Brooklyn Bridge so audaciously thrown over the East River.

None of these is comparable to this tumultuous pouring over of the waters of Lake Erie into Lake Ontario by the Niagaran channel. It is the St Lawrence that passes, cleaving itself on the head of Goat Island to form on one side the American Fall, on the other the Canadian Fall, in the shape of a horse-shoe. And those furious leapings at the feet of both cataracts, those verdant excavation in the centre of the second, after which the pacified river sweeps its tranquil waters for three miles to the suspension bridge, where it breaks again into those terrible rapids! Formerly, Terrapin Tower rose on the outermost rocks of Goat Island surrounded by whirlpools, the pulverized spray of which formed over its head — rainbows by the sun in day-time, rainbows by the moon at night. But it has had to be taken down, for the fall has cut back a hundred feet in a century and a half, and it would have ended by falling into the abyss. A daring foot-bridge thrown from one bank to the other of the noisy river allows of the double stream being admired in all its splendour. Harris T. Kymbale, escorted by numerous visitors, American and Canadian, placed himself in the middle of this bridge, taking care not to encroach upon the part that belongs to the Dominion. Then raising a cheer which a thousand voices shouted across the uproar of the waters, he returned to the village of Niagara Falls, the surroundings of which are now becoming hideous with too many factories. But what would you have when there is a power of a hundred million tons to be utilized?

The reporter did not stray off among the verdant thickets of Goat Island, nor did he descend into the Cave of the Winds under the island, nor did he venture behind the deep sheets of the Horse Shoe Fall — which he could only do from the Canadian shore; but he did not forget to call at the post office in the village, where he sent off a cheque for a thousand dollars to Tornbrock's order — a cheque which the *Tribune* cashier would hasten to pay as soon as presented.

In the afternoon, after a magnificent luncheon in his honour, Harris T. Kymbale was back in Buffalo, which he left that same evening to accomplish the second part of his journey within the prescribed time.

As he stepped into the car, the mayor of the city, the Honourable H. V. Exulton said to him in a serious tone, — "It is all very well for once, sir, but do not amuse yourself any more by taking it easy on the road as you have done up to now"

"And if it pleases me," said Harris T. Kymbale, who did not seem to quite like the observation, although coming from so elevated a quarter, "I think I have the right — "

"No, sir, no more than a pawn has the right to take things easy on the chess-board"

"What? I belong to myself, I suppose?" Quite a mistake, sir! you belong to those who have backed you, and I am on for five thousand dollars."

The Honourable H. V. Exulton was undoubtedly right, and in his own interest, the *Tribune* reporter, even though his reports might suffer, had but one thing to do — to get to his place by the shortest and quickest way.

Besides, Harris T. Kymbale had nothing to learn in this State of New York, which had been many times visited by him. Between its metropolis and Chicago communications are as numerous as they are easy. It is a matter of a day for these Americans, whose trains hold the record for a thousand miles in twenty-four hours.

It was the 11th of May, and he must be in Santa Fé on the 21st at latest, before noon. Now as the two states were from fifteen to sixteen hundred miles away from each other, they were not exactly neighbours.

On leaving Buffalo, Harris T. Kymbale had proposed to return to Chicago so as to take the Grand Trunk to the west. But as there was no branch putting it in direct communication with Santa Fé, this would have been a mistake, as it would have meant a long carriage journey in a country badly furnished with transport facilities. Fortunately his colleagues on the *Tribune* had made a profound study of this part of the Far West and drawn up an itinerary, which they sent by telegram to Buffalo.

This telegram was in the following terms: —

"Return from Niagara Falls to Buffalo and come down as far as Cleveland. Cross Ohio obliquely by Columbus and Cincinnati, Indiana by Lawrenceburg, Madison, Versailles and Vincennes, Missouri by Salem, Belley and St. Louis. Choose the Jefferson line for Kansas City. Leave Kansas by the more southern line, Lawrence, Emporia, Toleda, Newton, Hutchinson, Plum Buttes, Fort Zarah, Larned, Petersburg, Dodge City, Fort Atkinson, Sherbrock, then east of Colorado by Grenade and Las Arimas. Take the branch at Pueblo, and by Trinidad reach Clifton, on the frontier of New Mexico. Then by Cimarron, Las Vegas and Galateo reach the short line which runs to Santa Fé. Do not forget that the sender of this has put a hundred dollars on you, and that by any other way you will risk making him lose them. — Brennan S. Bickhorn.

How could this one of the Seven, whose friends served him with such zeal, who helped him with such precision in the accomplishment of his task, fail to have the best chance of getting in first? But provided he followed the advice of the Honourable V. H. Exulton, that is to say, not to delay in unseasonable admirations.

"Agreed, my brave Bickhorn," said Harris T. Kymbale," that is the road I will go, and I will not budge from it in the least! There is nothing to worry about with regard to the railroads. Be easy; if there are delays they will not arise from my heedlessness, nor my negligence, and your hundred dollars will be as energetically defended as the five thousand of his Highness the first magistrate of Buffalo! I don't forget that I carry the colours of the *Tribune.*"

A jockey could have said no better. This jockey, it is true, was a centaur and ran on his own account.

And in this way, by a judicious combination of trains, without hurrying, and by managing to stop at night at the best hotels, Harris T. Kymbale covered in sixty hours the five states of Ohio, Indiana, Illinois, Missouri, Kansas and Colorado, and in the evening of the 19th stopped at Clifton, on the border of New Mexico.

There, if the reporter exchanged but 546 shakes of the hand, it was that there were only 273 humans in this little village lost in the depths of the immense plains of the Far West.

He reckoned on having a good night at Clifton. But when he alighted from the car, what was his disappointment to find that on account of important repairs the railroad traffic would be stopped for some days. And he was yet 125 miles from Santa Fé, and had only thirty-six hours to do them in. The wise Brennan S. Bickhorn had not foreseen that.

Fortunately, as he came out of the railway station he found himself in the presence of a man, half American, half Spaniard, who was waiting for him. As soon as he saw the reporter this man gave three-cracks with his whip, a triple crack with which he was probably accustomed to salute people. And in a language reminding one more of Cervantes than Cooper:

"Harris T. Kymbale?" he said.

"I am."

"Would you like me to take you to Santa Fé!"

"Would I not!"

"Agreed."

"Your name?"

"Isidorio."

"Isidorio will do."

"My carriage is there, ready to start."

"Let us start, and do not forget, my friend, that if a carriage moves owing to its horses, it is owing to its driver that it arrives."

Did the Hispano-American comprehend all the hidden meaning of this aphorism? Perhaps.

He was a man of from forty-five to fifty, of a very tawny skin, a very clear eye, and with a jeering expression about his face — one of those wide-awake rascals who are not easily rolled over. As to thinking that he was proud of driving a personage who had one chance in seven of becoming the owner of sixty millions of dollars, the reporter did not doubt it for a moment.

Harris T. Kymbale was the vehicle's only passenger. It was not a stage coach with six horses, but a simple carriole that would have to take fresh horses at the villages on the way. It dashed forth on to the rocky road of Aubey's Trail, cut by numerous creeks which it passed at the fords, took in provisions at the relays, and rested during a few hours of the night.

At dawn the carriole had covered forty miles up to Cimarron, skirting the base of the White Mountains without any mishap. There was nothing to fear from the Apaches, the Comanches, and other tribes of Redskins who formerly roamed over the country, some of which have been allowed by the federal government to retain their independence.

In the afternoon the carriage passed Fort Union, Las Vegas, and was traversing the defiles of Moro Peaks, a route, mountainous, difficult, and even dangerous — in any case little suitable for rapid driving. In fact, from these lower plains they had to ascend to 4800 feet, which is the height of Santa Fé above the level of the sea.

Beyond this huge backbone of New Mexico extends the basin watered by the numerous tributaries which form the Rio Grande del Norte, one of the most magnificent streams on the western slope of America. There you meet with the important road from Chicago to Denver which is the trade route with the provinces of Mexico.

During this night of the 20th the progress of the carriole was very slow and the road very rough. The impatient traveller, not without reason, was afraid of not arriving in time. Consequently incessant exhortations and objurgations were hurled at the phlegmatic Isidorio.

"But you are not moving".

"What would you like, Mr. Kymbale? We have only wheels, we have not got wings."

"But you do not understand how interested I am in getting to Santa Fé on the 21st."

"Good! If we are not there to-day, we shall be there tomorrow."

"But it will be too late."

"My horse and I will do all we can, and you cannot require more from beast or man."

Then Harris T. Kymbale had an idea. He would give this man a more direct interest in the game he was playing. And so while the carriole was going up one of the most rugged valleys of the chain, through thick forests of green trees, following the windings of a labyrinth strewn with rough heaps and trunks fallen through age, he said to his automedon:

"Isidorio, I have a proposal to make!"

"Make it, Mr. Kymbale."

"A thousand dollars for you — if I am to-morrow, before noon, at Santa Fé."

"A thousand dollars, you say?" said the Hispano-American, winking an eye."

"A thousand dollars — on condition, be it understood, that I win the game."

"Ah!" said Isidorio, "on the condition that — "

"Evidently."

"Be it so — it will be all the same," and he gave his horse a triple cut with the whip.

At midnight the carriole had only reached the top of the pass, and the anxieties of Harris T. Kymbale redoubled. He could contain himself no longer and said:

"Isidorio," giving him a slap on the shoulder, "I have a new proposal to make to you."

"Make it, Mr. Kymbale."

"Ten thousand — yes! ten thousand dollars if I arrive in time."

"Ten thousand, you say"

"Ten thousand!"

"That is, if you win the game."

"Certainly."

To descend the range, without going to Galisteo to take the short stretch of a railroad — which would have lost a little time — then to follow the valley of the Rio Chiquito and reach Santa Fé, was about fifty miles, and he had only twelve hours to spare.

It is true the road was fairly good, not very hilly, and it would have been difficult to get a better horse than the one from Tuos; so it was possible to reach the end within the time if no stoppage were made and the weather continued favourable.

The night was magnificent, the moon seemed to have been ordered by the obliging Bickhorn, the temperature agreeable, a lovely refreshing breeze from the north, a fair wind which did not hinder the progress of the vehicle.

The horse pawed the ground with impatience at the door of the inn, a beast full of fire, of the Mexico-American race, bred in the corrals of the western provinces.

As to him who held the reins of the carriole, a better could not be found. Ten thousand dollars in his hand — even in his wildest dreams he had never seen the glitter of so much. But Isidorio did not somehow seem so very much astonished at the stroke of fortune that had come to him — at least so thought Harris T. Kymbale.

"Does the brigand want more?" he said to himself; "ten times more, for example? After all, what are a few thousand dollars among the millions of William J. Hypperbone? — a drop of water in the sea! Well! If it must be, I will go to a hundred drops."

And just as they were starting:

"Isidorio, he said in his ear, it is not now ten thousand dollars — "

"What — are you going to withdraw from your promise?" asked Isidorio sharply.

"No, my friend, no. Very much on the contrary! It is a hundred thousand dollars for you if we are in Santa Fé before midday."

"A hundred thousand dollars, did you say?" repeated Isidorio, half closing his left eye.

Then he added:

"If you-win?"

"Yes — if I win."

"Could you write that on a piece of paper, Mr. Kymbale — only a few words — "

"With my signature?"

"With your signature."

Clearly in an affair of this importance mere word of mouth would not suffice. Without hesitation Harris T. Kymbale opened his note-book and on one of its leaves wrote a promissory note to pay a hundred thousand dollars to Mr. Isidorio, of Santa Fé — a promise that would be faithfully kept if the reporter became the sole heir of William J. Hypperbone. Then he signed it with his usual flourish and handed it up to its destined owner.

Isidorio took it, read it, folded it carefully, stuffed it into his pocket and said:

"Come on."

Ah! The dashing wild gallop, the vertiginous rush, of the carriole down the road along the Rio Chiquito, And in spite of all efforts, at the risk of smashing up the vehicle, of being thrown into the river, Santa Fé could not be reached until ten minutes to twelve.

There are not more than 7000 inhabitants in this capital. New Mexico was annexed in 1850, but its admission to the number of fifty states had taken place only a few months before, so that the eccentric deceased had been able to get it on his board.

Manifestly it remained Spanish in manners and aspect and did not assume the Anglo-American character very quickly. As to Santa Fé, its position among silver-bearing deposits assures it a prosperous future. According to the inhabitants the town itself rests on a thick bed of silver, and from the subsoil of its streets you can dig out an ore giving two hundred dollars to the ton.

The town has few attractions for tourists. There are the ruins of a church built by the Spaniards nearly three centuries before, and a governor's palace, a humble building of one storey which is ornamented with small columns of wood. Its houses, Spanish and Indian, are built of adobe or unburnt bricks, a few being but a cube of masonry pierced with irregular embrasures like those met with in the native pueblos.

Harris T. Kymbale was welcomed as he had been throughout his journey. And he had no time to reply to the seven thousand hands which were stretched out to him otherwise than by a general acknowledgment of thanks. In fact, it was already 11.50, and he must be at the telegraph office before the town clock, struck twelve.

Two telegrams awaited him; sent that morning, and almost at the same time, from Chicago. The first, signed by Tornbrock, notified him of the second throw of the dice with which he was concerned. By ten, made up of five and five, he was sent to the twenty-second square, South Carolina.

Well, this intrepid, this indefatigable traveller, who dreamt of wild itineraries, had certainly got what he wanted! Fifteen hundred good miles to cover towards the Atlantic slope of the States! He made but one remark: Had it been Florida, I should have had a few hundred miles more!

At Santa Fé the Hispano-Americans wished to welcome the presence of their compatriot by organizing meetings, banquets, and other ceremonies of that kind. But to his great regret the reporter-in-chief of the *Tribune* refused. Taught by experience, he had resolved to follow the advice of the worthy Mayor of Buffalo and to delay on no pretext, to travel by the shortest way and be free to ramble when he had reached his post.

In addition to this, the other telegram, sent him by the careful Bickhorn, contained a new itinerary, as carefully worked out as the first, to which his comrades begged him to conform by starting at once. And he decided to leave the capital of New Mexico that very day.

The coachmen of the town were not unaware of what this ultra-generous traveller had done for Isidorio; and in consequence they all offered their services in the hope that they would be as well provided for as their comrade.

Doubtless you will be astonished at Isidorio not claiming the honour — almost the right — of taking the reporter to the nearest railway station, and, who knows? with the thought of adding perhaps another hundred thousand dollars to those promised by Harris T. Kymbale. But it is likely that this very practical personage was no less satisfied than fatigued. He came, however, to say goodbye to the journalist, who had engaged another man, and was preparing to start at three in the afternoon.

"Well, my brave fellow," said Harris T. Kymbale," are you all right?"

"I am all right, sir."

"And now I have not done with you, for I have associated you in my fortune — "

"Thank you, Mr. Kymbale, I do not deserve it."

"But you do — I have to thank you, for without your zeal, your devotion, I should have arrived too late — I should have been put out of the game, and if we had failed by those ten minutes — "

Isidorio listened to this eulogistic appreciation calmly and banteringly as usual.

"If you are pleased, Mr. Kymbale, I am."

"And the two of us make a pair, as our friends the French say, Isidorio."

"Then that is like two horses in a team."

"Exactly. Now that paper that I gave you, keep it carefully. When you hear me announced to the world as the winner of the Hypperbone match, the road will then be working, I suppose; go down to Clifton, take the train to Chicago, and come along for the cash! You need not be uneasy, I will honour my signature."

Isidorio nodded his head, scratched his forehead, winked his eye, like a man who was undecided and wished to speak and hesitated to do so.

"What is up?" asked Harris T. Kymbale. "Do you think you are not sufficiently rewarded?"

"To be sure, I am," replied Isidorio, "but these hundred thousand dollars — are always if you win — "

"Think, my dear fellow, think. Could it be otherwise?"

"Why not?"

"See here — it would be impossible for me to pay such a sum if I do not pocket the heritage."

"Oh! I understand, Mr. Kymbale, I understand very well! And I should prefer — "

"What?

"A hundred good dollars."

"A hundred instead of a hundred thousand?"

"Yes," replied Isidorio placidly, "I do not care to trust to chance — and a hundred good dollars which you could give me now — there would be something in it — "

Perhaps at the bottom he regretted his generosity, anyway Harris T. Kymbale quickly drew from his pocket a hundred dollars and handed them over to the wise man, who tore up the note and handed him back the pieces.

The reporter departed, accompanied by noisy good wishes, and disappeared at a gallop down the main street of Santa Fé. This time the new driver would doubtless be less philosophic than his comrade.

When Isidorio was asked about the decision he had made:

"Good he said, a hundred dollars — it is a hundred dollars! Then I had no confidence in him! — a man so sure of himself! Look here — I would not put twenty-five cents on him!"

CHAPTER XI . THE ANXIETIES OF JOVITA FOLEY

Lizzie Wag, in numerical order, was the fifth to start. Nine days had to elapse between that on which Max Real left Chicago and that on which she had to leave the city.

In what a state of impatience did she pass this apparently interminable week, or, to tell the truth, did Jovita Foley pass it in her place. Lizzie Wag could not succeed in keeping her quiet. She ate no more, she slept no more, she lived no more. She had finished her preparations the day after the first throw of the dice, the first of the month, at eight o'clock in the morning, and the next day she had made Lizzie Wag accompany her to the Auditorium, where the second throw had taken place in the presence of a crowd quite as numerous and quite as excited. Then the third and fourth throws were announced on the 5th and 7th of May. In forty-eight hours destiny would decide regarding the two friends, for they would not separate from each other, the two girls would be one and the same person.

But it must be understood that it was Jovita Foley who absorbed Lizzie Wag, the latter being, reduced to the position of mentor, prudent and reasonable as could be listened to.

Of course, the holiday given by Mr. Marshall Field to his sub-cashier and leading saleswoman had begun on the 16th of April, the day after the reading of the will. The two girls were no longer obliged to attend at the shop in Madison Street. This, however, was the cause of some anxiety to the wiser of the two, for if this absence were prolonged for weeks or months, could their employer dispense with their services for so long?

"We have made a mistake," said Lizzie Wag.

"Agreed," said Jovita Foley, "and we will continue to make a mistake as long as is necessary."

And so saying, the nervous and impressionable personage went on walking backwards and forwards in the little apartment in Sheridan Street. She opened the only bag which contained the clothes for the journey; she made sure that nothing had been forgotten for a tour of long duration, perhaps; she counted and re-counted the disposable money — all their savings converted into paper or cash, which the hotels, railways and carriages, and the unexpected would devour, to the great desolation of Lizzie Wag; and she talked about it all with the other lodgers, so numerous in these immense bee-hives of Chicago, seventeen stories high. And she went down and up in the lift each time she heard of something new in the newspapers or from the shouters in the street.

"Ah, my dear," she said one day. "He has gone, this Mr. Real; but where is he? He has not even let anyone know his route to Kansas."

And in fact, the smartest detectives of the local press had been unable to get on the track of the young painter, of whom they did not expect to get any news before the 15th, that is to say, a week after Jovita Foley and Lizzie Wag had been sent forth on to the railroads of the Union.

"Well, to speak frankly," said Lizzie Wag, "of all our competitors, this young man interests me most — "

"Because he wished you a pleasant journey, is it not?" asked Jovita Foley.

"And also because he seems to me to be worthy of all the favours of fortune — "

"After you, Lizzie, I imagine."

"No, before me."

"I understand," replied Jovita. "If you were not one of the seven, your good wishes would be for him."

"And they are, all the same."

"Quite so; but as you are playing in the game, and I also as your intimate friend, before imploring heaven for this Max Real, I beg that you will implore it for me. Besides, I tell you we do not know where he is — not far from Fort Riley, I suppose, unless some accident — "

"Let us hope not, Jovita."

"Let us hope not is understood, my dear; it is understood — "

And in this way Jovita Foley most often replied, ironically, to the observations of the timorous Lizzie Wag.

Then, getting excited again, she said to her, "You never talk to me about that horrible Tom Crabbe, for he is on the road with his keeper — to Texas? Have you no good wishes for the crustacean?"

"I hope, Jovita, that fate will not send us into countries too far away."

"Bah, Lizzie!"

"See, Jovita, we are only women, and a neighbouring State would suit us better — "

"Agreed, Lizzie; but if fate does not push gallantry so far as to spare our weakness — if it sends us to the Atlantic Ocean — to the Pacific Ocean — or to the Gulf of Mexico, we shall be obliged to submit — "

"We shall submit, because you wish it."

"It is not because I wish it, but because it must be done, Lizzie. You think only of the departure, never of the arrival — the grand arrival, the-sixty-third square — and I think of it night and day, and of the return to Chicago — where the millions await us in the safe of this excellent notary — "

"Yes. These famous millions of the heritage," said Lizzie Wag, smiling.

"Look here, Lizzie. Have the other players made so much fuss about accepting it? Are not the Titburys on the road to Maine?"

"Poor people! I pity them."

"Ah, you will make me angry!" exclaimed Jovita Foley.

"And you, if you do not keep quiet, if you continue to make yourself so nervous as you have been doing during the last week, you will make yourself ill, and I shall have to stay here to look after you. I warn you — "

"Me! 111! You are mad! It is my nerves which will keep me going, which will give me endurance, and I shall be nervous all through the journey!"

"Well, then, Jovita, it will not be you who will go to bed, but I shall do so."

"You! You! Well — do think better of being ill!" exclaimed the very excellent and too expansive damsel, throwing herself on Lizzie Wag's neck.

"Then be calm," answered Lizzie Wag, replying to her kisses, "and all will go well."

Jovita Foley, with great effort, contrived to control herself, alarmed at the thought of her young friend being laid up on the day of departure.

On the 7th, in the morning, when she returned from the Auditorium, Jovita Foley brought the news that the fourth to start Harris T. Kymbale, had got six points, and had to go first to the State of New York, to the bridge of Niagara, and then to Santa Fé in New Mexico.

Lizzie Wag made but one remark with regard to this, and that was that the *Tribune* reporter would have to pay a fine.

"That will hardly cause his journal any trouble," said Jovita.

"No, Jovita, but it would give us very much trouble if we were obliged to pay a thousand dollars at the beginning, or even in the course, of our journey."

And the other replied as usual by a toss of the head signifying, "That will not happen. No! That will not happen."

Really this was what worried her most, although she would not let it be seen. And every night during a troubled sleep which often kept Lizzie awake, she raved in a loud voice of the bridge, the inn, the labyrinth the well, the prison, those unfortunate squares where the players had to pay fines, single, double, treble, to be allowed to continue the game.

At last the 8th of May arrived, and next day the young travellers would start on their journey; and with merely the live coals that Jovita Foley had been playing with for a week or more they could have fired an express locomotive that would have taken them to the extremity of America.

It need not be said that Jovita Foley had bought a general guide to journeys across the United States, the best and most complete of the guide-books, which she turned over and read and re-read incessantly, although she was not in a position to study one route more than another.

But to be quite up-to-date it was only necessary for her to consult the newspapers of the metropolis or any other town. Communications were opened at once between each State as it was introduced into the game, and especially between the places indicated by William J. Hypperbone. The post, the telephone, the telegraph, were working all day long. Morning papers, evening papers, containing columns of information, more or less veracious, more or less fantastic even, it must be confessed. It is true that the reader and the subscriber were agreed on one point: rather false news than no news at all.

It will be understood that this information depended on the players and their way of procedure. For instance, with regard to Max Real, if the information was not trustworthy it was because he had taken nobody but his mother into his confidence. Not having been recognized at Omaha or Kansas City, or on board the *Dean Richmond*, the reporters had sought for trace of him in vain and knew not what had become of him.

A no less profound obscurity still enveloped Hermann Titbury. There was no doubt that he had started on the 5th with Mrs. Titbury, and that he was no longer at the house in Robey Street, nor was the servant, the female molossus we have mentioned. But what they did not know was that they were travelling under an assumed name, and the reporters were helpless to discover them on their journey. Apparently there would be no certain news of this couple until the day when they went to the post-office at Calais to receive the telegram.

The information was more complete with regard to Tom Crabbe. Starting on the 3rd from Chicago in a very ostentatious fashion, Milner and his companion had been viewed and interviewed in the principal cities on their route, and finally at New Orleans, where they had embarked for Galveston in Texas. The *Freie Presse* had been careful to remark that the steamer *Sherman* was of American nationality, that is to say, a piece of the mother country; and in fact, as it was forbidden to the players to leave the national territory, it would not do to take passage on a foreign ship, even though it remained on the waters of the Union.

As to Harris T. Kymbale, there was no want of news on his account. It came in showers like rain in April, for he spared neither telegram, article, nor letter that would benefit the *Tribune*. Thus people had learnt of his passing through Jackson and Detroit, and readers were impatiently awaiting the account of the receptions organized in his honour at Buffalo and Niagara Falls.

The 7th of May arrived. The next day but one, Tornbrock, assisted by George B. Higginbotham, would announce in the Auditorium the result of the fifth throw of the dice. Still thirty-six hours and Lizzie Wag would know her fate.

It can easily be imagined with what impatience Jovita Foley would have passed these two days if she had not been a prey to anxieties of the deepest gravity.

During the night of the 7th, Lizzie Wag was suddenly seized with a very violent sore throat, and she was in a high state of fever when she awoke her friend, who slept in the next room.

Jovita Foley at once arose, did what she could to help her, gave her some soothing drinks, covered her up warmly, and said to her in anything but a confident way:

"It will be nothing, my dear; it will be nothing,"

"I hope so," answered Lizzie Wag, "for it would be to fall ill at a bad time."

That was the opinion of Jovita Foley, who did not even think of going to bed again, but stayed to watch by the girl, whose sleep was very painfully troubled.

Next morning at dawn the whole house knew that the fifth player was so unwell that it had been necessary to send for a doctor; and the doctor came again at nine o'clock.

The house was informed of what had occurred, then the street, then the quarter, then the section, then the town, for the intelligence spread with that electric swiftness that is characteristic of bad news.

What was there to be astonished at in that? Was not Miss Wag the woman of the hour — the personage most in view since the departure of Harris T. Kymbale? Was not public attention fixed on her — the only heroine among the six heroes of the Hypperbone match?

And here was Lizzie Wag ill — seriously ill, perhaps — on the eve of the day on which destiny was to decide with regard to her!

The doctor, D. M. P. Pughe, was announced a little after nine o'clock. To begin with, he asked Jovita Foley about the patient's temperature.

"Excellent," he replied.

The doctor then went and sat by the bedside of Lizzie Wag; he looked at her attentively, he made her put out her tongue, he felt her pulse, he listened to her, he auscultated her. Nothing wrong with the heart, nothing wrong with the liver, nothing wrong with the stomach. At last, after a conscientious examination which to him was worth four dollars a visit, he said:

"It will not be serious, unless grave complications intervene."

"Are these complications to be feared?" asked Jovita Foley, troubled at this declaration.

"Yes and no," replied D. M. P. Pughe. "No if the malady is checked at the outset — yes if, in spite of our care, it is not and assumes a development which the remedies are powerless to affect — "

"But" interrupted Jovita Foley, whom these evasive replies rendered more and more anxious, "can you say definitely what is the matter with her?"

"Yes, decidedly."

"Tell me then, doctor."

"Well, I have diagnosed simple bronchitis. The bases of the two lungs are attacked. There is a slight rattle, but the pleura is not affected — so — up to now — there is no fear of pleurisy — but — "

"But what?"

"But the bronchitis may degenerate into pneumonia, and pneumonia into pulmonary congestion. That is what I call grave complications."

And the practitioner prescribed the usual remedies, drops of spirit of aconite, soothing syrups, warm infusions, rest — rest above everything. Then promising to return in the evening, he left the house in a hurry to return to his consulting-room, which the reporters were already besieging without doubt.

Would the possible complications occur, and if they occurred, when would it be?

In the presence of this event, Jovita Foley was nearly losing her head. During the hours that followed, Lizzie Wag appeared to suffer more and be more depressed. Shivering announced a second attack of fever, the pulse beat with irregular frequency and the prostration increased.

Jovita Foley, as much overcome mentally as the patient was physically, did not leave the bedside, interrupting herself only to look at her, to wipe her heated forehead, to pour the spoonfuls of draught, while she abandoned herself to the most distressing reflections and just recriminations against such conspicuous misfortune.

"No!" she said to herself, "no! It is not a Crabbe, it is not a Titbury, who would have had an attack of bronchitis on the eve of the start, nor a Kymbale, nor a Max Real! And neither will it be this Commodore Urrican who will have such ill-luck! It must be my poor Lizzie, whose health is so good — and it is to-morrow — yes! tomorrow, that the fifth throw is to take place! And if we are sent far away — far away — and if a delay of five or six days only prevents our being at our post — and even if the 23rd of the month arrives before we leave Chicago — and if it is too late to do so — and if we are shut out from the game without having begun it — "

If! If! This unlucky conjunction tossed itself about in Jovita Foley's brain.

Towards three o'clock the attack of fever decreased. Lizzie Wag emerged from this profound prostration, and the cough appeared to be more marked. When her eyes opened Jovita Foley was bending over her.

"Well," she asked, "how do you feel? Better — do you not? What would you like me to give you?"

"A little to drink," replied Lizzie in a voice much altered by her sore throat.

"There, my dear — a nice drink of this in some warm milk. And then — the doctor has ordered it — there will be a few — "

"As you please, my good Jovita."

"Then it will do by itself — "

"Yes, by itself."

"You seem to be a little better."

"You know, dear friend" replied *Lizzie* Wag, "that when the fever leaves you, you are very low-spirited, but you feel a little better."

"That is convalescence!" exclaimed Jovita Foley. "Tomorrow there will be no signs of it."

"Convalescence — already — " murmured the patient, trying to smile.

"Yes — already — and when the doctor returns he will say if you can get up."

"Between us — confess, my good Jovita, that I have indeed no chance."

"No chance — you — "

"Yes, and fate made a mistake in not choosing you in my place. To-morrow you will be at the Auditorium, and you will start the same day — "

"I start — leaving you in this state! Never!"

"I know how to make you!"

"That is not the point," said Jovita Foley; "I am not the fifth player — I am not the future heiress of the late Hypperbone — you are! But think a little. No harm will be done even if we start two days late. There will still remain thirteen days for the journey, and in thirteen days you can go from one end of the United States to another."

Lizzie Wag did not care to say that her illness might last a week, and — who knows — perhaps beyond the regulation fortnight. She contented herself with saying:

"I promise, Jovita, to get well as soon as possible."

"And I ask no more. But — for the moment — you have talked enough. Do not tire yourself — try to sleep a little. I am going to sit there, near you — "

"You will end by falling ill yourself — "

"I! Never fear. And besides, we have good neighbours who would take my place if it were necessary. Sleep in all confidence, Lizzie."

And after pressing her friend's hand, Lizzie turned over and soon became sleepy.

But what disquieted and annoyed Jovita Foley was that in the afternoon the street presented a scene of animation quite unusual in this tranquil quarter. The noise was enough to trouble the repose of Lizzie Wag, even on the ninth floor of the house. Spectators moved about the pavement. Business men stopped and inquired of each other at the door of No. 19. Carriages arrived noisily and departed, at full trot towards the chief quarters of the town.

"How is she?" said some.

"Not so well," replied the others.

"They say it is gastric fever."

"No, typhoid."

"Ah! poor girl! There are people who are indeed out of luck."

"Yet, she is one of the Seven in the Hypperbone match."

"A fine thing if you cannot take advantage of it."

"And even when she is fit to go by train, is she capable of standing the fatigue of so much travel?"

"Perfectly, if the game finishes in a few throws — and that is possible — "

"And if it lasts for months?"

"How can you reckon with chance?"

And a thousand sayings of that sort.

It need hardly be said that a number of inquirers presented themselves at Jovita Foley's door. Insist as they might, she refused to see them. Whereupon contradictory news, manifestly exaggerated or false in every way, spread through the town. But Jovita held out, contenting herself with approaching the window and anathematizing the noise in the street. The only exception she made was in the case of one of Marshall Field's, staff, to whom she gave very reassuring news — a cold — a mere cold.

Between four and five o'clock in the evening, as the uproar redoubled, she put her head out and recognized amid a group in great agitation — whom? — Hodge Urrican. He was accompanied by a man of about forty, who looked like a sailor, vigorous, thick-set, fidgety, gesticulating. You would have taken him to be more violent, more irascible than the terrible commodore.

Certainly it was not out of sympathy for his young competitor that Hodge Urrican was that day in Sheridan Street, that he was walking under her windows, that he devoured them with his look. And Jovita Foley noticed distinctly that his companion, more demonstrative, shook his fist like a man who cannot control himself.

When those around him assured him that the illness of Lizzie Wag was reduced to a mere indisposition:

"What imbecile says that?" he yelled. The personage called upon did not make himself known for fear of an unlucky blow.

"Bad — she is bad!" declared the commodore.

"Worse and worse," added his companion. "And if any one says the contrary — "

"Come, Turk, restrain yourself."

"Restrain myself!" replied Turk, rolling his tiger's eyes in fury. "It is easy for you, my commodore, who are the most patient of men! But I — to hear people talking like that — drives me out of my mind — and when I am like that — "

"Good — that will do!" ordered Hodge Urrican, getting his arm away from him with a shake.

From these few phrases it was to be believed — what no one thought probable — that there existed a man below compared with whom Hodge Urrican would pass as an angel of gentleness.

In any case, if the two were there, it was in the hope that they would get some bad news and make certain that the Hypperbone match would be contested by no more than six players.

That was what Jovita Foley thought, and she restrained herself from going down into the street. How she would have liked to treat these two individuals as they deserved, at the risk of being devoured by the wild beast with the face of a man!

In short, from this state of affairs it resulted that the news in the early papers, published about six o'clock in the evening, was full of the strangest contradictions.

According to some, Lizzie Wag's indisposition had yielded to the doctor's first remedies, and her departure would not be delayed for a single day.

According to others, the illness was not of a serious character, but a certain amount of rest would be necessary, and Miss Wag would not be able to start before the end of the week.

Now it was the *Chicago Globe* and the *Chicago Evening Post*, with whom the girl was a favourite, who were the most alarmist: consultation of the princes of science — an operation necessary — Miss Wag had broken — an arm, said the first — a leg, said the second. In fact a letter, signed "Jovita Foley" had been sent to Mr. Tornbrock, testamentary executor of the deceased, informing him that the fifth competitor renounced her share in the heritage.

The *Chicago Mail*, whose editor seemed to espouse the sympathies and antipathies of Commodore Urrican, did not hesitate to declare that Lizzie Wag had taken her last breath between 4.45 and 4.47 that afternoon.

When Jovita Foley heard this news she felt anything but well. Fortunately, Dr. Pughe, at his evening visit, reassured her in a certain measure.

"No," he repeated. "It is only simple bronchitis. There is no symptom of the terrible pneumonia, nor of the terrible pulmonary congestion — at present, at least. A few days of quiet and repose will be enough — "

"How many?"

"Perhaps seven or eight."

"Seven or eight!"

"And on condition that the patient is not exposed to currents of air."

"Seven or eight days!" repeated the unhappy Jovita Foley, twisting her hands.

"That is, if serious complications do not occur!"

The night was not a very good one. Fever came on again — the attack lasting till morning and causing an abundant perspiration. But the sore throat was better.

Jovita Foley did not go to bed. These interminable hours she passed at the bedside of her poor friend. What nurse could have surpassed her in care, attention, and zeal! But she would not have yielded her place to any one.

The next day, after a few minutes of sickness and morning restlessness, Lizzie Wag went to sleep.

It was the 9th of May, and the fifth throw of the dice was to take place in the Auditorium.

Jovita Foley would have given ten years of her life to be there. But to leave the patient — no — it was not to be thought of. But it came about in this way. Lizzie Wag awoke, and calling her companion, said to her:

"My good Jovita, ask our neighbour to take your place near me — "

"You wish me — "

"I wish you to go to the Auditorium. It is at eight o'clock — is it not?"

"Yes, eight o'clock."

"Well, you can be back in twenty minutes afterwards. I should like to know you were there — and if you believe in my chance — "

"If I believe in it!" Jovita Foley had exclaimed three days before. But now she made no answer. She put a kiss on her patient's forehead and called the neighbour, an excellent woman, who installed herself at the side of the bed. Then she went down, threw herself into a carriage, and was driven to the Auditorium.

It was a quarter to eight when Jovita Foley arrived at the door of the theatre, which was already crowded. Recognized as soon as she entered, she was assailed with questions.

"How is Lizzie Wag?"

"Perfectly well," she declared, asking to be allowed to pass on to the stage — which she did.

The girl's death had been formally affirmed by the morning newspapers, and some of the people were astonished that her most intimate friend had come — and not even in mourning.

At ten minutes to eight the president and members of the Eccentric Club, escorting Tornbrock, always with his aluminium spectacles, appeared on the stage and sat down before the table.

The board was opened under the notary's eyes. The two dice lay near the leather-covered box. Five minutes more and eight o'clock would strike.

Suddenly a voice of thunder broke the silence which had been obtained, not without difficulty.

This voice was that of the commodore. Hodge Urrican asked permission to make a simple observation, which was accorded him.

"It seems to me, Mr. President," said he, louder and louder as the sentence developed, "it seems to me that to conform to the precise wishes of the deceased, it will not be correct to make this fifth throw, inasmuch as the fifth competitor is not in a state — "

"Yes! Yes!" yelled a few of those in the group around Urrican, one voice more enraged than the others being that of the violent man who had accompanied him beneath Jovita Foley's windows the night before.

"Be quiet, Turk, be quiet!" said the commodore as if he were talking to a dog.

"Quiet, indeed — "

"This moment."

Turk resigned himself to silence beneath the thunderous look of Hodge Urrican, who continued:

"And if I make this proposition, it is because I have serious reasons for believing that the fifth competitor will not be able to start either to-day — to-morrow — "

"Not even in eight days?" shouted one of the spectators at the back.

"Nor in eight days, nor in fifteen, nor in thirty," affirmed Commodore Urrican, "for she died this morning at forty-seven minutes past five."

A long murmur followed this declaration. But above it was immediately heard a feminine voice repeating three times:

"It is false — false — false — for I, Jovita Foley, left Lizzie Wag twenty-five minutes ago, alive and well."

Then the clamour recommenced, and renewed protests from the Urrican group. After the formal declaration of the commodore, Lizzie Wag evidently did not know how to behave properly. He had said she was dead, and she certainly ought to be dead.

But now it would be difficult to take notice of Hodge Urrican's observation. Nevertheless that irrepressible personage insisted on modifying his argument as follows: —

"Be it so — the fifth competitor is not dead, but she is almost as bad. And so, under these circumstances, I demand that my throw of the dice be advanced forty-eight hours, and that the throw about to be announced should be that of the sixth competitor, who for the future shall be ranked as the fifth."

Renewed thunder of shouts and shuffling of feet on the part of Urrican's partisans, who were well worthy of sailing under his flag.

At last Tornbrock managed to calm this noisy assembly, and when silence was established he said:

"The proposal of Mr. Hodge Urrican is based on an erroneous interpretation of the wishes of the testator and is opposed to the rules of the Noble Game of the United States of America. Whatever the state of health of the fifth competitor, and whether this state will be such as to remove her from the number of the living, my duty as testamentary executor of the late William J. Hypperbone is none the less to proceed to this throw on this 9th of May, and on behalf of Miss Lizzie Wag. In a fortnight, if she is not at her post, dead or not, she will be deprived of her rights, and the game will continue to be played by the six competitors."

Vehement protests from Hodge Urrican. He contended in a furious voice that Tornbrock had falsely interpreted the will, although the notary's action was approved by the Eccentric Club. And in shouting his threatening phrases, the commodore, red with anger as he was, appeared pale beside his companion, whose face had become scarlet.

But he felt he must restrain Turk to prevent a disaster. He seized him as he was trying to get away."

Where are you going?" he asked.

"There," replied Turk, pointing to the stage with his fist.

"To?"

"To take that Tornbrock by the skin of his neck and throw him out like a porpoise — "

"Here — Turk — here!" commanded Hodge Urrican.

And you could hear in Turk's inside a deep growling like that of a subdued wild beast who would gladly have devoured his subduer.

Eight o'clock struck.

Instantly a deep silence fell on all.

Then Tornbrock — perhaps a little more excited than usual — took the box in his right hand, put into it the dice with his left, and shook it up and down. The little cubes of ivory could be heard clicking against each other against the side of the box, and when they escaped they rolled on the board to the edge of the table.

Tornbrock invited George B. Higginbotham and his colleagues to verify the number thrown, and in a clear voice he said:

"Nine, by six and three!"

A lucky number, for it took the fifth competitor at a bound to the twenty-sixth square, the State of Wisconsin.

CHAPTER XII . THE FIFTH PLAYER

"Ah! dear Lizzie, what a fortunate — what a marvellous throw!" exclaimed the impetuous Jovita Foley.

She was entering the room without a thought, careless girl, of how she might disturb the patient, who perhaps was asleep.

Lizzie Wag was awake, looking very pale, and exchanging a few words with the good old lady seated near her bed.

As soon as the announcement was made by Tornbrock, Jovita Foley had left the Auditorium, leaving the crowd to its reflections and Hodge Urrican furious at not having profited by such a throw.

"And what is the number of points?" asked Lizzie Wag, half rising.

"Nine, my dear, nine by six and three — which takes us at a bound to the twenty-sixth square — "

"And that square?"

"State of Wisconsin. Milwaukee — two hours — two hours only by express."

For a start nothing better could be wished for.

"No — no — "repeated the enthusiastic personage, "Oh! I know well, with nine by five and four you could go right away to the fifty-third square. But that square — look at the board — is Florida! And we should have been obliged to start for Florida — that is to say, the end of the world."

And flushed and panting for breath, she used the board as if it were a fan.

"Well, you are right," replied Lizzie Wag. "Florida — is rather far — "

"All the chances, my dear," affirmed Jovita Foley, "to you all the good chances, and to the others — well — all the bad ones."

"Be more generous — "

"If it pleases you, I except Mr. Max Real, because he has your good wishes — "

"Certainly."

"But let us return to business, Lizzie. The twenty-sixth square — do you see the start it gives us? The leader up to now was the journalist, Harris T. Kymbale, and he is only at the twelfth square, while we — want thirty-seven points — only thirty-seven points — and we-reach the end!"

Feeling some annoyance at Lizzie Wag not sharing her enthusiasm, she exclaimed:

"But you do not look as though you were pleased."

"But I am, Jovita — and we will go to Wisconsin — to Milwaukee — "

"Oh! we have time, my dear Lizzie! Not to-morrow, nor even the day after. In five or six days, when you have quite recovered, and even in a fortnight if necessary, provided we are there on the 23rd in the forenoon."

"Well — all is for the best, and as you are content — "

"And I am, my dear, just as contented as the commodore is discontented! That horrible man would have thrust you out of the game — would have made Mr. Tornbrock give him the fifth throw, on the pretext that you could not profit by it — that you would be in bed for weeks and weeks. And even that you were no longer of this world! Ah! The abominable-sea-wolf. You know — I do not wish evil to anybody — but this commodore, I hope he will lose himself in the labyrinth, fall into the well, go mouldy in the prison, pay fines, single, double, treble — in short, all the disagreeable things that the game has in store for those who have no luck and do not deserve any! If you had heard Mr. Tornbrock reply to him! Oh! that excellent notary — I could have kissed him!"

Setting aside her customary exaggeration, there was no doubt Jovita Foley was-right. This throw of nine by six and three was one of the best that could have occurred at the beginning. Not only had it put her ahead of her four preceding competitors, but it gave Lizzie Wag time to recover her health.

The State of Wisconsin borders on that of Illinois, from which it is separated on the south by the 42nd line of latitude or thereabouts. It is bounded on the west by the course of the Mississippi, and on the east by Lake Michigan, of which it forms the western border, and, in part, on the north by Lake Superior. Madison is its capital, Milwaukee is its metropolis. Situated on the shore of the lake, at less than two hundred miles from Chicago, Milwaukee is in prompt, regular and frequent communication with all the commercial centres of Illinois.

Thus, this day of the 9th, which might have been entered upon so badly, began in the happiest manner. True, the excitement she experienced caused some trouble to the patient, and when Dr. Pughe came to see her in the morning he found her rather more agitated than on the previous evening. The cough, occasionally very hacking, was followed by a lengthy prostration and some appearance of fever, but nothing could be done except to follow the treatment prescribed.

"Rest — rest above all," he said to Jovita Foley, as she was showing him out. "I advise you to save Miss Wag from all fatigue! Let her remain alone; let her sleep — "

"Sir, you are not more anxious?" asked Jovita Foley, seized with new apprehensions.

"No — I repeat it — it is only bronchitis, and it is taking the usual course! Nothing on the side of the lungs — nothing on the side of the heart! Above all things be careful of draughts. Ah! let her have a little nourishment — forcing her to it, if necessary — milk — beef tea — "

"But, doctor, if there are no serious complications — "

"Which it is always good to foresee, miss — "

"Yes — I know — could we hope for our patient to be well in a week?"

The doctor only replied by a shake of the head which was not too encouraging.

Jovita Foley, in great trouble, consented not to remain in Lizzie Wag's room, and kept in her own, leaving the door half-open. There, before her table, on which was spread the board of the Noble Game of the United States of America, turning over the leaves of her guide-book incessantly, she persistently studied Wisconsin to its remotest villages, as regards its climate, salubrity, habits and customs, as if she thought of installing herself there for the rest of her existence.

The newspapers of the Union had naturally published the results of the fifth throw. Many mentioned the Urrican incident, some to sustain the claims of the ferocious commodore, some to blame him. On the whole the majority was against him. No! He had no right to claim this throw for himself, and Tornbrock was praised for having applied the rules in all their rigour.

Besides, whatever Hodge Urrican may have said, Lizzie Wag was not dead, nor was she at her last breath. A sudden change, natural enough, came over the public with regard to her. She began to become more interesting, although it was difficult to believe that she could stand the fatigue of such travels to the end. As to her malady, it was not even bronchitis, not even laryngitis, and within twenty-four hours nothing more would be heard of it.

But as the reader is exacting in the matter of news, a bulletin of the fifth player's health was published morning and evening, neither more nor less than if she had been a princess of the blood royal.

This day of the 9th had brought no change in the state of the patient. She got no worse during the following night or during the day of the 10th of May. Jovita Foley at once drew the conclusion that a week would suffice to set her friend on her feet. But when one's recovery requires ten — eleven — twelve — even thirteen days — even fifteen! It was only a journey of two hours. Providing they were at Milwaukee on the 23rd in the forenoon, they would conform to the rules of the Hypperbone match. And after that, if it were necessary to take more rest, they could get it there.

The night of the 10th was calm enough. Lizzie Wag had but two or three slight shivers, and it seemed as though the period of fever was at an end. The cough, however, continued to be very exhausting, but the chest was gradually relaxing, the sound was less raucous, the respiration easier. There was, therefore, no new complication.

It follows from this that Lizzie Wag found herself decidedly better when in the morning Jovita returned after an absence of an hour. Where had she been? She had said nothing, not even to the neighbour, who could not answer Miss Wag when she was asked about it.

As soon as Jovita Foley entered the room she went, without taking off her hat, and impressed a loud kiss on Lizzie Wag's forehead, who, at the sight of the face so animated, the eyes so sparkling with malice, could not help saying:

"What have you been doing this morning?"

"Nothing, my dear, nothing! I wanted a little fresh air for the sake of my health. And it is so fine — a beautiful May sun — you know — those lovely rays you can almost drink in — that you breathe! Ah! if you could only remain for an hour at the window. Eh? A good dose of sun! I am sure that would cure you at once. But — no imprudence — for fear of serious complications — "

"And where did you go?"

"Where did I go? I went first to Marshall Field's to give news of you. Our employers sent to say that we might take all the time, and I went thank them."

"You did well, Jovita. They have been very good to give us this holiday — and when it comes to an end — "

"Agreed — agreed, my dear. They will not give our situations to anyone."

"And then — after?"

"After?"

"Did you not go somewhere else?

"Somewhere else?"

And it seemed as though Jovita Foley hesitated to speak. But she could not restrain herself for long, particularly as Lizzie Wag asked her:

"Is not to-day the 11th of May?"

"The 11th of May, my dear," she replied in a loud voice, "and in two days we shall be at a hotel in this beautiful town of Milwaukee, if we are not kept here by bronchitis."

"Well," continued Lizzie Wag, "as it is the 11th of May, the sixth throw of the dice ought to have taken place."

"Certainly"

"And then?"

"And then! Oh, I never was so pleased. Never. There, let me kiss you. I would not tell you because it might make you excited but it is too strong for me — "

"Speak then, Jovita."

"Fancy — my dear — he has got nine also — but by four and five!"

"Who?"

"Commodore Urrican — "

"It seems to me that his throw is better — "

"Yes — for he goes at the first throw to the fifty-third square — a great advance on all the others — but it is also very bad — "

And Jovita abandoned herself to a burst of merriment no less extraordinary than inexplicable.

"And why is it bad?" asked Lizzie Wag.

"Because the commodore is sent to the devil."

"To the devil?"

"Yes! to the depths of Florida."

Such was in fact the result of the throw that morning, announced with visible satisfaction by Tornbrock, who was still irritated against Hodge Urrican. In what way had the commodore accepted the result? In a fury, no doubt, and perhaps he had had to interfere to prevent Turk going to some extremity. On this subject Jovita Foley could say nothing, as she had left the Auditorium immediately.

"To the depths of Florida," she repeated, "to the very depths of Florida — more than two thousand miles from here!"

But somehow the news did not cause the patient anything like the excitement that her friend feared. Her good nature led her, rather, to pity the commodore.

"And that is how you take the news?" said her impetuous companion.

"Yes — poor man!" murmured Lizzie Wag.

The day was not a bad one, although convalescence had not commenced. However, there was no more fear of those serious complications of which a prudent doctor always foresees the possibility.

On the 12th Lizzie Wag began to take a little nourishment. As she was not allowed to leave her bed, and as the fever had gone and the time appeared long to both of them — particularly to Jovita Foley — Jovita went to sit in the room, and if not in the form of dialogue, at least in that of monologue, the conversation did not languish.

And of what would Jovita Foley not talk if it was not of this Wisconsin, according to her the most beautiful and most curious of the States of the Union. With her guidebook under her eyes she was inexhaustible. And if Lizzie Wag was delayed till the last day and only stayed there a few hours, she would know as much about it as if she had spent many weeks there.

"Fancy, my dear," said Jovita Foley in an admiring tone, "it was formerly called Mesconsin, on account of the river of that name, and there is no part of the country which can be compared with it. In the north you still see the remains of the ancient pine forests which covered the whole territory. And it possesses hot springs superior to those of Virginia, and I am certain that if your bronchitis — "

"But," said Lizzie Wag, "is it not to Milwaukee we have to go?"

"Yes — Milwaukee, the principal town of the State, the name of which in an old Indian language signifies 'beautiful country' a city of two hundred thousand people, my dear, a large number of them Germans, so that it is called the Germano-American Athens. Ah! if we were there, what delightful walks we should have on the cliffs, where the superb houses are built along the border of the river — none but elegant and clean quarters — nothing but buildings in brick of a milky white — which give it its name. Can you guess it?"

"No, Jovita."

"Cream City, my dear — the city of cream — you can dip your bread in it. Ah! why does this wretched bronchitis hinder us from going there?"

Wisconsin had a number of other towns they would have had time to visit if they could have started on the 9th. Madison, built on its isthmus as on a bridge between Lake Mendota and Lake Monona, which flow into each other; then other towns with strange names: Fond-du-lac on the Fox River, on soil pierced with artesian wells — a regular colander; and a beautiful place they call Eau Claire, with a fine torrent that justifies the name; and Lake Winnebago; and Green Bay; and the anchorage of the Twelve Apostles off Ashland Bay; and the Devil's Lake, one of the natural beauties of this marvellous Wisconsin.

And in a voice of enthusiasm Jovita Foley read the pages of her guide-book and related the different changes of the country, formerly overrun by Indian tribes, discovered and colonized by French Canadians, up to the time it was known as the Badger State.

In the morning of the 13th, the curiosity of the public redoubled. The newspapers had worked up the excitement to its highest point. The Auditorium was as crowded as it had been on the day of the reading of William J. Hypperbone's will. In fact, at eight o'clock was to be announced the seventh throw, which was on behalf of that mysterious and enigmatic personage designated by the letters XKZ. :

In vain had they endeavoured to discover the incognito of this competitor. The cleverest reporters, the shrewdest ferrets of the local press had failed. On several occasions they thought they had got a trustworthy clue and followed it to find it worthless. At first it was thought that by the codicil the deceased wished to designate one of his colleagues of the Eccentric Club and give him a seventh chance in the match. The name of George B. Higginbotham was even announced, but the worthy member formally contradicted the report. When Tornbrock was interrogated on the subject he declared he knew nothing about it, and that all he had to do was to send to the post offices of the places where he ought to be, the result of the throws regarding the "masked man" — as he was popularly called.

But it was hoped — not without reason, perhaps — that on this occasion Mr. XKZ would reply to the call in the Auditorium. Hence this crowd, of which a small portion only had found room before the stage on which appeared the notary and the members of the Eccentric Club, while spectators in thousands thronged the neighbouring streets and spread beneath the shady trees of Lake Park.

Their curiosity was, disappointed, quite disappointed. Masked or not, no individual presented himself when Tornbrock rolled out the dice on the board and announced in a loud voice:

"Nine by six and three, twenty-sixth square, State of Wisconsin."

Strange coincidence! This was the same number as Lizzie Wag had obtained; produced in the same way by six and three. But — circumstance of extreme gravity for her — according to the rule established by the deceased, if she was still at Milwaukee the day XKZ arrived there, she would have to yield her place to him and return to her own — which meant beginning the game again. And not to be able to go there, and to be nailed to Chicago!

The crowd would not leave; they waited for nobody. They had to resign themselves to it. But it was a general disappointment which the evening journals expressed in articles that were anything but complimentary to the unlucky XKZ. A whole population was not to be played with in that way!

The days went by. Every forty-eight hours the throws took place regularly under the usual circumstances, and the results were sent by telegraph to those interested, wherever they ought to be at the time stated.

In this way the 22nd of May arrived. No news of XKZ, who had not yet appeared in Wisconsin. It is true that it would be enough if he were at the post office of Milwaukee on the 27th. Then, could not Lizzie Wag go at once to Milwaukee and, according to the rule of the game, leave it before XKZ arrived there? Yes, as she was nearly well again. But then there were grounds for fearing that Jovita Foley, who was suffering from a violent nervous attack, might fall ill in her turn. An attack of fever came on and she had to take to her bed.

"I warned you of this, my poor Jovita," said Lizzie Wag. "You are not reasonable."

"It will be nothing, my dear. Besides, the position is not the same. I am not in the game, and if I cannot go, you can go alone — "

"Never, Jovita!"

"But you must!"

"Never, I tell you! With you, yes, though that is not common sense. Without you — No!"

And undoubtedly, if Jovita Foley could not accompany her, Lizzie Wag had decided to abandon all chances of becoming the sole heiress of William J. Hypperbone.

There was no need for anxiety. Jovita Foley was all right again after a day's dieting and repose. In the after-

noon of the 22nd she was able to get up and buckle the bag of the two travellers who were to travel about the United States.

"Ah!" she exclaimed, "I would give ten years of my life to be already on the way."

With the ten years she had already given on many occasions, and the ten years she would give again and again in the course of the journey, there would remain very little of the time she was to spend in this lower world!

The departure was fixed for the next day, the 23rd, by the train which arrives in two hours at Milwaukee, where Lizzie Wag would find the telegram from Tornbrock. Now this last day would have ended without incident if a little before five o'clock the two friends had not received a visit which they never expected.

There was a ring at the door. Jovita Foley went to open it.

The lift had just deposited an individual on the landing of the ninth floor.

"Miss Lizzie Wag?" asked the individual, turning to the girl.

"She is here, sir."

"May I see her?"

"But," replied Jovita Foley, hesitating, "Miss Wag has been very ill, and — "

"I know — I know — " said the visitor, "and I have reason to believe she is quite well again — "

"Quite, sir, and we are going to start to-morrow morning."

"Ah! Then it is to Miss Jovita Foley I have the honour of speaking — "

"To herself, sir; and with regard to your business, can I replace Lizzie?"

"I would prefer to see her — to see her with my own eyes — if it is possible — "

"May I ask why?"

"I have nothing to hide from you with respect to what brings me here. I intend to have a little speculation on this Hypperbone match — to venture a considerable sum on the fifth player — and you understand — I would like — "

If Jovita Foley understood — and so was delighted! Here at last was some one to whom Lizzie Wag's chance appeared good enough to risk some thousands of dollars on.

"My visit will be short — very short," added the gentleman with a bow.

He was a man about fifty, with greyish beard, his eyes bright behind his glasses, brighter even than usual at his age, the air of a gentleman, a distinguished face, upright figure, voice of extreme sweetness. Although persisting in seeing Lizzie Wag, he did it with perfect politeness, excusing himself from disturbing her "just on the eve of a journey of such importance — "

In short, Jovita Foley did not think it would be in the least inconvenient for her to receive him, as his visit was not to be a long one.

"May I know your name, sir?"

"Humphrey Weldon, of Boston, Massachusetts" replied the gentleman.

And he entered the first room, of which Jovita Foley had just opened the door, and then went to the second room, in which was Lizzie Wag.

On seeing the visitor, she would have risen. "Do not disturb yourself, miss," said he. "You will excuse my importunity, — but I wished to see you — oh! — only for a moment — "

However, he accepted the chair which Jovita Foley placed near him, "An instant — only an instant!" he repeated. "As I have said, my intention is to venture on an important speculation with regard to you, for I believe in your final success, and I wish to assure myself that your state of health — "

"I have quite recovered, sir," said Lizzie Wag, "and I thank you for the confidence you show in me. But indeed, my chances — "

"An affair of presentiment, miss," said Mr. Weldon in a decided tone.

"Yes — of presentiment," added Jovita Foley.

"That admits of no discussion," affirmed the honourable gentleman.

"And what you think of Lizzie," exclaimed Jovita Foley, "I think also. I am sure she will win."

"I am no less sure — from the moment that nothing opposes her departure," declared Mr. Weldon.

"To-morrow," said Jovita Foley, "we shall both go to the railway station, and the train will land us before noon at Milwaukee — "

"Where you can rest a few days, if necessary," observed Mr. Weldon.

"Oh, not at all," replied Jovita Foley.

"And why not?"

"Because we must not be there when Mr. XKZ arrives, or we shall have to begin the game again."

"That is true."

"But where this second throw will send us," said Lizzie Wag, "is what makes me anxious."

"Eh! What does it matter, my dear!" said Jovita Foley, swooping on her as if on wings.

"Let us hope, Miss Wag," said the gentleman, "that the second throw of the dice will be as fortunate for you as the first has been."

And then the excellent man spoke of the precautions to take on the journey, of the necessity of care in allowing sufficient time for changing from train to train in the network of lines which covers the Union.

"And," added he, "I see with great satisfaction, Miss Wag, that you do not start alone."

"No, my friend accompanies me — or to speak truly, drags me with her."

"And you are right, Miss Foley," said Mr. Weldon. "It is better for two to travel together It is more agreeable."

"And it is more prudent, when you have got to catch trains," declared Jovita Foley.

"And so," added Mr. Weldon, "I reckon on you to make Miss Wag win."

"You can depend upon me."

"Then, my good wishes to you, ladies, for your success guarantees mine."

The visit had lasted twenty minutes, and after asking permission to shake hands with Lizzie Wag and with her amiable companion, Mr. Humphrey Weldon was shown back to the lift, from which he gave a parting salute.

"Poor man," said Lizzie Wag, "and when I think that I am to make him lose his money."

"All right," said Jovita Foley, "but remember what I tell you, my dear — these old gentlemen are full of good sense. They have a scent which never deceives them! And this worthy gentleman in your game — will bring you luck."

The preparations were finished — and how many times, we know — there was nothing to do when night came but to go to bed and get up first thing next morning. But they had to wait for the last visit of the doctor, who had promised to call in the evening. Dr. Pughe was not late in arriving, and declared that his client's state of health left nothing more to be desired, and that all fear of serious complications was at last at an end.

At five o'clock next morning, the more important of the travellers was up and about. And in a final attack of nerves this astonishing Jovita Foley imagined quite a series of hindrances and misfortunes, delays and accidents. If the carriage that was to take them to the railway station were to turn over — if a block stopped them on the way — if there had been a change in the time of the train — if the train were thrown off the line — "

"Calm yourself, Jovita, Calm, yourself, I pray," again and again did Lizzie Wag ask.

"I cannot — I cannot, my dear."

"Are you going on like that all through the journey?"

"All the time."

"Then I shall stop here."

"The carriage is below, *Lizzie*. Let us be off — let us be off."

The carriage was waiting, ordered an hour earlier than was necessary. The two friends went down, followed by the good wishes of the whole house, at the windows of which even at this early hour of the morning appeared several hundred heads, The vehicle went along North Avenue to North Branch, down the right bank of Chicago River, crossing it by the bridge at the end of Van Buren Street, and deposited the travellers at the station at ten minutes past seven.

Perhaps Jovita Foley experienced a certain amount of disappointment in noticing that the departure of the fifth player had not attracted a large crowd of spectators. Decidedly, Lizzie Wag was not the favourite in the Hypperbone match. But the bashful girl did not complain, and much preferred to leave Chicago without provoking public attention.

"Even Mr. Weldon is not here!" Jovita Foley could not help remarking.

And in fact the visitor of the previous afternoon had not come to hand to the car the player in whom he took so great an interest.

"You see," said Lizzie Wag, "he also abandons me!"

The train started at last, without any notice whatever being taken of Lizzie Wag. No cheers, except those which Jovita Foley gave *in petto* in her own honour!

The railroad skirts the shore of Lake Michigan. Lake View, Evanston, Glenoke, and other stations were passed at full speed. The weather was superb. The waters sparkled in the offing, alive with steamers and sailing vessels — the waters which from lake to lake, Superior, Huron, Michigan, Erie, Ontario, flow down the great artery of the St. Lawrence into the vast Atlantic. After leaving Vankegan, an important town on the coast, the train leaves Illinois at State Line station to enter Wisconsin. A little further north it halts at Racine, a large manufacturing city, and it was not ten o'clock when it stopped at Milwaukee.

"We are here — we are here!" said Jovita with such a sigh of satisfaction that her veil stretched like a sail in the breeze.

"And two good hours in advance" observed Lizzie Wag, looking at her watch.

"No, fourteen days behindhand," replied Jovita Foley as she jumped out on to the platform.

Then she busied herself in finding the portmanteau among the heap of luggage.

The portmanteau had not gone astray — as Jovita had feared, one knows not why. A carriage approached. The travellers got in and ordered it to drive to a suitable hotel which was mentioned in the guide-book. And when she was asked if she was going to stay at Milwaukee, Jovita Foley replied that she would tell them when she returned from the post office, but that probably she would leave during the day. Then turning to Lizzie Wag, she said:

"Are you not hungry?"

"I should be glad to have some breakfast."

"Well, let us breakfast, and then we can take a walk — "

"But you know that at twelve o'clock — "

"As if I did not know!"

They sat down in the dining-room and did not remain more than half an hour at the table.

As they had not given their names, refraining from doing so until their return from the post office, Milwaukee had no notion that the fifth player in the Hypperbone match was within its walls.

At a quarter to twelve they went to the post office and Jovita Foley asked if a telegram had arrived for Miss Lizzie Wag.

At the name the man looked up with an expression of lively satisfaction in his eyes.

"Miss Lizzie Wag?" he said.

"Yes — of Chicago," replied Jovita Foley-

"The telegram is waiting for you," he added, handing it over.

"Give it to me — give it to me!" said Jovita Foley. "You are too long in opening it — and I shall have an attack of nerves,"

With her fingers trembling with impatience, she tore open the envelope and read these words:

"Lizzie Wag, Post Office, Milwaukee, Wisconsin.

"Twenty, by ten and ten doubled, forty-sixth square, State of Kentucky, Mammoth Caves. — Tornbrock."

CHAPTER XIII . THE ADVENTURES OF COMMODORE URRICAN

IT was at eight o'clock in the morning of the 11th of May that Commodore Urrican knew the number of the throw that concerned him, and at twenty-five minutes past nine he left Chicago.

There was no time lost, you see, and he had none to lose, considering that within a fortnight he had to find himself at the extreme end of the peninsula of Florida.

Nine by four and five, one of the best throws of the game! At the first bound the fortunate player had been sent to the fifty-third square. It is true that on the board arranged by William J. Hypperbone it was the State of Florida which occupied this square, the furthest to the south-east of the North American Republic.

Hodge Urrican's friends — or rather his partisans, for he had no friends, though certain people believed in the chances of a man of such violent speech — wished to congratulate him as he came out of the Auditorium. "And why, if you please?" he replied in that peevish tone which gave such a charm to his conversation. "Why load me with compliments just as I am starting? It may make me have to pay excess luggage!"

"Commodore," said one to him, "five and four is a superb beginning — "

"Superb — I fancy it is — particularly for those who have business in Florida!"

"Observe, commodore, that you are a long way in front of your competitors — "

"And that is only fair, I think, as luck made me the last to start."

"Evidently, Mr. Urrican; and it will now be enough for you to get ten points to reach the end and win the game in two throws."

"That is true, gentlemen! And if I get nine I shall not be able to win next time, and if I get more than ten, I shall have to go back — does anyone know where?"

"Never mind, commodore; anyone else in your place would be satisfied — "

"Perhaps — but I am not"

"Think of it — sixty millions of dollars — perhaps — on your return."

"Which I could just as well put in my pocket if the State had been next to ours!"

Nothing could be more true, and although he refused to admit it, he had a real advantage over his five competitors. It was impossible for them to reach the last square at their next throw, to which he could go with ten points.

Though Hodge Urrican shut his ears to the language of reason, it is probable that he would have done the same if he had been sent to either Indiana or Missouri, which border on Illinois.

Growling and cursing, Commodore Urrican returned to his house in Randolph Street with Turk, whose recriminations became so violent that his master ordered him to be silent.

His master? Was then Hodge Urrican the master of Turk, when on the one hand America had proclaimed the abolition of slavery, and on the other hand the said Turk, although brown in hue, could not have passed for a negro?

Was he then his servant? Yes and no.

To begin with, Turk, although he was in the commodore's service, received no wages, and when he was in want of money — oh! very little! — he asked for it and was given it. He was more of a companion, as they say of ladies who are in the suite of princesses. But the social distance which separated Hodge Urrican from Turk did not permit of his being considered as a companion.

Turk, whose real name was Turk, was an old sailor of the federal navy who had risen through the grades of boy, ordinary seaman, able seaman, quartermaster. It is noteworthy that he had served on board the same vessels in which Hodge Urrican had successively become cadet, ensign, lieutenant, captain, and commodore. Thus these two knew each other well, and Turk was the only one of his like with whom the fiery officer could get on. Possibly this was because he was the more violent of the two, espousing Urrican's quarrels and always ready to do an ill-turn to those who had not the luck to please him.

During his voyages Turk was often of particular service to Hodge Urrican, who appreciated his abilities and ended by being unable to do without him. When the hour of retirement had struck, Turk left the navy, rejoined the commodore, and attached himself to his person on the conditions above given. In this way he had been for three years in the house in Randolph Street as a manager who managed nothing, or, if you will, as an honorary steward.

But one thing we have not said — and no one would have suspected it — Turk was really the gentlest, most inoffensive, least quarrelsome and easiest to live with, of men. Never on board had he got into a dispute; never had he taken part in the fights of the sailors; never had he lifted his hand against anyone, not even when he had drunk uncounted glasses of whisky — and yet he carried as much sail as a sixty-gun frigate.

Whence then had he obtained the notion that he, a man placid and tranquil, should appear to exceed in violence the most violent man in the world?

Turk had a real affection for the commodore in spite of his unsociability. He was one of those faithful dogs who, when their master is angry with them, bark with all the more fury. But if with the dog it is according to nature, with Turk it was contrary to it. The habit of storming out on all occasions, and more loudly than Hodge Urrican, had in no way altered the mildness of his character.

His rage was a feint, he played a part. It was out of pure affection for his master and with the object of restraining him that he surpassed him and alarmed him by the lengths to which he went. And whenever he intervened to calm Turk, Hodge Urrican finished by calming himself. When one spoke of giving some ill-bred fellow a talking to, the other spoke of a smack in the face, and when the commodore spoke of a smack in the face, Turk spoke of leaving him dead on the spot. Then the commodore tried to make Turk listen to reason, and in this way Turk had often put an end to matters from which the commodore would perhaps not have emerged without damage.

And finally as regards his being sent to Florida, when Hodge Urrican wished to quarrel with the notary — as if Tornbrock had had anything to do with it — Turk had raised a great uproar that the notary had cheated, and swore he would wring off both his ears to make a buttonhole in honour of his master.

Such was the original, clever enough to never let his game be detected, who on this morning accompanied Commodore Urrican to the central railway station of Chicago. At the departure of the sixth player there was a crowd, and amongst this crowd, we repeat, if there were no friends, there were at least some people who had resolved to risk their money on him. Did it not seem as though a man of such violent character would be capable of compelling fortune to be kind to him?

And now what was the itinerary adopted by the commodore? Assuredly that which offered the least risk of delay, besides being the shortest.

"Listen, Turk," said he, as soon as he had got back to his house in Randolph Street, "listen and attend."

"I am listening and attending."

"This is the map of the United States I am putting under your eyes."

"Very good — the map of the United States — "

"Yes. Here is Illinois with Chicago, there is Florida — "

"Oh! I know," replied Turk, growling to himself. "We have sailed and fought in these parts, commodore."

"You understand, Turk, that if we had only to go to Tallahassee, the State capital, or to Pensacola, or even to Jacksonville, it would not be difficult and would not take long to work out the different trains that would take us there."

"It would not be difficult and would not take long," repeated Turk, "And," continued the commodore, "when I think of that Lizzie Wag, that saucy baggage, getting off with going from Chicago to Milwaukee — "

"The wretch!" growled Turk.

"And that this Hypperbone — "

"Oh! If that fellow is not dead — " said Turk, lifting his fist as if he would smash the unhappy defunct.

"Calm yourself, Turk; he is dead. But why did he have the absurd idea of choosing in all Florida the most distant point of it, the end of the tail of the peninsula which dips into the Gulf of Mexico — "

"A tail with which he deserves to be thrashed until the blood comes!" declared Turk.

"For it is to Key West, to this islet of the Pine Islands that we have to carry our traps! An islet, and even quite a 'bone' as the Spaniards say, good enough only to carry a lighthouse, and on which they have built a town — "

"A bad neighbourhood, commodore," replied Turk; "and as to the lighthouse, we have sighted it several times before entering the Straits of Florida."

"Well, I think," continued Hodge Urrican, "that the best, the shortest, and also the quickest way would be to effect the first part of our journey by land and the second by sea; that means nine hundred miles to reach Mobile and five or six hundred to reach Key West."

Turk made no objection, and in truth the very reasonable proposal did not deserve one. In thirty-six hours by the railway Hodge Urrican would be at Mobile, in Alabama, and he had left twelve days for the voyage from there to Key West.

"And if we do not get there," declared the commodore, "it is that boats no longer move on water"

"Or that there is no more water in the sea!" replied Turk in a tone that boded ill to the Gulf of Mexico, These two eventualities were little to be feared, it must be admitted, As for not finding at Mobile a vessel starting for Florida, they never thought of it. The port is much frequented, its movement of shipping is considerable, and on the other hand, owing to its position between the Gulf of Mexico and the Atlantic, Key West has become a port of call for nearly all passing ships.

The itinerary was somewhat similar to that of Tom Crabbe. If the Champion of the New World had gone down the basin of the Mississippi to New Orleans, in the State of Louisiana, Commodore Urrican was going down south to Mobile, in the State of Alabama. On arriving at the port the first had gone west to the shores of Texas, the second was going east to the shores of Florida.

Preceded by a heavy portmanteau, Hodge Urrican and Turk had reached the station at nine o'clock in the morning. Their clothes, jackets, belts, boots, caps, showed them to be seafarers. And they were armed with the Derringer six-shooter, which always peeps from the trouser-pocket of a genuine American.

No incident occurred at their departure — which was greeted with the usual cheers — except that the commodore had a very lively conversation with the station-master owing to the train being three and a half minutes late. The train was soon going at full speed, and in this way the travellers crossed Illinois. At Cairo, near the frontier of Tennessee, where Tom Crabbe had followed the line that ends at New Orleans, they took that which follows the frontier of Mississippi and Alabama and ends at Mobile.

Commodore Urrican did not travel for the sake of travelling, but to arrive with the shortest delay possible at his post, to be there on the day fixed. Thus there was nothing of the tourist about him. And natural curiosities, landscapes, towns, and such things had no interest for an old seaman like Turk.

At ten o'clock in the evening the train stopped in Mobile station, having completed its long run without accident or incident. And it is worthy of remark that Hodge Urrican had not a single opportunity of getting into a quarrel with the drivers, stokers, guards, and other railway people, or with his travelling companions. But he did not conceal who he was, and the whole train knew that they had with them in his noisy person the sixth starter in the Hypperbone match.

The commodore went to a hotel near the harbour. It was too late to inquire about a ship being about to sail. To-morrow at break of day Hodge Urrican would leave his room, Turk would leave his, and if he found a vessel bound for the Straits of Florida, they would embark that very day.

In the morning at sunrise they were together on the quays of Mobile. It was not without reason that Commodore Urrican had thought that the means of getting to Key West would not fail him. Such is the importance of Mobile that at least five hundred vessels enter it in a year.

But there are people whom fate rarely spares, who cannot escape bad luck, and this time Hodge Urrican had an opportunity to be justifiably angry.

He had come to Mobile when a strike was on — a general strike of dockers declared the day before! And it threatened to last many days. And of the outward bound ships not one could go out before an agreement had been come to with the shipowners, who were resolute to resist the demands of the strikers.

And so in vain did the commodore wait during the 13th, 14th, and 15th for a ship to finish loading. The cargoes remained on the quays, the boiler fires were not lighted, the cotton bales encumbered the docks, and navigation could not have been more immobile if the Bay of Mobile had been frozen over. This abnormal position might be prolonged for a week or more. What was to be done?

The commodore's partisans made the very reasonable suggestion that he should go to Pensacola, one of the important towns of the State of Florida, which adjoins Alabama. By going up the railroad to the north and coming down again along the coast it would be easy to reach Pensacola in twelve hours.

Hodge Urrican — it is necessary to recognize this gift — was a man of decision. On the 16th, in the morning, he was in the train with Turk, and that evening they were at Pensacola. He now had nine days, and this was more than the voyage to Key West required, even by sailing ship.

But the bad luck continued. There was no strike at Pensacola, it is true, but not a single vessel was preparing to leave the port, at least in a south-westerly direction, neither for the Antilles nor the Atlantic, and consequently none stopping at Key West.

"Decidedly," said Hodge Urrican, biting his lips, "this will not do — "

"And there is no one to lay the blame on," replied his companion, throwing a fierce look around him.

"We cannot stay anchored here for a whole week."

"No; we must get under way, cost what it may!" declared Turk.

Agreed, but how were they to transport themselves from Pensacola to Key West.

Hodge Urrican did not lose an hour, going from ship to ship, steam or sailing, obtaining only vague promises. They would sail — when they had got their goods on board, or when they had completed their cargoes. Nothing definite, except the high price the commodore offered for his passage. Then he wanted to know the reason why, as they say, of these captains, and even of the dock manager, at the risk of being given into custody.

In short, two days elapsed, until the evening of the 18th, and then he could only try by land what he could not try by sea. And what fatigue, what delays there were to be feared!

Consider! It was necessary — by railroad be it understood — to cross Florida in almost its entire breadth from west to east by Tallahassee to Live Oak and then return south to reach Tampa or Punta Gorda or the Gulf of Mexico. About six hundred miles in trains whose times nowhere fitted in.

A miserable region, barely habitable and thinly inhabited, is that portion of Florida which lies along the shore of the gulf up to Cedar Key. Would there be any means of transport — stage coaches, carriages, horses — that could take passengers to the extreme end in a few days? And supposing these could be procured at a high price, what a slow, painful, even dangerous journey, through these interminable forests, under the thick foliage of gloomy cypresses, occasionally impenetrable, half-drowned in the stagnant waters of the bayous, at the mercy of the floating meadows of the grassy pistia, through the depths of those masses of gigantic mushrooms which explode at a shock like fireworks, through the mazes of marshy plains and lakes and pools swarming with alligators and manatees, and with the most formidable serpents of the ophidian race, the trigonocephali, whose bite is fatal.

Such is this abominable country of the Everglades, the last refuge of the Seminole tribes, those handsome and ferocious Indians who, under their chief Osceola, struggled so valiantly against the Federal invasion. These natives alone could live, or rather vegetate in this warm and humid climate, so suitable for the development of marsh fevers which in a few hours will bring down men of the most vigorous constitution — even commodores of the stamp of Hodge Urrican.

If this part of Florida had been comparable to that which extends to the east about the 29th parallel, if he had only had to go from Fernandina to Jacksonville and to St. Augustine, in that country where there is no want of towns or villages or ways of communication!

It was the 19th of May. He had only six full days. And this overland route it was impossible to dream of.

That morning Commodore Urrican was accosted on the quay by one of those coasting captains, half American, half Spanish, who carry on the trade along the coast of Florida.

The said captain, named Huelcar, spoke to him with a touch of the cap to begin with.

"Still no vessel for Florida, commodore?"

"No," replied Hodge Urrican. "And if you know of one, there are ten piastres for you."

"I know of one.

"Which?"

"Mine!"

"Yours?"

"Yes, the *Chicola,* a smart schooner of forty-five tons, three men in the crew, which does her nine knots in anything of a breeze!"

"Of American nationality?"

"American!"

"Ready to start?"

"Ready to start, and at your orders," replied Huelcar.

About five hundred miles from Pensacola to Key West — in a straight line it is true — with an average of five knots only and allowing for deviations from the course or unfavourable winds, that ought to be done in six days.

Ten minutes afterwards Hodge Urrican and Turk were on board the *Chicola,* which they examined as experts. She was a little coasting craft, of light draught, designed for working along the coast between the shoals, and beamy enough to carry a good spread of canvas.

Two sailors, like the commodore and the old quartermaster, were not the men to trouble themselves about the dangers of the seas. For twenty years Huelcar had been working his schooner from Mobile to the Bahamas through the Straits of Florida, and he had many times put in at Key West.

"How much for the voyage?" asked the commodore.

"A hundred piastres a day."

"Including provisions?"

"Including provisions."

It was dear, and Huelcar took advantage of the position.

"We will start at once," commanded Hodge Urrican.

"As soon as your baggage is on board."

"At what time is the ebb?"

"It is beginning, and in less than an hour we can be out at sea."

To take passage on the *Chicola,* that was the only way of arriving at Key West, where the sixth player had to be on the 25th by noon at latest.

At eight o'clock, the hotel bill paid, Hodge Urrican and Turk embarked. Fifty minutes later the schooner went out into the bay between Forts MacRae and Pickens, formerly built by the French and Spaniards; and she was headed for the open sea.

CHAPTER XIV. COMMODORE URRICAN'S ADVENTURES, CONTINUED

The weather was uncertain. The breeze blew rather fresh from the east. The sea, defended by the long breakwater of the Florida peninsula, was not yet affected by the long Atlantic rollers, and the *Chicola* bore herself well.

There was no fear of either the commodore or Turk being troubled by the sea-sickness of which Tom Crabbe had been such a victim; and they were ready to help Huelcar and his three men in working the schooner if she got into difficulties.

The *Chicola,* with the wind ahead, went off on the starboard tack, so as to keep in shelter of the land. The voyage would be long, no doubt; but the storms in the gulf are dangerous, and a small vessel could not venture far from the ports, bays, creeks and estuaries that are so numerous on the Florida coast, and which are accessible to vessels of small tonnage. The *Chicola* could always find a creek or a gap in which to take refuge for a few hours. This would be time lost, it is true, and Hodge Urrican had little to lose.

The breeze held all day and all night, with a tendency to weaken. If it had increased, it would have meant more speed and a better voyage. Unfortunately, on the morrow it gradually died away. On the surface of the calm white sea the *Chicola* though covered with sail, only made about twenty miles to the south-east. It was necessary to get out the sweeps, so as not to be drifted out into the gulf. Here were forty-eight hours of navigation and practically no progress whatever. The commodore, devoured with impatience, spoke to nobody — not even to Turk.

On the 22nd, however, drifting on the Gulf Stream, they were in the latitude of Tampa, a port of five or six thousand inhabitants, where vessels of a certain tonnage find safe shelter along the coast, which is strewn with reefs and shoals; but it was fifty miles to the east, and the schooner could not get near it without a good deal of delay.

Besides, after yesterday's calm, it looked, from the aspect of the sky, as though there was going to be a change in the weather.

Commodore Urrican and Turk thought the same as the crew of the schooner.

"A change of weather probably," they said that morning.

"It is bound to help us," said Turk, "if the wind settles in the west."

"The sea feels something," said Huelcar. "See the long heavy waves and the surge in the offing beginning to show green."

Then, looking attentively at the horizon, he shook his head and added:

"I do not like it when it comes from that quarter."

"But it is good," said Turk; "it can blow as hard as it likes if it sends us where we want to go."

Hodge Urrican said nothing. He was evidently uneasy at the symptoms which were becoming more marked in the west and south-west. It is all very well to have a good breeze providing you can keep afloat, but with this vessel of only forty tons, and only half-decked — No! Never will it be known what was passing in the excited mind of the commodore; and if there was bad weather out in the offing, then there was bad weather within Hodge Urrican.

In the afternoon the wind, settled in the west, came up in big squalls varied with short periods of calm. The upper sails had to be sent down. On this sea, which began to run in sharp furrows, the schooner lifted like a feather at the will of the waves.

The night was bad, in the sense that it was necessary to further reduce the sail.

Now the *Chicola* was being driven in towards the coast more than was agreeable. As there was no time to run in for safety, she had to be kept at all cost heading south-east, in the direction of the point.

The captain handled her like a seaman. Turk, at the helm, kept the schooner up as much as possible as she rolled. The commodore assisted the crew in taking in a reef in the fore-spencer and main-sail, and setting the small fore stay-sail. It was difficult to keep her out against the wind and current, which were both sending her towards the land.

And in fact, in the morning of the 23rd the coast, low as it was, appeared amid the wreathing mists of the horizon.

Huelcar and his men recognized it.

"It is Whitewater Bay" they said.

This bay is deeply cut into the coast, and is only separated from the Straits of Florida by a tongue of land defended by Fort Poinsett, at the end of Cape Sable.

Another twelve miles before the schooner would be abreast of it.

"I am afraid we shall have to put in," said Huelcar.

"Put in — and never be able to get out in this wind!" exclaimed Turk.

Hodge Urrican remained silent.

"If we do not run for shelter," continued Huelcar, "and if when off Cape Sable the stream takes us into the Straits, it is not at Key West that we shall drop our anchor, but at the Bahamas, out in the Atlantic."

The commodore continued silent, and perhaps his throat was so full and his lips so shut that he could not articulate a word.

Huelcar saw clearly enough that if she ran for Whitewater Bay the *Chicola* would be weather-bound for several days. And it was the 23rd of May, and it was necessary to reach Key West in less than forty-eight hours.

Then the crew with equal boldness and skill kept up the little ship against the squalls from the offing at the risk of bringing down the masts or splitting the sails. They tried to fetch the cape with a small fore stay-sail and a try-sail aft.

The schooner lost three or four miles during that day and the following night. If the wind did not haul round to the north or south she could not keep on against it and next day she would go ashore.

And this was only too evident when, in the early morning of the 24th, the land, bristling with rocks and reefs, was sighted about five miles from the terrible crags of Cape Sable. In a few hours the *Chicola* would be driven through the Straits of Florida.

But with renewed effort, and taking advantage of the rising tide, it would be possible to get into Whitewater Bay.

"It must be" said Huelcar.

"No," said Commodore Urrican.

"Eh! I am not going to risk my vessel and ourselves as well in obstinately trying to keep her out."

"I will buy your boat."

"She is not for sale."

"A boat is always for sale when she is bought for more than she is worth."

"How much will you give for her?"

"Two thousand piastres."

"Agreed," said Huelcar, enchanted at so good a bargain.

"It is double her value," said Commodore Urrican. "There will be a thousand for her hull, and a thousand for you and your men."

"Payable?"

"With a cheque I will give you at Key West."

"Done, my commodore."

"And now, Huelcar, keep her out."

All that day the *Chicola* struggled gamely, sometimes nearly covered by the waves, her bulwarks half under water. But Turk steered her with a firm hand, and the crew handled her with as much courage as skill.

The schooner had begun to head off from the coast, owing mainly to a slight change in the wind, which had shifted a little towards the north. When night arrived the wind began to go down and a thick fog came on.

The perplexity was extreme. It had been impossible to work out the position during the day. Was the schooner in the latitude of Key West, or had she passed the assemblage of reefs which prolongs the tail of the peninsula towards the Marquesas and the Tortugas?

In Huelcar's opinion the *Chicola* was very near this string of islets.

"We should certainly see the lighthouse at Key West if it were not for the fog," said he, "and we must take care that we are not thrown on the rocks. Better wait until daylight, and if the fog disperses — "

"I will not wait," replied the commodore.

And in fact he could not wait if he wished to be at Key West by noon next day.

The *Chicola,* then, was continuing to keep to the south over a calm sea in a fog, when, at five o'clock in the morning, there was a shock, and then another shock.

The schooner had touched on a reef. Lifted for the third time by an irresistible blow from the surge, and partly smashed, with her bow driven in, she capsized on her port side.

At this moment a cry was heard.

Turk recognized the voice of the commodore.

He called and received no response.

The mists were so thick that they could not see the rocks round the schooner.

Huelcar and his three men were standing on the reef.

With them was Turk, despairing, searching, shouting all the time.

Vain the shouts, vain the search.

But perhaps the mists would disperse. And perhaps Turk would find his master still living? He dared not hope to do so. Great tears rolled down his cheeks.

Towards seven o'clock the fog began to lift a little, and the sea was visible for a few cable lengths around.

It was a mass of whitish rocks against which the *Chicola* had struck; and her boat had been crushed in and was useless. From east to west over a quarter of a mile the bank ran out in reefs divided by pools, and this surf was beating over them with violence.

The search was resumed, and one of the sailors ended by discovering the body of Commodore Urrican jammed between two points of rock. , Turk ran up; he threw himself on his master, he seized him in his arms, he lifted him up, he spoke to him without obtaining any reply.

But a gentle sigh escaped from Hodge Urrican's lips, and his heart was distinctly beating.

"He lives! he lives!" exclaimed Turk.

In truth, Hodge Urrican was in a piteous state. In falling his head had struck against an angle of the rock, but the blood had ceased to flow.

The wound, which had closed itself, was bandaged with a piece of rag, after being washed with some fresh water brought from the schooner. Then the commodore, without recovering consciousness, was carried to a higher portion of the island, which the rising sea would not cover.

The sky becoming quite clear from mist, the view extended for many miles.

It was twenty minutes past nine, and at this moment, Huelcar, stretching his arm out to the west, shouted:

"The lighthouse of Key West!"

In fact, Key West was only four miles off in that direction. If the night had been clear they would have sighted the light in time, and the schooner would not have come to be lost on those dangerous reefs.

And, now, was not the game over so far as the sixth player was concerned? He had no means of traversing the distance which separated the islet on which the *Chicola* had been wrecked from Key West, and all he could do was to wait for a passing ship.

A melancholy position for these poor fellows, on the surface of this whitish mass which looked like a field of bones rising not more than five or six feet above the water at high tide. Around them were twined masses of seaweed of a thousand colours, gigantic phycoeans, tiny algae torn from the submarine depths by the currents of the Gulf Stream.

In the creeks swarmed a hundred species of fishes of all dimensions and all forms, sheeps'-heads, angels, wrasses, sea-wolves, klephtics of marvellous shades, garter-fishes of silver, and cavaliers striped with multicoloured bands. And also swarming there were mollusks and crustaceans — shrimps, prawns, lobsters, crabs and crawfishes.

And on every side at the top of the water, attracted by the wreck and prowling round the reefs, were multitudes of voracious, sharks — principally hammer-headed ones, from six to seven feet long, with enormous jaws, the most formidable of monsters.

In the air were innumerable flocks of birds — egrets, crab catchers, herons, gulls, grebes, terns, cormorants. A few tall pelicans stood midway in the water, fishing with as much seriousness, and perhaps more success than those who fish with the line, and calling in a cavernous voice what sounded very much like "encore". The men need not be without food on this reef. They had only to hunt the legions of turtles either in the water or on the little sandy beaches among the islands which bear the name of these crawling reptiles.

However, time was passing, and in spite of all that could be done the unfortunate commodore seemed no nearer to recovery. The prolongation of his unconsciousness gave Turk the keenest anxiety. If he could take his master to Key West and hand him over to a doctor, he might perhaps be saved, considering his vigorous constitution. But how many days might pass before they left the island, for it was impossible to get the schooner afloat, to repair the hull, which was crushed in below, and which the first bad weather would break up.

It need scarcely be said that Turk was under no illusion as to the result of the Hypperbone match. The game was lost so far as Hodge Urrican was concerned. What a burst of rage there would be if he returned to life, and this time would it be unpardonable, considering the wretched bad luck?

It was a little after ten o'clock when the sailors of the *Chicola* on the look-out at the extremity of the rocks shouted:

"Boat ahoy!"

A fishing boat running before the easterly wind was approaching the rocks.

At once Huelcar made a signal, which was observed by the men in the boat, and half an hour afterwards the shipwrecked party were on board and on the way to Key West.

Then hope returned to Turk, and perhaps it would also have returned to Hodge Urrican if he had emerged from the state in which he knew nothing of external things.

In the freshening breeze the boat rapidly covered the four miles, and at a quarter past eleven was moored in the harbour.

The town has risen on this island of Key West — which is two leagues long and one league wide — like a vegetable grown under glass. It is already a considerable city, which is connected with the mainland by its telegraph lines, and with Havana by a submarine cable; a city with a great future, the prosperity of which is bound to increase, owing to a shipping trade of 300,000 tons; a city half Spanish, sheltered beneath magnolias and other magnificent trees of the tropical zone.

The sloop ran up to the end of the harbour, and immediately many hundred inhabitants — Key West possessed eighteen thousand at this period — surrounded the shipwrecked party. They were expecting Commodore Urrican: and in what a condition he presented himself, or rather, was presented to their eyes.

Decidedly the sea was not kind to the players in the Hypperbone match. Tom Crabbe arrived in Texas as an inert mass; the commodore had arrived as a corpse, or as near to one as possible.

Hodge Urrican was taken to the harbour office, and a doctor sent for.

The sixth competitor still breathed, and though his heart beat feebly, it did not seem as though any of his organs were injured. But when he was pitched out of the schooner his head had struck against a pointed rock, and the blood had flowed abundantly, so that there might be some damage to the brain.

In spite of all that was done, and the rubbings to which he was subjected — and Turk did not spare them, as we may imagine — the commodore, although he sighed two or three times, did not recover consciousness.

The doctor suggested that he should be taken to some room in a comfortable hotel, or it would be better to take him to the hospital, where he would have every attention.

"No" replied Turk, "neither to the hospital, nor to the hotel — "

"Where, then?"

"To the-post office."

Turk had an idea which was understood and adopted by those around him. As Hodge Urrican had arrived before noon at Key West on this day, the 25th of May — and that against wind and tide, as it were — why should not his presence be officially notified in the very place where he ought to be found at this date?

A stretcher was procured, a mattress thrown on it, the commodore was laid on that, and away they went to the post office amid a crowd that constantly increased.

Great was the astonishment of the staff, who thought at first some mistake had been made. Had the post office been taken for a mortuary? But when they learnt that the body was that of Commodore Urrican, one of the competitors in the Hypperbone match, their astonishment gave place to emotion. He was here, then, in front of the telegraph desk, he whom the throw of the dice by five and four had sent so far — and in what a state!

Turk came forward, and in a loud voice, heard by all, inquired:

"Is there a telegram here for Commodore Urrican?"

"Not yet," replied the clerk.

"Well, sir," continued Turk, "will you certify that we were here before it arrived?"

And the fact was at once written down and signed by numerous witnesses.

It was then a quarter to twelve, and they could do no more than to wait for the telegram, which without doubt had been sent off that morning from Chicago.

They did not wait long.

At 11.53 the bell of the telegraphic apparatus began to ring, the mechanism to work, the paper to unroll.

As soon as the clerk could, he read the address, and said:

"A message for Commodore Hodge Urrican."

"Present!" replied Turk for his master, in whom the doctor at this moment could not perceive the slightest sign of intelligence.

The telegram was in these words: —

"Chicago, Illinois, 8.30 a.m., 25th May. — Five by three and two, fifty-eighth square, State of California, Death Valley. — TORNBROCK."

State of California! At the other extremity of the republic, which it would be necessary to cross from southeast to north-west!

And not only did a distance of more than two thousand miles separate California from Florida, but this fifty-eighth square was that of the Noble Game of Goose in which figures the death's head. And after making his appearance in this square the player had to return to the first to begin the game over again.

"Well," said Turk to himself, "better my poor master should not recover, for he will never get up again after a blow like that!"

CHAPTER XV. THE SITUATION ON THE 27TH OF MAY

IT will not have been forgotten that originally, according to the will of William J. Hypperbone, the number of players of the Noble Game of the United States of America had been fixed at six, chosen by lot. These "six," at the instructions of Tornbrock, had figured at the funeral around the car of this eccentric personage.

Neither will it have been forgotten, that at the meeting on the 15th of April in which the notary had read the will in the Auditorium, a very unexpected codicil had brought in a seventh competitor known only under the letters XKZ. Had this new-comer come out of the urn like the rest, or had he been brought in solely at the wish of the deceased? No one knew. Whichever way it might be, the codicil was so carefully drawn that no one would think of evading it. My lord XKZ — the masked man — enjoyed the same rights as the original six, and if he gained the enormous heritage no one would think of disputing his possession of it.

It was in accordance with this clause that on the 13th of the month, at eight o'clock in the morning, Tornbrock had proceeded to a seventh throw of the dice, and the number of the points obtained, nine by six and three, obliged XKZ to go to Wisconsin. Unless the unknown player was possessed by that immoderate desire for travel and love of running about which devoured the reporter of the *Tribune,* if he had no mania for locomotion, he ought to have been satisfied. In a few hours by railway he could reach Milwaukee, and, if she were there when he arrived, Lizzie Wag would have to give place to him and begin the game again. It was not known if the masked man would hasten to get to Milwaukee as soon as he had heard the result of the seventh throw, although he had a fortnight to do so.

At first the public had been much concerned about the introduction of this new personage into the match. Who was he? A Chicago man, as the testator had only admitted to the competition people who lived in Chicago. But no more was known, and curiosity was, as a consequence, all the greater.

And so on the 13th of the month, the day of the seventh throw, there had been a crowd at the railway station when the trains departed from Chicago to Milwaukee.

They hoped to recognize this XKZ by his walk, his bearing, by some singularity or originality. They were completely deceived; they saw nothing but the usual travellers of every social rank, distinguished in no way from ordinary mortals. Each time, at the moment of departure, somebody was taken for the masked man, and, very much confused, became the object of an ovation he did not deserve.

Next day there was again a large number of inquisitive people, the day after not so many, and very few on the following days, and never was anybody noticed who looked as though he were in the running in the Hypperbone match.

One thing that could be done and was done by those who were attracted by the mysterious side of this XKZ, and desirous of venturing large sums on him, was to question Tornbrock with regard to the matter. And thus this personage was overwhelmed with questions.

"You ought to know who this XKZ is!" they said to him.

"By no means," he replied.

"But you do know?"

"I do not know him; and if I did know him, I should probably not be permitted to reveal his incognito."

"But you ought to know where he lives — it he lives in Chicago or elsewhere, for you have sent him the result of the throw?"

"I have sent him nothing. Either he has learnt it from the newspapers and posters, or he heard it at the Auditorium"

"But you must send him a telegram informing him of where the dice are going to send him on the 27th of this month?"

"I will send it to him, without doubt."

"But where?"

"Where he will be; that is to say, where he ought to be — at Milwaukee, Wisconsin."

"But at what address?"

"Post Office, letters XKZ."

"But if he is not there?"

"If he is not there, all the worse for him, as he will be thrown out of the game."

To all their "buts" it will be seen Tornbrock had but one reply: he knew nothing and could tell them nothing.

It followed that the interest so greatly excited at first by the man of the codicil soon began to diminish, and it was left to the future to establish the identity of this XKZ. Besides, if he won, if he became the sole heir of Hypperbone's millions, his name would be known all over the world. On the contrary, if he did not win, was it worthwhile to know if he were old or young, tall or short, stout or slim, dark or fair, rich or poor, and under what patronymic appellation he had been inscribed in the registers of his parish?

Meanwhile the vicissitudes of the game were followed with extreme attention in the world of speculation. The financial bulletins gave the position day by day, as if they were treating of the prices on the Stock Exchange.

The principal cities, New York, Boston, Philadelphia, Washington, Albany, St. Louis, Baltimore, Richmond, Charleston, Cincinnati, Detroit, Omaha, Denver, Salt Lake City, Savannah, Mobile, New Orleans, San Francisco, Sacramento, opened special betting agencies, whose business throve immensely. It looked as though these would double, treble, and even increase to ten times in the same proportion as the adventures caused by the dice of which Max Real, Tom Crabbe, Hermann Titbury, Harris T. Kymbale, Lizzie Wag, Hodge Urrican, and XKZ were in turn the beneficiaries or the victims. Regular markets were started, with brokers and quotations, in which there were inquiries and offers, in which people bought and sold at prices varying with the chances of one player or another.

It was inevitable that this current could not be contained within the United States of America. It passed the frontier and ramified across the Dominion by Quebec, Montreal, Toronto, and the other important towns of Canada. It had also flowed towards Mexico, towards the smaller states bathed by the waters of the Gulf. Then it overflowed down South America, Colombia, Venezuela, Brazil, Argentina, Peru, Bolivia, Chile. The game fever ended by becoming endemic throughout the New World.

Decidedly, if the defunct member of the Eccentric Club of Chicago had not made much noise during his lifetime, he had made a considerable stir after his death. The Honourable George B. Higginbotham and his colleagues could not but be proud at being associated with so much posthumous glory.

At the moment, who was the favourite?

It was difficult to say up to now, owing to the small number of throws, but it seemed that the fourth player, Harris T. Kymbale, had most supporters. Most of the attention was directed to him. It was of him that the newspapers most frequently spoke, for they followed him step by step, getting their information from his daily correspondence. Max Real, with the reserve that rarely left him, Hermann Titbury, who had begun by travelling under an assumed name, Lizzie Wag, whose departure had been delayed till the last day, could not approach in the public esteem the brilliant and blustering reporter of the *Tribune*.

At the same time it should be noted that Tom Crabbe, well-advertised by John Milner, had a large number of supporters. It seemed natural that the enormous fortune should go to this enormous brute. Chance amuses itself with likes and unlikes, as you please, and if it has no habits, at least it has caprices, which ought to be considered.

Commodore Urrican had begun to rise in the market at first. With his throw of nine by five and four, which took him to the fifty-third square, what a magnificent beginning! But at the second throw sent to the fifty-eighth square, to California, and obliged to begin the game again, he went quite out of favour. Besides, it was known that he had been shipwrecked near Key West, that his landing had taken place under deplorable conditions, and that on the 23rd at noon he had not recovered consciousness. Would he ever be in a state to go to Death Valley, and was he not twice dead both as a man and as a player?

There remained the seventh competitor, XKZ, and there were already signs that the clever people whom some special disposition of the brain leads them to discover good things would end by supporting him. That he was not attracting much notice at the moment was because it was not known if he were on the way to Wisconsin or not. But this question would be solved when he presented himself at the Milwaukee post office to receive his telegram.

And this day was not far off. The 27th of May was approaching, the date of the fourteenth throw, which would concern the masked man. That day, after the throw, Tornbrock would send a message to Milwaukee, where the personage ought to be before noon. One can easily imagine that there would be a crowd at the office eager to see the man of letters. If they did not learn his name, at least they would see what he was like, and instantaneous photographs could be taken which the newspapers would publish that very day.

It should be observed that William J. Hypperbone had distributed the different states of the Union on the board in a purely arbitrary manner. They were placed in neither alphabetical nor geographical order. Thus Florida and Georgia, which are adjacent, occupied one the twenty-eighth square, the other the fifty-third. And thus Texas and South Carolina were numbered ten and eleven, although they were separated by a distance of eight or nine hundred miles. The same with all the others. The distribution did not seem to be due to any system, and perhaps the places had been filled up by lot by the testator.

Anyhow, it was in Wisconsin that the mysterious XKZ would await the telegram announcing the result of the second throw. And as Lizzie Wag and Jovita Foley had not reached Milwaukee till the 23rd, in the morning, they had to hurry up to get away again immediately, so as not to run against the seventh competitor, when he appeared at the telegraph office of the town.

At last the 27th of May arrived, and attention was recalled to this personage, who, for one knew not what motives, abstained from revealing his name to the public.

The crowd hastened, then, on this occasion, to the Auditorium, and, doubtless, would have been much greater if thousands had not taken the morning trains for Milwaukee to be present at the post office and gaze on this mysterious XKZ.

At eight o'clock, solemn as usual, surrounded by members of the Eccentric Club, Tornbrock shook the box, rolled the dice on the table, and amid the general silence proclaimed in a sonorous voice:

"Fourteenth throw; ten, by four and six." And these were the consequences:

XKZ being at the twenty-sixth square, Wisconsin, the ten points would have sent him to the thirty-sixth, if they had not to be doubled, for this thirty-sixth square was

occupied by Illinois. Thus it was to the forty-sixth square he had to betake himself after leaving Wisconsin. And on Hypperbone's board this meant the District of Columbia.

In truth, fortune singularly favoured this enigmatic personage. At the first throw, an adjacent state, at the next, three states only to cross, Indiana, Ohio and West Virginia, to reach the District of Columbia, and Washington, its capital, which is also the capital of the United States of America. What a difference to the majority of the players, who had been sent to the further ends of the country!

Assuredly such a lucky fellow was worthy of support — that is, if he existed.

This morning, at Milwaukee, there was no more doubt as to his existence. A little before noon, around and in the post office, the crowd opened their ranks to give passage to a man of medium height, of healthy appearance, greyish beard, and wearing a double eye-glass. He was in a travelling suit, and carried a Gladstone bag.

"Have you a telegram for XKZ?" he asked the clerk.

"It is here," said the clerk.

"Then the seventh player — for it was really the man — took the message, opened it, read it, folded it again, put it into his pocket-book, without showing any sign of satisfaction or discontent, and went back through the excited and silent crowd.

They had seen him at last, this last to start on the Hypperbone match! He existed! But who he was, his name, his trade, his social position, they knew not! Arrived without noise, he had gone again without noise! It mattered not, for as he had been found that day at Milwaukee, so would he be found on the stated day at Washington! Was it, then, necessary to know all about him? No! There was no doubt he would fulfil to the letter all the conditions of the will, inasmuch as he had been nominated by the testator himself. Why trouble to know more? Supporters could put their money on him without hesitation! He might become first favourite; for, to judge by his first throws, it seemed as though the Goddess of Fortune was going to accompany him on his travels.

To sum up. On this date, the 27th of May, the state of the game was as follows: —

Max Real, on the 15th of May, had left Fort Riley, Kansas, for the twenty-eighth square, that of Wyoming.

Tom Crabbe, on the 17th of May, had left Austin, Texas, for the thirty-fifth square, that of the State of Ohio.

Hermann Titbury, having been released in time, on the 19th of May left Calais, Maine, for the fourth square, the State of Utah.

Harris T. Kymbale, on the 21st of May, left Santa Fé, New Mexico, for the twenty-second square, that of South Carolina.

Lizzie Wag, on the 23rd of May, left Milwaukee, Wisconsin, for the thirty-eighth square, the State of Kentucky.

Commodore Urrican, if he were not dead — and it was to be wished that he was not — had received two days before, the 25th of May, the message which sent him to the fifty-eighth square, the State of California, whence he would return to Chicago to recommence the game.

Finally, XKZ, on the 27th of May, had been sent to the forty-sixth square, the District of Columbia.

The universe had to wait for the further incidents and results of the succeeding throws, which were to take place every other day.

An idea started by the *Tribune* achieved a great success, and it was adopted not only in America but throughout the world.

As the players were only seven in number, why not — as was done by jockeys on the race-course — give each of them a special colour? And why not choose the seven primitive colours in the order they occupy in the rainbow?

Let Max Real have the violet, Tom Crabbe the indigo, Hermann Titbury the blue, Harris T. Kymbale the green, Lizzie Wag the yellow, Hodge Urrican the orange, and XKZ the red.? And in this way, each with their own colour, little flags were daily stuck in the squares occupied by the players in the Hypperbone match, on the board of the Noble Game of the United States of America.

CHAPTER XVI . THE NATIONAL PARK

It was at noon on the 15th of May, at the post office of Fort Riley, that Max Real had received the telegram sent that morning from Chicago. Ten, by five and five, such was the number of points at the second throw of the first player.

Reckoning from the eighth square, Kansas, with ten points, the player alighted in one of the squares of Illinois; and as the rule in such cases obliged him to double the number, he had to go on ten more to the twenty-eighth square, that of Wyoming.

"A lucky chance!" said Max Real, when he and Tommy returned to the hotel.

"If my master is pleased," replied the boy, "I ought to be — "

"He is," declared Max Real, "and for two reasons: first, that the journey will not be long, for Kansas and Wyoming almost touch at one of their angles; secondly, that we shall have time to visit the most beautiful region of the United States, that marvellous National Park of the Yellowstone, which I have not yet seen. That is my lucky star, you see. To have got exactly the ten which gives me a double stride and puts Wyoming on my route! Do you understand, Tommy, do you understand?"

"No, master," replied Tommy.

212

And the truth is that Tommy did not yet understand these ingenious combinations of the Noble Game of the United States of America which enchanted the young painter.

That mattered little, however, and Max Real could congratulate himself on his second throw, although he was still behind Lizzie Wag and Commodore Urrican — the latter, as we know, being condemned to begin the game again. Not only would the journey be without fatigue, but it would give the first player an opportunity of visiting this wonderful corner of Wyoming.

Wishing to devote to it as much time as possible, and having only a fortnight at his disposal, from the 15th to the 29th of May, he decided to leave the little town of Fort Riley immediately.

It was at Cheyenne, the capital of Wyoming, that he would find the next telegram sent to him — unless the game had been won before then. And if Hodge Urrican were to get a ten it would take him to the sixty-third and last square, for at the first throw he had reached the fifty-third, a great advance on his competitors.

"He is quite capable of it, this terrible man!" said Max Real, when the newspapers published the result. "Then no more of the heritage, and I cannot buy you, my poor Tommy! At any rate I shall have visited the regions of the Yellowstone! Vile slave, buckle up our bags, and let us start for the National Park!"

The vile slave, much honoured, set about the preparations for departure in all haste.

If Max Real had been obliged to go from Fort Riley to Cheyenne, he would have done the journey of four hundred and fifty miles in a single day by the railroads which unite the two towns. But as he intended to go to the north-western angle of Wyoming occupied by the National Park, he had to reckon on this distance being at least doubled.

As soon as he received the telegram, Max Real had studied the routes of the iron network in order to choose the shortest. The study resulted in his finding that the two lines of the Union Pacific were about equal as far as time was concerned.

The first runs from Kansas to Nebraska, and by Marysville, Kearney City, North Platte, Ogalalla, Antelope, reaches the south-east angle of Wyoming and leads to Cheyenne.

The second by Salina, Ellis, Oakley, Monument, Wallace, touches the frontier of Colorado at Monotony, runs on towards Denver, the State capital, and by Jersey, Brighton, La Salle, Dover, reaches the frontier of Wyoming to stop at Cheyenne.

It was to the latter route that the violet flag — this, it will be remembered, was the colour of the first player — gave the preference. When he reached Cheyenne he would work out another, so as in the shortest delay to reach the quadrilateral of the National Park.

In the afternoon of the 16th Max Real started with his painter's outfit, Tommy carrying the bag. Immense, without a ridge or a slope, are these western plains of Kansas, watered by the course of the Arkansas, which descends the White Mountains of Colorado. How easy was the making of the railways. As the rails were laid on the sleepers, the locomotive advanced on them, and in this way the line was made at the rate of several miles a day. It is true that these interminable steppes offered nothing very attractive to the eyes of an artist, but the country becomes varied, strange, and superb in the mountainous part of Colorado. During the night the train crossed the geodetic frontier between the two states, and it arrived early in the morning at Denver.

To see this town would take an hour, but Max Real had not the time. The train for Cheyenne was about to start, and to miss it meant the loss of a day. A hundred miles, leaving to the west the magnificent panorama of Snowy Ranges, dominated by the summits of Long's Peak, and the journey was over.

What is Cheyenne? It is the name of a river and a city; it is also that of the Indians who formerly inhabited the country — or rather the "Chiens" or dogs, which the popular language corrupted into Cheyenne.

The town originated in one of the camps of the early gold-seekers. To the tents succeeded huts; to the huts, houses bordering the roads and squares. The iron network formed around it, and now Cheyenne contains nearly twelve thousand inhabitants. Built at an altitude; of six thousand feet, it is a station, and an important station, on this great Pacific railway.

Wyoming has no natural boundaries. It is reduced to that which geometry has fixed for it, namely, four straight lines forming a long square. It is a country of imposing mountains and deep valleys, among which the Colorado, the Columbia, and the Missouri have their sources. And when a region has given birth to these three rivers of so much importance in American hydrography, it is worthy of adding a star to those which shine so brilliantly in the flag of the United States.

As was customary with him, Max Real maintained the completest incognito. Cheyenne knew not that on that day it possessed one of the players in the Hypperbone match, whom it did not expect so soon, and knew it would find at his post on the 29th. He avoided the receptions, indigestible banquets, tedious ceremonies, of which he would have been the object on the part of a population, among whom would certainly have figured the women who have the right to vote in this happy State of Wyoming.

Arriving in the morning of the 16th of May, Max Real prepared to reach the National Park without delay. With more time at his disposal he would have made the journey in a carriage, in stages, stopping where fancy led him, exploring this region of the Laramie Ranges, these elevated plains of which the clayey subsoil was formerly that of an immense lake, crossing at fords the innumerable creeks, the capricious affluents of the North Fork and Platte rivers, penetrating the magnificent orographic system, the sinuous valleys, the thick forests, and the network of the tributaries of the Columbia, in short all that country dominated at more than 12,000 feet by Union Peak, Hayden Peak, Fremont Peak, and the wild Mount Ouragans of the Wide Water Mountains, whence came, perhaps, the name of Oregon, and which for its storms and squalls might perhaps rival the no less wild Commodore Urrican.

Yes, to travel in this way in a carriage, on horseback, on foot, in perfect liberty to stop at leisure in the most beautiful places, to pitch one's tent here and there without being hurried by the hours, what could be more delightful for a painter, and with what enchantment would not Max Real have pursued the journey under such conditions! But could he forget that in him the artist was doubled by a player, that he was not his own master, that, as the plaything of chance, he was at its mercy, that he depended on a throw of the dice, that he had to manoeuvre within fixed dates, and was treated like a pawn on the chessboard!

"A pawn which fate moves at its will," he said to himself, "I am nothing else! I have abandoned all human dignity for one chance in seven of pocketing the heritage of this eccentric defunct. I blush to my forehead when this nigger of a Tommy looks at me. I ought to have sent this Tornbrock to Jericho, and never taken part in this ridiculous game, from which it would be wise for me to retire, to the great satisfaction of the Titburys, the Crabbes, the Kymbales, and the other Urricans. I say nothing of the sweet and modest Lizzie Wag, for that girl did not seem to be particularly charmed at figuring in the group of seven. Yes — to Jericho — and I would do it this moment, and would stay in Wyoming at my convenience if it were not for my dear old mother, who would never pardon me for having deserted! Well, as I am in this extraordinary country of the Yellowstone, let us see all we can see in a dozen days!"

Thus reasoned Max Real, and it was not bad reasoning after a study of the route best adapted for the circumstances. Besides, to travel as he would have liked would have been to expose himself to delays and to dangers. These plains and valleys of central Wyoming are far from being safe when traversed without escort. Besides the possible encounters with wild bears and other carnivores which frequent them, there are reasons for fearing an attack from Indians, from the wandering Sioux who are not already settled in their reserves.

In the government expedition organized in 1870 to explore the country of the Yellowstone, Messrs. Doane, Langford and Dr. Hayden were accompanied by military to ensure their safety. And it was two years afterwards, on the 1st of March, 1872, that Congress formed as a National Park this region, worthy in more than one respect of being denominated the eighth wonder of the world.

That evening, as unknown at their departure as at their arrival, Max Real and Tommy installed themselves in the train, and crossed the long lacustrine plains of Laramie, and were in imperturbable sleep when they reached Benton City, one of those towns that spring up from the ground of the Far West like mushrooms — a little poisonous, perhaps, at their birth, but soon made antitoxic by their excellent culture. Then, without their awaking, the train left behind Laramie, Rawlins, Halville, Granger, Separation, Buttes Noires, Green River, which joins Grand River to form the Colorado; then following the course of the Muddy Fork to Aspen station, near the frontier of Utah, they entered the state of that name, and in the morning of the 27th stopped at Ogden.

There the Union Pacific, before skirting Salt Lake by its upper curve to go west, throws off a branch of 450 miles to Helena City. At the same point it throws off one towards the south uniting Ogden with Salt Lake City, the state capital, the great Mormon city which has had so much said about it, not always to its advantage.

What an opportunity had Max Real, without going more than thirty-six miles out of his way, of visiting this famous town! He refrained, however, and who knows if the chances of the game might bring him back to the City of the Saints, made illustrious by the matrimonial exploits of Brigham Young and his polygamous compatriots?

The whole of the 17th was spent in running up through Idaho, leaving to the east the frontier of Wyoming, along the base of the Bear River Mountains, by Utah Hot Springs, the train crossing the boundary of Idaho at Oxford.

Idaho belongs to the basin of the Columbia, rich in mining deposits, attracting a tumultuous crowd of gold-washers, but farmers will have utilized the southern plains in the near future. Boise City with its two thousand five hundred inhabitants is the capital of this territory, which possesses certain reserves assigned to the Blackfeet, Nez-Percés, Cœurs-d'Alene, without reckoning the Chinese mingled in such great numbers with the white population.

Montana is a country of mountains, as its name indicates. One of the largest in the Union, unfitted for culture but favourable for the raising of cattle, it is rich in deposits of gold, silver, and copper. Of all the states it is that in which the Indians occupy the largest reservations of the Far West, Flatheads, Crows, Modocks, Cheyennes, Assiniboines, whose turbulent proximity the American endures with difficulty.

Virginia City, the State capital, seemed at first to be bound to prosper, like so many other towns of these western territories; but it has been left behind by Butte City and Helena, although the first has experienced a decrease in the number of its inhabitants.

Of course, rapid and comfortable means of communication exist between the National Park and Monida station, where the first player stopped, and they are still increasing for the benefit of the legions of tourists from the old and new world invited by the Federal Government to visit the domain of the Yellowstone.

Max Real left Monida immediately in one of the coaches, and a few hours afterwards, accompanied by Tommy, he arrived at his destination.

The national parks are to the territory of the Republic what squares are to great cities. Besides the Yellowstone, others have been made, or will be made without delay — such as that of Crater Lake in the volcanic region of the North-West, such as the American Switzerland, the Garden of the Gods magnificently situated in the mountainous zone of the Colorado.

At the end of February, 1872, the Senate and the House of Representatives considered a report on a proposal to be made to Congress with regard to withdrawing from occupation and putting under the protection of the State, a part of the land of the Union measuring fifty-five miles by sixty-five miles, situated near the sources of the Yellowstone and the Missouri. This region would become henceforth a National Park whose full and complete enjoyment should be reserved to the American people.

After declaring that the space comprised within the limits indicated was not capable of productive culture, the report added:

"The proposed law would make no diminution in the revenue of the Government, and would be regarded by the entire civilized world as a step of progress and an honour to Congress and the Nation."

The conclusions of the report were adopted. The National Park of the Yellowstone passed under the administration of the Secretary of the Interior, and if the whole world has not yet visited it, the future will probably realize the wishes of Congress.

In this privileged corner of the United States there is, it appears, nothing to be expected from culture, neither on the table-lands, nor in the valleys, nor on the plains placed at a mean altitude of seven thousand feet. Then the climate is extremely severe, there not being a month without frost. And so there is no raising of cattle, which could not stand these severe temperatures, nothing beyond the mineral yield of a soil, generally volcanic, strewn with eruptive matters, devoured by plutonian heat, and encompassed by a frame of mountains whose crests rise six thousand feet above the level of the sea.

It is thus the most useless country in the world, though one of the most celebrated, and its only value is due to its beauties, to its natural peculiarities, to which the hand of man could add nothing.

This hand has intervened, however, with the object of attracting excursionists from the five parts of the world whom the official report provides for. Communications are facilitated by carriage roads through the chaotic labyrinth. Hotels have been built, wherein elegance disputes with comfort. The whole domain can be traversed in perfect security. The fear is that it will become a thermal station, an immense watering-place, in which will swarm the invalids attracted by the hot springs of the Fire Hole and the Yellowstone.

And besides, as has been observed by Elisée Réclus, these national parks have already become great hunting-grounds for the directors of financial companies who possess the railways running to them and the principal hotels. In this way the establishment of Mammoth Terrace is the centre of a regular principality. Who would have believed it? A principality in the great North American Republic! It was there — and unfortunately at this time of the year a number of visitors encumbered the caravansary — that all the time was spent which Max Real had to dispose of. Fortunately, no one suspected him to be one of the starters in the Hypperbone match, for he would have been escorted, or rather assailed, by intruders in thousands. He could thus come and go as he liked, admiring the natural attractions, which in no way, it must be confessed, provoked the admiration of Tommy, and sketching in several canvases, which the young negro found infinitely superior to what they represented. Never would Max Real forget the unforgettable marvels of the National Park.

"And suppose," he would say to himself sometimes, "suppose I were to miss the appointment at Cheyenne on the 29th. What would my dear good mother say?"

It is truly magnificent, this Valley of the Yellowstone — marked out with basaltic masses from which a whole palace could be carved — with its slashed peaks rising around; its white summits, down which the snows run in a thousand ramifications of rios and creeks through the depths of the forests of pines; its canyons with their vertical walls closely approaching each other and forming the interminable corridors that furrow this domain. There on every side are the wildest convulsions of nature. There stretch the lava fields, the plains on which accumulates the tribute of the volcanoes. There stand the groups of columns carved in blackish cliffs, striped with red and yellow bands, and forming models for a polychrome architecture. There lie in heaps the remains of forests petrified beneath the ejections of craters now cold. There is still felt the formidable subterranean energy whose action is manifested through the soil by the escape of two thousand hot springs.

And what shall we say of the lake of the Yellowstone, with its banks strewn with obsidian, scooped in a tableland more than seven thousand feet high? This basin of water, pure as crystal, of an area of three hundred and thirty square miles, has its mountainous islands, and in many places the cloud of its vapours hangs not only over its beach but over its surface. It is a sheet of water deep and calm, where trout swarm in myriads, and is girt by an orographic system of incomparable splendour.

And so Max Real, without thinking of the hours and days that went by, secured many imperishable memories of these magnificences. He visited the environs of Yellowstone Lake, the pools of purple waves close by, with their patches of brightly-coloured algae. He went north to that startling display of basins at Mammoth Springs. He bathed in these basaltic piscinas that are arranged in a semi-circle, filled with tepid water and wreathed with vapours. He was deafened by the tumultuous uproar of the two cataracts of the Yellowstone, which for half a mile in chutes, and rapids, and cascades pour over a narrow bed rugged with volcanic rocks to end amid a vast cloud of spray in a leap of a hundred and twenty feet. He walked between the fiery hollows which border the torrent of the Fire Hole. There in the valley worn by the impetuous tributary of the Madison can be counted in hundreds springs, mud fountains, and geysers which rival the most famous ones of Iceland.

And what a panorama develops to the view along the banks of this sinuous and capricious Fire Hole, emerging from a lagoon and flowing towards the north. On every shelf of the massive strata that descend in steps to its bed, stand in succession the craters in which spout the geysers whose names are so descriptive. Here is "Old Faithful," with its regular jets, whose fidelity begins to decrease on account of less precise intermittences. Here is the "Castle" on the banks of a marshy pool, in the form of an old donjon, whose waters are inundated by the rain of its condensed vapours. Here is the "Beehive," a prodigious well, whose margin rises above the ground like the stump of a tower; here is the "Grand Geyser," which has an interval of thirty-two hours between its eruptions; here is the "Giant," with its cloud of vapour floating a hundred and twenty feet overhead, less powerful than the "Giantess" which sends up hers to more than double that height.

In the upper basin is the "Fan" with its watery bars decorated with all the shades of the rainbow, as they refract the solar rays. Not far off is "Excelsior" with its central column twenty yards through, rising to 360 feet, throwing out stones and lavas torn from the terrestrial crust. A mile away is the "Grotto" which crowns with its aqueous plumes enormous blocks that arch over the orifices of the dark caves in which the plutonian forces are constantly at work. And finally the "Blood Geyser," spurting from a crater in the reddish clay walls, which check its outflow so that it seems to expand in a spout of blood.

Such is the district, without arrival in this world, in which Max Real explored the valleys, the canyons, the lakes, going from marvel to marvel, from admiration to admiration. In this angle of Wyoming watered by the Fire Hole and the upper Yellowstone, where the ground thrills beneath the feet like the plates of a boiler, telluric substances mingle, amalgamate and combine under the action of internal fires inexhaustibly fed from the central furnace that utters its roar through a thousand mouths. There occur the most unexpected phenomena, like the scenic effects of a pantomime produced by the wand of the magician, amid the prodigies of this National Park of the Yellowstone, for which no equivalent can be found in no matter what other country of the globe.

CHAPTER XVII . ONE TAKEN FOR THE OTHER

"I do not believe he has arrived." —

"And why do you not believe it?"

"Because my newspaper has said nothing about it."

"Your newspaper is badly served, then, for in mine I have the news at length."

"Then I shall stop my subscription."

"And you will not do wrong."

"Assuredly, for it is not to be permitted, when a fact occurs of this importance, that a journal should have no mention of it, and that its readers should be unaware of it."

"It is unpardonable."

The conversation was between two citizens of Cincinnati who were walking on the suspension bridge, 120 yards long, thrown over the Ohio near the mouth of the Licking, between the metropolis and the two suburbs of Newport and Covington, built on the shore of Kentucky.

It is the Ohio, the "Beautiful River," which separates on the south and southeast the state of this name from Kentucky and West Virginia. Geodetic boundaries are common to it on the east with Pennsylvania, on the north with Michigan, on the west with Indiana; and the waters of Lake Erie bathe its coast.

By crossing the bridge, which is as elegant as it is strong, you get a view of the industrious city extending for nine miles along the right bank of the river, to the summit of the hills which shut it in on that side. There the view extends beyond Eden Park on the east, and over a suburb of villas and cottages almost concealed beneath their verdant foliage.

The Ohio may justly be compared to European rivers, with its European trees and villages in the European style. Fed in its upper course by the Alleghany and the Monongahela, in its middle course by the Muskingum, the Sicoto, the two Miamis and the Licking, in its lower course by the Kentucky, the Green River, the Wabash, the Cumberland, the Tennessee and other tributaries, it flows to join the Mississippi at Cairo.

As they were talking, the two citizens, of whom posterity with regret will know neither the names nor social position, looked between the thousand bars of the bridge at the ferry-boats which ploughed the river, the steamboats, the barges that passed under the viaduct above stream, or the two viaducts below, by which the railways are put in communication with the neighbouring states.

Further, on this 28th day of May, other citizens, no less unknown than the preceding, were indulging almost everywhere in animated conversation — in the industrial and commercial quarters, in the workshops and factories, of which there are nearly seven thousand at Cincinnati, in the breweries, flour mills, refineries, slaughter-houses, in the markets, and in the precincts of the railway stations, where very noisy and demonstrative groups were stationed. But to tell the truth, it did not seem as though these worthy citizens were of any of the superior classes, or of the learned and artistic class which attends university courses and rich libraries and visits valuable collections and the museums of the metropolis. No! The excitement was chiefly noticeable in the lower part of the town, and did not extend to the sumptuous quarters, to the fashionable streets, to the squares, to the parks shaded with magnificent trees — among others the chestnuts, which have led to Ohio being called the Buckeye State.

Moving among the groups listening to the conversation, you would have heard remarks of this nature:

"Have you seen him?"

"No. He arrived very late in the evening; he was put into a closed carriage and his companion accompanied him — "

"Where?"

"That is not known, and it would be so interesting to know — "

"But he has not come to Cincinnati not to be shown! They will exhibit him, I suppose — "

"Yes — the day after to-morrow — they say — at the great meeting at Spring Grove."

"There will be a crowd."

"Yes, a regular crush."

But this way of judging the hero of the day was not the only one. In the vicinity of the slaughter-houses, where physical properties — the stature, the vigour, the muscular strength of individuals — are more appreciated than moral or intellectual qualities, a number of sturdy slaughtermen shrugged their shoulders.

"An exaggerated reputation," said one.

"We know how to take it at its value," said another.

"Over six feet, to believe the reports."

"Six feet, but not of twelve inches, perhaps."

"We must see."

"But it seems that up to now he has had the luck to beat all others."

"Bah! They say he holds the record. A way of attracting the public. And the public is taken in — "

"Here we shall not be taken in."

"Is it true that he comes from Texas?" asked a big jolly fellow with massive arms spotted with the blood of the slaughter-house.

"From Texas, straight," replied one of his comrades, quite his equal in strength.

"Then we will wait."

"Yes — wait. There is more than one already that has come to us from a distance who had much better have stayed at home."

"After all, if he wins! It is possible, and it would not astonish me."

Here was a divergence of appreciations, as you see, which, on the whole, would not have satisfied John Milner, who had arrived the evening before at Cincinnati with the second player, Tom Crabbe, whom the second throw of the dice had sent from the capital of Texas to the metropolis of Ohio.

It was at Austin at noon on the 17th of May that John Milner had received telegraphic advice of the throw relative to the blue flag, the famous pugilist of Chicago.

Decidedly Tom Crabbe could say he was in great form, and even with more reason than Max Real, although the latter had made a great advance owing to his doubled number. But for Crabbe, Tornbrock had thrown twelve, the highest number obtainable by two dice; and as this twelve put him into one of the Illinois squares, he had to double it, and with twenty-four he moved from the eleventh to the thirty-fifth square. And the result was to take him across the most populous provinces of the Central States, where communications are rapid and easy, instead of sending him to the confines of the republic.

For this reason, before leaving Austin, John Milner was heartily congratulated. That day the bets grew larger. Tom Crabbe went up in the betting not only in Texas but in many another state — principally in the markets of Illinois, where the agencies quoted him at five to one; and this put him above Harris T. Kymbale, who was favourite up to then.

"And take care of him — take care of him — " they said to John Milner; "he may have a constitution of meteoric iron and muscles of chrome steel, but do not expose him! He must get to the end without damage."

"Depend upon me," declared the trainer sharply. "It is not Tom Crabbe who is in the skin of Tom Crabbe, but John Milner."

"And," added they, "no more sea passages, neither long nor short, for sea-sickness puts him into such a state of decomposition, physical and mental — "

"Who has not experienced it?" replied John Milner; "but have no fear. No more navigation between Galveston and New Orleans. We shall reach Ohio by the railroads leisurely, as we have a fortnight to get to Cincinnati."

That same day, encouraged, petted, caressed by his partisans, Tom Crabbe was conducted to the railway station, hoisted into a car, and enveloped in good wraps as a precaution, considering the difference of temperature between Ohio and Texas. Then the train started for the frontier of Louisiana. The two travellers stayed a day at New Orleans, where they were welcomed more warmly than the first time. That was because the famous boxer was rising in the betting. Tom Crabbe was in demand everywhere. A delirium, a fury, had set in. The newspapers estimated that at least 1,500,000 dollars were laid on the player who was on his journey between the capital of Texas and the metropolis of Ohio. '

"What a success!" said John Milner to himself. "And what a welcome awaits us at Cincinnati! It ought to be a triumph. I have an idea!"

And this was John Milner's idea — which would not have been disavowed by the illustrious Barnum — to excite the curiosity and redouble the public enthusiasm with regard to Tom Crabbe.

It was not, as one might be led to believe, to announce with much advertisement the arrival of the Champion of the New World and to challenge the boldest boxers of Cincinnati to some contest from which Tom Crabbe would evidently emerge victorious to resume the course of his peregrinations. John Milner might try that some day. if opportunity presented itself.

What he intended was, on the contrary, to arrive in the strictest incognito, to leave the crowd without news of his favourite to the last day, to let them think he had disappeared, that he would not be in time on the 31st. And then he would produce him.

John Milner had learnt from the newspapers that there would be a great cattle show on the 30th at Cincinnati — a show at which horned cattle and others would be exhibited for the prizes to which people seemed to attach so much importance. What an opportunity for exhibiting Tom Crabbe at Spring Grove, at this meeting, when they had lost all hope of seeing him again, and that on the eve of his appearing at the post office.

Useless to say, John Milner did not consult his companion on this matter, and for a good reason. And thus it was that at night, the two, without informing anybody, got out at the first station after leaving New Orleans. What had become of them? That is what the whole town was asking next morning.

John Milner did not return by the route he had followed in leaving Illinois for Louisiana. The network of railroads is so close in these parts of the States that it seems to cover the maps of the guide books like a spider's web. And thus it was that without hurry, without the presence of Tom Crabbe being reported anywhere, travelling by night, sleeping during the day, careful not to attract attention, the blue flag and his trainer crossed Mississippi, Tennessee and Kentucky, and stopped on the 20th at daybreak at a modest hotel in the suburb of Covington. They had only to cross the Ohio to tread the soil of Cincinnati.

Thus John Milner's idea had been happily realized. Arrived at the gates of the metropolis, Tom Crabbe had come incognito. The newspapers and the best informed people knew not what had become of him. They had lost all trace of him after he left New Orleans. And they would have asked what it meant, and what John Milner thought, if they had had the opportunity.

Assuredly he had cause to reckon on a great effect among the population of Cincinnati, despairing of seeing him at his post on the 31st, when, on the eve of the day in question, and after they had vainly sought for news of him in all the echoes of the Union, he suddenly appeared among the crowd at Spring Grove.

But who can say that John Milner might not have done better during the two weeks from his departure from Texas in conducting his phenomenon across the territories of Ohio? Does not this state hold the fourth rank in the North American Republic, with its population of three million seven hundred thousand? And as much from the point of view of the Hypperbone match as from that of the supporters of prize-fighting, would it not have been wiser to take him from town to town, from village to village, to exhibit him in the chief cities of Ohio? And they are numerous and prosperous, and Tom Crabbe would have received the best of welcomes.

Next morning John Milner decided to take a tour round the town, unaccompanied of course by his curious beast. Before leaving the hotel he said:

"Tom, I leave you here, and you will wait for me."

As it was not with a view of consulting him that John Milner made this recommendation, Tom Crabbe had nothing to say.

"You will not go out of your room under any pretext," added John Milner.

Tom Crabbe would have gone out if he had been told to go out, and when he was told not to go out he would not go out.

"If I am late in coming back," John Milner added, "they will bring you your first breakfast, then your second, then your lunch, then your dinner, then your supper. I am going to give the orders, and you need not be uneasy about your food."

No, certainly. Tom Crabbe would not be uneasy, and under these circumstances he would patiently await John Milner's return. Then directing his enormous mass towards a large rocking chair, he placed himself in it, and giving a gentle balancing to his seat, retired into the vacancy of his thoughts.

John Milner descended to the office of the hotel, arranged the bill of fare of the substantial meals that were to be served to his companion, went out of the door, walked towards the Ohio through the streets of Covington, crossed the river in a ferry-boat, landed on the right bank, and with his hands in his pockets lounged up into the commercial quarter of the town.

He could not help noticing that there was great excitement about. He tried to overhear a few words of the passing conversation. He had no doubt the people were much interested in the approaching arrival of the second player.

Behold John Milner, then, going up one street and down another among the crowd, who were evidently discussing something, stopping near groups of them, in front of the shops, wherever the excitement was manifesting itself by the noisiest talk. Among the crowd were many women, and in America they are no less demonstrative than in any country of the old world.

John Milner was quite satisfied, but he would have liked to know to what a pitch of impatience they had risen at not having yet seen Tom Crabbe at Cincinnati. That was why that, noticing the worthy Dick Wolgod, pork butcher, in a tall hat, a black coat and working apron, standing at the door of his shop, he entered and asked for a ham, of which, as we know, he could easily dispose. After paying for it without bargaining at all, he said as he went out:

"The meeting is to-morrow?"

"Yes — a fine show," replied Dick Wolgod, "and it will be a credit to the city."

"There will be, doubtless, a great crowd at Spring Grove?" asked John Milner.

"All the town will be there, sir," replied Dick, with that politeness which no proper pork butcher would deny to a customer who had just bought a ham. "Consider, sir, such an exhibition — "

John Milner pricked up his ears. He was puzzled. How could anyone doubt that he intended to exhibit Tom Crabbe at Spring Grove?

And then he said:

"Then — there is no anxiety about the delays — which might occur — "

"None."

And as a customer entered at this moment, John Milner departed, a prey to more perplexity.

He had not gone a hundred yards when, at the corner of the fifth cross-road, he suddenly stopped, lifted his arms to the sky, and let the ham drop on the footpath.

There at the corner of a house was a poster, on which was displayed in large letters:

HE ARRIVES! HE ARRIVES!! HE ARRIVES!!!

HE HAS ARRIVED!!!!

That beat everything! How did they know that Tom Crabbe was at Cincinnati? They knew the date the Champion of the New World was to appear! Was this the explanation of the joy that animated the town and the satisfaction displayed by the pork butcher Wolgod?

Decidedly it is difficult — let us say impossible — for a celebrated man to escape the inconveniences of celebrity, and for the future he would have to give up throwing the veil of incognito over the shoulders of Tom Crabbe.

Besides, there were other posters explicitly stating not only that he had arrived, but that he had come from Texas to figure at the Spring Grove show.

"Ah! This is too strong" said John Milner. "They know my plans of bringing Tom Crabbe here! But I have not said a word about it to anybody. I must have spoken to Crabbe, and Crabbe, who never speaks, must have spoken on the way. I cannot understand it otherwise."

Thereupon John Milner went back to Covington, entered the hotel for a second breakfast, said nothing to Crabbe of the indiscretion he must have committed, and, persisting in not showing himself again, spent the rest of the day with him.

Next day at eight o'clock both of them walked to the river, crossed the suspension bridge, and went up the streets of the town.

It was in the north-west, in the enclosure of Spring Grove, that the great show of cattle was to be held. Already the people were on their way there in large numbers, and — as John Milner was obliged to notice — they showed no sign of anxiety. On all sides were crowds of joyous, noisy people, whose curiosity was soon to be gratified.

Perhaps John Milner thought that before he reached Spring Grove, Tom Crabbe would be recognized by his stature, his build, his face, which his photographs had reproduced thousands of times in the farthest villages of the Union! Well, no! Nobody took any notice of him, nobody looked round as he passed, nobody seemed to imagine that this colossus who suited his pace to that of John Milner was the celebrated pugilist as well as the competitor in the Hypperbone match whom twenty-four points had sent to the thirty-eighth square, State of Ohio, Cincinnati.

They reached Spring Grove as nine o'clock was striking. There was already a great crowd there. To the tumult of the spectators were added the lowing and bleating and grunting of the animals, of which the most favoured were to figure, to their great honour, in the official prize lists.

There were assembled splendid examples of bovine, ovine, and porcine species, a number of sheep and pigs of the best breeds, milch cows, cattle of which America in a year furnishes England with more than four hundred thousand. There paraded with the breeding kings, the cattle kings reckoned among the most worthy citizens of the United States. In the centre was a platform on which agricultural products were exhibited.

And then an idea occurred to John Milner to make his way through the crowd to reach the foot of the platform, to make his companion mount it and to shout to the crowd:

"Behold Tom Crabbe, the Champion of the New World, the second player in the Hypperbone match!"

What an effect this unexpected revelation would make in the presence of the hero of the day towering above the excited crowd!

And so, pushing Tom Crabbe in front, and as if towed by this powerful tug, he forged through the waves of the populace and reached the platform.

The place was taken! And who occupied it? A pig — an enormous pig, the colossal product of the two American breeds, the Poland, China, and the Red Jersey — a pig sold when three years old for two hundred and fifty dollars and then already weighing 1320 lbs. — a phenomenal pig, his length nearly eight feet, his height four, around the neck six, around the body seven and a half, his present weight 1954 lbs.!

And it was this specimen of the Suide family that had been brought from Texas! It was his arrival at Cincinnati that the posters announced! He it was who this day absorbed all the public attention! He it was whom his fortunate owner presented to the applause of the crowd!

Behold, then, before what new star had paled the star of Tom Crabbe! A monstrous pig that was to win a prize at the Spring Grove meeting!

John Milner, astounded, recoiled. Then, making a sign to Tom Crabbe to follow him, he returned to the hotel by the side streets, and, disappointed, humiliated, he shut himself up in his room and went out no more that day.

And if ever Cincinnati had occasion to regain its nickname of Porkopolis, which had first been taken from it by Chicago, it was on the 30th of May, 1897.

CHAPTER XVIII . THE PACE OF THE TORTOISE

"Received of Mr. Hermann Titbury, of Chicago, the sum of three hundred dollars in payment of the fine to which he was sentenced on the 14th of May, instant, for infringement of the law as to alcoholic drinks.

"Calais, Maine, 19th of May, 1897.

"Walter Hoek, *Registrar.*"

And so Hermann Titbury had had to give in, not without a long resistance that lasted to the 19th of May. Then, the amount being paid, the identity of the third player duly established, the proof given that it was Mr. and Mrs. Titbury who were travelling under the name of Mr. and Mrs. Field, Judge R. T. Ordak, after three days in prison, had remitted the rest of the sentence. It was time.

That very day, the 19th, at eight o'clock in the morning, Tornbrock had made the sixth throw of the dice, and sent the notification by wire to Calais.

The inhabitants of this little town, annoyed at one of the players in the Hypperbone match hiding himself under a false name, did not show themselves very hospitable, and even laughed at the misadventure. They had been delighted that in Maine, Calais should have been the place chosen by the late Mr. Hypperbone, and could not forgive Titbury for not making his arrival known. It follows that his real name, when it was revealed, produced no impression. As soon as the gaoler had set him at liberty, Hermann Titbury took the road to the inn. No one accompanied him, no one even turned round to look at him. And, besides, the Titburys did not care for the acclamations of the crowd, which Harris T. Kymbale sought, and they had but one wish: to leave Calais as soon as possible.

It was nine o'clock in the morning, and three hours would elapse before the time came for them to present themselves at the telegraph office. And so before the tea and toast of their breakfast, Mr. and Mrs. Titbury occupied themselves in putting their accounts in order.

"How much have we spent since our departure from Chicago?" asked the husband.

"Eighty-eight dollars and thirty-seven cents," replied the wife.

"As much as that — "

"Yes, and we have not wasted our money on the road."

Without the blood of Titbury in your veins you might be astonished that the expenses had been reduced to this point. It is true that the amount had been increased by the three hundred dollars fine — which brought up the sum sufficiently to make a heavy drain on the Titburyan treasury.

"And supposing the telegram we are to receive from Chicago does not oblige us to leave for the other end of the country!" sighed Mr. Titbury.

"We shall have to pay what is necessary," said Mrs. Titbury decidedly.

"I would rather give it up — "

"Again!" exclaimed the imperious lady. "Let it be the last time, Hermann, that you talk of giving up this chance of winning sixty millions of dollars!"

The three hours went by, and at twenty minutes to twelve the couple, installed at the post office, waited, with what impatience can be imagined. Hardly half a dozen people had come in to look at them.

What a difference to the excitement of which their competitors were the object at Fort Riley, at Austin, at Santa Fé, at Milwaukee, at Key West!

"Here is a message for Mr. Hermann Titbury, of Chicago," said the clerk.

The personage called upon was seized with weakness at the moment his lot was about to be decided. His legs bent, his tongue was paralyzed, and he could not reply.

"Here!" said Mrs. Titbury, giving her husband a shake and pushing him by his shoulders.

"You are really the person for whom this message is intended?" asked the clerk.

"As if he were not!" exclaimed Mrs. Titbury.

"As if I were not!" replied the third competitor at last. "Go and ask Judge Ordak! It cost me dear to prevent them cheating me out of my identity!"

In fact there was no doubt on the subject. The telegram was handed to Mrs. Titbury, and opened by her, for the trembling hand of her husband could not manage it.

And this is what she read, in a voice that died away to silence before she articulated the last words:

"Hermann Titbury two, by one and one. Great Salt Lake City, Utah. — Tornbrock."

The couple fainted amid the ill-restrained raillery of the crowd, and had to be placed on one of the seats in the room.

The first time, by one and one, sent to the second square, at the end of Maine; the second time, again by one and one, to be sent to the fourth square, that of Utah! Four points in two throws! And to crown it all, after coming from Chicago to one extremity of the Union, to go nearly to the other extremity in the west!

When they had got over the few minutes of weakness, which were quite, intelligible, it will be admitted, Mrs. Titbury recovered herself, became once again the resolute virago who dominated the household, took her husband by the arm and dragged him towards the inn.

The bad luck was indeed too pronounced! What an advance had already been made by the other players, Tom Crabbe, Max Real, Harris T. Kymbale, Lizzie Wag, without mentioning Commodore Urrican! They were running like hares, and the Titburys were going like tortoises! To the thousands of miles travelled between Chicago and Calais there would now be added the two thousand two hundred miles which separate Calais from Great Salt Lake City.

But if the Titburys were not going to abandon the match, it would not do for them to delay in Calais if they were to rest a few days in Chicago, for they had to reach Utah before the 2nd of June. And as Mrs. Titbury would not hear of giving up the game, the couple left Calais that same day by the first train, accompanied by all the good wishes of the people — for their competitors.

The unfortunate couple had no occasion to trouble themselves about their route, for they had only to go back by that which had brought them to Maine. Arrived at Chicago, they would have the Union Pacific trains which by Omaha, Granger, and Ogden run to the capital of Utah.

In the afternoon the little town was relieved of the presence of these uncongenial people who had made so sorry a figure there. And the townsfolk hoped that the chances of the Noble Game of the United States of America would never bring them there again — a hope in which they themselves shared, as may be imagined.

Two days later the Titburys stepped out of the train at Chicago, almost knocked up by these long journeys, which were ill-suited to their age and habits. They were able to stay a few days at their house in Robey Street. Mr. Titbury was seized on the road with an attack of rheumatism, which he usually treated with contempt — an economical kind of treatment very much in keeping with his native meanness. In fact he quite lost the use of his legs, and he had to be carried home from the railway station.

The newspapers, of course, announced his arrival. The reporters of the *Staats Zeitung,* who were favourable to his chance, called on him. But seeing him in such a state, they had to abandon him to his ill-luck, and the agencies found no more takers, not even at seven to one.

But all the time they reckoned without Kate Titbury, that masterful woman, and she let them see it. It was not with indifference that she treated her husband's rheumatism, but with violence. Aided by her dragon of a servant, she rubbed him with such vigour as to leave hardly any skin on his legs. Never was horse or ass currycombed in this fashion. Needless to say, neither doctor nor druggist was called in, and perhaps the patient was no worse for it.

The delay lasted only four days. On the 23rd, arrangements were made to continue the journey. Several thousand paper dollars had to be drawn from the bank, and on the 24th, in the morning, husband and wife were off together, having all the necessary time to reach the Mormon capital.

The railroad runs direct from Chicago to Omaha; thence the Union Pacific goes off to Ogden, and under the name of the Southern Pacific continues to San Francisco. All things considered, it was fortunate that the Titburys had not been sent to California, which would have increased the journey by a thousand miles.

In the afternoon of the 28th they reached Ogden, an important station which a branch line puts in communication with Great Salt Lake City.

Then occurred a meeting — not between two trains, we hasten to say — but between two competitors, a meeting which had curious consequences.

In the afternoon, Max Real, returning from his visit to the National Park, had just entered Ogden. Thence he was going next day, the 29th, to Cheyenne to receive the result of his third throw of the dice. As he was walking along the platform of the railway station he found himself face to face with this Titbury in whose, company he had followed the funeral of William J. Hypperbone, and figured on the stage of the Auditorium during the reading of the will of the eccentric deceased.

The couple had again resolved to travel under a fictitious name. They would not again expose themselves to the inconveniences of which they had been the victims at Calais. They could keep themselves incognito during the journey and enter themselves under their real name at the hotel in Great Salt Lake City. What was the use of revealing on the journey his position as the future heir of sixty millions? It would be enough to do that in the capital of Utah, and then if anyone tried to make use of the information, Mr. Titbury would know how to defend himself.

Judge, then, of the disagreeable surprise experienced by the blue flag when, in the hearing of a large number of people who had got out of the train, he heard himself addressed in this way by the violet flag:

"If I am not mistaken, it is Mr. Hermann Titbury, of Chicago, my competitor in the Hypperbone match, to whom I have the honour of speaking?"

The couple jumped back in unison. Visibly annoyed at being signalled out for public attention, Mr. Titbury turned back and did not appear to remember having ever seen the intruder, although he recognized him at once.

"I do not know, sir," he replied. "Are you addressing yourself to me?"

"Pardon," continued the young painter. "It is not possible for me to be mistaken. We were together at the famous funeral — at Chicago — Max Real — the first to start — ".

"Max Real?" said Mrs. Titbury, as if she heard the name for the first time. |

Max Real began to get impatient. "Come, sir," he said, "are you, or are you not, Mr. Hermann Titbury, of Chicago?"

"Sir," said the other sharply. "By what right do you permit yourself to catechize me?"

"That is how you take it," said Max Real. "You do not wish to be Mr. Titbury, one of the seven, sent first to Maine and then to Utah — be it so! That is your affair! As for me, I am Max Real, on my return from Kansas and Wyoming! And with that, good evening!"

Then, as the train was just starting for Cheyenne, he jumped on to one of the cars with Tommy, leaving the Titburys confused at the adventure, and cursing those good-for-nothings who call themselves artists.

At this moment a man who had been looking on at this little scene, not without evident interest, approached. This individual, who was fairly well dressed, was about forty years of age, and had a frank physiognomy which could not but inspire confidence even with the most suspicious.

"There," said he, with a. bow to Mrs. Titbury," we have an impertinent fellow who deserved to be punished for his insolence! And if I had not been afraid of interfering in what did not concern me — "

"I thank you, sir," replied Mr. Titbury, flattered at seeing so distinguished a man come to his defence.

"But," continued the man so distinguished, "is that really Max Real, your competitor?"

"Yes — I believe so — quite so," replied Mr. Titbury," although I scarcely know him."

"Well," added the traveller, "I wish him everything unpleasant for having spoken in so free and easy a way with such infinitely respectable people, and that you, sir, will beat him in this game — him and the others, be it understood!"

One would have had to be very churlish not to welcome the advances of a man of such politeness, and even such obsequiousness, a gentleman who was so much interested in the success of Mr. and Mrs. Titbury.

Who was this man? Mr. Robert Inglis, of Great Salt Lake City, who was returning there this very day — a commercial traveller on a large scale who knew the district thoroughly from having been everywhere about it for a number of years. After mentioning his name and occupation, he offered very politely to pilot the Titburys, and undertook to find a hotel that would suit them.

How could they refuse the services of Mr. Robert Inglis, who stated, in addition, that he had ventured a very heavy sum on the chances of the third partner? He took Mrs. Titbury's smaller luggage and put it in one of the cars of the train just leaving Ogden. Mr. Titbury was particularly pleased that Mr. Inglis had treated Max Real as the rascal deserved. And he could not help congratulating himself on meeting so pleasant a travelling companion to be his guide in the capital of Utah.

All was for the best. The travellers took their scats in the car, and never, it may be affirmed, did time pass more quickly for them than during this journey of about fifty miles.

Mr. Inglis was as interesting as he was inexhaustible. What appeared to please the excellent lady was that he was the forty-third child of a Mormon household, before, be it understood, polygamy had been forbidden by the decree of the President of the United States.

"Ah, my friends," he said in a voice that almost drew tears from Mrs. Titbury's eyes," if you had known Brigham Young, our venerated pope, with his hair in a tuft, his grey beard fringing his cheeks and his chin, his lynx eyes; and George Smith, cousin of the prophet and historian of the church; and Hunter, president of the bishops; and Orme Hyde, president of the twelve apostles; and Daniel Wells, second counsellor, and Eliza Snow, one of the spiritual wives of the pope — "

"Was she beautiful?" asked Mrs. Titbury.

"Abominably ugly, madame; but what is beauty in a woman?"

And she whom he addressed gave him a little smile of approval.

"What age now is the celebrated Brigham Young?" asked Mr. Titbury.

"None — for he is dead! But if he had lived he would be a hundred and two."

"And you, sir," asked Mrs. Titbury with a slight hesitation," are you married?"

"My dear madame! What is the use of being married now polygamy is forbidden! One wife is more difficult to manage than fifty!"

And Mr. Inglis laughed so gaily at his repartee that the couple joined in his hilarity.

The country crossed by the Ogden branch is flat and barren, of sand and clay mingled with salts which cover it with whitish efflorescence, as in the great desert to the west of the lake. It grows little but thyme, sage, rosemary, heaths and prodigious quantities of yellow sunflowers. Towards the east rise the distant and misty summits of the Wahsatch mountains.

It was half-past seven when the train stopped at Great Salt Lake City station.

A magnificent city, Robert Inglis had said, and assuredly he would not let his new friends leave it until they had seen it, a town of fifty thousand inhabitants — he exaggerated by five thousand — a magnificent town enclosed on the east by magnificent mountains, which the magnificent Jordan puts in communication with the magnificent Salt Lake; a town healthier than all others, with its houses, its cottages surrounded by masses of verdure, their orchards, their kitchen gardens planted with pears, plums, apricots, peaches, yielding the most beautiful fruit in the world! And bordering its streets, magnificent shops, built of stone and magnificent in aspect! And its public buildings, magnificent specimens of Mormon architecture, the magnificent presidency where once resided Brigham Young, the magnificent Mormon Temple, the magnificent Tabernacle, a marvel of carpentry, in which eight thousand faithful could find places!. And formerly what magnificent ceremonies, the pope and the apostles on a magnificent platform, around them the crowd of saints. Men, women, children — oh! what a number! — assisting at the reading of the bible written by the magnificent hand of Mormon himself! In short, everything was magnificent.

The truth is that Mr. Robert Inglis, for love of his native city, allowed himself a good deal of exaggeration. The town of Great Salt Lake City does not merit such praises. It is too large for its population, and if it possesses some natural beauties it has no artistic ones. The famous Tabernacle is but an enormous dish-cover placed flat on the ground.

In any case there could be no question of visiting Great Salt Lake City that evening. The most pressing thing was to choose a hotel, and as Mr. Titbury did not wish to pay an exorbitant price, his guide proposed one out of the town, the *Cheap Hotel* The very name was attractive to the couple, and reassuring; and leaving their portmanteau at the station, to be fetched if the *Cheap Hotel* proved suitable, he followed Mr. Inglis, who had offered to carry the bag and rug of the excellent and worthy dame.

They went down towards the lower quarters of the city, of which the Titburys could see nothing, as it was already nearly night; they reached the right bank of a river which Mr. Inglis said was Crescent River, and they walked for nearly three miles.

Perhaps the Titburys found the walk rather long; but they thought that the hotel would be cheaper the farther it was from the town and did not complain.

At last about half-past eight, amid complete darkness, the sky being overcast, the travellers arrived in front of a house of the appearance of which they were unable to judge, A few minutes later, the hotel-keeper — a fellow of somewhat savage mien, it must be confessed — ushered them into a whitewashed room on the ground floor, furnished with a bed, a table and two chairs. That would do for them, and they thanked Mr. Inglis, who took his departure, promising to return next morning.

Very tired, Mr. and Mrs. Titbury, after sharing a few provisions that remained in the bag, went to bed. And soon asleep side by side, they dreamt that the prognostics of this obliging Mr. Inglis had come true, and that the approaching throw of the dice had put them on twenty squares.

They awoke at eight o'clock, having passed a good, restful night. They rose leisurely, having nothing to do but to wait for their guide to visit the town with him. It was not that they were inquisitive by nature — oh, no! — but how could they refuse the offers of Mr. Robert Inglis, who wished to show them the marvels of the great Mormon city?

At nine o'clock, nobody. Mr. and Mrs. Titbury, dressed, ready to go out, looked out of the window on to the main road before the *Cheap Hotel*.

This road, their obliging cicerone had told them the evening before, was the old Emigrants' Road. It ran along by Crescent River. There formerly went the waggons laden with merchandise for the camps of the pioneers when it took many months to go from New York to the western territories.

The *Cheap Hotel* stood evidently by itself, for by leaning out of the window Mr. Titbury could see no house on either bank of the river. Nothing but the sombre masses of a pine forest that rose in terraces on the flanks of a high mountain.

At ten o'clock, still nobody. Mr. and Mrs. Titbury began to get impatient and hungry.

"Let us go out," said one.

"Let us go out," said the other.

And opening the door of their room, they entered a central room, the bar of a roadside inn, with the door opening on to the road.

There on the threshold were two men, shabbily dressed, of doubtful aspect, drunken-eyed, who seemed to be guarding the door.

"You cannot pass!"

Such was the injunction conveyed in a rough voice to Mr. Titbury.

"What do you mean by 'you cannot pass'?"

"Not — without paying."

"Paying?"

This word was evidently, in all the English language, that which pleased Mr. Titbury the least when it was addressed to him.

"Paying?" he repeated. "Paying to go out? It is a joke."

But Mrs. Titbury, suddenly seized with anxiety, did not take matters in that way, and asked:

"How much?"

"Three thousand dollars."

The voice she recognized. It was the voice of Robert Inglis, who appeared at the door of the hotel.

Mr. Titbury, however, less perspicacious than his wife, began to laugh.

"Eh!" he exclaimed. "There is our friend."

"In person," replied he.

"And always in a good humour — "

"Always."

"And really it is very funny, this claim for three thousand dollars."

"What you would have, my dear sir," answered Mr. Inglis," that is the price for a night at the *Cheap Hotel.*"

"You speak seriously?" asked Mrs. Titbury, turning pale.

"Quite seriously, madame."

Mr. Titbury, in a burst of anger, tried to rush through the doorway.

Two strong arms were laid heavily on his shoulders and he could not move.

This Robert Inglis was simply one of those rascals of whom there are so many in the distant parts of the Union always lying in wait for opportunities which are so frequent. More than once already many a traveller had been plundered by this pretended forty-third child of a Mormon marriage, aided by accomplices such as the two individuals of this wretched *Cheap Hotel* An abominable cut-throat, or rather cut-purse, put on a good scent by the questions of Max Real, he had offered his services to the Titburys, and having learnt from them that they had with them three thousand dollars — a most imprudent admission, it must be confessed — he had brought them to this isolated dram shop, where they would be entirely at his mercy.

Mr. Titbury understood, but too late.

"Sir," he said, "I understand that you will not let us go out just now. I have business in the town — "

"Not until the 2nd of June, the day when the telegram should come," said Mr. Inglis, with a smile," and this is only the 29th of May."

"Then do you intend to keep us here five days?"

"And even longer, and even much longer," replied the affable gentleman, "at least until you hand me over three thousand dollars in good notes on the Bank of Chicago."

"Wretch!"

"I am polite with you," observed Mr. Inglis; "will you be the same with me, Mr. Blue Flag?"

"But this money — it is all that I have."

"It will be easy for the rich Hermann Titbury to have as much sent to him from Chicago as he may require! His cash-box is well lined, this wealthy Hermann Titbury! Observe, my dear guest, that these three thousand dollars you have with you I could take out of your pocket. But, by Jonathan! we are not thieves. It is merely the amount of the *Cheap Hotel* bill, and you would do well to settle it"

"Never."

"As you please."

At this the door was shut, and the Titburys remained imprisoned in the low room.

And then what recriminations on this accursed journey, on the tribulations, to say nothing of the dangers, that had fallen on the travelling pair! After the fine of Calais, the robbery of Great Salt Lake City! How unlucky to have encountered this bandit Inglis!

"We owe this to that rascal Real!" said Mr. Titbury. "We did not want our name to be known until we arrived, and the beggar shouted it out at Ogden all over the platform! And it happened that this brigand overheard it! What is to be done?"

"Sacrifice the three thousand dollars," said Mrs. Titbury.

"Never — never!"

"Hermann!" That was all that was said by the imperious and peevish woman.

But it must come to this dire extremity if Titbury remained obstinate, the scoundrels could compel him to do it. And if they wanted to seize his money, and then throw him into Crescent River, and his wife, after him, who was to bother about strangers whom nobody knew were in the town?

Yet Mr. Titbury resisted. Perhaps relief might come — a detachment of militia passing along the road, or at least some passersby he could call to his assistance. Vain hope! A minute afterwards both of them were put in a room with a window opening on to an interior court. The ferocious innkeeper brought some food. Decidedly for the price demanded it was not too much to be not only lodged but boarded at the *Cheap Hotel* Twenty-four, forty-eight hours went by in this way. The degree outrage reached by the prisoners we do not know. They had not even the opportunity of seeing Mr. Inglis, who kept away discreetly, no doubt, so as not to seem to exercise any pressure on his guests.

At last the 1st of June was inscribed on the calendars of the Union. Next day, before noon, the third player must appear in person at the post office in Great Salt Lake City. In default of his being present, he would lose all his rights to continue the game, which up to then had been so disastrous to him.

Well, no! Mr. Titbury would not give in — he would not give in. But, urged on by the delay, Mrs. Titbury intervened with rare vigour in the endeavour to impose her will upon him. Supposing Mr. Titbury had by the caprice of the teetotum been sent to the inn, to the labyrinth, to the prison, would he not have paid the fines, double or treble? Would he have hesitated to do so? No. Yet it was just as obligatory under the present circumstances, for if it is well to keep money, it is still better to keep alive, and their existence was in the hands of these rascals. So — he must pay.

Mr. Titbury resisted for seven hours in the hope of a providential succour that never came.

Exactly at half past seven Mr. Inglis came in, as amiable and polite as ever.

"To-morrow is the great day," said he. "It will be better, my dear guest, for you to go this evening to Great Salt Lake City."

"And who is hindering me but you?" said Mr. Titbury, almost choking with rage.

"Me?" replied Mr. Inglis, always smiling. "But all you have to do is pay your bill."

"There it is," said Mrs. Titbury, handing Mr. Inglis the bundle of bank notes.

Mr. Titbury nearly died when he saw this scoundrel take the bundle and count the notes. And he could make no answer when the brigand added:

It is useless for you to give me a receipt for this money — is it not so? But have no fear; I will put it to your account, my dear guest. And now it remains to me to wish you, with a sympathetic good evening, a good chance of gaining the millions of the Hypperbone match!"

The door was opened, and without hearing any more the couple rushed outside.

It was nearly night and the place was difficult to identify. How then could they inform the police of the scene of this tragi-comedy? The urgent matter was to regain Great Salt City, the lights of which they could see three miles away up Crescent River. And an hour afterwards Mr. and Mrs. Titbury reached the *New Sion,* where they went into the first hotel they came to. It could not cost them more than the *Cheap Hotel.*

Next morning, the 2nd of June, Mr. Titbury went to the sheriffs offices, so as to lay his complaint and ask for the police to be sent in search of Mr. Robert Inglis. Perhaps there might still be time for him to recover his three thousand dollars.

The sheriff — a most intelligent magistrate — listened with great interest to what the robbed had to say about the robber. Unfortunately Mr. Titbury could give but vague information regarding the whereabouts of the hotel. He had been taken there in the evening; he had left there in the evening. When he mentioned *Cheap Hotel*, on the banks of the Crescent River, the sheriff replied that he knew of no hotel of that name and that there was no Crescent River in the district. It would thus be difficult to lay hands on the thief, who, besides, had probably tied with his accomplices. As to sending a brigade of detectives after him in this country of woods and mountains, it would end in nothing.

"You say, Mr. Titbury," asked the sheriff, "that this man calls himself — "

"Inglis — the scoundrel — Robert Inglis — "

"Yes — that is the name he gave you! But now I think of it I have no doubt he is the famous Bill Arrol. I recognize his style of workmanship. This is not the first time."

"And you have not yet arrested him?" exclaimed Mr. Titbury furiously.

"Not yet," replied the sheriff, "we have only got as far as having him under observation. He will be taken some day — or another, and he will be electrocuted — if he is not hanged."

"But my money, sir, my money?"

"What would you have? We must apprehend this rascal, Bill Arrol, and that is not an easy thing. All I can promise you, Mr. Titbury, is to send you a piece of the rope, if he is hanged, and, supposing the game is not finished, you are sure to win with such a fetish!"

And that is all Mr. Titbury could get out of this original sheriff of the Mormon city.

CHAPTER XIX. THE GREEN FLAG

The green flag was that of Harris T. Kymbale, the flag that was assigned to the fourth player on account of the place this colour occupies in the solar spectrum. The reporter-in-chief of the *Tribune* was quite satisfied with it. Was it not the colour of hope?

It would have been in very bad taste for him to complain of the lot which had fallen to him as tourist and player. After having been, by the first throw of twelve, sent to New Mexico, his throw of ten, by four and six, had sent him to the twenty-second square, South Carolina, on the coast of the Union, and in particular to Charleston, its metropolis. He had from the 21st of May to the 4th of June to get to South Carolina, and as the journey could be done by railroad all the way after leaving Clifton Station, he had plenty of time to spare.

Harris T. Kymbale left Santa Fé, then, on the 21st, and this time he escaped with a handsome gratuity and had not to dazzle his driver's eyes with hundreds of thousands or even hundreds of dollars. He arrived in the evening at the station at Clifton, whence the iron road, after crossing the parallel which bounds Colorado on the south, took him to Denver, the capital of the said State.

"Here I am in one of the finest States of the Union, the Rocky Mountains to the west, to the east plains of marvellous fertility, a soil paved with lead, silver, and gold, across which petroleum flows in streams, a region to which flock emigrants attracted by the natural riches and idlers invited by the luxurious watering-places, the salubrity of its climate, the purity of its atmosphere! Then I do not know this superb country and I have an opportunity of knowing it. Can I hope the chance will bring me here in the course of the game? Nothing is less likely! On the other hand, to reach South Carolina, I have to cross three or four States I have already visited. They offer nothing new to me. The best I can do is to devote to Colorado all the time I have at my disposal, and that is what I will do. Provided I am at Charleston on the 4th of June, before noon, I do not see that my backers can reproach me. Besides, I can do as I please, and those who do not like it, &c., &c."

And that is why, instead of continuing his journey by the line which runs through Oakley, Topeka and Kansas, Harris T. Kymbale on the 21st made choice of a comfortable hotel in the capital of Colorado.

He spent but five days in the state — up to the evening of the 26th — but a reporter can do in a short time what no one else can do in double the time. It is a matter of professional training.

The afternoon of the 26th the green flag passed in the splendid capital. A reception took place in his honour at the residency. In the States, as we know, a man is valued according to his money value, and in the mind of the Coloradans Harris T. Kymbale was worth sixty millions of dollars. He beheld himself entertained, then, according to his merit by these ostentatious Americans, who have gold not only in their strong boxes, in their pockets, in their soil, but even in the names of their principal cities!

Next day, the 27th of May, the fourth player took his leave of the governor amid a great crowd of his supporters, who cheered him loudly. The train left Denver, reached the frontier at Fort Wallace, crossed Kansas from west to east, then Missouri by way of its capital, Jefferson City, and at its eastern frontier stopped at the railway station of St. Louis on the evening of the 28th.

It was not his intention to stay in this large town, which he already knew, and he hoped he would never be sent there by fate, for it was the city of the fifty-second square, and occupied the place of the prison in the Noble Game of Goose. And so he proposed to choose one of the best hotels at St. Louis to devote a night to the rest he required, and to start early in the morning by the first train.

It appeared as though nothing would hinder his journey or prevent his being at Charleston on the day named. And yet he might never have arrived, and might even never have been able to travel again, owing to an incident which no one could have foreseen.

About a quarter past seven he was walking along the platform of the railway station to ascertain when the train started, when suddenly he knocked up against, or was knocked up against by, an individual hurrying out of one of the offices.

Immediately these amenities were exchanged: —

"Booby!"

"Brute!"

"Why don't you look where you are going?"

"Why don't you!"

The words came like revolver bullets, for the men were both of them quick-tempered and irritable.

One of them was so in the highest degree, and you will not be surprised to hear he was Hodge Urrican.

Harris T. Kymbale recognized his competitor.

"The commodore!" he exclaimed.

"The journalist!" was the reply, in a voice as if from the mouth of a gun.

It was indeed the commodore, without his faithful Turk this time, and it was better that Turk was not there to intervene in the affair that he might have pushed to extremes.

So Hodge Urrican had not only survived his shipwreck, but he had found an opportunity of leaving Key West? In what way? Anyhow his journey must have been rapidly accomplished, for he was still in Florida on the 25th. Quite a resurrection, assuredly, and after his landing at Key West in the state we know his competitors might have imagined that the match of the Seven would go on with only six!

But here was Hodge Urrican at St. Louis in flesh and bone, as his competitor could prove by the collision, but in a humour considerably worse than usual. That could be understood. Was he not on his way to California with the obligation to return to Chicago, so as to recommence the game after paying a triple fine?

However, Harris T. Kymbale, like a good fellow, endeavoured to say something pleasant.

"My compliments, Commodore Urrican, for I see you are not dead."

"No, sir, not even after this blow from a clumsy fool, and quite capable of burying those who would doubtless be glad at never seeing me again."

"Do you say that to me?" asked the reporter with a frown.

"Yes, sir," replied Hodge Urrican, looking straight into his eyes; "yes, Mr. Favourite!"

And he seemed to chew the word, to grind it between his teeth.

Harris T. Kymbale, who was never particularly patient, began to get warm, and replied:

"It does not seem to improve your politeness to have to go to California to return to Chicago — "

This was touching the commodore in a sensitive place.

"You insult me, sir!" he exclaimed.

"You can take it as you please!"

"Well, I take it as an insult, and you shall give me satisfaction for it!"

"This very moment, if you like!"

"Yes — if I had the time," yelled Hodge Urrican." but I cannot"££

"Then take it."

"What I am going to take is this train, which is off, and which I must not miss."

The train was whistling, and in a cloud of smoke began to move. Not a second to lose. The commodore jumped on to the gangway between two of the cars, and roared out in a terrible voice:

"Mr. Journalist, you shall hear from me — you shall hear — "

"When?"

"This very evening — at the European Hotel."

"I will be there," said Harris T. Kymbale.

But the train had hardly gone when he made this reflection:

"Good! That is where he makes a mistake, the animal! That is not the Omaha train he has got into! He has gone the wrong way! After all, that is his affair."

And in fact the train in question was going east, the way Harris T. Kymbale would go to reach Charleston.

But Hodge Urrican had made no mistake. He was returning to the next station, to Herculaneum, where Turk was waiting for him. His bag had been left behind, and a lively scene had occurred between the commodore and the station-master at Herculaneum — a discussion in which Turk threatened to introduce the said station-master, all alive oh! into the furnace of one of the locomotives. His master had quieted him down, and, taking advantage of a train that was just starting, had gone off to claim the bag at St. Louis. The matter was arranged without difficulty, the bag would be telegraphed for; and it was just as Hodge Urrican was coming out of the office to return to Herculaneum that he had come into contact with the reporter.

Having seen his adversary depart, Harris T. Kymbale thought no more of the incident. He went back to the European Hotel, which happened to be the one at which he had put up. After dinner he took a long walk through the town, and as he entered the hotel on his return a letter was given him which had come from Herculaneum by the last train.

It could only have been a brain of the chemical composition of that which fermented beneath the cranium of Hodge Urrican that would have written such a letter as this from this astonishing man: —

"mr. fourth competitor, — Doubtless you have a revolver, as I have. To-morrow morning at seven o'clock I take the train leaving Herculaneum for St. Louis. I request that you will take the train leaving St. Louis for Herculaneum at the same time. This will make no change in your road or in mine. These two trains will pass each other at seventeen minutes past seven. If you are not a man who knocks up against people and then insults them without giving them satisfaction, you can be, at that precise moment, alone, on the gangway behind the last car which precedes the luggage van, as I shall be on the gangway of the last car of my train. There will then be an opportunity of exchanging a few bullets.

"hodge urrican, *Commodore.*"

There you have the man, always terrible, who had said nothing to Turk about this quarrel, nor of this challenge, for fear of making things worse.

But to find an adversary worthy of him, he could not have done better than to write to the reporter of the *Tribune,* who at once rose to the occasion.

"Well!" he exclaimed, "if this salt-water sailor imagines I am going to retreat, he is mistaken! I shall be on the gangway at the time named, seeing that he will be on his! And the Green Flag of a journalist will not strike to the Orange Flag of a commodore!"

And it may be observed that in all this there would be nothing astonishing in this astonishing country of America.

Next morning, a little before seven o'clock, Harris T. Kymbale went to the railway station to catch the train to Columbus, on the borders of Tennessee, which passes through Herculaneum. Taking his place in the last car, which communicates by a gangway with the luggage van, he sat down. Seventeen minutes were to elapse before he had to occupy his fighting post.

The weather was chilly, the wind searching, and evidently no one would be tempted to stay outside while the train was in motion. The car in which he sat had only about a dozen people in it.

When the reporter consulted his watch for the first time it was five minutes past seven. He had only twelve minutes to wait, and he waited with a calm probably much greater than that of his adversary.

At fourteen minutes past seven, he rose, went out on to the gangway, drew the revolver from his trousers pocket, examined it to see that it was fully charged, and waited.

At sixteen minutes past seven an increasing roar was heard on the other line by which the train from Herculaneum was coming towards him at full speed.

Harris T. Kymbale held up the revolver level with his eye, ready to lower it.

The engines crossed each other, leaving behind them a volume of white vapour.

Half a second afterwards two detonations were heard simultaneously.

Harris T. Kymbale felt the wind of a bullet against his cheek, to which he replied, shot for shot.

Then the trains lost each other in the distance.

It need not be supposed that on hearing these two shots the travellers in the car were in any way disturbed. No! There was nothing in it to trouble them. And so Harris T. Kymbale returned tranquilly to his seat without knowing if the commodore had been hit on the wing.

And then the journey continued by Nashville, the capital of Tennessee, on the Cumberland River, a commercial and industrial city of 66,000 inhabitants, by Chattanooga — a name which in Cherokee signifies Crow's Nest — a nest of the first order at the entrance of the passes through which Sherman took the Federal army. Then the route continued through the State of Georgia, the position of which has led to its being called the "Keystone State of the South," as Pennsylvania is known as the "Keystone State of the North."

Since the War of Secession, Atlanta has become the capital of Georgia, in memory of its long resistance. Situated at a height of nine hundred feet on the border of the practicable gorges of the Appalachians, this town in increasing prosperity is the most populous in the State.

After crossing Georgia to the town of Augusta, on the river Savannah, in which are many cotton mills, the line ran through South Carolina by Hamburg, which is opposite Augusta, and continued to its terminus at Charleston.

It was on the 2nd of June, in the evening, that the reporter reached this famous town, after a journey of about 1500 miles from Santé Fé, in New Mexico.

Then he read in the newspapers of the arrival of the two inseparables, the commodore and Turk, at Ogden on the 31st of May, travelling express towards the distant regions of California.

"Well," said he, "all is for the best. I am not sorry I missed him. He may be a bear, and even a sea-bear, but he is a bear in human shape all the same."

The newspapers made no allusion to the duel on the railway, which was known only to those who took part in it, and would never be known unless one of the two spoke.

without a guide. There exists no more complicated labyrinth except those of Lemnos or Crete.

By a wide corridor the tourists attained one of the most spacious caverns, to which has been given the name of the Gothic Church.

Gothic? Is it really the ogival style which characterizes the architecture? It matters little. It is marvellous, with the stalactites from the vault above, the stalagmites below, the columns fantastically moulded, the shapes taken by the terraced rocks with the crystal concretions the light puts in relief, here an altar heaped with liturgical ornaments, there an organ with the pipes rising to the ribs of the arches, there a balcony, or rather a chair from which preachers of eminence have more than once addressed congregations of five or six thousand people.

Needless to say, the party of excursionists shared in the amazement of Jovita Foley.

"See, Lizzie, do you regret the journey?"

"No, Jovita, it is very beautiful."

"But it is all the work of nature, the hand of man did not make these caves, and we are right down underground!"

"And I am afraid," said Lizzie Wag, "at the thought we might get lost — "

"And here we should be in the Mammoth Caves and miss the telegram from good Mr. Tornbrock."

They had already come a mile and a half from the entrance to reach the Gothic Church. Continuing the exploration, they found it many times necessary to stoop, to crawl even along narrow tunnels to reach the Hall of Apparitions. But there, to Jovita Foley's disappointment, appeared none of the phantoms her imagination dreamt of evoking in these subterranean caverns.

In reality the Hall of Apparitions is a halting-place, lighted by torches, in which is a well-furnished bar where luncheon is served by the staff of the Mammoth Hotel.

The hall ought to be called the Sanatorium, for to it come the invalids who ascribe some therapeutic virtue to the atmosphere of the caves. They had come here for the day to the number of twenty, and had installed themselves in front of a gigantic skeleton of a mastodon from which the caves derive their name of Mammoth.

Hereabouts ended the first visit, to be followed by many others, the extreme point reached being a little chapel like a small edition of the Gothic Church. It contains an unfathomable abyss, into which the guides throw burning papers to light its gloomy depths. This is the Bottomless Pit, in the wall of which is the Devil's Chair, to which more than one legend is attached.

After this fatiguing day the tourists were glad to enter the gallery that led them back to the entrance, in preference to another outlet by the dome of Ammath, nearer the hotel, but which could only be reached by going a long way round.

An excellent dinner and a long night's rest gave the two friends the strength necessary to resume their explorations next day.

One would generously pay with fatigue to traverse these marvellous caves — a walk through the enchanted world of the Arabian Nights — even without meeting with demons or gnomes, and Jovita Foley was only too pleased to admit that the spectacle exceeded the limits of human imagination.

For five days this energetic person, exhibiting an endurance exceeding that of most of the other excursionists and of the guides themselves, imposed on herself the task of exploring all that was known of these famous caves, and regretted being unable to launch on the unknown. But what she did her friend was incapable of doing, and Lizzie Wag had to ask for mercy after the third day. Do not forget that she had recently been very ill, and that it would never do for her to be unable to continue the journey. And so Jovita Foley was not accompanied by Lizzie Wag during her last excursions.

In this way she visited the cave of the Giant Dome, which rises to a height of four hundred and fifty feet; the Starry Chamber, the walls of which seem encrusted with diamonds and other precious stones glittering in the light of the torches; Cleveland Avenue, carpeted with lace and mineral flowers; the Ball Room, with its walls as white as snow furrowed with creamy leakages; the Rocky Mountains, great masses of blocks and lofty peaks, as if the chains of Utah and Colorado extended their branches into the interior of the globe; the Fairies' Grotto, so rich in sedimentary formations, maintained by subterranean springs, with arches, pillars, even a sort, of gigantic tree, a palm in stone which rises to the cupola of this hall situated some twelve miles from the principal entrance to the Mammoth Caves.

And what remembrances must the indefatigable visitor have had of the occasion when, entering the doorway of the dome of Goran, she embarked in a boat on the Styx, which, like the Jordan, flows into the Dead Sea. But if it is true that no fish can live in the waters of the biblical river, it is not true of this large subterranean lake. In myriads you find the siredons and cypronidons whose optical apparatus is completely atrophied, as in the eyeless species of some of the Mexican waters.

Such are the incomparable wonders of these caves, which have only given up a part of their secrets. We know not what they may have in reserve, and some day may we not discover quite an extraordinary world in the bowels of the terrestrial globe?

The last hours were striking of the five days that Jovita Foley and her companion had to stay at Mammoth Caves. It was on the 6th of June that the message was to come to the office of the hotel. Owing to the interest taken by this gathering of tourists in the fifth player, the morning of the day before was spent in feverish expectation — an impatience which Lizzie Wag was perhaps the only one not to feel.

That evening the toasts were given with more enthusiasm than ever at the dinner. And how the people cheered when John Hamilton, following the rule adopted by governors in admitting ladies to their staffs, conferred on Lizzie Wag the rank of colonel, and on Jovita Foley that of Lieutenant-colonel in the Illinois Militia.

If one of the new officers, always modest, felt herself rather embarrassed by so many honours, the other welcomed them as if she had always worn the uniform. And that night when they had both retired to their room:

"Well!" said Jovita, making the military salute, "have you had enough of it, colonel?"

"It is pure folly!" replied Lizzie Wag, "and it will end badly, I am afraid — "

"Will you be silent, my dear? or I shall forget that you are my superior officer, and may fail to treat you with respect."

And thereupon, with a good kiss, she went to bed, and was soon dreaming she had been made a general.

From eight o'clock onwards next morning the people in the hotel crowded round the office, waiting for the message sent from Chicago by Tornbrock.

It would not be easy to depict the emotion of the sympathetic throng that surrounded the two friends. Whither was fate sending them? Were they going to the end of America? Would they go a long way ahead of their competitors?

Half an hour afterwards the bell began to ring.

A message was arriving for Lizzie Wag, Mammoth Hotel, Mammoth Caves, Kentucky.

A profound — it might almost be said a religious — silence reigned around the office.

And what was the stupefaction, the disappointment, the despair even when Jovita Foley read in a trembling voice:

"Fourteen by seven doubled, fifty-second square, St. Louis, State of Missouri. — tornbrock."

It was the square of the prison, where, after paying a triple fine, the unfortunate Lizzie Wag would have to remain until some no less unfortunate competitor came to deliver her by taking her place.

CHAPTER XXI . DEATH VALLEY

On the 1st of June, in the morning, coming out of a little Californian town situated in the ancient lacustrine basin of the San Joaquin, a train was running at high speed towards the south-west.

The train, which consisted only of an engine, a car and a van, was not mentioned in the time-table, and had started three good hours before that which traverses the southern regions of California from Sacramento to the frontier of Arizona.

The country through which the special train was running did not seem to attract the notice of the passengers. But were there any? Yes, assuredly, for from time to time two heads would appear at the windows and then disappear immediately, two bearded faces, which might almost be called ferocious. Several times the window was lowered, and a large hairy hand passed out, holding a short pipe from which it shook the ashes, and was instantly drawn in again.

Who, then, were these indifferent travellers? Whence came they, whither went they? Were they ardent Californians suddenly called out by the discovery of new pockets of gold? were they seekers of new placers? For there is always ground for hope that the six milliards of francs extracted during forty years have not exhausted all the deposits of this auriferous soil. And it contains other valuable mines, particularly in the vicinity of the coast range, mines of cinnabar, red sulphide of mercury, native vermilion, which in the workings at New Almaden between 1850 and 1886 are said to have yielded about a hundred thousand tons.

These passengers may perhaps be originators of "bonanza farms," members of some great syndicate for agricultural development, people formidable to the small farmers by the abundance of capital provided them by England. And why should not money be attracted there, where the vine yields grapes that weigh several pounds, and the pear-tree pears that measure a foot and a half in circumference?

Anyhow, these people ought to be very rich and very much pressed for time, for they are indulging in the luxury of a special train, although they had at their disposal the ordinary trains of the Southern Pacific. These would have cost them but half a day's delay, and not the several thousand dollars they have not cared to save.

It was eleven o'clock in the morning when the engine began to slow a quarter of a mile before it reached the station at Keeler, where it was going to stop.

Two men jumped out on to the platform with luggage reduced to the absolutely necessary, a portmanteau and a basket of provisions which did not seem to have been opened. Each of them carried a hand-bag and had a carbine slung over his shoulders.

One of the men went along to the engine and said to the driver, "Wait," as if he were a coachman and they had left a carriage to pay a visit.

The driver gave an affirmative gesture, and prepared to shunt into the siding so as to leave the main road clear.

The traveller, followed by his companion, went to the exit from the station and found there an individual who was awaiting his arrival.

"Is the carriage here?" he asked shortly.

"Since yesterday."

"Ready?"

"Ready."

"Let us start."

A minute afterwards the two travellers were installed in a comfortable motor-car, driven by powerful mechanism, and were running rapidly in an easterly direction.

The travellers were Commodore Urrican and his faithful Turk, who had had no occasion to abandon themselves to their natural irascibility, the engine-driver having been punctual to the minute and the motor-car being at its post.

And now by what miracle had Hodge Urrican, half dead in the post office of Key West on the 25th of May, reappeared eight days afterwards in this little Californian town nearly 1500 miles from Florida? Under what really exceptional circumstances had he made such a journey in such limited time? How had the sixth player, pursued by such terrible ill luck, who seemed to be in no condition to continue the game, managed to get here, more resolute than ever to play it out to the end?

Shipwrecked on the *Chicola,* he had been taken without recovering consciousness to the telegraph office of Key West. The telegram sent that morning from Chicago had arrived at noon precisely. And what a deplorable result it announced. A most miserable throw — five by two and three.

By this throw the commodore was moved from the fifty-third square to the fifty-eighth, from Florida to California, the whole width of the Union to cross from south-east to north-west! And, circumstance still more disastrous, it was the square of Death which had been chosen by William J. Hypperbone, it was Death Valley to which the player had to come and pay a triple fine and then return to Chicago! And that after beginning so well!

When Hodge Urrican had been recalled to life by energetic frictions and no less energetic potions, and had been informed of the contents of the telegram, he received a shock which ended in the most terrible fit of anger that Turk had ever seen. That put him on his feet.

Fortunately for the people present, there was no one with whom the commodore could quarrel, and Turk had not, according to custom, to exceed him in violence.

Hodge Urrican uttered but one word, one only, one of those words which from their appropriateness acquire a historic value.

"Start!"

A glacial silence greeted the word. Turk had to tell his master where he was and how he was there. For the first time Hodge Urrican learnt of the shipwreck of the schooner, the transport of the passengers and crew to Key West, where no ship could be found to take them to one of the ports of Alabama or Louisiana.

The commodore was nailed like Prometheus to his rock, and his heart was to be devoured by the vulture of impatience.

He had a fortnight to travel from Florida to California and from California to Illinois. Decidedly the word "impossible" is in all languages, even in the American, although it is generally reported to have been erased from the dictionary by the audacious Yankees.

In thinking of the consequences of losing the game by being unable to leave Key West that very day, Hodge Urrican indulged in a second crisis, with vociferations, imprecations and threats that made the very windows shiver. But Turk succeeded in mastering it by betaking himself to such deeds of fury that his master had to quiet him.

Yet it was a cruel necessity and a cruel wound to a competitor's self-respect to have to retire from the contest and lower the Orange Flag before the Violet, Indigo, Blue, Green, Yellow and Red.

Well, as we know, there is nothing but good luck and bad luck in this world! The good chances and the bad chances rustle against each other all through life, and sometimes succeed each other with electric rapidity. And in this way, by really providential intervention, the situation, desperate as it appeared, was saved.

At thirty-seven minutes past twelve the harbour semaphore of Key West signalled a vessel five miles out at sea.

The crowd of spectators assembled before the telegraph office ran off, Hodge Urrican and Turk at their head, to the high ground where the view embraced the open sea.

A ship was seen in the distance with her smoke drifting along the horizon in long dark clouds. And those interested said: "Is that ship coming to Key West?"

"And if she comes, will she put in, or start again this very day?"

"And if she sails again, will it be for a port in Alabama, Mississippi or Louisiana, New Orleans, Mobile, Pensacola?"

"And if her destination is one of those ports, is her speed sufficient to take her there in two days?"

Here, as will be seen, were four indispensable conditions to fulfil.

They were all fulfilled. The *President Grant* was to stop at Key West but a few hours; she was to start that very evening for Mobile; and she was a steamer of great speed, being one of the fastest in the American mercantile marine.

Needless to add that Hodge Urrican and Turk were received as passengers, that Captain Humper was as much interested in the commodore as the captain of the *Sherman* in Tom Crabbe; and that on a favouring sea with a light breeze from the north-east, the *President Grant,* at her maximum speed of twenty miles an hour, arrived at Mobile in the night of the 27th.

The passage money being generously paid, Hodge Urrican and Turk jumped into the first train, which in twenty hours covered the seven hundred miles between Mobile and St. Louis.

There occurred the incidents we know — the difficulty with the station-master at Herculaneum, the necessity for Hodge Urrican to go to St. Louis to claim his portmanteau, the meeting with Harris T. Kymbale, the return to Herculaneum, the challenge sent to the reporter, the revolver shots exchanged as the trains crossed, the arrival at St. Louis. Thence the railway took the commodore to Topeka on the 30th, thence by the Union Pacific to Ogden on the 31st, thence to Reno, whence he started at seven o'clock in the morning for Keeler.

But when the commodore was at Keeler he was not at Death Valley, the point he had to reach in the State of California.

Now if there was a more or less practicable carriage road between Keeler and Death Valley, there was no service of vehicles. No relays of horses, no stage-coaches. Could it be done on horseback in so short a time, nearly four hundred miles there and back? Considering the windings of the road in so hilly a country, it would have been impossible.

When at St. Louis, Hodge Urrican had the excellent idea of telegraphing to Sacramento if they could supply him with a motor-car and send it to Keeler to await his arrival.

The reply was in the affirmative. The motor-car was at Keeler station waiting for Commodore Urrican. Two days would suffice to reach Death Valley, two days to return, and in this way he could be at Chicago before the 8th of June. Decidedly fortune favoured this old sea-wolf.

An excellent vehicle, this motor-car from Sacramento, designed on the Adamson principle, which is most generally adopted in America. It was worked by petroleum, and could carry enough fuel for a week. The commodore and Turk were seated in a sort of comfortable coupe, the driver in front with an assistant. This time the commodore remained wrapped up in himself, and Turk could not get a word from him. He thought of nothing but the object to be obtained, hypnotized by this sixty-third square, now so distant, which he had approached so closely. He did not trouble about the money it would cost him, the expense of the special train, the hire of the motor-car, to say nothing of the triple fine, the three thousand dollars he would have to pay before beginning the game again. No! it was a question of self-respect and honour; it was the shame, yes! the shame of seeing himself distanced by six others and — it must be confessed — the fear of losing Hypperbone's heritage.

The motor-car ran swiftly and easily along the road, which the driver knew, having been to Death Valley along it before. It passed several villages isolated beyond the ancient ramifications of the Sierra Nevada, dominated by Mount Whitney, whose summit rises nearly fourteen thousand feet in the air.

Passing several creeks at the fords, the motor-car turned off towards the south-east, crossing the river Chayopoovapah to the village of Indian Wells at the outlet of the passes of the Walker.

Up to there the country was not absolutely deserted. The farms were a long way apart, it is true. Occasionally they met labourers going from one to the other, and a few groups of Indians, who were the former owners of the district. And these people, who appear astonished at nothing, regarded without surprise the vehicle they probably saw for the first time. The ground was not yet bare of vegetation; there were still a few bushes and clumps of yuccas and giant cactuses, some of them four-and-twenty feet high. It was not the famous district of Calaveras or Mariposa with its phenomenal trees, the "Father of the Forest" and the "Mother of the Forest," giants of a height exceeding three hundred feet.

And if, instead of being sent to Death Valley, Hodge Urrican had gone to the Yosemite Valley in the central part of the Sierra Nevada, or rather if Max Real had had the good fortune to go there, what souvenirs he would have retained — even after the National Park of Wyoming — of those natural beauties with their significant designations, the "Grand Falls" of six hundred feet, the "Vernal Fall,"

"Mirror Lake," the "Royal Arches," the "Cathedral' "Washington's Column," so much admired by thousands of tourists.

At last the motor-car reached the desert at the end of which the depressions of Death Valley have been formed. There, nothing but an immense solitude. Men and animals do not frequent it. A burning sun falls on its extensive plains. Scarcely is there a trace of vegetable life. Neither horses nor mules can feed there, and it was fortunate that the motor-car had no want of petroleum vapours to drive it. Here and there only a few foothills, mere hillocks of moderate height, surrounded by chapparals, which are thickets of half-starved shrubs. To the fierce heat of the day succeed the Californian nights, dry and cold, whose rigours the dew never comes to soften.

It was thus that on the 3rd of June Commodore Urrican reached the southern extremity of Telescope Range, which bounds Death Valley on the west.

It was three o'clock in the afternoon. The journey had taken fifty hours, without rest and without accident.

This desolate country, with its clayey soil covered in places with saline efflorescences, is appropriately named the land of Death. The valley, which terminates almost on the boundary of Nevada, is really a canyon nineteen miles wide and twenty long, pierced with abysses that go down to a hundred and eighty feet below the level of the sea. On its borders are a few under-sized poplars, willows of sickly paleness, yuccas dry and like sharp bayonets, stinking mugworts, and many tufts of that cactus known in California as petalinas, without leaves, all in branches, regular funereal candelabra placed on the field of death.

Death Valley was evidently at an earlier geological period the bed of a river which is lost to-day in Soda Lake and is now only watered by the creek of the Amargosa. Its declivities bristle with needles of salt, borax accumulates in its cavities, and a few sand-hills mingle their sandy dust with the atmospheric currents that occasionally sweep through it with extreme violence.

Yes! The Valley of Death had been well chosen by the eccentric testator to receive the unhappy player pulled up in full career at the fifty-eighth square.

Commodore Urrican had then reached the end of his difficult journey. He halted at the foot of the east of the Funeral Mountains, so called in memory of the caravans that perished in these mournful regions. It was at this spot that he took the precaution of writing a document, recording his presence in Death Valley on the 3rd of June — a document that was put under a stone after being signed by Turk and the two motor-car men.

He stayed barely an hour on the threshold of the Valley. All he had to do was to leave the place as soon as possible and return to Keeler by the same road. Then, opening his mouth for the first time, he uttered but one word:

"Start!"

And the motor-car started, favoured all the time by the weather, across the upper region of the desert and down the passes of the Nevada, and without accident reached Keeler station two days afterwards, on the 5th of June, at eleven in the morning.

In three words, but three energetic words, Commodore Urrican thanked the driver and his companion who had showed such zeal and skill in the accomplishment of their fatiguing task; and turning to Turk: "Start!" he said.

The special train was in the station awaiting the commodore's return. Hodge Urrican went straight to the guard.

"Start!" he repeated.

And with a whistle the engine began to move on the rails, worked up quickly to its highest speed, and seven hours later reached Reno.

The Union Pacific behaved in the most correct fashion under the circumstances. The train crossed the Rocky Mountains, Wyoming, Nebraska, Iowa, Illinois, and reached Chicago on the 8th of June, at 9.37 a.m.

What a welcome was that which Commodore Urrican received from those who remained faithful to him in spite of all! And it seemed as though good luck returned to him with the throw of the dice that took place the very morning of his arrival in Chicago.

Nine by six and three, the third time the number had been scored since the match began — the first time by Lizzie Wag, the second by the unknown XKZ, the third time by the commodore.

And after having been sent to Florida, then to California, Hodge Urrican had but a step to take to reach the twenty-sixth square, the State of Wisconsin, which adjoins Illinois, and was not then occupied by any of the players.

CHAPTER XXII . THE HOUSE IN SOUTH HALSTED STREET

ON the 1st of June the door of No. 3997, South Halsted Street, Chicago, opened at eight o'clock in the morning to a young man carrying a painter's knapsack on his shoulder and followed by a young negro, bag in hand.

What was the surprise and also the joy of Madame Real when her dear son entered the room and she could clasp him in her arms.

"You, Max — what — is it you?"

"In person, mother."

"And you are at Chicago instead of being — "

"At Richmond?" said Max Real. "Be easy, mother, I have time to get to Richmond, and as Chicago was on my road, I thought I was entitled to stay a few days here and spend them with you."

"But, my dear boy, you are running the risk of a failure — "

"Well, I should not always fail to embrace you on my way dear mother! Think, for two long weeks I have not seen you!"

"Ah, Max, I am anxious for this game to end."

"And so am I."

"To your advantage, understand!"

"Do not be anxious. It is as if I already possessed the word, of the strong-box of this worthy Hypperbone," replied Max Real, laughing.

"Well, I am glad to see you, my dear son, very glad."

Max Real was at Cheyenne in Wyoming, when on the 29th of May he had returned from his excursion to the National Park of the Yellowstone and received the telegram referring to his third throw — eight by five and three. Now the eighth square after the twenty-eighth occupied by Wyoming was assigned to Illinois. The eight had consequently to be doubled, and the number sixteen took the young painter to the forty-fourth square, that of Virginia, Richmond City.

Between Chicago and Richmond there was a network of railways by which the distance between the two places could be run in twenty-four hours; and as Max Real had a fortnight — from the 29th of May to the 12th of June — he could, as they say, take things easy, and stay for a week with his mother.

Leaving Cheyenne in the afternoon, he was at Omaha two days afterwards, and at Chicago the next day in excellent health — in excellent health also the anti-abolitionist Tommy, always as much embarrassed at his position as a free citizen of free America as a poor fellow whose clothes are too large for him.

During his stay Max Real proposed to finish two of the pictures he had sketched in on the road — one a view of Kansas River near Fort Riley, the other a view of the cascades of the Fire Hole in the National Park. Being sure of selling these pictures at a good price, they would enable him to discharge his liabilities if ill-luck condemned him to pay many fines in the course of his travels.

Madame Real, enchanted to have her son with her for a few days, accepted all these reasons and once again pressed Max to her heart.

They talked and laughed, and made one of those good breakfasts which have so many charms with mother and son. Although he had written many times to Madame Real, he had to begin the story of his travels from the beginning, narrating the different incidents, the adventure of the thousands of horses wandering on the plains of Kansas, the meeting with the Titburys at Ogden. Then his mother told him of the lamentable tribulations of this couple at Calais in Maine, how in consequence of the law against alcoholic drinks Mr. Titbury had been prosecuted, and what were the pecuniary consequences.

"And now," asked Max Real, "how stands the game?"

To make it clearer to him, Madame Real took him to her room and showed him a board open on the table in which were stuck flags of different colours.

While running about the country Max Real had not thought much about his competitors, very seldom reading the newspapers at the hotels and railway stations. But he had only to look at this board and learn the colours and he could easily see how matters were. Besides, his mother had followed the vicissitudes of the Hypperbone match from the beginning.

"Who is the blue flag which is ahead?" he asked.

"That is Tom Crabbe, whom yesterday's throw sent to the forty-seventh square, Pennsylvania."

"That ought to please his trainer, John Milner! And this red flag?"

"That is the flag of XKZ on the forty-sixth square, District of Columbia."

In fact, owing to a throw of ten, doubled, that is twenty, the masked man had made a leap of twenty squares from Milwaukee, Wisconsin, to Washington, the capital of the United States — an easy and rapid journey in this part of the country where the railway network is so close.

"Do not they suspect who this unknown is?" asked Max Real.

"Not at all, my dear boy."

"I am sure he must figure well in the betting list and have big supporters."

"Yes. Many people believe in his chances, and I myself am rather afraid of them."

"That is the advantage of being a mysterious personage!" declared Max Real.

Was this XKZ at Chicago, or had he already left for the District of Columbia? Nobody could say. Washington, if it is only an administrative centre without industry, without commerce, is well worth spending a few days in; but if the last player had arrived there, no newspaper had as yet reported his presence.

"And this yellow flag?" asked Max Real, pointing to the one in the thirty-fifth square.

"That is Lizzie Wag's flag."

Yes, the flag was then floating on the Kentucky square, for at this date, the 1st of June, the fatal throw which sent her into prison in Missouri had not been made.

"Ah, the charming girl!" said Max Real. "I saw her all embarrassment and blushes at the funeral of William Hypperbone; then on the stage of the Auditorium! Of a certainty, if I had met her on the way I should have renewed my wishes for her final success."

"And yours, Max?"

"Mine also, mother! Both winning the game! We could share it! Eh? Would that be good enough?"

"Is it to be feared?"

"No, it is not to be feared, but such extraordinary things happen in this world — "

"You know, Max, that it was thought Lizzie Wag would not start?"

"Yes, the poor girl was ill, and there were more than one among the Seven who rejoiced at it! Oh, not I, mother! Luckily she had a friend who looked after her well and brought her through — this Jovita Foley — as resolute in her way as Commodore Urrican! And when is her next throw?"

"In five days, on the 6th of June."

"Let us hope that my pretty competitor will avoid the dangers of the road, the labyrinth of Nebraska, the prison of Missouri, the Californian Death Valley! I wish her luck with all my heart!"

Decidedly Max Real must sometimes think of Lizzie Wag — often even, and perhaps too often, said Madame Real to herself, rather surprised at the heat with which he spoke.

"Do you not ask, Max, who is the green flag?"

"That on the twenty-second square?"

"That is Mr. Kymbale's flag."

"A good fellow, that journalist," declared Max Real. "From what I hear he is taking advantage of the opportunity to see the country."

"Just so, my child, and the *Tribune* publishes his letters every day."

"Well, mother, his readers ought to be satisfied. If he goes to Oregon or Washington he will tell them curious tales."

"But he is rather behind."

"That is of little consequence in the game we are playing," answered Max Real; "a lucky throw may put you right in front."

"That is so, my son."

"Now whose flag is this in the fourth square?"

"Hermann Titbury's."

"Ah! The horrible man!" exclaimed Max Real. "Let him rage at being last — and a good last!"

"He is to be pitied, Max, really to be pitied, for he has only scored four in two throws, and after being sent to Maine has had to go all the way to Utah."

At this date, the 1st of June, it could not be known how the Titburys had been robbed of all they had after their arrival in Great Salt Lake City.

"And yet I do not pity them," declared Max Real. "No! A pair of misers are not at all interesting, and I am sorry they have not had a heavy fine to pay — "

"But do not forget he had to pay a fine at Calais," said Madame Real.

"So much the better. All I wish is that he may get the minimum of points, one and one! That will take him to Niagara, and the toll of the bridge will cost him a thousand dollars!"

"You are cruel on these Titburys, Max!"

"Abominable people, mother, who got rich on usury and deserve no pity. Fortune would make a mistake in making them Hypperbone's heirs — "

"Everything is possible," replied Madame Real.

"But, tell me. I do not see the flag of the famous Hodge Urrican."

"The orange flag? No, it is nowhere on the board, for bad luck sent the commodore to Death Valley, whence he has to come back to Chicago to begin the game again."

"Rather hard for a naval officer to have to strike his flag!" said Max. "What a storm of anger he must have got into, and how it must have made his hull shake from keel to truck!"

"That is probable."

"And when is the throw for XKZ?"

"In nine days."

"It was a curious idea of the dead man to conceal the name of this last of the Seven."

Max Real now knew the position of the game. After the dice had sent him to Virginia, he knew he occupied the third place, being behind Tom Crabbe and XKZ, for whom, it is true, the third throw had not yet been made.

This did not worry him much, although Madame Real and even Tommy thought a good deal about it. While he remained in Chicago he passed some of his time in his studio, where he finished the two landscapes, the value of which would be increased in the eyes of the American amateur by the conditions under which they had been painted.

It happened then that until his approaching departure Max Real thought very little about the match, and of those whom it was hurrying about over the United States. Really he was playing the part so as not to oppose his excellent mother — no less indifferent, in fact, than Lizzie Wag, who was only participating in the game so as not to annoy Jovita Foley.

Nevertheless during his stay he necessarily heard of the three throws that took place at the Auditorium. Hermann Titbury's was deplorable, as it took him to the nineteenth square, that is the State of Louisiana, where there was the inn in which he had to stay for two throws without playing. A throw of ten was welcomed by Harris T. Kymbale, as it was doubled by landing him in Illinois and thus took him to the forty-second square, Nebraska, whence he had to return to the thirtieth square, that occupied by the State of Washington.

At last on the 6th, at eight o'clock, Tornbrock proceeded to throw for Lizzie Wag, and that morning Max Real, who was much interested in the girl's fate, went to the Auditorium, whence he came back in deep dejection.

Deep was his vexation when on returning to his mother he saw her stick the yellow flag in the midst of this Missouri transformed into a prison — partly by the will of the eccentric defunct, and, for Lizzie Wag, by the will of destiny. He was much concerned, and did not hide it. This throw into the prison, like that into the well, was the worst that could happen during the game. Yes! more serious than that into the Valley of Death, of which Hodge Urrican had just been the victim! At least, the commodore experienced only a delay, and was able to continue the strife. Who could say if the match would not be finished before the prisoner was rescued?

Next day, June 7th, Max Real prepared to leave Chicago. His mother renewed her warnings, and made him promise not to delay on the road.

"Let us hope," said she, "that the telegram you are to get at Richmond will not send you to the end of the world."

"I will come back, mother, I will come back," replied Max. "Even from prison! Isn't it all very ridiculous? To be exposed like a common racehorse, to be defeated by half a length! Yes! Ridiculous!"

"No, my child, no! Go, and may Heaven protect you!"

And it was quite seriously, under the sway of sincere emotion, that the excellent dame said these things.

He promised his mother to go by the most direct line to Virginia. But provided he was at Richmond on the morning of the twelfth, who could blame him for preferring to take not a straight line, but a curved line or one with a break in it? However, he had resolved not to stray from the states he had to cross — Illinois, Ohio, Maryland, Western Virginia, Virginia — to get to Richmond.

Here is a letter received by Madame Real, dated the 11th of June, four days after his departure, which summarizes the incidents of his journey. To say nothing of the observations on the countries passed through, the towns visited, the meetings that occurred, it contains certain remarks that made her reflect and caused her some anxiety as to her son's state of mind.

"Richmond, Virginia, 11th June.

"My dear and good mother, — Here am I at the end, not of this brute of a game, but of the journey forced on me by the third throw of the dice. After Fort Riley, Kansas; after Cheyenne, Wyoming; now Richmond, Virginia. So have no apprehension for the being you cherish the most in this world, and who returns your love with all his heart. He is at his post in good health.

"I wish I could say the same of Lizzie Wag, whom a prison bed awaits in the great Missourian city. I don't hide from you, mother, that although I ought to see in her only a rival, she is so charming, so interesting that I am quite sorry for her unhappy fate! The more I think of that deplorable throw — seven by three and four, doubled — the more I regret that the yellow flag so valiantly borne up to now by the intrepid Jovita Foley on account of her friend should be hoisted on the wall of this prison! And until when will it be there?

"I left you on the 7th, in the morning. The railroad runs along the southern shore of Lake Michigan and affords several beautiful views over its waters. But, between ourselves, I know that lake a little, and also the country that bounds it. Besides, in this part of the United States, as in Canada, it is permitted to be a little wearied of lakes; their blue waters which are not always blue, their sleeping waters which do not always sleep!

"In part I followed the same road as Harris Kymbale when he went from Illinois to New York, from Chicago to Niagara. But on arriving at Cleveland City in Ohio, I left it to go south-east. There are railroads everywhere; a pedestrian would not know where to put his feet down.

"Do not ask me to tell you the times of my arrivals and departures during the journey. It would not interest you. I will indicate a few places where our locomotive blew off clouds of steam. In these industrial countries they are as plentiful as the cells in a beehive! But the chief ones only:

"From Cleveland I went to Warren, an important centre of Ohio, so rich in springs of petroleum that a blind man would recognize it, provided he had a nose, from its sickening atmosphere. The air would burst into flame if you lighted a match. And then what a country! On plains as far as you can see, nothing but scaffolds and pit-mouths, as also on the slopes of the hills, the borders of the creeks. Lamps all these, lamps from fifteen to twenty feet high. You only want a match.

"You see, mother, this country is not like our poetic prairies of the Far West, nor the wild valleys of Wyoming, nor the distant perspectives of the Rockies, nor the deep horizons of the great lakes and oceans. Industrial beauties are good, artistic beauties are better, natural beauties are best.

"Between ourselves, dear mother, I will confess that if I had been favoured at the last throw — favoured by the choice of country, be it understood — I would have taken you with me. Yes, Madame Real, to the Far West, for instance. It is not that there are not interesting spots in the Alleghanies' I have crossed — but Montana, Colorado, California, Oregon, by the word of a painter, it is not to be compared with them.

"Yes, we would have travelled together, and if we had met Lizzie Wag on the way, who knows — chance? Well, you would have made her acquaintance — It is true she is now in prison, at least is on her way there, poor girl!

"Ah! If at the next throw a Titbury, a Crabbe, an Urrican comes to deliver her. Our terrible commodore, you see, after so many trials falling on to the fifty-second square! He would be capable of abandoning his Turk to the ferocious instincts of the tiger!

"Once in a way a Lizzie Wag might be sent, although it would be regrettable, to the inn, to the labyrinth! But the well, the horrible well — the prison, the horrible prison — they are for representatives of the stronger sex. Decidedly destiny forgot to be gallant on that day!

"But let us leave off divagating and continue the journey. After Warren I followed the Ring River, crossed the frontier of Ohio, and was in Pennsylvania. The first important town was Pittsburg, on the Ohio, with its annexe of Alleghany, the Iron City, the Smoky City, as it is called, in spite of the thousand miles of subterranean conduits by which it delivers its natural gas. This is the place to get dirty! You get your hands and face black in a few minutes, hands and face like a negro's!

"I put on my window a little water in the bottom of a glass and next morning I had ink. With this chemical mixture, mother, I am writing to you now.

"I have just seen in a newspaper that Urrican's throw on the 8th sent the thundering commodore to Wisconsin. Unfortunately, if next throw he gets twelve, even if he doubles it he will not get to the fifty-second square, where the young prisoner is in distress.

"I continued to go south-east. I passed numerous stations on each side of the road — towns, villages — and through these districts not a corner of nature that had been left to itself! Everywhere the hand of man and his noisy tools. It is true that in Illinois it is the same, and Canada is not free from it. Some day the trees will be of metal, the prairies of felt, and the beaches of iron filings. That is progress.

"Yet I have had a few pleasant hours in running through the passes of the Alleghanies. A chain, picturesque, capricious, occasionally wild, covered with blackish coniferous trees, abrupt slopes, deep gorges, sinuous valleys, tumultuous torrents which, manufacturers have not yet utilized for works and which are still allowed to form cascades with their original freedom.

"Then we skirted the small corner of Maryland watered by the Upper Potomac, to reach Cumberland, more important than its capital, modest Annapolis, which is of little account compared with invading and imperious Baltimore, in which is centred all the commercial life of the state. It rests on a base of iron and coal, and in a few strokes of the pickaxe the vegetable soil is dug through.

"Now we are in West Virginia, and — do not get uneasy, mother — Virginia is not far off. I should have been there already if the question of slavery had not divided the old state, which had to be cut in two during the Secession War. Yes! while the east attached itself more strongly to the inhuman doctrines of slavery — Tommy is asleep, be it understood — the west, on the contrary, separated from the Confederates to range itself under the Federal flag.

"It is a hilly, if not mountainous, region furrowed in its eastern part by the different chains of the Appalachians, agricultural, mining, with iron, coal, and also salt for seasoning the cookery of the whole confederation for centuries.

"I did not go to Charleston, capital of West Virginia — not to be confounded with the other great Charleston of South Carolina, where my competitor Kymbale has gone, nor with a third Charlestown of which I am about to speak. But I stopped a day at Martinsburg, the most important city of West Virginia on the eastern side.

"Yes, a whole day; and do not growl at me, dear mother, for I could get to Richmond in a few hours by railroad. Why did I stop at Martinsburg? Solely to make a pilgrimage; and if I did not take Tommy with me, it was because he would only have held in horror the hero I went to honour.

"John Brown, dear mother, John Brown, who was the first to raise the anti-slavery flag at the outset of the war of Secession! The Virginian planters trapped him like a wild beast. He had but twenty men and endeavoured to seize the arsenal at Harper's Ferry. This name is that of a little town situated on the escarpment of a hill between the Potomac and Shenandoah, a marvellous position, but more celebrated for the terrible scenes of which it was the theatre.

"It was there in 1859 that the heroic defender of the great and holy cause had taken refuge. The militia attacked him there. After prodigies of courage, seriously wounded, he was taken prisoner, dragged to the neighbouring town of Charlestown and there hanged on the 2nd of December — a death which the gallows could not make infamous, and the glorious renown of which will be perpetuated from age to age.

"It was to this martyr of liberty, of human emancipation that I wished to tender my patriotic homage.

"Finally, here I am in Virginia, mother, pre-eminently the Slave state, which was the principal theatre of the War of Secession. Richmond is a fine city, the ex-capital of separatist America, the key of Virginia, which the Federal Government eventually pocketed. It occupies a site with seven hills on the bank of James River, and at the opposite bank stretches a hand to Manchester, a double town like so many others in the United States, after the example of certain stars. I repeat it is a city to be seen, with its capitol, a sort of Greek temple from which is absent the Attic sky and the Athenian horizons of the Acropolis as is the Parthenon at Edinburgh. But there are too many factories, too many works — to my taste at least, and there are at least a hundred manufacturing tobacco. In one of the fashionable districts, Leonard Height, stands the monument to Lee, the general of the Confederates, who deserves the honour, if not for the cause he defended, at least for his personal qualities.

"At present, dear mother, I have not visited the other towns in the state. They are, however, somewhat alike, as are all American towns. I have just read the result of the throw on the 10th of June. It is Minnesota which, with five by two and three, is assigned to our famous unknown XKZ. From the forty-sixth he jumps to the fifty-first square, and he is now ahead of us all. But who is this man? He seems to me to be singularly lucky, and it is not certain that my throw to-morrow will put me in front of him.

"With that, dear mother, I end this long letter, which cannot but interest you as it comes from your son, and I embrace you with all my heart in signing my name, which after all is only that of a racehorse on the Hypperbone turf.

"MAX REAL."

CHAPTER XXIII . A CHALLENGE AND ITS CONSEQUENCES

If anyone appeared less indicated by nature for the forty-seventh square, State of Pennsylvania, for Philadelphia, the chief city of the state, the most important city in the Union after Chicago and New York, it was assuredly this Tom Crabbe, brute by nature and boxer by trade. But instead of Max Real, Harris T. Kymbale, or Lizzie Wag, all capable of admiring the magnificence of this metropolis, it was that stupid being who had been sent there with his trainer. Never could the deceased member of the Eccentric Club have foreseen that.

It could not be helped, however. The dice had spoken in the early hours of the 31st of May. Twelve by six and six had been sent by wire from Chicago to Cincinnati, and the second player had to take measures for immediately leaving the ancient Porkopolis.

"Yes, Porkopolis!" exclaimed John Milner in a tone of the deepest contempt. "The day the celebrated Tom Crabbe was honouring it with his presence its population were going in crowds to that disgusting cattle show! To the pig the whole public attention was directed, and there was not a single cheer for the champion of the New World! Well, let us pocket Hypperbone's big bag and I will know how to be avenged!"

How to effect this vengeance John Milner would have been embarrassed to explain. And under any circumstances it depended on his winning the game. And that is why Tom Crabbe, in conformity with the instructions in the telegram received that morning, had to take the train for Philadelphia.

He had ten times enough time to do the journey. The states of Ohio and Pennsylvania adjoin. As soon as the eastern frontier of one is passed you are in the other. Between the two cities there are hardly six hundred miles, and there were several routes for the travellers to choose between. Twenty hours would suffice for the journey. Here was good fortune such as did not fall to Commodore Urrican and would not be envied by the young painter or the *Tribune* reporter in search of long distances.

But John Milner did not complain, as he did not intend to stay a day longer than he could help in this city so partial to phenomena of the porcine race. When he stepped into the train he contemptuously shook the dust off his feet. No one had taken any notice of Tom Crabbe's presence at Cincinnati, no one had come to interview him at his hotel in Covington, and the post office was deserted when he presented himself to receive Tornbrock's telegram. But thanks to his throw of twelve he had gone three squares ahead of Max Real, and was a square ahead of the masked man.

This time public attention would not be diverted from him. He would return the man of the day. John Milner would know how to bring him into the light and force the great city to take some notice of the personage who held so considerable a place in the pugilistic world of North America.

It was about ten o'clock in the evening of the 31 st of May that Tom Crabbe made his entry into the "City of Brotherly Love," in which he and his trainer passed their first night incognito.

In the morning John Milner would see how the wind blew. Did it blow from a good quarter, and had it blown the name of the illustrious boxer to the banks of the Delaware?

As was his custom, John Milner had left Tom Crabbe at the hotel after taking the necessary measures with regard to the two breakfasts.

This time, again, as at Cincinnati, he had not entered their names and vocations in the visitors' book. A walk through the city seemed advisable. As the result of the last throw had been known since the evening before, he might discover if the populace were interested in Tom Crabbe's arrival.

You can walk through a town of the third or fourth rank in a few hours, but here was an agglomeration comprising the suburbs of Manaynac and Germanstown, Camden and Gloucester, containing two hundred thousand houses and eleven hundred thousand people. Lying from north-east to south-west along the course of the Delaware, Philadelphia is about eighteen miles in length, and its area is large, owing to the Philadelphians living in their own houses. Enormous buildings with hundreds of tenants, as in Chicago and New York, are rare there. It is pre-eminently the city of "home."

The city is, in fact, immense, magnificent also, open, airy, regularly built, with some of the streets a hundred feet wide. It has houses with frontages of brick and marble, trees that have survived since the sylvanian epoch, gardens kept up luxuriously, squares, parks — and one of the largest in the States, Fairmount Park, a bit of country of three thousand acres on the banks of the Schuylkill, in which the ravines have retained their wild aspect.

In any case, during this first day John Milner could only visit that part of the town situated on the right bank of the Delaware, and he went along towards the west, following the Schuylkill, an affluent of the river flowing from northwest to south-east. On the other side of the Delaware extends New Jersey, one of the small states of the Union to which belong the suburbs of Camden and Gloucester, which for want of bridges communicate with the city by ferry-boats.

It was not on this day that John Milner traversed the centre of the city from which radiate the principal arteries, around the Town Hall, a vast edifice of white marble built at the cost of millions, the tower of which when it is finished will support an enormous statue of William Penn six hundred feet in the air.

If during his sojourn in the city John Milner could not help noticing its monuments, he never thought of looking for them. He had not come to see Philadelphia. He was not expected to paint pictures like Max Real, or write articles like Harris T. Kymbale. His business was to take Tom Crabbe where the last throw obliged him to present himself. But he intended to get something out of the trip for the benefit of Tom Crabbe, in case he did not win the sixty millions of dollars and was obliged to continue his trade.

Patrons of this kind of sport were not wanting in Philadelphia, where there are hundreds of thousands of workmen in the various metal mines, in the machine shops, in the refineries, the chemical works, the textile factories — more than six thousand manufactories of all sorts — and also the labourers in the harbour trades employed by the exporters of coal, petroleum, grain and manufactured articles, the shipping business being only second to that of New York.

Yes, Tom Crabbe would be estimated at his true value among these people, by whom the physical qualities are more thought of than the intellectual ones. And even among the other classes claiming to be superior, how many gentlemen might not be found who knew how to appreciate a good straight hit in the face and the dislocation of a jawbone in a scientific manner!

John Milner noticed, with real satisfaction, that the market-place, which is said to be the largest in the world, was not devoted to a cattle show. In this particular his companion had no rival to fear as at Cincinnati, and the indigo flag would not have to. be lowered before the majesty of a phenomenal pig.

On this subject John Milner was relieved from anxiety at the very beginning. The Philadelphia newspapers had announced, with a good deal of fuss, that Pennsylvania might expect the approaching arrival of the second partner during the coming fortnight. The betting agencies had begun to make a stir, and Tom Crabbe had risen in the list owing to his being in front of his competitors and requiring only two lucky throws to win, &c., &c.

And when next day Tom Crabbe was taken through the more frequented streets by his trainer, he would have had every reason to be satisfied with himself if he had only been able to read.

Everywhere were huge posters, as big as those about the pig at Cincinnati, with the name of the second player in letters a foot high and marks of exclamation escorting it like a guard of honour, to say nothing of the handbills distributed by the vociferous agents of the bookmakers.

TOM CRABBE! TOM CRABBE!! TOM CRABBE!!!

The Famous Tom Crabbe, Champion of the new world!!!

The Great Favourite of the Hypperbone Match!!!

Tom Crabbe, who has beaten Fitzsimmons and Corbett!

TOM CRABBE!

Who is beating Real, Kymbale, Wag, Urrican and XKZ!!!

Tom crabbe, who leads!!!

Tom Crabbe, who is but sixteen squares from the end!

Tom Crabbe, who will hoist the indigo flag on the Heights of Illinois!!

Tom Crabbe is within our walls!!!

THREE CHEERS FOR TOM CRABBE!!!!

It will be understood how proud was John Milner when he exhibited his triumphant subject in the streets of Philadelphia, in the principal squares, at Fairmount Park, and in the market-place. What revenge for the vexations of Cincinnati! What a pledge of final success!

But on the 7th, amid this delirious joy, John Milner had a spasm of the heart, provoked by the following unexpected incident. It was the prick of the pin that threatened to burst the balloon before it rose in the air.

A poster, no less enormous, had been put up by a rival, if not an opponent in the Hypperbone match.

Cavanaugh against Crabbe.

Who was Cavanaugh? Oh, he was well known in the city. He was a prize-fighter of renown who three months before had been beaten in a memorable contest by Tom Crabbe in person without having been able to obtain his revenge in spite of his persistent attempts. And these words on the poster below the name of Cavanaugh:

challenge for the championship!

challenge!! challenge!!!

It must be admitted that Tom Crabbe had something else to do than to reply to this provocation, and that was to quietly wait for the approaching throw. But Cavanaugh — or rather those who were pitting him against the champion of the New World — did not intend to be replied to in that way. Who could say if it were not the move of some opposition agency to stop the most advanced of the players?

John Milner should have shrugged his shoulders. Tom Crabbe's partisans even came to tell him to despise a challenge which was clearly put forward from interested motives.

But on the one hand John Milner knew the indisputable superiority of his man over Cavanaugh, and on the other he made this reflection: if at the end Tom Crabbe did not win the game, if he were not enriched by the millions of the will, if he did not continue to fight in public, would he not lose his reputation for having refused this revenge demanded under such peculiar circumstances?

In short, after a fresh lot of posters more provoking still and going so far as to impeach the honour of the champion of the New World, there could be read on the walls of Philadelphia:

THE CHALLENGE ACCEPTED!

CRABBE AGAINST CAVANAUGH!!

We can imagine the effect!

What? Tom Crabbe going to fight? Tom Crabbe at the head of the "Seven," going to risk his position in a pugilistic revenge? Had he forgotten in what game he was engaged? Well, yes! "Besides," said John Milner to himself, "it is not a jaw knocked out or an eye knocked in that will prevent Tom Crabbe resuming his route and making a good figure in the Hypperbone match!"

If the revenge was going to take place, the sooner it took place the better.

But it so happened that as meetings of this nature are forbidden, even in America, the Philadelphian police interfered and threatened the heroes with fine and imprisonment if the fight took place. To be confined in the Western Penitentiary, where the prisoners are obliged to learn a musical instrument and play on it all day long — and what a lovely concert it must be with the mournful accordion heard above all! — would not, it is true, be a very severe penalty, but the detention would mean the impossibility of starting on the day named, and to expose himself to the same delay as Hermann Titbury had fallen a victim to in Maine.

But there remained a method of procedure without fear of the sheriff. Would it not do to go to some spot in the district and keep the place and time secret, so as to settle this great question of the championship outside Philadelphia?

This is what was done. Only the seconds of the two boxers and a few amateurs of so-called high respectability were informed of the arrangements.

The preliminaries being arranged, the provocations by poster were put an end to and the rumour spread about that the meeting would not take place till after the match — which might lead people to believe it would not take place at all.

But, all the same, on the 9th, about eight o'clock in the morning, in the small town of Arondale, some thirty miles from Philadelphia, a certain number of people found themselves together in a room secretly hired for the event.

Photographers and cinematographists accompanied them, so as to preserve for posterity every phase of the enthralling contest.

Among the personages figured Tom Crabbe in fine form, with his arms about on the level with his adversary's head, and Cavanaugh, though less in height, just as broad of shoulder and exceptionally strong — both men good for twenty or thirty rounds at the least. The first was looked after by John Milner, the second by his private trainer. Amateurs and professionals surrounded them, eager to criticize the action and effect of these two machines of two fist-power each.

But scarcely had the men squared up to one another than there appeared on the scene the sheriff of Arondale, Vincent Burck, accompanied by a Methodist minister, the Reverend Hugh Hunter. Accidentally hearing of what was taking place, they had both hurried down to the scene to stop the degrading encounter, one in the name of Pennsylvanian law and the other in the name of a higher law.

Naturally they were not well received, either by the champions or their friends or the spectators. They tried to speak, but no one would allow them to be heard. They tried to separate the combatants, and were thrust back. What could they do against these muscular men, who seemed strong enough to send them rolling twenty feet with a back-hander?

Doubtless the two interlopers had the strength of their official position. They represented the authorities, terrestrial and celestial, but they had not got the police, who are usually in attendance to help them.

So Tom Crabbe and Cavanaugh again put up their fists.

"Stop!" shouted Vincent Burck.

"Take care!" shouted Hugh Hunter.

No notice was taken and a few, feints were made, and — Well — and then ensued a scene that provoked the surprise and then the admiration of those who were its witnesses.

Neither the sheriff nor the clergyman was tall or of much breadth — they were thin, little men. But what they had not in strength they had — or seemed to have — in suppleness, address, and agility.

In a moment they were on the two boxers. John Milner, trying to keep back the minister, received a smack in the face that sent him staggering on to the ground, where he remained half dazed.

The next moment Cavanaugh was gratified with a nasty knock the sheriff administered to his left eye, while Mr. Hunter performed the like kind office for Tom Crabbe's right eye.

The two professionals turned on their assailants, who, in dodging their attacks, capered and jumped about like monkeys, and luckily escaped unhit. The crowd began to applaud and then to cheer. Suddenly the minister got in his right fist on to Tom Crabbe's left eye, and made a blind man of him for the time being.

A moment afterwards the police rushed in, and the whole assembly — principals, seconds, and spectators cleared out at a run, leaving the field to the sheriff and the minister.

And John Milner, with a swollen cheek, led back Tom Crabbe to Philadelphia. And there they hid their shame in their rooms, waiting for the arrival of the next telegram.

CHAPTER XXIV. TWO HUNDRED DOLLARS A DAY

A FETISH for the Titburys? Certainly they wanted it; and if it were only the end of the rope which hanged this brigand, Bill Arrol, it would have been welcome. But, as the magistrate of Great Salt Lake City had said, he would have to be caught before he was hanged, and it did not look as though that would happen very soon.

Assuredly the fetish which would make Hermann Titbury win the game would not have been dear at the three thousand dollars he had been robbed of at the *Cheap Hotel* But meanwhile the blue flag did not possess a cent, and furious and no less disappointed at the ironical replies of the sheriff, he left the police station to rejoin Mrs. Titbury.

"Well, Hermann," she asked, "this rascal, this wretch of an Inglis?"

"His name is not Inglis," answered Mr. Titbury, falling back into a chair," it is Bill Arrol — "

"Is he arrested?"

"He will be."

"When?"

"When they can put their hands on him."

"And our money? Our three thousand — "

"I would not give half a dollar for it."

Mrs. Titbury collapsed into an arm-chair in ruins. But this masterful woman was soon herself again; she rose, and when her husband, in the last stage of dejection, said:

"What is to be done?"

"Wait."

"Wait — for what? Till this bandit, Arrol — "

"No — Hermann — wait for Mr. Tornbrock's telegram, which will not be long in coming. Then we can think matters over — "

"And the money?"

"We have time to get it sent to us even if we are sent to the end of the States."

"That would not astonish me, with the run of bad luck that pursues us."

"Follow me!" answered Mrs. Titbury resolutely. And they went out of the hotel to go to the telegraph office.

All the town had heard of the misadventures of the Titburys. It is true that Great Salt Lake City did not seem to have more sympathy for them than the town of Calais, from which they had arrived direct. If, then, a few persons were at the post office when the couple arrived, they were only there out of curiosity, or rather had come to laugh at the "good last," as the unfortunate Titbury had been popularly designated.

But chaff did not trouble him, still less did it trouble Mrs. Titbury. He cared not whether he rose or fell in the betting lists, for who knew whether he might not recover at once by a superb throw? In fact, by studying the board, Mrs. Titbury had discovered that if they threw ten, they would have to double on the fourteenth square, that of Illinois, and go at a bound to the twenty-fourth, which was that of Michigan, adjoining Illinois, which would take them back towards Chicago. This would be — there was no doubt of it — the best throw they could get. Would they get it?

At forty-seven minutes past nine, with automatic regularity, the telegram came out of the instrument.

The throw was disastrous.

It will be remembered that the same day, June 2nd, Max Real, then with his mother at Chicago, had known of it immediately, as in the following days he knew the number which sent Harris T. Kymbale to Washington, Lizzie Wag to Missouri, and Commodore Urrican to Wisconsin.

Deplorable as it was for Hermann Titbury, it was none the less singular, and he must have been in a vein of terrible bad luck for it to have occurred.

The number was five, by two and three, which took him from the fourth square to the ninth. The ninth square was Illinois, and he had to double, which brought him to fourteen, another Illinois square; so he had to triple it, and that gave him in all fifteen points and put him on the nineteenth square, Louisiana, New Orleans, marked as the inn on Hypperbone's board.

In truth it would have been impossible to be more unfortunate.

Mr. and Mrs. Titbury, returned to their hotel amid the pleasantries of the crowd, walking as if they had received a formidable blow on the head. But Mrs. Titbury had a harder head than her husband, and did not, like him, remain overwhelmed on the spot.

"To Louisiana! To New Orleans!" repeated Mr. Titbury, seizing his hair. "Ah! Why have we been so foolish as to run about like this — "

"And we will still run!" declared Mrs. Titbury, crossing her arms.

"What — you think — "

"Of starting for Louisiana."

"But it is thirteen hundred miles to do!"

"We will do it!"

"But we shall have to pay a fine of a thousand dollars — "

"We will pay it."

"But we shall have to remain for two throws without playing — "

"We will not play."

"But there will be six weeks to spend in this town, where the cost of living is very high — "

"We will spend them."

"But we have no more money!"

"We will have some sent."

"But I do not wish it!"

"And I do!"

Kate Titbury had a reply for everything, it will be seen. Evidently she had in her the spirit of an old gambler, and it had got the upper hand. The mirage of those sixty million dollars had attracted her, fascinated her, hypnotized her.

Hermann Titbury did not attempt to resist. It would have been of no use. The consequences he had deduced from this unfortunate throw were only too correct — a long and expensive journey, the States to be almost entirely traversed from north-west to south-east, the dearness of living in this opulent and ruinous city of New Orleans, the time that would have to be passed there, the rule that obliged him to miss two throws before resuming the game.

"Perhaps," said Mrs. Titbury," luck may send one of our opponents there, and then we should have to take his old place — "

"But which one," asked Mr. Titbury," seeing they are all in front of us?"

"And why should they not be obliged to go back after passing the end — and recommence the game like that abominable Urrican?"

No doubt it might occur — but the chances were against it.

"And then," added Mr. Titbury," as the crowning misfortune, we are not allowed to choose the hotel to which we are to put up!"

In fact, after the words," nineteenth square, Louisiana, New Orleans, "the unlucky telegram added, *Excelsior Hotel*"

There could be no discussion. Whether the hotel was of the first or twentieth class, it was that ordered by the imperious deceased.

"We will go to the *Excelsior Hotel,* that is all!" so said Mrs. Titbury.

Such was this woman, as resolute as she was avaricious. Yet, the agony she went through in thinking of the losses that had already befallen them, the three hundred dollars fine, the three thousand dollars theft, the expenses up to the present, the expenses in the future! But the heritage dazzled her eyes and made her blind.

There was plenty of time for the third player to get to his post. It was the 2nd of June, and it would suffice if the blue flag were hoisted in the metropolis of Louisiana on the 15th of July. But, as Mrs. Titbury had observed, another of the "Seven" might be sent there any day, and it was necessary for them to be in the nineteenth square to be replaced by him. Better not waste time in Great Salt Lake City, then. And so it was decided to start as soon as the money arrived that had been demanded by telegram from the bank where Mr. Titbury kept his current account.

This operation took but two days. In the morning of the 4th of June he drew from the bank in Great Salt Lake City five thousand dollars, which, alas! would never more yield interest.

On the 5th of June, Mr. and Mrs. Titbury left Great Salt Lake City amid general indifference, and unfortunately without that piece of rope which would have put them in luck if Bill Arrol had been hanged.

It was the Union Pacific — decidedly much used by the players in the Hypperbone match — which took them across Wyoming to Cheyenne, and across Nebraska to Omaha.

Thence, for the sake of cheapness — the fares by steamboat being less than by railway — the travellers went down the Missouri to Kansas, as Max Real had done at his first move; from Kansas they reached St. Louis, where Lizzie Wag and Jovita Foley would soon take up their quarters to spend their time in prison.

To leave the waters of the Missouri for those of the Mississippi you require only a change of boat. Steamers are numerous on these rivers, and if you are satisfied to travel third class, the voyage can be done very cheaply. By providing your own food — easily done at the stopping places — you can still further diminish your daily expenses. And this was done by the Titburys, who spent as little as possible in preparation for the bills they would have to meet for a probably lengthened stay at the *Excelsior Hotel.*

The steamboat *Black Warrior* received them on board to take them to the Louisianan capital. They had but to follow the "Father of Waters" between the states of Illinois, Missouri, Arkansas, Tennessee, Mississippi, and Louisiana, to which the great river gives a more natural frontier than the degrees of longitude and latitude on their other sides.

Seven days after leaving Great Salt Lake City they arrived at New Orleans in the evening.

As they came down the gangway they saw a carriage superbly horsed which was evidently waiting for some of the passengers of the *Black Warrior.* Their intention was to walk to the hotel, leaving their luggage to be brought on by a porter. What was their surprise — a surprise to which was added a pang of alarm — when a footman approached, a negro of the most beautiful black, who said to them:

"Mr. and Mrs. Titbury, I think?"

"We are," said Mr. Titbury.

Then the newspapers had announced their departure from Utah, their journey to Omaha, their voyage on board the *Black Warrior,* their imminent arrival at New Orleans. They had hoped to be left without such attentions; could they never escape the always costly inconveniences of celebrity?

"And what do you want with us?" asked Mr. Titbury gruffly.

"The carriage is waiting for you."

"We did not order any carriage."

"People do not come to the *Excelsior* in any other way," replied, with a bow, the negro of the most beautiful black.

"It begins well!" murmured Mr. Titbury with a big sigh.

But as it was not customary to go in a simpler fashion to the hotel named, the best thing to do was get into the carriage. The couple took their seats, and an omnibus took their bag and portmanteau. Arrived at Canal Street before a noble building, a palace in fact, along the front of which shone the words,

EXCELSIOR HOTEL COMPANY, LIMITED, and the hall of which was resplendent with lights, the carriage stopped, and the footman hastened to open the door.

The Titburys, tired and bewildered, hardly noticed the ceremonious reception given to them by the hotel staff. A major-domo in a black suit conducted them to their rooms. Absolutely dazzled, their haggard eyes saw nothing of the magnificence which surrounded them, and they postponed till the morning the reflections that such extraordinary pomp would inspire.

In the morning, after a night spent in the calm of this comfortable room, protected by the double windows which kept out all the noise of the street, they awoke under the subdued light of an electric night-lamp. The transparent dial of an expensive timepiece showed that it was eight o'clock.

Within reach of the hand at the side of the huge bed where they had so tranquilly reposed, a series of buttons awaited but the pressure of the finger to summon the chamber-maid or the groom of the chambers. Other buttons commanded the bath, the early breakfast, the morning papers, and — what persuaded the travellers to press it — the light of day.

It was on this button that Mrs. Titbury placed her crooked finger.

Instantly the thick blinds of the windows rolled up mechanically, the sun-blinds dropped down outside and the rays of the sun flooded the room.

Mr. and Mrs. Titbury looked at one-another. They dared not utter a word for fear that every sentence would cost them a piastre a word.

The luxury of the room was beyond all reason, everything of incomparable richness, furniture, draperies, carpets, the walls hung with brocaded silk.

The couple arose and passed into an adjoining room of most marvellous comfort; washing-stands with taps for hot water, tepid water, or cold water at will, pulverizers ready to spout their perfumed sprays, soaps of different colours and odours, sponges of exceptional softness, towels as white as snow.

As soon as they were dressed, the Titburys ventured into a further series of rooms, a suite complete, dining-room with the table glittering with silver and china, reception room furnished with unheard of luxury, electrolier, brackets, pictures by famous artists, art bronzes, lamp shades ornamented with gold — madame's boudoir, piano with music, table with fashionable novels, albums with Louisianan photographs — the gentleman's room with American reviews, the best newspapers of the States, a case of stationery with the hotel note-heading, and even a typewriter ready to work at the touch of the traveller's finger.

"It is the cave of Ali Baba!" exclaimed Mrs. Titbury, absolutely fascinated.

"And the forty thieves are not far off!" added Mr. Titbury.

At this moment his eyes caught sight of a notice in a golden frame, with the list of the different departments of the hotel, and the times of the meals for those who preferred not to take them in their rooms.

The suite occupied by the third player was No. 1, and had this notice against it: "Reserved for the players in the Hypperbone match by the Excelsior Hotel Company."

"Ring, Hermann," Mrs. Titbury contented herself with saying.

He pressed the button, and a gentleman in black coat and white cravat presented himself at the door of the reception room.

And to begin with, in studied phrase, he tendered them the compliments of the Excelsior Hotel Company and its manager, honoured at having as guest one of the most popular competitors in the great national game. As he had some time to spend in Louisiana, and especially at New Orleans, with his worthy wife, they had endeavoured to surround them with all possible comfort. The routine of the hotel, if it was convenient for them to conform to it, was early breakfast at eight o'clock, breakfast at eleven, luncheon at four, dinner at seven, evening tea at ten. The style of cookery would be English, American, or French, as they pleased. The wines were of the best foreign vintages. During the day a carriage was at the disposal of the great Chicago banker *(sic)*, an elegant steam yacht was kept ready to start for excursions to the mouth of the Mississippi or trips on Lake Borque or Lake Pontchartrain. A box had been, engaged at the opera, where one of the best French companies was then performing.

"How much?" asked Mrs. Titbury abruptly.

"A hundred dollars."

"For the month?"

"For the day."

"And for each, of course?" added Mrs. Titbury in a tone in which irony, contended with anger.

"Yes, madame, and the price was arranged on the most reasonable terms as soon as the newspapers informed us that the third player and Mrs. Titbury were to stay some time at the *Excelsior Hotel.*"

Hither had their ill-luck brought this unfortunate couple — and they could not go elsewhere — and Mrs. Titbury could not even install herself in some humble lodging-house! It was the hotel designated by William J. Hypperbone, and there was nothing to be surprised at in the arrangement, as he was one of the principal shareholders. Yes! two hundred dollars a day for the pair of them, six thousand dollars for thirty days if they remained the month in this tavern.

And whether they liked it or not, they had to put up with it. To leave the hotel was to leave the game, the rules of which were indisputable! It was to renounce all hope of coming back to it — and coming into the millions.

As soon as the major-domo had retired, "Let us be off!" said Mr. Titbury. "Let us get our baggage and return to Chicago. I will not remain a minute longer here — at eight dollars an hour!"

"Indeed!" replied the imperious dame.

The "Crescent City," as they call the Louisianan metropolis, was founded in 1717 in the bend of the great river which bounds it on the south, and may be said to absorb all Louisiana. The other towns, Baton Rouge — the state capital — Donaldsonville, Shreveport, have only from eleven to twelve thousand people. Situated over 1700 miles from New York and 107 from the mouth of the Mississippi, nine railroads run into it, and fifteen hundred steamboats ply on its web of waters.

It was in this vast city of two hundred and forty-two thousand inhabitants, much diversified by the mingling of races, in which the blacks, if they rejoice in all political rights, have not gained social equality — it was amid this hybrid population of French, Spanish, English, Anglo-Americans, in the heart of Louisiana, that there had been thrust into an existence they had never even imagined, this pair of Titburys so strangely torn from Chicago. But as bad luck necessitated it, the best thing to do — unless they went home — was to get all they could for their money. At least, so said Mrs. Titbury.

And so every day their magnificent equipage took them about in great pomp. A noisy crowd accompanied them with its ironical cheers, for the people knew them to be downright misers who had been as unpopular at Great Salt Lake City as at Calais, and as at Chicago. What did it matter? They did not notice it, and nothing occurred to lead them to think that they were not the great favourites of the match.

In this way they exhibited themselves in the northern wards, the suburbs of Lafayette, Jefferson, Carrollton, those elegant neighbourhoods in which the mansions and villas and cottages stand embowered in the foliage of the orange and magnolia and other trees then in full flower.

They drove on the substantial levee a hundred yards wide which protects the town against inundation, on the quays bordered by a four-deep row of steamers, steamboats, tugs, sailing vessels, coasting craft, which take away 1,700,000 cotton bales a year. In this way they saw Algiers and Gretna, by crossing the river to the left bank, where the workshops, factories and warehouses are mainly to be found.

In this way they drove in their gorgeous vehicle along the beautiful streets, bordered with houses of brick and stone which have taken the places of those of wood which were destroyed in the numerous fires; and often in Royal Street and St. Louis Street, which cross each other in the French quarter — and there, what charming habitations with green blinds, with their courts in which the fountains murmur in their basins and the plants flourish in their window boxes.

It was thus that they honoured with a visit the Capitol, an old building transformed during the War of Secession into a legislative palace where sat the Chambers of Senators and Deputies. Thus they visited the very architectural palace of the University, the gothic cathedral, the Custom House, the Rotunda with its immense hall. There the reader finds a collection of the best assorted reading, the lounger a promenade arranged under the open galleries, the speculators in stocks and public funds an animated exchange. Many excursions they went on their elegant steam yacht on the placid waters of Lake Pontchartrain and among the channels of the Mississippi. At the opera the admirers of the great lyric masterpieces saw them in the box placed at their disposal, trying desperately to appreciate the chords of the orchestra with ears absolutely closed to all musical comprehension.

Thus they lived as in a dream, but what an awakening there would be when they fell back into reality!

A singular phenomenon occurred in their case. Yes! These niggards, these skinflints, these misers, became accustomed to this new life, they were bewildered by this abnormal situation, they grew intoxicated, in the physical sense of the word, at this table which was always luxuriously served and of which they would not lose a crumb at the risk of future dyspepsia, for they wanted their money's worth out of those two hundred dollars a day.

Time rolled on. Their stay at the hotel was not interrupted. Thirteen throws had to take place at Chicago before they had the right to start again. Every two days the throws were announced in the Rotunda, as they had been a few minutes before in the Auditorium.

None of them took an opponent to Louisiana; neither that of the 12th, concerning Max Real, nor that of the 14th, concerning Tom Crabbe. On the 16th — the date reserved for Hermann Titbury before misfortune sent him to the nineteenth square — no throw took place. On the 18th, it was for the fourth player, Harris T. Kymbale, that Tornbrock rolled the dice on the table of the Auditorium.

The Titburys were thus apparently doomed to continue this existence which was as agreeable as ruinous to the purse and health during the six weeks of seclusion. And perhaps before they were free to move some competitor might arrive at the sixty-third square!

That, however, was the secret of the future. Meanwhile, the days rolled on, and if the match ended, all Mr. and Mrs. Titbury had to do was to return to Illinois after paying the formidable bill of the *Excelsior Hotel*, added to the previous expenses, and think of what it had cost them to figure among the "Seven" of the Hypperbone match!

CHAPTER XXV. THE PEREGRINATIONS OF HARRIS T KYMBALE

If the Titburys and Commodore Urrican had reason to complain of the bad luck that followed them, it would seem that the chief reporter of the *Tribune* had a right to do so in some measure. To begin with, he had been sent to Niagara, in New York, made to pay a fine, and sent on immediately to Santa Fe, in New Mexico. And now he was obliged to come from South Carolina to Nebraska, and then go to Washington, at the north-western extremity of the States.

At Charleston, in South Carolina, where he had been so warmly welcomed, he had received the telegram on the 4th of June. The throw was ten by six and four, and that being doubled, took him from the twenty-second square to the forty-second.

This last was Nebraska, chosen by the deceased as the labyrinth of the Noble Game of Goose. And — this was serious — when the player had got there and paid a double fine, he had to go back to the thirtieth square, which was occupied by Washington State. It is true that the itinerary from South Carolina to Washington passed through Nebraska.

When the throw was announced his partisans gathered in great numbers at the Charleston Post Office were thunderstruck, and the reporter saw himself in danger of losing his position as first favourite, which most of the agencies had given him, a little too hastily it must be admitted.

But the man, as clear-headed as he was resolute, had soon reassured those who supported him.

"Eh! my friends," he said, "do not despair! You know I am not afraid of long journeys. From Charleston to Nebraska, from Nebraska to Washington is a matter of two strides, and I have a fortnight in which to do the four thousand miles. I shall have railroads all the way. As to the fine to pay, that concerns the cashier of the *Tribune,* and all the worse for him if he makes a face at it! The trouble is not the going from Nebraska to Washington, but the returning from the forty-second to the thirtieth square! Bah! The loss of twelve squares is not worth talking about, and I shall soon pick up what chance made me put down!"

How could people not have confidence in a man who showed himself so confident? How could they hesitate to risk putting their money on him? How could they deny him the applause to which he was so justly entitled? And they did not spare it him, and this morning saw the renewal of the triumphs of the evening at the famous Astley banquet at which had figured the monster pie that had occasioned 1577 cases of indigestion.

At the same time Harris T. Kymbale was in error in affirming that he could go all the way by railroad from Charleston to Olympia, the capital of Washington, mentioned in the telegram. No, there was a solution of continuity, which was certain to be noticed by Brennan S. Bickhorn. Half the journey, that to Nebraska, could, however, be rapidly accomplished by the lines in connection with the Union Pacific.

Nevertheless, there was no time to lose, considering the possible delays. The wise thing to do was to leave Charleston that evening, and this the Green Flag did. His enthusiastic supporters cheered him up to the minute the train started to cross the plains of South Carolina.

The first part of the route several of the "Seven" had followed when they crossed their regions, and probably some would follow it again. Harris T. Kymbale went through Tennessee, and in the evening of the 5th reached St. Louis, where Lizzie Wag and Jovita Foley went to find a prison. Then, fearing to lose too much time by taking the steamboat to Omaha, he picked out the quickest trains and reached Omaha, by way of Kansas City, next evening.

He spent the night in Omaha, where, Max Real on his first journey had spent a few hours. Here a telegram reached him from the *Tribune* which told him day by day the stages and the manner in which he could reach Olympia, in Washington, in the forenoon of the 18th. This is what it said: —

"1. Leave Omaha in the morning of the 7th by Union Pacific, 8.35 train, to reach, ninety miles from there, Julesburg Junction at 6.30 in the evening.

"2. Find there a coach ready horsed, provisioned, with relays arranged along the road of a hundred miles to the Bad Lands of Nebraska. Arrive there next morning, report your presence, and return by coach to Julesburg.

"3. At Julesburg, take the 10 p.m. train to California, by Union and Southern Pacific, which reaches Sacramento in the evening of the 12th, and pass the night in that town.

"4. In the afternoon of the 12th take the line going north and stop at Shasta station, in Upper California, three hundred miles from Sacramento — repairs interrupting the traffic up to Roseburgh, in Oregon.

"5. In this mountainous country where coaches cannot run, travel the two hundred and forty miles on horseback so as to reach Roseburgh station on the 17th at latest, the journey taking four days, at 75 miles every 24 hours.

"6. In the afternoon of the 17th take the train at Roseburgh for Olympia, arriving there early next morning after a run of 350 miles."

The message was long, but clear, explicit, and positive. The receiver had but to conform to its prescriptions and he would be at his post on the day named. It was to be hoped, however, that there would be no delay, for even half a day lost would ruin the result of the journey.

We may be sure Harris T. Kymbale was resolved to use all diligence. If he passed the night at Omaha, it was because the next train did not start till the morning. He caught it right enough, and in the evening was at Julesburg Junction, near the spot where the line skirts the frontier of Colorado, not far from the South Platte River.

This time, on leaving Charleston, the journalist had taken the precaution not to say who he was, so as to avoid receptions and their inconvenient consequences. At Julesburg he could not preserve his incognito, as the coach that had been ordered was awaiting his arrival.

His partisans assembled at the station understood that they must not delay him on any pretext, that his hours were numbered, that this excursion to the Bad Lands of Nebraska must be accomplished in the time fixed. They were the first, when the reporter got out on the platform, to advise him to start at once. And even a dozen of these Anglo-Americans who, with the emigrants and a certain number of Sioux, become citizens of the States, compose the Nebraskan population, had made arrangements to accompany him. This escort was not to be despised in these regions, where wild beasts of four legs and two legs were still to be found.

"As you please, gentlemen," replied Harris T. Kymbale, shaking the hands extended towards him," but on condition that the coach can hold you all."

"Our places are taken — and we can pile in!" replied one of these enthusiasts.

The vehicle was a transcontinental coach belonging to Wells, Fargo and Co., which formerly carried the overland mails. It was painted a bright red and hung on leather straps, and contained a single compartment with nine seats, arranged in threes. The fourth player and eight of his supporters occupied the inside, ready to replace in turns the four others, two of whom sat at the back outside and two near the driver, who had a team of six horses.

Instead of roads there were only the tracks made by the waggons. But were roads necessary on these interminable plains on which the railroads have only to lay their sleepers? From time to time they crossed several creeks in the vicinity of the Raymond and Cole lagoons, the Boardman River, the Niobrara, which was crossed at the ford, and also a few hamlets where the horses of the relays were waiting.

It was in this way that on the evening of the 8th, after a forty hours' journey in favourable weather, the coach arrived at the Bad Lands. No villages there, nothing but prairies where the horses could take their fill of pasture. Harris T. Kymbale and his companions were comfortable enough, the lockers in the coach being well filled with provisions.

After a night under a clump of trees, the coach was left in charge of the driver, and they descended the slopes of the wild, valley. William J. Hypperbone had good reason for choosing Nebraska as the labyrinth of his forty-second square.

Between the furthest undulations of the Rockies, in the neighbourhood of the Black Hills, covered with fir trees, lay this deep depression of the ground, thirty-six miles wide and eighty-five long, which extends into Dakota. On all sides rose the rings of rocks, with their thousand pyramids, needles, pinnacles; belfries, of stone. It was indeed a labyrinth, one of the most complicated, this region of the Bad Lands, where for over hundreds of square miles through strata of clays and ferruginous sands rise the earth-sculptured pillars of prismatic rock, with here and there a seeming bastion, a fort, a castle, gleaming brick-red on the white surface of the ground.

This corner of North America seems to have formed a world apart. In prehistoric times it was frequented by herds of elephants, mammoths, mastodons, whose bones are still found as fossils or reduced to dust, the hypothesis being that the depression was formerly filled with the waters coming down from the Rockies and the Black Hills which have flowed away through underground fissures, the altitude of the region being considerably above the level of the sea; and the empty reservoir became an ossuary where the fossil fragments have accumulated in surprising quantities.

There was no need to penetrate far into the sinuosities of the Bad Lands. It was enough that the fourth player was present in person at the entrance to the labyrinth, and that his presence had been certified in some authentic way. No document was left behind under a stone, as had been done by Commodore Urrican before leaving Death Valley. A paper was drawn up by Harris T. Kymbale and signed by his twelve companions, which was sufficient evidence of his arrival in this Nebraskan region. A last repast was taken under the shadow of the trees and his health was drunk with loud cheers.

"The reporter-in-chief of the *Tribune!* The favourite of the match! The heir of the sixty millions of dollars of William J. Hypperbone!"

Decidedly, Kymbale had reason to be confident. His supporters would not abandon him. They forgot, they wished to forget, that to go from Nebraska to Washington was to go back, if not on the map of the United States, at least on the board of the deceased. And when he returned to the thirtieth square he had only in front of him Max Real on the forty-fourth, XKZ on the forty-sixth, Tom Crabbe on the forty-seventh. The camp was raised at three o'clock in the afternoon, and at ten o'clock next morning the party had returned to Julesburg Junction.

An hour afterwards the Union Pacific train arrived, to stop ten minutes. Only ten minutes to stop, and if Harris T. Kymbale had missed the train, he would have imperilled the rest of his journey, for only two trains a day stop at the station — and he had not an hour to lose.

We know what States the line passes through on its way to the west. Max Real had been there on the way to Cheyenne, Hermann Titbury in going to Great Salt Lake City, Commodore Urrican in going to Death Valley. So the reporter went through Wyoming, Utah and Nevada and part of California to reach the Californian capital, during the night of the 11th, fit, cheery and confident.

He had an excellent welcome. His supporters in great numbers were there to greet them, but did not think of detaining him for an instant, the train leaving Sacramento at one o'clock in the afternoon.

Among others there to meet him out of interest or sympathy was the correspondent of the *Tribune,* Will Walter, who said to him:

"Sir, I was informed that you were to arrive to-day, and I sincerely congratulate you in having met with no delay."

"That is so," replied Harris T. Kymbale. "Not the least delay between Charleston and Sacramento, and I reckon it will be the same between Sacramento and Olympia."

"There is no reason to fear it will not be," said Will Walter. "It is a nuisance that the line should be temporarily closed, but the train will take you to Shasta station, where you will find the horses ready. A guide, who knows the country well, will take you by the shortest way to Roseburgh, and there you will get the Southern Pacific for Olympia."

"Then all I can do is to thank you for your kindness."

"Not at all, Mr. Kymbale; it is I who have to thank you, for I have backed you."

"At what price?"

"Five to one."

"Then, my dear comrade, let us have five good grips of the hand by way of gratitude — "

"Double it, if you like; and now, Mr. Kymbale, a pleasant journey."

The engine whistled, the train moved off, and disappeared at the curve in the direction of Marysville.

It was annoying that the train did not go faster. It stopped at every station, at Ewings, at Woodland, and so on, the gradient being a rising one all the time, so as to reach in Upper California a considerable height above sea-level. And it was not until eight o'clock in the morning of the 13th that it reached Shasta, up to time.

Beyond this, it will be remembered, the line was closed for repairs, and to resume his railway journey Harris T. Kymbale would have to ride northwards with the guide and horses provided by the *Tribune*. He had five clear days to reach Olympia, four of which must be spent on horseback, travelling about seventy-five miles a day. There was nothing impossible in this, but it meant much fatigue for both horses and riders.

Three horses were at the station, the one destined for Harris T. Kymbale, the others for the guide and a groom who accompanied him. Needless to say the reporter was accustomed to riding.

The guide, named Fred Wilmot, was a man about forty, with all the strength of his age.

"You are ready?" asked Harris T. Kymbale.

"Ready."

"And we shall get there?"

"Yes, if you are a good horseman. By the coach it would have taken double as long."

"I can answer for myself."

"Then to the saddle."

The horses went off at a swinging trot. There was no need to worry about food, for there were numerous towns and villages on the road.

The weather promised to continue fine, with a certain freshness that became more noticeable among the mountains. The day was broken by a halt of two hours, and they rested during a part of the night.

The road followed the right bank of the Sacramento, and after stopping for a meal at a farm, they reached a country of mineral springs, of which there are so many in America. Seven hours of sleep at an inn, and the travellers were off at daybreak to lunch at Yreka. A hundred miles to the east they could see Mount Shasta, whose crater opens at more than twelve thousand feet between the two summits. Solidly seated on its base, cut deep into by verdant ravines, this mountain is considered one of the finest in the States," with its rosy lavas enamelled like glass, "as an enthusiastic traveller has said. Harris T. Kymbale had to postpone his admiration for another journey.

A grand State is this Oregon, the ninth in the Union. With very few people as yet, it possesses vast pasturages, its principal industry being salmon fishing, though the extreme fertility of its western lands is making it much sought after by farmers.

During this day the reporter had his eyes rejoiced by the sight of many magnificent landscapes. A passing look was all he could spare, to his great regret. In him the tourist was effaced by the player. In the evening, having come over Pilot Rock Pass, the men and horses, all in fair condition, rested at the town of Jackson, which should not be confused with its numerous homonyms. Next day, after a journey which rather tried the horses, and the second stage of which lasted till near midnight, the guide pointed out the lights of Roseburgh.

Thus ended the ride without an accident, without an incident, with the regularity of an express. Neither thanks nor dollars were spared to Fred Wilmot, and in the morning at daybreak Harris T. Kymbale "leapt " — the word was used by the *Tribune* reporter — into the first train bound for Olympia.

The line passes through the principal towns and villages of this rich valley of the Villamette, Winchester, Eugene City, Harrisburg, Albany; Salem, the State capital, a basket of flowers and verdure; Oregon City, with its powerful waterfalls that work its paper mills, its sugar refineries, and its textile works; Portland, with seventy-five thousand people, the headquarters of the trade of Oregon, of which the Columbia has made a busy seaport.

At last the train crossed the river which separates Oregon from Washington and stopped on the right bank above the confluence of the Villamette at Vancouver, at eight o'clock in the morning of the 18th. This is the Washington Vancouver, be it understood, not the Vancouver of British Columbia, which is a hundred miles further north. Harris T. Kymbale left it at 8.10 a.m. to finish the last stage of his journey.

No obstacle, no delay to fear. Nine stations and the train would arrive a little after eleven at Olympia station. The intermediate stations were successively left behind. The train ran rapidly along through this region watered by the numerous affluents of the Columbia. At last, at three minutes past eleven, it stopped at the little town of Tenino, about forty miles from the capital.

There — disagreeable news for the travellers and disastrous for Harris T. Kymbale — they were informed of an accident which the careful Bickhorn could not have foreseen. The train could not go beyond. At ten miles from the station a bridge had fallen in an hour before, and the traffic had to be stopped on that portion of the line.

A fatal blow, if ever there was one; and the fourth player could not recover from it. And yet he might!

Three young men who had got out of the train came up to him.

"Mr. Kymbale," said one, "do you know how to ride a bicycle?"

"Yes."

"Come along here, then."

Nothing else was said. You see they had to go straight to the point, as became practical American men.

It was not a bicycle, but a triplet which was taken out of the luggage van and placed on the platform.

"Mr. Kymbale," said the young man, "one of us will give you his place in the middle, the other will take the back seat, and I will take the front, and there is a chance of our getting to Olympia before twelve."

"Your names, gentlemen?"

"Will Stanton and Robert Flock."

"And yours, sir, you who have given up your place to me?"

"John Berry."

"Well, Messrs. Stanton, Flock and Berry, thank you — and let us be off, and may St. Cycle, the patron of the bicyclists, protect us."

Forty-five miles in less than an hour! The record had not yet been achieved on the road by any professional.

"Gentlemen," said Harris T. Kymbale as they started," I don't know how I can ever thank — "

"By winning," said Stanton curtly.

"We have put our money on you," added Flock from behind.

The triplet was a machine made by Camden and Co. of New York, which had been used in an international race at the Chicago velodrome. Will Stanton and Robert Flock were natives of Washington, and well-known long distance riders. Harris T. Kymbale on the intermediate seat had only to let himself be taken along, but he well knew how to add his muscular power to that of his trainers — that is the word — and pedal on his own account.

The departure was magnificent. The splendid machine went like greased lightning along the well-kept road, which was quite a velodrome track minus the raised corners, the country being very flat in this part of Washington bordering on the coast. The three cyclists did not speak, for their mouths were shut, the lips with a piece of quill between them, which, without allowing the air to reach the lungs too strongly, assisted the respiration through the nose.

And they did not hesitate to "scorch" from the very beginning. The wheels ran with the speed of a dynamo driven by a powerful motor, and the motor had three pairs of legs acting as connecting rods, which drove the machine with all their strength. The triplet carried a cloud of dust behind it, and when it crossed a ford it cut the water into a furrow with its wheels. The bell kept ringing to clear the road, and the people pulled up on the roadside to see the thing go by.

In the first quarter of an hour fifteen miles were run, and the rate must be kept up if the effort were not to be in vain.

It seemed as though no obstacle would arise, when, as they were running over a wide plain, a furious howling was heard.

An exclamation escaped from the mouth of Robert Flock, who dropped his quill to make it.

"Coyotes!"

Yes, coyotes, a score of prairie wolves. Mad with hunger, these ferocious animals came running faster than the cyclists, and threw themselves on their flank.

"You have a revolver?" asked Will Stanton, without slowing the triplet for a moment.

"Yes," replied Harris T. Kymbale.

"Be ready to use it, then — you also, Flock, get yours out. I will steer. Keep on pedalling, and we may get ahead of them."

Get ahead of them? It was soon evident that it was impossible.

The coyotes leapt after the triplet, ready to precipitate themselves on the reporter and his companions, who would be lost if they were upset.

Two shots were heard, and two wolves, mortally wounded, rolled, howling on to the road. The others in a fury flew at the machine, which could only avoid the shock by a sudden turn, which nearly threw Kymbale off his saddle.

"Pedal! pedal!" shouted Stanton, and the legs worked with such vigour that the teeth of the gearing absolutely hummed.

Another quarter of an hour, and fifteen more miles had been reeled off. But more than ever the coyotes must be settled, for they were leaping at the back wheel, and the grind of their claws could be heard against the spokes as they struck them. The revolvers had been emptied of all their shots; and twelve of the pursuers, dead or dying, had been left behind. Then Harris T. Kymbale let go the handle bar, loaded his revolver, fired; and of the shots none missed, and the coyote danger was over.

It was ten minutes to twelve. About six miles off appeared the first houses of Olympia.

The triplet devoured the distance at the speed of an express, it reached the town, and in defiance of the police regulations, at the risk of smashing some of the five thousand inhabitants, it stopped at the post office as twelve o'clock began to strike.

Harris T. Kymbale got off. Tottering, almost breathless, he stepped through the crowd, who were expecting his arrival, and appeared before the counter as the clock was striking for the tenth time.

"Here is a telegram for Harris T. Kymbale — " shouted the telegraph clerk.

"Here!" replied the reporter-in-chief of the *Tribune,* falling unconscious on to a seat.

The favourite of St. Cycle had arrived in time, thanks to the devotion and energy of his companions; and Will Stanton and Robert Flock, with forty-five miles in 46 minutes 33 seconds, easily beat the record, and are still unbeaten.

CHAPTER XXVI . THE PRISON OF MISSOURI

IT was on the 6th of June, at the *Mammoth Hotel,* after the six days spent in the caves, that Lizzie Wag received the fatal news. Seven, by four and three; doubled, had sent her to the fifty-second square, Missouri.

The journey would be neither tiring nor long. The two States adjoined at the angle near Cairo. From Mammoth Caves to St. Louis was hardly two hundred miles, eight or ten hours by railway, not more. But what disappointment, what ruin!

"How unfortunate! How unfortunate!" said Jovita Foley." Better to have been sent like Commodore Urrican to the end of Florida, or like Mr. Kymbale to the depths of Washington! At least, we should not have been knocked out of this abominable game — "

"Yes, abominable, that is the word, my poor Jovita!" replied Lizzie Wag. "But why did you want to play it?"

The disconsolate damsel did not reply, and what could she have replied? Even if she went to Missouri and waited until an opponent came — by an unfortunate throw for himself but a fortunate one for her — to deliver Lizzie Wag from the prison and take her place, she could only do so by paying the triple fine to the pool which was to belong to him who came in second! And did she possess these three thousand dollars? No. Could she get them? No.

Some of the supporters of the yellow flag might have advanced the amount of the fine if her chance had not been so damaged. When Hodge Urrican got the "Death Number" he was free to begin again. Hermann Titbury could come out of the inn on the day fixed and resume his turn. Neither one nor the other was excluded from the match for an unlimited time, whereas this poor Lizzie Wag —

"How unfortunate! How unfortunate!" repeated Jovita Foley, who seemed to be unable to say anything else.

"Well — what are we to do?" asked her companion.

"Wait — wait, my poor dear."

"Wait? What for?"

"I do not know! We have a fortnight before we need go to prison."

"But not to pay the fine, Jovita; it is that which troubles us most."

"Yes, Lizzie, yes! We'll wait — "

"Here?"

"No. Of course not."

And the "no" came from her heart, not without reason, for the manner of the guests of the *Mammoth Hotel* had changed wonderfully towards them. Since that deplorable throw of the dice Lizzie Wag had been put in the cold. Favourite of the evening, she was no favourite of the next morning. Those who had ventured any money on her would willingly have covered her with curses. She would go to prison and the game would certainly end before she was set free. From the first hour a void opened around her. Jovita Foley saw this clearly, and it was only human, was it not?

That day most of the tourists went away, among them the governor of Illinois. And it is not unlikely that at that hour John Hamilton regretted the titular rank he had bestowed on the two friends. Colonel Wag and Lieutenant-Colonel Foley would make a sorry figure in the Illinois Militia.

In the afternoon they paid their bill at the *Mammoth Hotel,* and took the train for Louisville, there to await — what?

"My dear Jovita," said Lizzie Wag as they were getting out of the train, "do you know what we are going to do?"

"No, Lizzie, I have lost my head! I do not know what I am about."

"Well, let us continue the journey to Chicago, go quietly home, and go back to work at Marshall Field's. Would not that be wise?"

"Very wise, my dear, very wise! But I would rather be deaf than hear the voice of wisdom!"

"That is madness."

"Well — I am mad! I have been so since the game began, and I want to be so till the end."

"Come! It is ended for us, Jovita, well ended!"

"You do not know, and I would give ten years of my life to be a month older!"

And she gave them, and she had given them so many times, that if we reckon them up we find that she had already given away 130 years of her life for nothing!

Did she still hope? In any case she obtained from Lizzie Wag, who had the weakness to listen to her, a promise not to abandon the game. They spent several days at Louisville. Had they not from the 6th to the 20th of June to get to Missouri?

It was here at a humble hotel in Louisville that they would bury their disappointment — at least, Jovita Foley would, for her companion had easily resigned herself to it, having never believed in her final success.

The 7th, the 8th, the 9th went by. There was no change in the position, and such were the insistences of Lizzie Wag that she made Jovita consent to return to Chicago.

The newspapers — even the *Chicago Herald,* who had always supported the fifth player, now "dropped" her. Jovita Foley was so enraged as she read them that she tore them up. Lizzie Wag was no longer quoted in the betting; she had fallen to zero or below it. In the morning of the 8th, the two friends had learnt that Commodore Urrican had got nine, by six and three, which sent him at a bound to Wisconsin, the twenty-sixth square.

"There is a good start for the second time!" exclaimed the unhappy Jovita.

On the 10th it was announced by telegraph that the masked man had by ten points been sent to Minnesota, the fifty-first square.

"Decidedly," she said, "he has the best chance, and he will be the heir of the millions of this Hypperbone!"

It will be noticed that the eccentric deceased had fallen considerably in her esteem since the dice had made a prisoner of dear Lizzie Wag!

At last it was agreed that that very evening the two friends would take the train to Chicago. Although the Louisville newspapers had mentioned the hotel at which the friends were staying, it is needless to add that not a single reporter had visited them. If this was to the great satisfaction of one, it was to the extreme disgust of the other, for, as she bitterly repeated," it is as if we no longer existed."

But it was written that they were not to return just yet. Something most unexpected occurred to allow them, perhaps, to recover their chances in the match, which they would have to abandon in default of paying the fine.

About three o'clock in the afternoon the postman presented himself at the hotel and went up to the room occupied by the two girls. As soon as the door was opened:

"Miss Lizzie Wag?" he asked.

"Yes. I am Miss Wag."

"I have a letter addressed to you, if you will sign the receipt — "

"Give it to me!" said Jovita Foley, her heart beating ready to break.

The signature was given; the postman retired.

"What is in the letter?" asked Lizzie Wag.

"Money, Lizzie."

"And who could have sent it?"

"Who?" said Jovita Foley.

She broke the seals of the envelope and drew out a letter which contained a piece of folded paper.

The letter contained only these lines:

"Herein enclosed is a cheque for three thousand dollars on the Bank Of Louisville, which Miss Lizzie Wag will please accept for the payment of her fine — on behalf of Humphry Weldon."

Jovita's joy exploded like a firework. She jumped into the air; she laughed till she nearly choked; she spun round like a teetotum; and she shouted:

"The cheque — the cheque for three thousand dollars! It is the worthy gentleman who came to see us when you were ill, my dear! It is from Mr. Weldon!"

"But," said Lizzie, "I do not know if I can — if I ought to accept it."

"If you can — if you ought! Don't you see that Mr Weldon wishes you to continue the game. There! In spite of his respectable age, I could marry him — if he would have me! Come, let us cash the cheque!"

And they went to cash the cheque, and it was paid instantly. As to thanking this worthy, this excellent, this delightful Humphry Weldon, it was impossible, as they did not know his address.

That evening Lizzie Wag and Jovita Foley left Louisville without saying anything to anyone of the letter so opportunely received, and on the morning of the 11th they arrived at St. Louis.

Assuredly, it is well to remember, Lizzie Wag's position in the match was not promising, as she could take no part in the spins until one of her competitors had replaced her in the fifty-second square. But that would not fail to happen — to believe this confident, too confident, I Jovita — and anyhow, she was not excluded from the game for not paying her fine.

Here they were then in the State of Missouri, of which none of the "Seven" could think without a shudder. The first thing to do was to choose a hotel — and it was to the *Cleveland* they went, to occupy the same room, in the afternoon of the 11th of June.

"Well," said Jovita, "we are here in this horrible prison, and I confess that for a horrible prison St. Louis seems rather pleasant."

"A prison it must be, Jovita, from the moment we are not allowed to leave it."

"Be easy, we shall get out of it, my dear!"

All her former confidence had returned to Jovita Foley — and at the same time her natural cheerfulness — since the arrival of those three thousand dollars from the excellent Humphry Weldon, which were sent off that day by cheque to the order of Mr. Tornbrock, notary, of Chicago.

The two girls employed their leisure in the afternoon in walking about the town, which a ravine parallel to the course of the Mississippi cuts into two unequal parts. Next morning Jovita's impatience can be imagined. She was awake at sunrise, for on that day at eight o'clock Tornbrock was to proceed to another throw.

Leaving Lizzie Wag asleep, she went out of the hotel in quest of information.

Two hours. Yes! She was away for two hours, and what an awakening for the fifth player, who jumped up at the noise of a door violently thrown open and the boisterous entry of Jovita, shouting:

"Released, my dear, released!"

"What do you say?" „

"Eight by five and three. He has — "

"He?"

"And as he was at the forty-fourth square, behold him sent to the fifty-second."

"Who?"

"And as the fifty-second is the prison, he comes here to take our place — "

"But who?"

"Max Real, my dear, Max Real!"

"Ah! The poor young man!" replied Lizzie Wag. "I would much rather have remained — "

"Of course!" exclaimed the triumphant Jovita, jumping like a wild goat at the remark.

Nothing could be more correct. This throw of the dice set Lizzie Wag at liberty. She would be replaced at St. Louis by Max Real, whose place she would take at Richmond, Virginia, seven hundred and fifty miles, twenty-five to thirty hours' journey.

To get there she had from the 12th to the 20th, more time than she required. This did not prevent her impatient companion, incapable of restraining her joy, from saying:

"Let us go."

"No — Jovita, no!" replied Lizzie Wag decidedly.

"No. And why?"

"I think it is only right for us to wait here for Mr. Real. We at least owe that to this unfortunate young man.

And Jovita had to acquiesce, but on condition that the prisoner would not delay more than three days in crossing the threshold of her prison.

Now it was on the next day, the 13th, that Max Real arrived at St. Louis railway station. There existed, no doubt, some mysterious chain of suggestion between the first and fifth player, for if she had not wished to go until he arrived, he had wished to arrive before she went.

Poor Madame Real! In what a state that excellent mother must have been at the thought of her son thus unluckily stopped on the road to success!

Max Real knew from the newspapers that Lizzie Wag was staying at the *Cleveland Hotel* As soon as he called he was received by the two friends, while Tommy awaited his master's return in a neighbouring hotel.

Lizzie Wag, much more moved than she wished to appear, rose to greet the young painter:

"Ah! Mr. Real," she said. "We are so sorry for you — "

"From the bottom of our hearts!" added Jovita Foley, who was not the least in the world sorry, and whose eyes could not be got to express pity, though she tried.

"But no, Miss Wag," answered Max Real, when he had recovered his breath after a too rapid ascent. "No! I am not to be pitied — or rather I do not wish to be — for I have the happiness of releasing you."

"And you are right!" declared Jovita Foley, who could not restrain this reply, which was as frank as it was disagreeable.

"Excuse Jovita," said Lizzie Wag. "She does not reflect enough, Mr. Real; and for my part, believe me, I am really very sorry."

"Without a doubt," said Jovita Foley. "Besides, do not despair, Mr. Real! What has happened to us may happen to you! It would have been preferable if some of the others had come to prison, this Tom Crabbe, for instance, or Commodore Urrican, or Titbury! We should have received their, visit with more pleasure — than yours — that is to say — well, you understand. Anyhow, they may come to release you."

"That is possible, Miss Foley," replied Max Real, "but we must not count on it. Believe me, I accept this mishap with great philosophy. As far as the game goes I have never thought I should win it."

"Nor have I, Mr. Real," Lizzie Wag hastened to say.

"But she has — she has," interrupted Jovita, "'or at least I have thought so for her."

"As I also hope," said the young man.

"And I hope you will win, Mr. Real," said Lizzie.

"Come, come, you cannot both win!" broke in Jovita.

"It is impossible, of course," said Max Real, laughing. "There can be only one winner."

"Well, then," said Jovita Foley, "if Lizzie wins, she will have the millions; and if you come in second, you will get the pool."

"How you arrange things, my poor Jovita!" observed Lizzie.

"We must wait, and let fate do its work. If it is in your favour, Miss Wag — "

He evidently thought her more and more charming. That was only too clear. And Jovita, who assuredly was not a fool, said to herself aside:

"Well, well, and why not? It would simplify matters, and it would then make little difference which of them won!"

Ah! how she knew the human heart, and particularly that of her friend!

The three began to talk about the circumstances of the match, the incidents during the journeys, the beauties of nature they had admired in going from one state to another, the wonders of the National Park, of the Yellowstone, which Max Real would never forget, the wonders of the caves of Kentucky, which Lizzie Wag and Jovita Foley would always remember.

Then the girls told him how they had become possessed of the three thousand dollars. Without the generous remittance of Mr. Humphry Weldon, sent in terms which permitted of no refusal, Lizzie Wag would have had to retire from the game.

"And who is this Mr. Humphry Weldon?" asked Max Real, a little uneasy.

"An excellent and worthy old gentleman — who is interested in us — " replied Jovita Foley.

"In the betting way, no doubt — " added Lizzie.

"And one who is sure of winning his bets," declared Jovita.

And Max Real did not say that he himself had thought of putting this sum at the disposal of the young prisoner. But in what way could she have accepted it?

This day and the next Max Real and the two friends spent together in talks and walks. If Lizzie Wag showed herself extremely grieved at Max Real's ill-luck, he appeared quite happy that she had profited by it. And in fact, within twenty-four hours, a change had taken place among the speculators with regard to the fifth partner. And reporters began to come to the *Cleveland Hotel* to interview Lizzie Wag, who refused to see any of them. The result of her return to Virginia to the forty-fourth square, vacated by Max Real, was that she had in front of her only Tom Crabbe at the forty-seventh square and XKZ at the fifty-first.

"And this individual with the letters," asked Jovita. "Who is he?"

"Nobody knows," replied the young painter, "and he remains more mysterious than ever."

It is hardly necessary to say that Max Real, Lizzie Wag and Jovita Foley did not talk about nothing else than the Hypperbone match. They talked about their families — of the girl who had no parents left — of Madame Real, now residing at Chicago, and who would be pleased to see Miss Lizzie Wag if she would call — of Sheridan Street, which was not very far from South Halsted Street, &c., &c.

But at the same time Jovita tried her utmost to bring back the conversation to the game, and the throws that might happen.

"Perhaps," said she, "at the next throw you might plant the yellow flag on the last square."

"Impossible, Miss Foley, it is impossible," declared Max Real.

"And why?"

"Because Miss Wag has to take my place at the forty-fourth."

"Well, Mr. Real?"

"Well — the greatest number Miss Wag could obtain would be ten, which, doubled, would give her twenty points, and that would take her past the sixty-third square and bring her to the sixty-second. And then she could not win with the next throw, as you cannot get a one with two dice."

"You are. right, Mr. Real," said Lizzie Wag. "Then, Jovita, we must resign ourselves to wait — "

"But," continued the artist, "there is another throw which might be very bad for Miss Wag — "

"Which!"

"If she got eight, she would have to return to prison!"

"That! Never!" said Jovita Foley.

"However," replied Lizzie, smiling, "I should then have the pleasure of releasing Mr. Real!"

"Most sincerely, Miss Wag," affirmed the young man, "I do not wish it."

"Nor I!" declared the petulant Miss Foley.

"Then, Mr. Real," asked Lizzie Wag, "what is the best throw I can get?"

"Twelve, for it will send you to the fifty-sixth square, State of Indiana, and not to the distant regions of the Far West."

"Capital!" declared Jovita. "And at the next throw we could reach the end."

"Yes, with seven."

"Seven!" said Jovita, clapping her hands. "Seven, and the first of the Seven!"

"In any case," added Max Real, "you have only to fear the fifty-eighth square, that of Death Valley, where Commodore Urrican succumbed. But allow me once again to express the very sincere wishes regarding you that I told you at the start. That you may be victorious is what I should like better than anything else in the world."

Lizzie. Wag replied only by a look expressive of deep emotion.

"Decidedly," said Jovita to herself, "he is really very nice this Mr. Real, an artist of talent with a great future. And no one can say anything against Lizzie. She is charming, really charming, and she is quite as good as the millionaires' daughters who go hunting for titles in Europe without asking if the princes have principalities, or the dukes duchies, or if the counts are ruined, and the marquises in the bankruptcy court."

Thus reasoned this judicious though rather giddy young person, and, in her wisdom, she thought that it would not do to prolong this state of things unduly. So she returned to the question of departure.

Naturally Max Real trusted that there was no hurry for them to leave St. Louis. The two friends might wait till the 26th of June before going to Richmond, and next day was only the 13th. And perhaps Lizzie thought it was going away a little too soon. But she would not say so, and so gave in to Jovita's wish.

Max Real made no endeavour to conceal his regret at the separation. But he felt that he could say nothing more, and in the evening went to the station to see the two travellers off. There he again said:

"All my good wishes accompany you, Miss Wag."

"Thank you — thank you," replied Lizzie, shaking hands with him.

"And as to me?" asked Jovita. "Have you not a good word for me?"

"Yes, Miss Foley," replied Max Real, "for you have an excellent heart! Take great care of your companion until our return to Chicago."

The train began to move, and the young man remained on the platform until the lights of the last van disappeared in the night.

It was only too true that he was in love, and in love with this sweet and gentle Lizzie, whom his mother would adore as soon as he introduced her to her on his return. To be in serious danger of losing the game, to be imprisoned in this city with the very hypothetic hope of an early release, did not trouble him in the least.

He returned to the hotel very downhearted and lonely. Owing to his deplorable position in prison, he had been abandoned and had no more supporters; his price had gone down in the list like a barometer with a south-west wind, although he had met the demand for a triple fine.

Tommy was also in despair. His master would not win the millions of the match, and could not buy him to reduce him to the most cruel but most wished-for state of slavery.

Well, we are always wrong in not counting on chance. If it has no customs, as has been judiciously observed, it has caprices, and this observation was fully borne out on the morning of the 14th.

At nine o'clock a crowd of. spectators besieged the telegraph office at St. Louis to get the earliest possible information of the number thrown that day for the second player.

The result, which the special editions of the newspapers published immediately, was this: "Five, by three and two, Tom Crabbe."

Now Tom Crabbe, then in Pennsylvania, occupied the forty-seventh square, and this five sent him to square fifty-two, Missouri, St. Louis, prison.

Judge the effect produced by this unexpected throw of the dice! Max Real, who had taken the place of Lizzie Wag, was at once replaced by Tom Crabbe, and had in turn to replace him in Pennsylvania. Here was an upset for the bookmakers, which sent the agents and reporters rushing to the young artist's hotel; here was something to send him up in the world, bring back his partisans, and at this incredible piece of luck proclaim him the new great favourite of the Hypperbone match!

But what was the fury of John Milner, with whom nothing seemed to succeed! Tom Crabbe in prison at St. Louis and a triple fine to pay! Decidedly the pool was filling well, and the dollars were multiplying for the player who got in second.

Max Real was in no hurry to start. And why? Because he wished to hear of the throw on the 28th, which concerned Lizzie Wag. Perhaps she would be sent into one of the neighbouring states where it would be convenient for him *to* stay for a few days.

CHAPTER XXVII . A SENSATION FOR THE "TRIBUNE"

Harris T. Kymbale, it will be remembered, was present in the telegraph office at Olympia before noon on the 18th of June had become a thing of the past. He was at his post, knocked up with fatigue, exhausted in mind and body; and how could it be otherwise after this marvellous performance of the professional cyclists, Will Stanton and Robert Flock? He had just had time to say "Here!" when he fell unconscious on to a seat.

A few minutes later he had revived after a dose of his customary reviver, and read the telegram:

"Chicago, 8.13.

"Kymbale, Olympia, Washington, nine by five and four, South Dakota, Yankton. — tornbrock."

So the throw had been kept for the 18th of June, although it might have taken place two days before owing to Hermann Titbury being stopped at New Orleans, where he had to remain at the rate of two hundred dollars a day at the *Excelsior Hotel.* It had appeared reasonable to Tornbrock and the members of the Eccentric Club to make no change in the dates, so as to leave unaltered the times allowed the other players for their transit from place to place.

The reporter-in-chief of the *Tribune* could have little to complain of in this last throw of the dice. He was not obliged to return through a well-known portion of the States, but could traverse a region new for him on his way to South Dakota.

But it should be remarked that Harris T. Kymbale in taking possession of the thirty-ninth square, was behind XKZ in Minnesota, Max Real in Pennsylvania, and Lizzie Wag in Virginia. He was in the fourth place, in front of Commodore Urrican, who was in Wisconsin awaiting his approaching departure. Hermann Titbury was safe in Louisiana for the next twenty-eight days, and Tom Crabbe was doomed to grow rusty in prison at St. Louis until the end of the match, if none of the others came to his rescue.

Harris T. Kymbale recovered, it need hardly be said, all his confidence in his final success, and was even more certain of it than ever, as were also his partisans. Three stones of stumbling there were still on his road: the labyrinth of Nebraska, through which he had already passed, the prison of St. Louis, and Death Valley. But of these three dangers, one menaced XKZ, and two menaced Lizzie Wag and Max Real. But then, luck played so important a part in the Hypperbone match. The two throws the reporter had to dread were that of the twelve, which would send him to Nebraska, and that of the ten doubled, which would send him to pay his respects to Tom Crabbe in the prison of Missouri.

Although he had from the 18th of June to the 2nd of July to get to South Dakota, Harris T. Kymbale would not lose a day. Without waiting this time for the route, which the obliging Bickhorn would doubtless send him at Olympia, he arranged a very satisfactory one for himself.

South Dakota and North Dakota are separated from Washington by the two States of Idaho and Montana. In crossing Wisconsin, Minnesota, North Dakota, Montana and Idaho, the Northern Pacific puts Chicago, and consequently New York, in direct communication with Olympia. From Olympia to Fargo on the eastern frontier of North Dakota is a distance of 1300 miles, and from Fargo to Yankton in the south of South Dakota is another 400 — 1700 miles in all.

In ordinary work it is no rare thing for the American trains to run a thousand miles in thirty-two hours, and some of them do the distance in twenty-four hours. But here Harris T. Kymbale had to reckon with the crossing of the Rocky Mountains, and to admit the possibility of long delays; besides, he could easily spend his leisure at Yankton while waiting for the arrival of the next telegram on the 2nd of July. And so he very wisely decided to leave Olympia next day.

Four hundred miles divide Olympia from the range of the Rockies, then come two hundred miles from west to east through them; thus six hundred miles took him to Helena, the capital of Montana. Having a fortnight to get to South Dakota, he would arrive at Yankton well before the telegram, which he had no doubt would put him in a good position. In any case, the journey would furnish excellent copy for the *Tribune,* to the great satisfaction of its readers.

Leaving Olympia, the train ran to the north-east towards Tacoma and then south-east through the chain of the Cascade Mountains by Ellensburgh and Paxo Junction, where it crossed the Columbia River.

Standing on the gangway of his car, he viewed this marvellous country of which the scenery changed at every telegraph post, across the deep gorges through which foamed the tumultuous creeks of the Cascade Mountains, and further on where, leaving Mount Stuart to the north, the train skirted the Columbia, which flows from north to south to the elbow where it turns to join the Pacific and form the southern frontier of Washington.

Idaho, which belongs to the basin of the Columbia and abuts on the north on the Canadian Dominion, is still as rich in forests and pasturages as it was before the working of its placers. Its capital, Boise City, on the river of that name, is a town of 2300 people, and its metropolis, Idaho City, on an affluent of the Snake, commands the southern portion of this district. There the Chinese form a considerable part of the population, as do also the Mormons, who are not admitted as electors until they have renounced their custom of polygamy.

Beyond Idaho, in Montana, through the indescribable region of the Rockies, Harris T. Kymbale found more to astonish him, although his eyes might have been surfeited with the natural beauties of the sierras of New Mexico and Washington. Among the ravines and gorges of this state, for which meridians and parallels serve as geodetic boundaries, there run towards the north thousands of rios, creeks, rivers, watering vast pasturages favourable for the raising of cattle, which with its mines are its chief wealth, the climate being too rigorous for agriculture.

After passing Charles Fork River and the high peaks of Wiessner and Stevens, and then Eagle Peaks, which overlook them, the line descends towards

Helena, the capital of Idaho. This is a mountainous country, and assuredly it required the audacious genius of the Americans to make a railroad in this region. Unfortunately, the weather was not favourable. The sky was lowering, the electric tension of the atmosphere continued to increase for twenty-four hours. Heavy clouds were rising from the horizon, and Harris T. Kymbale was to witness the development of one of those terrible storms which are so grand in mountainous countries.

The storm soon assumed terrible proportions — one of those blizzards which blockade the inhabitants in their houses. The travellers were not free from anxiety, although the trains even at full speed are generally little exposed, the rails acting as conductors. But the frequency of the flashes, from second to second, the crashing and roaring of the thunder, repeated by the echoes in interminable rollings, the lightning striking the rocks and trees along the road, the detached masses leaping down in formidable avalanches, the scared animals, buffalo, deer, prongbuck, black bear, fleeing from all parts, formed an incomparable spectacle which the passengers could enjoy during the afternoon of the 20th.

And then it was that the reporter of the *Tribune* had not only the opportunity of sending his newspaper a most unexpected observation, but at the same time of recording a singular discovery regarding the zoology of the Rockies.

About five o'clock the train was slowly mounting a steep bank in the height of the storm. Harris T. Kymbale was outside on the gangway, while his companions remained inside on the seats of the car. At this moment he noticed a superb bear walking on its hind legs, troubled, no doubt, by this strife of the elements, which impresses animals so vividly. And the plantigrade, blinded by a brilliant flash raised his right paw to his forehead and drew it across.

"A bear making the sign of the — cross!" exclaimed Harris T. Kymbale. "It is not possible. My eyes must have deceived me."

No, they had not deceived him, and several times amid the blinding flashes he saw the bear making the sign with every token of terror.

Then the train arrived at the summit of the ascent, increased in speed, and soon left the bear behind.

Immediately the reporter made this entry in his notebook:

"Grizzly, new species of plantigrade. Makes the sign of the cross during storms. Name it, for the fauna of the Rockies, *Ursus christianus.*"

And this note, amplified, figured in the letter he sent from Helena next day to the *Tribune.*

Helena, situated at an altitude of 6000 feet on the eastern slope of the Rockies, on the bank of a tributary torrent of the Missouri, forms a vast emporium for mining products of the region, and contains from fourteen to fifteen thousand inhabitants. The Northern Pacific train stays there but a couple of hours, and then descends towards the plains furrowed by the course of the Yellowstone and its numerous affluents.

This country was formerly frequented by the Flatheads, Gros-Ventres, Blackfeet, Crows, Cheyennes, Modocs, and Assiniboines, now relegated to different reservations, whose neighbourhood is a constant source of complaint among the whites.

The railroad, running south-east by Bozeman, strikes the Yellowstone River at Livingston and passes from Montana into North Dakota at the 104th degree of west longitude. It crosses the Missouri at Bismarck, the capital of the state, and further east reaches Jamestown, on the James River, where Harris T. Kymbale might have changed for the branch which runs off south of Yankton. But for some whim of his own he went on by Valley City and Casselton to Fargo, where he arrived on the 23rd, in the morning, on the western frontier of Minnesota.

It was in this State, after the throw of the dice on the 10th, that that fantastic individual, XKZ, was waiting at St. Paul, the capital, for the throw on the 24th which would send him — to what square? Doubtless near the end, if not to the end — which, in spite of all his confidence, made the reporter of the *Tribune* most uneasy.

He spent the 23rd at Fargo without making himself known. Perhaps, yielding to his tourist proclivities, he would have visited the few villages on the left bank of the Red River and those on the other bank if an unexpected incident had not led him to change his plans.

While he was walking in the afternoon in the environs of the little town, he was accosted by an individual, assuredly American, of about fifty, medium height, sharp nose, blinking eyes, and not very prepossessing.

"Sir," said the man, "if I am not mistaken, I saw you alight this morning from the Northern Pacific train."

"Quite so, sir," replied Harris T. Kymbale.

"My name is Horgarth, Len Horgarth, Len William Horgarth."

"Well, Mr. Len William Horgarth, what do you want with me, if you please?"

"It is probable that you are going to Yankton?" was the reply.

"Just so — to Yankton."

"Then allow me to offer you my services."

"Your services? And what for?"

"A simple question, to begin with, sir. You have come alone?"

"Alone?" replied Harris T. Kymbale, somewhat surprised. "Yes, alone."

"Madame does not accompany you?"

"Madame?"

"Be it so; they can do without her. Here her presence is not necessary to divorce her — "

"To divorce her, Mr. Horgarth?"

"Undoubtedly, and I will undertake all the formalities for your divorce."

"But to be divorced you must be married, and, believe me, I am not."

"You are not married, and you are going to Yankton?" exclaimed Len Horgarth, who seemed extremely surprised.

"Ah! Who are you, then, Mr. Horgarth?"

"I am an inquiry agent and witness in divorce cases."

"Then I am sorry that your services are of no use to me," said Harris T. Kymbale.

The reporter need not have been astonished at the proposals of the worthy Len William Horgarth. If in Illinois divorces are so common that passengers can be greeted with, "Chicago, ten minutes to stop, time for divorce," it is still necessary for the dissolution of marriage to be surrounded with certain guarantees. But in South Dakota it is different. This is pre-eminently the country of divorces, it being only necessary for you to affirm by a witness that you have been domiciled there for six months to benefit by its advantages.

Hence this profession of inquiry agent and witness at the disposal of the lawyers. They pick up the client, witness in his favour, furnish him with a substitute, if he does not come in person and prefers to operate by procuration — in short, all the facilities imaginable. But Sioux Falls is even more advanced than Yankton in the record of matrimonial demolition.

"Well, sir," added Mr. Horgarth very obligingly, "I am infinitely sorry that you are not married."

"And so am I," replied Harris T. Kymbale," for I should have had an excellent opportunity of annulling my marriage."

"But if you are going to Yankton, do not fail to be there to-morrow before three o'clock, so as to be present at a meeting that is to be held there."

"A meeting — what about?"

"To demand that the delays of domicile should be reduced to three months, as in the State of Oklahoma, which has been an unfortunate competition for us. This meeting will be presided over by the Honourable Mr. Heldreth."

"Indeed, Mr. Horgarth! And who is this Mr. Heldreth?"

"A respectable commercial man who has already been divorced seventeen times — and has not yet finished, it is said!"

"Mr. Horgarth, I shall not fail to be at Yankton in useful time."

"I will leave you then, sir, putting myself at your disposal for the future."

"That is understood, Mr. Horgarth, and I will carefully make a note of so obliging an offer."

"One never knows when it may happen."

"As you say, Mr. Horgarth," replied Harris T. Kymbale.

And he took his leave, did this worthy witness and inquiry agent for Dakotan solicitors.

It remained to be seen if the meeting, presided over by the Honourable Mr. Heldreth would obtain the invaluable privileges in which Oklahoma rejoiced.

At six o'clock the following morning the reporter of the *Tribune* entered the train for South Dakota.

There is rather a complicated network of railways between the two states. But there are only two hundred and fifty miles between Fargo and Yankton, and he was sure of being there before the time of the meeting.

By good chance the last section of the line between Medary and Sioux Falls City had just been finished, and was to be open that very day. So that Harris T. Kymbale would not be under the necessity of doing by coach or on horseback a portion of the journey, as he had had to do in New Mexico and California.

It was about eleven o'clock when the train stopped near the little town of Medary on the bank of the Big Sioux River, and he saw all the passengers get out.

Addressing himself to the porter on the platform of the station, he said to him:

"Does the train stop here?"

"Yes, here," said the porter.

"Is it not to-day that they open the section between Medary and Sioux Falls City?"

"No, sir."

"When, then?"

"To-morrow."

This was rather annoying to Harris T. Kymbale, for the two stations are separated by some sixty miles, and if he took a vehicle he would arrive too late to be present at the meeting.

Just then he noticed in the station a train preparing to start in the direction of Yankton.

"And this train?" he asked.

"Oh, that train — " said the porter in a singular tone.

"Is it going to start?"

"Yes, at 12.13."

"For Yankton?"

"Oh! Yankton!" replied the porter with a toss of his head.

But at this moment the man was called by the station-master and could not finish his reply to the reporter.

The train was not a passenger train, and it was composed of two luggage vans, drawn by an engine which seemed to have steam up.

"My word!" said Harris T. Kymbale to himself. "Here is the very thing for me. They are not going to open the line till tomorrow. A goods train will do just as well to take me from Medary to Sioux Falls City. If I can get into one of those vans without being seen, I can explain matters when I get out."

And the confident reporter made no doubt that they would receive with perfect complaisance the explanations he would give as to being one of the celebrated players in the Hypperbone match, and offered to pay the price of this irregular trip.

His plan was favoured by the railway station being deserted at the time. All the travellers appeared to have been in a hurry to leave it. Not a porter was on the platform. There were only the driver and stoker on the engine, engaged in shovelling the coals into the fire-box.

Without being seen, Harris T. Kymbale was able to slip into a van, hide himself in a corner, and wait for the departure.

At thirteen minutes past twelve the train started with an unusual jerk.

Ten minutes elapsed, during which the speed continued to increase until it became excessive.

It was curious that when the train ran through the stations the driver did not whistle.

Harris T. Kymbale got up and looked through a little grated window in front of the van.

There was no one on the engine, which was belching out clouds of smoke and steam — no driver, no stoker.

"What does this mean?" asked Harris T. Kymbale. "Have they both fallen off — or has this wretched engine run away from the station, like a horse from his stable?"

Suddenly he uttered a cry of horror. On the same line, about two hundred yards in front, appeared another train coming in the opposite direction at equal speed.

A few seconds afterwards there was a frightful collision. The two locomotives, were telescoped with indescribable violence, smashing up the vans one against the other; and with a fearful explosion the two boilers flew in fragments into space.

And then amid the noise of the explosion came the excited cheering of thousands of people, massed on each side of the line at a safe distance from the scene of collision.

It was for the benefit of these spectators that this thrilling spectacle had been arranged at their expense, the meeting of two trains hurled against each other at full speed — a spectacle truly American if there ever was one.

And that is how the line of railroad was inaugurated between Medary and Sioux Falls City, the Eden of divorce in America.

CHAPTER XXVIII . THE LAST MOVES OF THE HYPPERBONE MATCH

Needless to depict Lizzie Wag's state of mind when she separated from Max Real to take his place at Richmond. Leaving in the evening of the 13th, she could not help thinking that next day fate would do for Max Real what it had done for her — that is to say, render him his liberty and give him an opportunity of getting on the move again along the vast race-course of the United States of America.

A prey to feelings she kept to herself, she ensconced herself in a corner of the car, and Jovita Foley, sitting near her, did not attempt to worry her companion with untimely conversations.

From St. Louis to Richmond is but seven hundred miles across Missouri, Kentucky, West Virginia, and Virginia. It was in the morning of the 14th that the two travellers reached Richmond to await the approaching telegram from Tornbrock. On the other hand, we know that Max Real had resolved not to leave St. Louis until the throw of the 20th had been announced, thinking he might meet Lizzie Wag on the way when going to Philadelphia to replace Tom Crabbe.

One can easily imagine the joy of the two friends — a joy great, but reserved with one, and noisy and demonstrative with the other — when, on their arrival, the Richmond newspapers announced the deliverance of Max Real.

"Now, do you not see, my dear," declared Jovita Foley, thrilling with excitement, "that there is a God! There are people who pretend there is not. The fools! If there were not, would this Crabbe ever have had a throw of five? No. God knows what He does, and we ought to give thanks to Him — "

"From the bottom of the heart!" finished Lizzie, a prey to profound emotion.

"After all," continued Jovita, "the happiness of one is often the unhappiness of another, and I have always thought that there is on earth a certain amount of happiness at the disposal of mankind, and that one takes his part of it to the detriment of another."

Notice this astonishing person with her philosophic views. In any case, if there had been a certain amount of gaiety to spend in this world, she would have left little for others after she had taken her share.

"There!" she continued, "now we have Crabbe in prison in place of Mr. Real. All the worse for him, unless Commodore Urrican is going to deliver him. But if that happens, I should not like to meet that bombshell on the road."

All they had to do now was to wait without impatience for the 20th. During these six days the time could be agreeably spent in going about this Richmond of whose beauty Max Real had so justly boasted to the two friends. Undoubtedly it would have seemed still more beautiful if the young painter had accompanied them during these walks. At least Jovita Foley said so, and it is not unlikely that Lizzie Wag shared this opinion.

They remained in the hotel as little as possible. That allowed them to escape the interviewers of the Virginian journals, which had, with great fuss, announced the presence of the fifth player in Richmond. To the great annoyance of Lizzie Wag, many of the journals had published her portrait as well as that of Jovita Foley — which did not displease "her other self," as she was called. And how did they manage to avoid replying to the marks of sympathy which greeted them during their excursions?

Yes! The two rich heiresses whom the people saluted, although they were not so far ahead as this inexplicable XKZ in whose existence numbers still refused to believe. Lizzie Wag was more and more in demand in all the betting agencies and on all the markets.

"I take Lizzie Wag!" „

"I back Kymbale against Wag."

"I have Titbury."

"Who wants Titbury?"

"Here is Titbury."

"Here is Crabbe in bundles."

"Who has Real?"

"Who has Lizzie Wag?"

Nothing was heard but that, and you can imagine the importance of the amounts ventured on the fifth player's chances of success. In two lucky throws she might reach the end and become the chief, or, if she shared with her companion, one of the richest heiresses of the country of dollars that figure in the Golden Book of America.

When the 16th of June arrived, as it only affected Hermann Titbury, plunged for another month in the delights of the *Excelsior Hotel,* a few of those interested had issued a proposal that the draw should take place on account of the fourth partner, that is to say of Harris T. Kymbale, and that each turn should be advanced two days. But such was not the opinion of Mr. George B. Higginbotham, nor of the other members of the Eccentric Club, nor of Mr. Tornbrock, who was entrusted with interpreting the wishes of the deceased.

On the 18th, it will be remembered, the reporter-in-chief of the *Tribune* had been sent from Olympia to Yankton, and the following morning the newspapers announced that he had left the capital of Washington by the Northern Pacific. But by his move from the thirtieth to the thirty-ninth square he in no way menaced Lizzie Wag, who was at the forty-fourth.

At last, on the 20th, before eight o'clock, Jovita Foley having compelled her to go with her, they were at the Richmond post office. There, half an hour afterwards, the wire brought them the result, twelve by six and six — the highest that could be given by two dice. This was a move of twelve squares, which took them to the fifty-sixth, Indiana.

The two friends returned in all haste to the hotel to escape the too obtrusive demonstrations of the public.

"Ah! my dear!" said Jovita, "Indiana and Indianapolis, its capital! Could such luck be possible! We get near our Illinois, and now you are at the head and are five squares in front of this intruder, this XKZ, and the yellow flag beats the red. You want only, seven points to win. And why should you not get seven? Is it not that of the branches of the biblical candlestick, that of the days of the week, that of the Pleiades (she did not dare say that of the capital sins), that of the players who are running after the heritage! May Heaven make the dice yield seven and let us win the game. You know, and you ought to know, what good use we will make of these millions — for the good — the good of all the world! We will found houses of charity, workshops, a hospital! Yes, the Wag-Foley Hospital for the sick of Chicago — in large letters! And I will have an institution for girls who cannot marry because they have no dowry, and I will be the manager, and you will see how I will administer it! Ah! of course you will never enter it, Mademoiselle Millionaire, because — oh! yes — I understand. And besides, marquises and dukes and princes will be seeking your hand!"

Positively, Jovita Foley was delirious! And she threw her arms around Lizzie Wag, who received with a vague smile all these promises of the future, and then she spun round and round and round like a whip-top.

The question now to be decided was if the fifth player should at once leave Richmond, as she had until the 4th of July to get to Indianapolis. And as she had already been in the Virginian city for six days, Jovita insisted that it would be best for them to start next morning for their new destination.

Lizzie Wag yielded to her arguments, particularly as the indiscretion of the public and the persistency of the reporters were getting more and more annoying. And as Max Real was not at Richmond, why prolong the stay there? To this argument, urged by Jovita Foley with a pertinacity that did not displease, what could Lizzie reply?

So in the morning of the 21st they went to the railway station. The train would cross Virginia, West Virginia, and Ohio, and deposit them the same evening in the capital of Indiana — a journey of four hundred and fifty miles.

But this is what happened. As they reached the platform they were spoken to by a most polite gentleman, who said to them, with a bow:

"It is to Miss Lizzie Wag and Miss Jovita Foley that I have the honour of speaking?"

"Just so," replied the more forward of the two.

"I am the major-domo of Mrs. Migglesy Bullen, and Mrs. Migglesy Bullen would be glad if Miss Lizzie Wag and Miss Jovita Foley would come into her train to be taken to Indianapolis."

"Come," said Jovita Foley, without giving Lizzie Wag time to reflect.

The major-domo accompanied them to a siding in which was waiting a train consisting of an engine, bright with paint and polish, a drawing-room car, a dining car, a sleeping car, and a second van in the rear, as luxurious within as without — a real royal, imperial, or presidential train.

It was in this way that Mrs. Migglesy Bullen, one of the most opulent Americans of the States travelled. A rival of the Waitmans, Stevenses, Gerry s,

Bradley s, Sloanes, Belmonts, e&c., who only travel in their own yachts and trains, until they make their own railroads, Mrs. Migglesy Bullen was an amiable widow of fifty, the owner of inexhaustible petroleum wells.

Lizzie Wag and Jovita Foley passed between a numerous domestic staff, drawn up on the platform, and were received by two lady companions, who conducted them to the drawing-room car, where they found the millionairess.

"Ladies," said she very affably, "I thank you for having accepted my offer and consented to accompany me during this journey. You will travel under more agreeable conditions than in the public train, and I am happy also to show the interest I take in the fifth player, although I have no interest in the game."

"We are infinitely honoured — by the honour you have done us, Mrs. Migglesy Bullen," said Jovita.

"And we tender you our grateful thanks," added Lizzie Wag.

"There is no need for that," replied the excellent dame with a smile, "but I hope, Miss Wag, that my company will bring you good fortune!"

The journey was charming, for, in spite of her millions, Mrs. Migglesy Bullen was the best of women, and they passed a pleasant time in the drawing-room, in the dining-room, and in walking from one end of the train to the other. The luxury of the furnishing and the richness of decoration were beyond imagination.

"And think," said Jovita Foley to Lizzie Wag at a moment when they found themselves alone, "that we may soon travel like this — in our own property — "

"Be reasonable, Jovita!"

"You will see!"

And really it was even the opinion, absolutely disinterested, of Mrs. Migglesy Bullen that Lizzie Wag would reach the end first of the Seven.

Towards the evening the train stopped at Indianapolis, and as it was going on to Chicago the two friends had to alight. In remembrance of the journey Mrs. Migglesy Bullen begged their acceptance of a beautiful ring each, and having thanked her, not without emotion, they took their leave, much impressed by this princely hospitality.

And then as quietly as possible they went to the *Sherman Hotel,* to which they had been recommended. But this did not prevent the Indianapolis newspapers next morning announcing their presence at the said hotel.

During the fortnight they had to spare they would have time to visit the principal places in the vicinity, and make an excursion to the Wyandotte Caves, between Evansville and New Albany, which are rivals to the Mammoth Caves. But Jovita Foley preferred to remain content with the remembrance of the marvels of Kentucky. Was it not in that charming spot she had won the grade of lieutenant-colonel in the Illinois militia? She thought of it sometimes, not without a strong temptation to laugh, and she also thought of the obligation imposed on both, when they returned to Chicago, to go in military fashion and report themselves to the governor —

And when she noticed her companion not sorrowful but thoughtful, she would repeat:

"Lizzie, I do not understand you — or rather I understand you very well! He is a nice young man — sympathetic — amiable — with all the gifts — and among others that of not displeasing you! But as he is not here, for he ought to be in Philadelphia in place of that unfortunate Crabbe, who cannot even walk sideways like the crustacean that bears the name, you should be reasonable, my dear; and if you think about him, you should also think about us too — "

"Jovita — you exaggerate."

"Come, Lizzie, be frank! Confess that you are in love with him!"

And the girl did not reply — which was doubtless a way of replying.

On the 22nd the newspapers announced the throw relative to Commodore Urrican.

The orange flag had had to begin the game again after the return from Death Valley, and by a happy throw had gone to the twenty-sixth square, Wisconsin. But like the days, the throws followed and did not resemble each other. Assuredly Tornbrock must have had an unlucky hand that morning, for by five, composed of one and four, he had sent Hodge Urrican to the thirty-first square, Nevada. And this was where William J. Hypperbone had placed the well, at the bottom of which the unfortunate commodore would have to remain until one of the competitors came to draw him up.

"He must have done it on purpose, this Tornbrock!" shouted Hodge Urrican in a paroxysm of fearful anger. And Turk having declared that on an early occasion he would wring Tornbrock's neck, his master made no attempt to calm him. Besides, it was a treble fine, three thousand dollars, which had to come out of the sixth player's pocket and fall into the pool.

The good-hearted Lizzie could not help pitying the unfortunate sea-wolf.

"Pity him!" said Jovita. "Yes, just enough to hope that when Mr. Titbury leaves his hotel he may get him out by getting in with a twelve. After all, the important thing is that Mr. Real is out of prison, and I have an idea we shall see him again sooner or later."

This perspicacious person was wiser than she thought. In fact, on returning from the walk which the two friends had taken that morning, on arriving opposite the *Sherman Hotel,* Lizzie Wag could not restrain an exclamation of surprise.

"Eh! what is the matter with you?" asked Jovita.

Then in turn she exclaimed:

"You — Mr. Real!"

The young artist was there in front of the door, and near him was Tommy. A little embarrassed, he endeavoured to excuse his presence.

"Ladies," he said, "I am going to my post in Philadelphia, and as Indiana happened by chance to be on the road — "

"A geographical chance," replied Jovita, laughing. "Anyway, a happy chance."

"And as it did not lengthen my journey — "

"For, Mr. Real, if it did lengthen it, you should not have run the risk of failing — ".

"Oh, I have till the 23rd, Miss Wag! Still six clear days, and — "

"And when one has six clear days in which one does not know what to do, the best thing is to spend them with the people in whom one takes an interest — a lively interest — "

"Jovita!" said Lizzie in an undertone.

"And chance," continued Jovita Foley, "always this fortunate chance, led you to select this very *Sherm.an Hotel* "The newspapers said the fifth player was here with her faithful companion — "

"And," replied the faithful companion, "from the moment the fifth player alighted at the *Sherman Hotel* it was quite natural that the first player should alight there also. Now if it had been the second or the third — but no! — it was precisely the fifth. And in all that, mere chance — "

"Nothing of the sort, and you know it, Miss Wag," avowed Max Real, pressing the hand that Lizzie held out to him.

"Come, that is more frank!" said Jovita. "And frankness for frankness, we are very glad of your visit, Mr. Real, but I warn you that you shall not remain here an hour longer than you ought to, and that we shall not let you miss the train for Philadelphia."

It is hardly necessary to remark that Max Real had waited at St. Louis until the newspapers announced the arrival of the two friends at Indianapolis, and that he intended to devote to them all the time he could.

Then they chatted "like old friends," as Jovita Foley said; they arranged walks across the city, which, owing to Max Rears presence, would be much more interesting to visit. However, the faithful companion insisted that they must sometimes talk about the game. Lizzie Wag was now ahead, and it was not this XKZ who would make her take second place. To arrive first, at the approaching throw this fortunate individual would have to throw twelve, and this could only be done by six and six, while the seven which would plant the yellow flag of Lizzie Wag on the sixty-third square could be obtained in three different ways, by three and four, two and five, one and six. Hence three chances to one — according to Jovita Foley.

Whether this reasoning was right or not, Max Real did not trouble about it. Between Lizzie Wag and him the match was hardly mentioned. They talked about Chicago, of the return there which would come shortly, of the pleasure — Madame Real would have in receiving the young friends, and a letter from this excellent lady — doubtless from information received — affirmed this in the most agreeable terms.

"You have a good mother, Mr. Real," said Lizzie Wag, whose eyes moistened as she read the letter.

"The best of mothers, Miss Wag; and who cannot help loving all those I love."

"And what a no less good mother-in-law she will make!" exclaimed Jovita, exploding with laughter.

The second part of the day was spent in walking in the better quarters of the town, principally on the banks of White River. To avoid the intruders who besieged the *Sherman Hotel* — and who all wished to espouse the future heiress of William J. Hypperbone, to believe Jovita — had become a veritable necessity. Prudently, Max Real had not said who he was, for their partisans had become legion.

And so Max Real waited till night had fallen before returning to the hotel, and the last meal over — supper rather than dinner — they had only to go to rest after the fatigues of so happy a day.

At ten o'clock Lizzie Wag and Jovita Foley regained their room, and Max Real retired to his, Tommy having a room close by. And while one abandoned herself to dreams "woven in silver and broidered in gold," perhaps the others met in similar thoughts without finding sleep. Yes, two of them thought only, of the return to Chicago by the line along the White River to Spring Valley, about twenty miles from Indianapolis, and come back by a different route. The happy trio started, then; Tommy, this time, being left at the hotel.

Now, although Max Real and Lizzie Wag were too much occupied to notice anything, Jovita Foley had remarked that five individuals had followed them since their departure. And not only had these people accompanied them to the station, but they had got into the same train, if not into the same car, for when Max Real and the two friends alighted at Spring Valley these people also got out.

This did not otherwise attract Jovita Foley's attention, as she was looking out of the windows of the car when she was not looking towards Max Real and Lizzie Wag.

Perhaps, suspecting that they had been observed, the five individuals separated as they came out of the railway station.

To be brief, Max Real and the two friends took a road which would bring them to the bank of the White River. Was there any risk of their losing themselves? None.

For an hour they walked in this way across this fertile country, watered by the creek, here cultivated fields, there thick woods, the remains of the old forests that had fallen before the civilizing axe of the woodman.

It was a very pleasant walk owing to the mildness of the temperature. Jovita flitted about quite joyously, first in front, then behind, teasing the young couple, who heeded her not. And did she not claim the respect due to a mother," and even a grandmother, "for was she not acting as such?

It was three o'clock when a ferry-boat took them across the White River. Beyond, under the large trees, lay a road leading to one of the numerous railroads which converge on Indianapolis. Max Real and his companions began to talk of other excursions in the vicinity of the city until the evening of the 27th, when to his disgust as well as that of his friends he would have to go by train to Philadelphia. And then — but it was better not to think of it.

After half an hour's walk along the road shaded by beautiful trees, Jovita Foley proposed a halt of a few minutes. There was plenty of time, provided they returned to the Sherman Hotel before dinner. Just there the road curved between two clumps of trees in full shadow, in full foliage.

At that very moment five men rushed out — the same who had left the train at Spring Valley.

What did these individuals want? What they wanted — for they were not professional murderers or thieves — was to seize Lizzie Wag, drag her away to some secret place, and there keep her so that she could not be at Indianapolis post-office on July 4th, when her telegram arrived. The result would be that she would be shut out of the game, on the eve perhaps, of her becoming the winner.

To this had been led some of these gamesters, these pernicious betting people who had enormous sums, hundreds of thousands of dollars, ventured on the match. Yes! These malefactors — can you call them otherwise? — did not recoil before such acts.

Three of the men threw themselves on Max Real, so as to prevent him defending his companions. The fourth seized Jovita Foley while the fifth tried to drag Lizzie Wag into the depths of the woods, where it would be difficult to discover any trace of her.

Max Real struggled, and seizing the revolver which an American always carries with him, he fired.

One of the men fell, wounded only.

Jovita Foley and Lizzie Wag shrieked for help, though they had no hope they would be heard.

They were, however, and behind a thicket at the left there was heard a sound of voices.

A few farmers in the neighbourhood — about a dozen — were out shooting in the woods, and a providential chance had brought them on the scene.

The five men made a final attempt. A second time Max Real fired at the one who was carrying off Lizzie Wag, and made him let the girl go. But he received a stab from a knife in his chest, and with a cry fell senseless on the ground.

The farmers came in view, and the aggressors, of whom two were wounded, realized that the attempt had failed and ran off under the trees.

There was something better to do than to pursue them; it was to carry Max Real to the nearest station, to send for a doctor, and to take him back to Indianapolis if his state would permit.

Lizzie Wag, distracted and in tears, went and knelt near the young man.

Max Real breathed, his eyes opened, and he said:

"Lizzie — dear Lizzie — it will be nothing — nothing. And you — you?"

His eyes closed again. But he lived — he had recognized the girl — he had spoken to her.

In half an hour the farmers had got him to the station, where a doctor was soon in attendance. After examining the wound, he said it was not mortal, and having washed it and dressed it, he assured them that Max Real could be taken back to Indianapolis without danger. So he was placed in one of the cars of the half-past five train, with Lizzie Wag and Jovita Foley on each side of him. He had recovered consciousness, he did not feel seriously hurt, and at six o'clock he was in bed in his room at the *Sherman Hotel*.

Alas! How long would he have to, remain there, and was it not only too certain that he could not be at Philadelphia post office on the 28th?

Well, Lizzie Wag would not abandon him who had been wounded in defending her. No! she would remain near him — she would look after him.

And it must be confessed, to her honour — though it meant the annihilation of all her hopes — that Jovita Foley approved of the conduct of her poor friend.

A second doctor who came to visit Max Real confirmed what his colleague had said. The lung had only been grazed by the point of the knife, but a very little more and the wound would have been fatal. He also was of opinion that Max Real would be at least a fortnight before he was able to move about again.

What did it matter? Did he dream of the fortune of William J. Hypperbone? Was Lizzie Wag vexed at sacrificing the chance she perhaps had of becoming the heiress of the eccentric deceased? No, it was of another future that both dreamed, a future of happiness quite independent of the sixty millions!

Yet, after long and bitter reflections, Jovita remarked to herself:

"After all, as this poor Mr. Real must remain here a fortnight, Lizzie will still be here on the 4th of July, at the date of her next throw, and if by good luck the seven comes — and may Heaven make it come! — she will win the game!"

This was true, and considering their past trials Heaven might very well do this for the fifth player!

It should be said that at Max Real's request his mother was not informed of what had occurred. He had not given his name at the hotel, as we know, and when the newspapers reported the attempt, indicating the motive that inspired it, they spoke only of Lizzie Wag.

When the news was known, its effect among the speculators can be imagined, and no one was surprised at the yellow flag being applauded throughout America.

But the matter, as we shall see, was to be cleared up more promptly and in quite a different fashion to what the immense majority of the public expected.

On the 24th, at half-past eight in the morning, the newsboys were running about Indianapolis with copies of the telegram in their hands, and announcing, or rather yelling, the result of the throw that morning on behalf of the seventh player.

The throw was twelve — six and six — and as this player then occupied the fifty-first square, State of Minnesota, he it was who had won the game.

So the winner was no other than the enigmatic personage designated as XKZ.

And it was the red flag that floated over this Illinois, fourteen times repeated on the board of the Noble Game of the United States of America.

CHAPTER XXIX. THE BELL AT OAKWOOD

A CLAP of thunder heard in every quarter of the terrestrial globe could not have produced more effect than the fall of the dice from the box in the hands of Tornbrock, as eight o'clock struck in the Auditorium on the 24th of June. The thousands assembled there — thinking it might be the last in the Hypperbone match — announced it all over Chicago, and thousands of telegrams spread it to the four corners of the New World and the Old.

It was, then, the masked man, the player of the last hour, the intruder of the codicil, in a word, or rather in three letters, this XKZ who had won the game, and with the game the sixty millions of dollars!

Let us see how this had been done by this favourite of fortune. While so many misfortunes had happened to the other players — one shut up in the inn, another obliged to pay toll on the bridge of Niagara, another lost in the labyrinth, another thrown into the well, three others sent to prison, all having fines to pay — XKZ had gone along at a steady pace from Illinois to Wisconsin, from Wisconsin to the District of Columbia, from the District of Columbia to Minnesota, from Minnesota to the end, without having to' pay a single fine, and within an easy radius necessitating few fatigues and expenses during his easy journeys.

Was that not an instance of luck beyond the ordinary and even wonderful, the luck of the privileged ones with whom everything succeeds in life?

It remained to be known who was this XKZ, and he would doubtless not delay in making himself known, so as to enter into possession of his enormous heritage.

There had of course been a crowd to see him when he presented himself at the post offices of Milwaukee, Washington and Minneapolis to receive his telegram, but they had seen a middle-aged man in one place, and a man over sixty in another, and each time he had immediately disappeared, leaving no trace behind him. But now they would soon know his real name, and the States would have another millionaire in place of William J. Hypperbone.

Nine days after the final throw the following was the position of the six other players: —

To begin with, it should be said that they had all returned to Chicago. Yes, all, some in despair, others furious — we can guess which — and two quite indifferent to the result of the match, which two it is also unnecessary to mention.

The week had just ended when Max Real, nearly healed of his wound, arrived in his native city, accompanied by Lizzie Wag and Jovita Foley. He went straight to South Halsted Street, while the two friends went to Sheridan Street.

And then Madame Real, who had already heard of the attack on Lizzie Wag, learnt, like the rest of the world, the name of the young man to whom the girl owed her safety.

"Ah, my boy — my boy!" she exclaimed, pressing Max in her arms, "it was you! it was you!"

"But as I am all right again, good mother, do not weep! What I did, I did for her — you understand, for her — whom you are going to know — and whom you will love as much as I love her and she loves me!"

In the course of that day Lizzie Wag, accompanied by Jovita Foley, came to visit Madame Real. The girl greatly, pleased the excellent dame, as she pleased the girl. Madame Real overwhelmed her with caresses, without forgetting Jovita, who was so different from her friend, but just as amiable in her own way.

Thus these three people became acquainted with each other, and what it led to we must wait a few days to learn.

It was after Max Real's departure that Tom Crabbe arrived in St. Louis. In what a state of fury and shame was John Milner! So much money expended for nothing — not only the cost of the journeys, but the triple fine he had to pay in this State prison of Missouri! Then the reputation of the Champion of the New World compromised in that encounter with the no less vexed Cavanaugh, of which the true victor was the Reverend Hugh Hunter of Arondale! As to Tom Crabbe, he continued to understand nothing of the part he was made to play, and went where his trainer took him. Was not the animal in him quite satisfied from the moment he was guaranteed his six meals a day? And how many weeks would John Milner be shut up in this city? Next morning he was at ease on that score, the game was over, and all he had to do was to get back to his house in Chicago.

And that also did Hermann Titbury. For fourteen days he had occupied the rooms reserved for him at the *Excelsior Hotel* in New Orleans — fourteen days during which he and his wife had eaten well, drunk well, had a carriage and a yacht at their command, and a box at the opera at their disposal, had lived, in fact, the life of the people who enjoy large incomes and know how to spend them. It is true this kind of life cost them two hundred dollars a day, and when the bill was presented it came like a blow from a sledge-hammer. But they raised the two thousand eight hundred dollars, and adding to them the fines in Louisiana, the fine in Maine, the robbery in Utah, and the expenses on the journeys as lengthy as they were costly, their expenses amounted to nearly eight thousand dollars.

Struck in the heart, that is to say in the purse, Mr. and Mrs. Titbury were brought to their senses, and on their return to their house in Robey Street indulged in grand scenes of violence, during which the lady reproached the gentleman for having launched her on this ruinous adventure in spite of all she could say, and conclusively proved that all the wrong was on his side. And Mr. Titbury ended by being convinced, as was his custom, all the more as the terrible servant took the side of her mistress, also as was her custom. At the same time it was agreed that the expenses of the house must be further reduced. But that did not hinder the happy couple from being haunted by the remembrance of the days spent among the delights of the *Excelsior Hotel.* And what a change was there when they fell out of their dreams into the abysses of reality!

"A monster, this Hypperbone, an abominable monster!" said Mrs. Titbury occasionally.

"You should have got his millions, or not meddled with them!" added the servant.

"Yes — not meddled with them! That is exactly what I was always telling Mr. Titbury! But you cannot talk reason to people like him!"

Harris T. Kymbale? Well, Harris T. Kymbale emerged safe and sound from that collision arranged for the opening of the Medary and Sioux Falls City Railway. Before the shock he had jumped out on to the line, and, not without a bounce as if he had been made of indiarubber, he remained unconscious at the foot of a rubbish heap in shelter from the explosion of the two engines. Undoubtedly it happens, even in America, that trains collide and telescope each other, but it is rare that the event is arranged in advance while spectators at a safe distance on each side of the line are able to be present at the incomparable entertainment.

Unfortunately, Harris T. Kymbale was not in a position to enjoy it.

Three hours later, when the railway men came to clear the line, they found a man unconscious, at the foot of the heap. They picked him up, they took him to the nearest house, they called in a doctor, who brought him round, questioned him, and discovered that he was the fourth player in the Hypperbone match. Then it became known how he had taken his place in the train doomed to destruction, and they favoured him with the reproaches he deserved, they made him pay his fare — for on the American lines you pay on the road or when you arrive — they telegraphed the incident to the editor of the *Tribune,* and they despatched this imprudent reporter by the shortest road to Chicago, where on the 25th he arrived at his house in Milwaukee Avenue.

And naturally the intrepid Kymbale declared himself ready to continue his travels and to go if need be from one end of the States to the other. But having learnt that the game had ended to the profit of XKZ, he had to content himself with remaining at home and writing interesting articles on the recent incidents in which he had taken part. In any case he had wasted neither his time nor his trouble, and he would never forget his rushes through New Mexico, South Carolina, Nebraska, Washington, South Dakota, nor the original manner in which had been inaugurated the Medary and Sioux Falls City Railway.

His self-respect as a well-informed reporter was, however, touched in a sensitive part by a revelation which brought on him the jokes and jeers of the petty press. It was with regard to that bear he had met within the passes of Idaho, the grizzly which had made the sign of the cross at each clap of thunder, the *Ursus christianus* for which he had formed so appropriate a name. It turned out to be merely a native of those parts, who was taking the skin of a magnificent, plantigrade to a fur merchant. As the rain was falling in torrents he had put the skin over him, and as he was afraid, he crossed himself, like a good Catholic, at every flash.

In short, Harris T. Kymbale ended by laughing at the occurrence, but his laughter was of the colour of the flag that Jovita Foley had not been able to wave triumphantly over the sixty-third square.

As to the fifth player, we know under what circumstances she had returned to Chicago with her faithful friend, Max Real, and Tommy, as disappointed at the non-success of his master as Jovita Foley at that of Lizzie Wag.

"But you must resign yourself to it, my poor Jovita!" said Lizzie Wag. "You know well that I never expected it — "

"But I did."

"You were wrong."

"After all you have nothing to complain of."

"And I do not complain," said Lizzie with a smile. If the Hypperbone heritage has escaped you, you are no longer a poor girl without a dowry."

"How is that?"

"Evidently, Lizzie! After XKZ, who has got to the end first, you are the nearest to him, and the amount of the fines will come to you."

"Well, Jovita, I never thought of that."

"But I thought of it for you, you careless Lizzie! and there is a nice little sum of which you are the legitimate proprietor."

In fact, the thousand dollars from Niagara Bridge, the two thousand from the inn at New Orleans, the two thousand from the Nebraska labyrinth, the three thousand from Death Valley, in California, and the nine thousand coming from the prison of St. Louis, made up seventeen thousand dollars, which incontestably belonged, by the terms of the will, to the second on the board, otherwise the fifth player. And yet, as Lizzie Wag had said, she had not thought about it, having something else to think about.

At the same time there was one person of whom Max Real could not be jealous, but of whom she did think occasionally. This person, it will be guessed, was the worthy Humphry Weldon, who had honoured her with a visit in Sheridan Street and to whom were due the three thousand dollars for the payment of the fine in the Missouri prison. Although he might be a gambler "following his money,' as they say, he had none the less generously helped the prisoner who had always intended to repay him when she won. And so she thought of him with proper gratitude and would have been glad to meet him. But he had not been seen again.

To complete this summary of the existing state of affairs, we must recall attention to Commodore Urrican.

On the 22nd of June there took place the throw which concerned him, and he was then in Wisconsin. It will not have been forgotten that by five, made up of one and four, he had been sent to the thirty-first square, State of Nevada. Another journey of twelve hundred miles, for Nevada lies between Oregon,

Idaho, Utah, Arizona, and California. And by an excess of ill-luck it was the State in which William J. Hypperbone had placed the well, to the bottom of which the unfortunate player might take a header.

The commodore's fury was beyond all bounds. He resolved to have satisfaction from Tornbrock — and Turk declared that he would leap at the notary's throat, strangle him with his teeth, open him up and eat his liver. But with the haste he brought to bear on everything, Hodge Urrican left Milwaukee on the 22nd, jumped into the train with his inseparable companion — after sending the notary the three thousand dollars which the last throw had cost him — and went off at full speed towards Nevada.

It was at Carson City, the capital, that the orange flag was to report himself on the 6th of July.

It should be noted that if Nevada had been chosen as the well by the testator, it was because wells there are so numerous — wells of mines; be it understood, and from the point of view of the production of gold and silver Nevada holds the fourth place in the Union. Improperly designated by the name, for the Nevada chain is beyond its boundaries, its principal towns are Virginia City, Gold Hill, Silver City — names that explain themselves. These towns are built above the silver veins, such as the Comstock Lode, and into these deposits the wells are sunk, some of them for a depth of two thousand seven hundred feet.

Wells of silver, if you please, but wells that justified the choice of the testator and also the anger of him whom fate had sent to them.

But he did not get there! At Great Salt Lake City, on the morning of the 24th, the great news reached him.

The game had ended to the advantage of XKZ, the winner of the Hypperbone match.

The commodore then returned to Chicago in a state more easily imagined than described.

It is no exaggeration to say that from the Atlantic to the Pacific people began to breathe again. And yet for all those who were interested in this national game — even platonically — there was a pardonable curiosity to satisfy.

Who was XKZ, and would he make himself known? There was no doubt about it. When one has to pocket sixty millions one does not remain incognito — one does not take refuge under letters! The fortunate winner must present himself in person, and he would so present himself.

But when and under what conditions? No time was mentioned in the will. And yet it was not likely to be long. The said XKZ was in Minnesota, at Minneapolis, when the telegram was sent to him, and he could come from Minneapolis to Chicago in half a day.

But a week elapsed, and then another, and no news of the unknown.

One of the most impatient — as a matter of course — was Jovita Foley. This nervous personage would have liked Max Real to go ten times a day for information, to remain permanently at the Auditorium, where the most fortunate of the Seven would certainly make his first appearance. But Max Real had his mind occupied with other things that interested him more.

And then Jovita Foley would exclaim:

"Oh, if I could only get hold of him!"

"Do not get so excited, my dear," said Lizzie Wag.

"I will get excited, Lizzie, and if I get hold of him I will ask him by what right he is allowed to win the game — a man whose name we do not even know."

"But, my dear Jovita," replied Max Real, "if you ask him that, he will be there, and we shall have no more to know."

We need not be surprised at the two friends not having yet returned to Marshall Field's to resume their duties. Lizzie would have to be replaced by some one else, and Jovita intended that the whole affair should be over before she went back, as she had no head for her old work just at present.

In every way, with her impatience, she faithfully represented the public opinion of the United States. As the time went by, imagination had full play. The press — particularly the sporting press — was bewildered. Numbers of people went to Tornbrock, and always the same reply. The notary affirmed that he knew nothing about the bearer of the red flag — he did not know him — he could not say where he had gone on leaving Minneapolis, where the message had been delivered into his own hands, and when they pressed him, when they insisted on knowing: "He will come when it pleases him!" was all that Tornbrock would vouchsafe.

Then the players, with the exception of Lizzie Wag and Max Real, judged it proper to interfere, and with some reason. In fact, if the winner did not declare himself, had they not reason to declare that the game was not won, that it should be resumed?

Commodore Urrican, Hermann Titbury, and John Milner by power of attorney from Tom Crabbe, absolutely intractable, and advised by their solicitors, announced their intention of bringing an action at law against the executor of the will. The newspapers that had supported them during the match did not abandon them. In the *Tribune* Harris T. Kymbale had a most lively article against XKZ, whose existence he denied, and the *Chicago Herald Chicago Inter-Ocean, Daily News Record, Chicago Mail*, and the *Free Press* defended the cause of the players with incredible violence.

All America became excited over this new matter. Besides, it was impossible to settle the bets until the identity of the winner had been certified officially, so long as it was not certain that the match was definitely over. One opinion soon came to the fore; it was that there should be a monster demonstration at the Auditorium. If XKZ did not appear shortly — Mr. Tornbrock would have to resume the throws. Tom Crabbe, Hermann Titbury, Harris T. Kymbale, Commodore Urrican, even Jovita Foley, if they would allow her to take Lizzie Wag's place, were ready to start for any of the States to which they might be sent.

At last the public, agitation attained such intensity that the authorities began to take steps — at Chicago above all. They had to afford protection to the members of the Eccentric Club and the notary whom the mob held responsible.

But on the 15th of July, three weeks after the last throw which had made the masked man the winner of the match, a most unexpected thing took place.

That day, at seventeen minutes past ten in the morning, a report spread that the bell was ringing full-swing at the, mausoleum of William J. Hypperbone in Oakwood Cemetery.

CHAPTER XXX. THE FINAL ECCENTRICITY

IT would be difficult to imagine the rapidity with which the news got about. If each house in Chicago had been in telephonic communication with the bell at Oakwood, the seventeen hundred thousand inhabitants could not have heard the news more promptly or more simultaneously.

In a few minutes the cemetery was invaded by the population of the neighbouring quarters. Then the crowd flowed in from all parts. An hour afterwards the traffic was all stopped from Washington Park onwards. The Governor of the State, John Hamilton, informed in all haste, sent a strong detachment of militia, who got into the cemetery with some trouble and cleared out a number of the crowd to leave the access clear.

And the bell went on ringing, ringing, ringing all the time in the tower of the superb monument to William J. Hypperbone.

It will be understood that George B. Higginbotham, the president of the Eccentric Club, and his colleagues and the notary, Tornbrock, had arrived in the cemetery. But how had they been able to get in front of the huge, tumultuous crowd unless they had been told beforehand? Certain it is that they were there as soon as the bell had been set going by the keeper of Oakwood.

Half an hour later came the six players in the Hypperbone match. That Commodore Urrican, Tom Crabbe towed by John Milner, Hermann Titbury pushed by Mrs. Titbury, and Harris T. Kymbale were in a hurry to get there was not surprising. But if Max Real and Lizzie Wag were there, and Jovita Foley with them, it was because the last had imperiously required it and they had to obey her.

All the players, then, were before the monument, guarded by a triple row of that militia which the two friends had the right to command, one as colonel, the other as lieutenant-colonel, for that rank had been conferred on them by the Governor of the State.

At last the bell stopped, and the door of the monument opened wide.

The interior hall was resplendent with the dazzling brightness of the electric lamps. Between the sconces appeared the magnificent tomb such as it had been three months and a half before, when the door was closed at the termination of the obsequies in which the whole town had taken part.

The Eccentric Club, the president at their head, entered the hall; Tornbrock in black suit, white cravat, and always with his aluminium spectacles, entered after them. The six players followed, accompanied by all the spectators the place would hold.

A profound silence reigned within as without the edifice — the sign of an emotion no less profound — and Jovita Foley was not the least moved of those present. It was vaguely felt that the word of the enigma, sought for in vain since the 24th, was at last to be pronounced, and that this word would be a name — the name of the winner of the Hypperbone match.

It was thirty-three minutes past eleven when a certain noise was heard in the interior of the hall. The noise came from the tomb, the mortuary cloth of which slipped on to the ground, as if drawn by an invisible hand.

And then, O Prodigy! while Lizzie Wag nestled against Max Real's arm, the lid of the tomb rose, the body it contained rose.

Then a man appeared, upright, alive, much alive; and the man was no other than the. defunct William J. Hypperbone!

"Good gracious!" exclaimed Jovita Foley, the exclamation being heard only by Max Real and Lizzie Wag amid the hubbub of stupefaction that rose from the crowd.

And with her hands stretched out, she added:

"It is the venerable Mr. Humphry Weldon!"

Yes, the venerable Mr. Humphry Weldon, but of an ageless venerable than when he paid his visit to Lizzie Wag.

This gentleman and William J. Hypperbone were one.

In a few words, the following is the story that in a few hours appeared in the newspapers. It explains all that seems inexplicable in this prodigious adventure.

On the 1st of April, at the club in Mohawk Street, while playing at the Noble Game of Goose, William J. Hypperbone had been seized with congestion. Carried to his house in La Salle Street, he died a few hours afterwards, or rather his doctors declared that he did.

But in spite of the doctors — and also in spite of those famous rays of Professor Frederick, of Elbing (Prussia), which corroborated their opinions — William J. Hypperbone was in a state of catalepsy, nothing more, but having every appearance of a dead man. In truth, it was fortunate that he had not wished in his will that he should be embalmed after his death, for assuredly if that operation had taken place he would never have come back.

The magnificent funeral took place as we know; and on the 3rd of April the gates of the monument were closed on the most distinguished member of the Eccentric Club.

Now in the evening, while the keeper was turning out the last lights in the hall, he heard a movement in the interior of the tomb. There were groans — and a stifled voice called him.

The keeper did not lose his head. He ran for his tools, he undid the lid of the tomb, and the first words uttered by William J. Hypperbone, awoke from his lethargic sleep, were:

"Not a word — and your fortune is made!" Then he added, with a presence of mind extraordinary in a man who had returned from so far:

"You alone must know that I am alive — you alone with my notary, Mr. Tornbrock, to whom you must go and tell him to come to me without losing an instant."

The keeper, without other explanation, ran from the hall in all haste to the notary's. And what was the surprise — oh! the most agreeable — of Tornbrock, when, half an hour later, he found himself again in the presence of his client, as well as he had ever been.

And this is what William J. Hypperbone had thought of since his resurrection.

As he had instituted by his will the famous game which would give rise to so many agitations, deceptions and surprises, he resolved that the game should be played out among the players designated by lot, and that he would submit to all the consequences.

"Then," replied Tornbrock, "you will certainly be ruined, for one of the six will win. As you are not dead — on which I sincerely congratulate you — your will becomes, void and its dispositions of no effect. Then why let the game be played?"

"Because I will take part in it."

"You?"

"Yes."

"And how?"

"I will add a codicil to my will and introduce a seventh player, who will be William J. Hypperbone under the letters XKZ."

"And you will play?"

"I will play like the others."

"But you must conform to the established rules."

"I will conform to them."

"And if you lose — "

"I shall lose, and all my fortune goes to the winner."

"Is that your decision?"

"It is. As I am not distinguished by any eccentricity up to now, I will show myself eccentric under cover of my supposed death."

We can guess what followed. The keeper of Oakwood, well rewarded, with a promise to be more so if he kept silence to the end of the adventure, had kept the secret. William J. Hypperbone, oft leaving the cemetery, went incognito to Tornbrock's, added to his will the codicil we know, and fixed on the place to which he was to go in case the notary had any communication to address to him. Then he took his leave of this worthy man, trusting to his extraordinary luck that had never abandoned him during his life, and which was to remain faithful to him, we might say, even after his death.

We know the rest.

The game began under the conditions determined on, and William J. Hypperbone was able to form his opinions with regard to each of the six. Neither that disagreeable fellow Urrican, nor that miser Titbury, nor that brute Tom Crabbe interested him or could interest him. Perhaps he felt some sympathy with regard to Harris T. Kymbale, but if he had to choose a winner other than himself it would be either Max Real or Lizzie Wag and her faithful Jovita. Hence during the illness of the fifth player his visit under the name of Humphry Weldon and the sending of the three thousand dollars to the prison of Missouri. And what satisfaction for this generous man when the girl was released by Max Real, and the artist replaced in turn by Tom Crabbe!

As to himself, with sure and steady step he had followed the vicissitudes of the match, served by that inexhaustible luck on which he had reckoned with, reason, which did not betray him once; and here he was first at the post, he, the outsider, having beaten all the favourites in this great national race.

This is what had happened, and what he almost immediately told those present. And that is why the colleagues of this eccentric personage clasped him affectionately by the hand, why Max Real did so too, why he received the thanks of Lizzie Wag and those of Jovita Foley — who asked and obtained permission to kiss him — and why, carried by the crowd, he was borne through the great city of Chicago as triumphantly as he had been taken three months and a half before to Oakwood Cemetery.

But were the players contented with the way the game ended? Yes, some of them, not all; and yet they had to be, whether they liked it or not.

Hermann Titbury was not pleased at having uselessly spent so much money in running from one end of the States to the other. But he would do his best to get it back. Agreeing with Mrs. Titbury, who insisted on it, he decided to go into business again, in other words, to resume money-lending, and woe to the poor fellows who got into the maw of that shark!

Tom Crabbe understood hardly anything about these adventures, unless it was that he had a revenge to take, and John Milner hoped that in an approaching fight he would resume his position in the front rank of pugilists and forget that little affair at Arondale.

Harris T. Kymbale took his defeat philosophically, for he retained the remembrances of his interesting journeys. He did not, however, hold the record, having covered but about ten thousand miles, while Hodge Urrican had done more than eleven thousand — but this did not prevent him writing in the *Tribune* a most eulogistic article in favour of the dead-come-to-life-again of the Eccentric Club.

The commodore went to see William J. Hypperbone, and said to him with his usual politeness:

"It was not fair, sir — no! it was not fair! When you are dead, you are dead, and you do not send people running about after your money when you are still in this world!"

"What would you have, commodore?" said William J. Hypperbone," courteously. "I could not help it."

"You could, sir, and you ought to have! If, instead of burying you in a tomb, they had put you into a crematorium, this would not have happened."

"Who knows — commodore? I am so lucky — "

"And as you have made a fool of me, and I do not tolerate that sort of thing, you shall give me satisfaction — "

"Where and when you please!"

As Turk had sworn by St. Jonathan he would devour Mr. Hypperbone's liver, his master did not endeavour to calm him, but sent him to the ex-deceased to fix the hour and day for a meeting.

But could it be Turk who at the opening of his visit mildly said to William J. Hypperbone:

"You see, sir, Commodore Urrican is not so bad as he wishes to appear. At bottom he is a good fellow — whom you can manage easily — "

"And you come from him — "

"To tell you that he regrets his vivacity yesterday, and begs you to accept his apology!"

And there the affair rested, for Hodge Urrican soon saw that he would cover himself with ridicule. But very fortunately for Turk, this terrible man never knew in what manner he had fulfilled his mandate.

The day before Max Real and Lizzie Wag were to be married — it was the 29th of July — they received a visit, not from the venerable Humphry Weldon, a little bent with age, but from William J. Hypperbone, smarter and younger than ever, as Jovita Foley observed. Having apologized for not letting Miss Wag win the game, he told her that whether she would like it or whether she would not, or whether it pleased or displeased her husband, he had just deposited a new will with Mr. Tornbrock by which he had divided his fortune into two parts, one of which would go to Lizzie Wag.

It were needless to repeat the replies to one who was as generous as he was original. At a blow Tommy was assured of being bought by his master at a reasonable price.

There remained Jovita Foley. Well, this lively, demonstrative and excellent person was in no way jealous of what had happened to her dear companion. What happiness for her to marry him who adored her, and to find in Mr. William J. Hypperbone such an excellent uncle to inherit from! As for her, after the wedding she would return to her duties as chief saleswoman at Marshall Field's.

The wedding took place next day, it might be said in the presence of the whole city. The governor, John Hamilton, and William J. Hypperbone were present at the magnificent ceremony.

When the newly-married couple and their friends had returned to Madame Real's William J. Hypperbone, addressing Jovita Foley, who made a charming bridesmaid, said:

"Miss Foley, I am fifty years old."

"You are flattering yourself, Mr. Hypperbone," she replied, laughing — as she knew how to laugh.

"No — I am fifty years old — do not disarrange my calculations — and you are twenty-five."

"Twenty-five I am."

"Now if I have not forgotten the first elements of arithmetic, twenty-five is the half of fifty."

What was this enigmatical, mathematical gentleman driving at?

"Well, Miss Foley, as you are half my age, if arithmetic is not a vain science, why should you not become half of myself?"

What could Jovita Foley say to a proposal so originally put, if it were not what any other girl would have said in her place?

And after all, in marrying this amiable and bewitching Jovita, if he proved himself as eccentric as his position as a member of the Eccentric Club required, did he not act with as much wisdom as good taste?

And to conclude, with regard to the perhaps rather unlikely events reported in this recital, will the reader kindly remember — by way of extenuating circumstances — that it all happened in America?

THE END

Made in United States
North Haven, CT
04 December 2022

27898236R00134